STRANGER AT THE GROVE

Strangers Book 2

A Regency Romance

by Mary Kingswood

Stranger at the Grove: Strangers Book 2

Published by Sutors Publishing

Cover design by: Shayne Rutherford of Darkmoon Graphics

Version 2

ISBN: 978-1-912167-35-7 (paperback)

Author's note:

this book is written using historic British terminology, so *saloon* instead of *salon*, *chaperon* instead of *chaperone* and so on. I follow Jane Austen's example and refer to a group of sisters as the Miss Wintertons.

Stranger at the Grove: Strangers Book 2

About this book: *an estranged brother is forced to return to his home and face up to his past.*

Malcolm Gage walked out of his brother's life sixteen years ago when they both wanted to marry the same woman. Malcolm lost that battle, and he's never forgiven his brother for it, preferring to live in poverty as a schoolmaster rather than swallow his pride and go home. But now an unusual condition in a will pushes him back into the family fold. If he can teach his nephew well enough to admit him to the Society of Gentleman Linguists, he will inherit a fortune and will never be poor again. The only catch — he has to stay under his brother's roof for three months.

But there's an unexpected benefit to his return to Great Maeswood, in the delightful shape of Marie Fournier, a French lady's maid. She speaks no English, and no one else in the village has bothered to get to know her. But Malcolm sees in her a kindred spirit, another outsider, and recruits her to help him with his teaching. As he gets to know her better, however, he begins to wonder if she's all she seems to be...

This is a complete story with a happy ever after. Book 2 of a 6 book series. A traditional Regency romance, drawing room rather than bedroom.

Isn't that what's-his-name? Regular readers will know that characters from previous books occasionally pop up. Lawyer Mr Willerton-Forbes, his flamboyant sidekick Captain Edgerton and the discreet Mr Neate have been helping my characters solve murders and other puzzles ever since *Lord Augustus*. Michael Chandry, first seen helping after the shipwreck in The Clerk and more recently in *The Duke*, is now a crime-solving partner to Captain Edgerton and his pals. Dr Butler, the headmaster of Harrow School, is a real person.

About the Strangers series*:* There's a famous saying attributed to John Gardner that authors like to quote: that there are only two plots - a stranger arrives in town, or a person goes on a journey. Most of my books have been based on the latter, in its loosest sense (sometimes a journey of discovery, rather than a literal journey, but a major change, of death or misfortune or even good fortune which propels the main character in a new direction). So I wondered what the other side of the coin would look like - a stranger arriving in town. And there was my series title - Strangers.

Book 0: Stranger at the Parsonage: a new parson arrives at the village of Great Maeswood, and tragedy strikes the baron's family. *(a novella, free to mailing list subscribers)*.

Book 1: Stranger at the Dower House: a widow moves into the long disused Dower House and makes a horrible discovery in the wine cellar.

Book 2: Stranger at the Grove: an estranged brother is forced to return to his home and face up to his past.

Book 3: Stranger at the Villa: a new physician arrives in the village, but is he all he seems?

Book 4: Stranger at the Manor: a destitute man comes looking for help from his cousin, and uncovers some mysterious goings-on.

Book 5: Stranger at the Cottage: an out-of-work governess tries to start a school in the village.

Book 6: Stranger at the Hall: the newly discovered heir to the barony arrives to claim his inheritance.

Want to be the first to hear about new releases? Sign up for my mailing list at http://marykingswood.co.uk/.

Table of Contents

The Principal Inhabitants Of Great Maeswood

At Maeswood Hall:

Lady Saxby (47), a baron's widow

Her step-daughter, Miss Cass Saxby (26)

Her daughters, Miss Agnes (20), Miss Flora (18), Miss Honora (16)

Her sons from her first marriage, Mr Jeffrey Rycroft (28), Mr Timothy Rycroft (24)

At the Dower House:

Mrs Edward Middlehope (Louisa, 30), a widow

Mademoiselle Marie Fournier (23), a lady's maid

At Cloverstone Manor:

Squire Winslade (52)

His third wife, Lilian (28), who is ill

His daughter, Miss Susannah Winslade (26)

His son, Mr Henry Winslade (24)

At Lower Maeswood Grove:

Mr Laurence Gage (40), a widower

His children, Henrietta (15), Edward (12)

His sister, Miss Viola Gage (46)

At Green Lawns:

Mr David Exton (28), a reclusive widower

At Whitfield Villa:

Dr Roland Beasley (54), a physician

His sister, Miss Phyllida Beasley (40)

At St Ann's Parsonage:

Mr Theodore Truman (28), a clergyman

At Bramble Cottage:

Mrs Cokely (84), widow of a previous parson to the parish

Her daughter, Miss Lucy Cokely (44), a milliner

Note: Hi-res versions of maps and family trees are available at my website http://marykingswood.co.uk/.

The Saxby Family

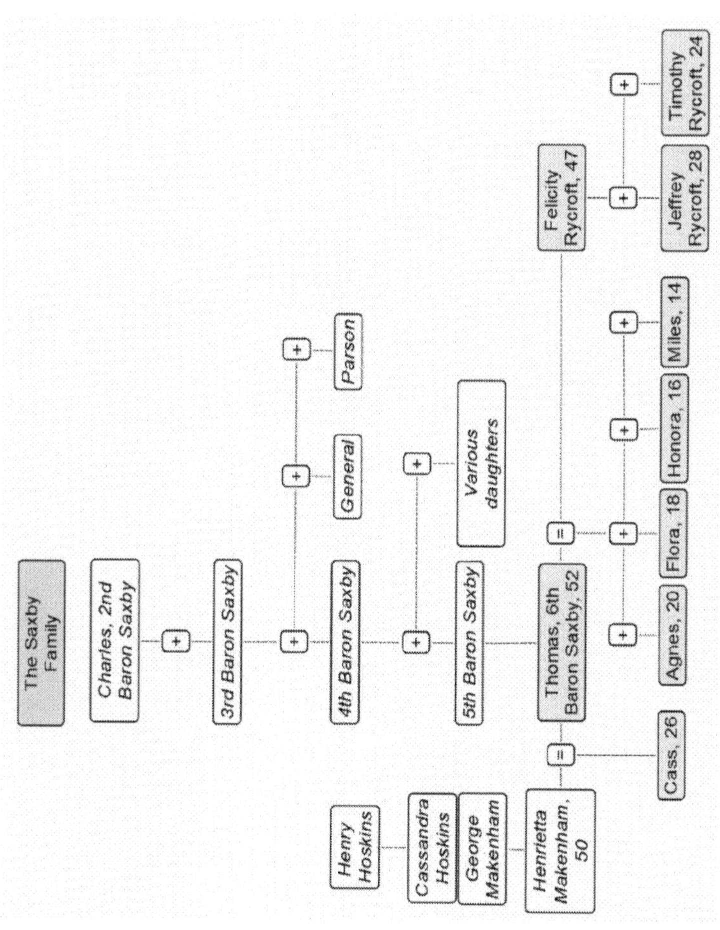

The Gage Family

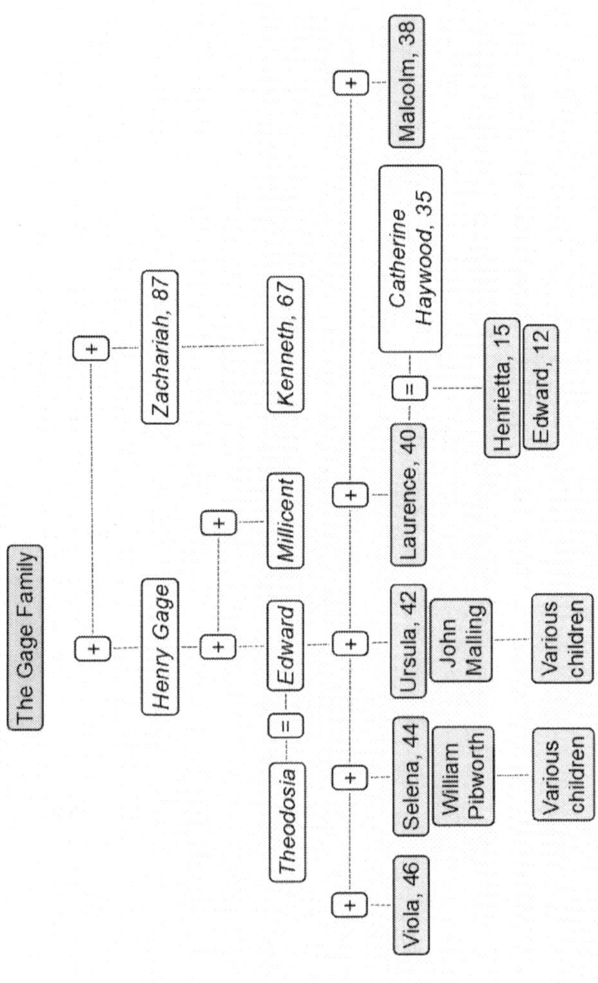

The Middlehope Family

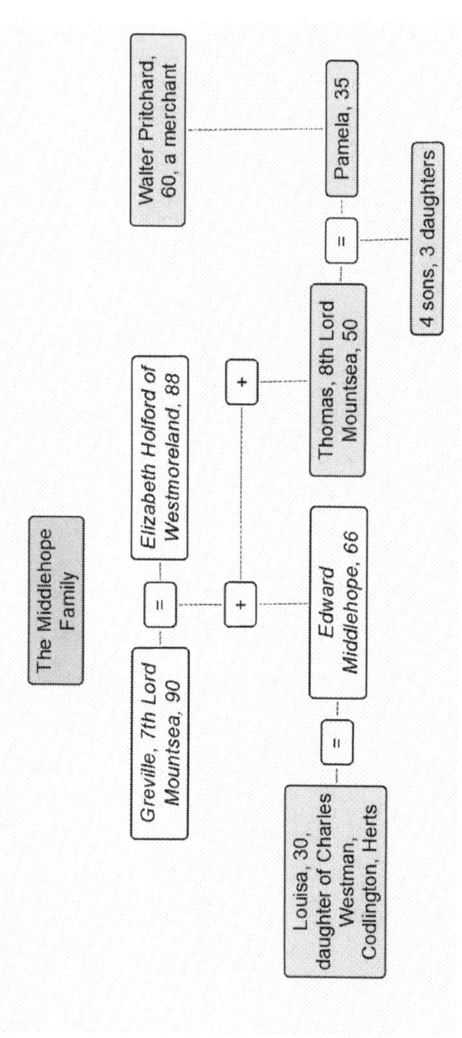

Great Maeswood Map

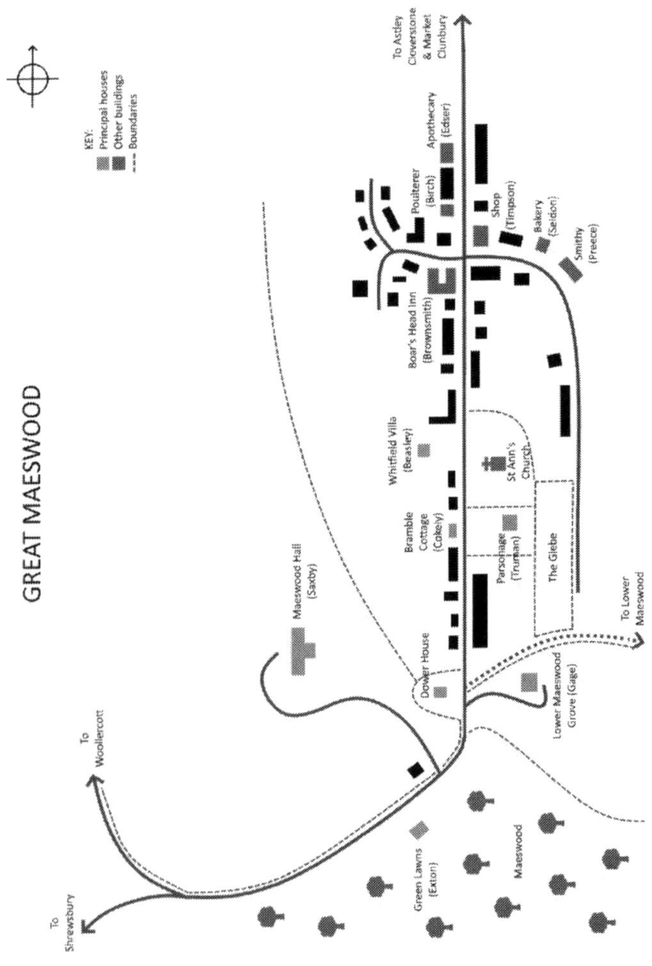

Great Maeswood Environs Map

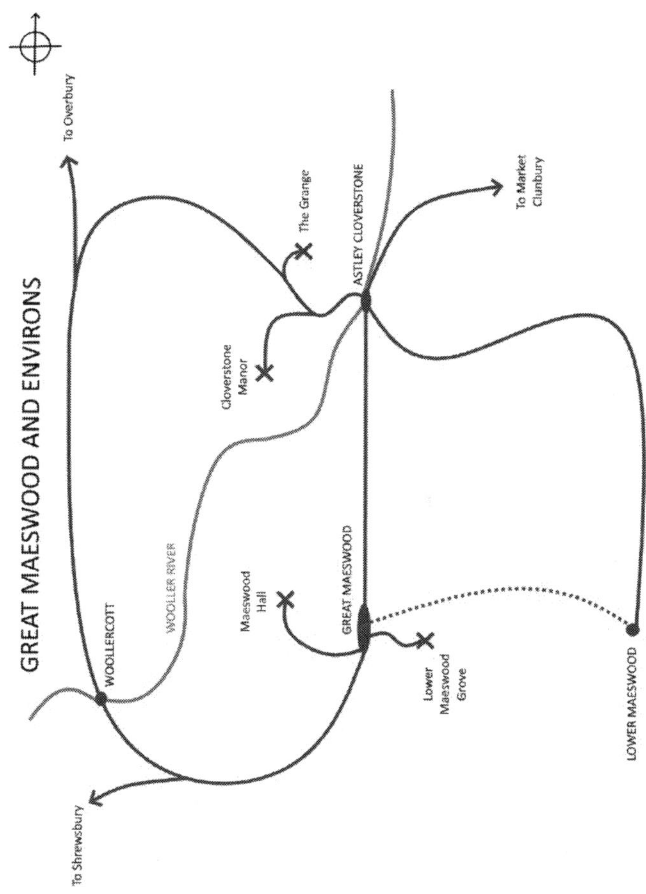

Prologue

'1st March. Well, here we are. Great Maeswood, although I am not at all sure what is so great about it. I have seen farms with almost as many buildings. An inn, a church, a smattering of tiny shops and no place to hide. It has to be said that the countryside is very pretty and less desolate than the north of England. So many trees! The primroses are out, and we passed several stands of daffodils on the drive here. Such cheerful flowers, with their bright yellow trumpets, waving about in the slightest breeze. They make me smile. The house is elegant, but so, so tiny. At Roseacre I could always find a quiet corner to tuck myself away out of sight. Here, there is nowhere, although the unused parlour has possibilities. Maybe I can requisition it for a sewing room. Madam seems to like it here, although I daresay we will not stay long. A few months and then she will long for a more public stage, but for now a secluded life suits her, and I have no objection to that. If only everyone will leave me alone! Still, I have managed to stay safe for this long, and no one on earth would think to look for me here, in this God-forsaken corner of England. Six hundred and forty.'

1: The Funeral

MARCH

The rain dripped over the brim of Malcolm's hat as he followed the little procession to the graveside. Why was there always rain at a funeral? As if it was not enough that a man had died to cause the participants to sink into despondency, without the grey gloom of relentless rain.

The parson began the familiar words. *"Man that is born of a woman hath but a short time to live, and is full of misery. He cometh up, and is cut down, like a flower; he fleeth as it were a shadow, and never continueth in one stay."*

Four working men in their Sunday best, no doubt paid a shilling apiece for their time, laboured to lower the coffin into the ground.

"In the midst of life we are in death: of whom may we seek for succour, but of thee, O Lord, who for our sins art justly displeased?"

Apart from the parson and Malcolm himself, only six men stood around the grave, silently watching. Two were his great-uncle's servants, almost as old and stooped as he had been.

Three others were his great-uncle's university colleagues, paying their respects. The sixth was Colville, the attorney.

"Yet, O Lord God most holy, O Lord most mighty, O holy and most merciful Saviour, deliver us not into the bitter pains of eternal death."

Some little distance away, and sensibly sheltering in the lee of one of the yew trees, a small group of neighbours and acquaintances, paying their last respects but not encroaching on the burial itself, since they were not invited. It amused Malcolm that they came anyway. How like his great-uncle to specify the precise details of his own funeral, down to the style of the coffin — plain wood, for economy's sake — to the refreshments to be offered the mourners afterwards. Only the official mourners, naturally. But the local people knew what was due to an Oxford man of renown, and so there they were, almost as wet and cold as the smaller group beside the grave.

"We therefore commit his body to the ground; earth to earth, ashes to ashes, dust to dust..."

Several of the mourners stepped forward to cast earth onto the coffin. Symbolic, they would say. Superstitious nonsense, Malcolm thought it. As soon as the clergyman began to move away, Malcolm strode off, glad that the whole business was over.

"Gage? May we offer you a lift?" One of the academics, spider-like in his black, pointed to a waiting carriage.

"Thank you, Monk, but I prefer to walk."

Malcolm's long legs carried him swiftly out of the churchyard and along the road. By the time the academics' carriage and the attorney's gig overtook him, he was already turning into the drive of Maitland House, past the high hedge that hid it from the world, or perhaps hid the world from the house. With Great-uncle Zachariah, either was equally likely.

The cook-housekeeper had the front door open already.

"Well, Mrs Staines, that is the old fellow settled in at the churchyard," Malcolm said.

She smiled at him, patting his arm in a motherly fashion. "Just the will-reading to get through now, Mr Malcolm, and then it will all be over. Goodness, you're wet! Go and have something to warm you up. It's all laid out in the parlour."

All over... that was true enough. The coming night would be his last under the roof of Maitland House, and when he left it, the connection would be severed absolutely. There would be no one left in his life. No family. Or none to speak of, anyway.

The two manservants came rushing in, puffing rather, to receive the gentleman mourners. The hall was already crowded, with a strong smell of damp wool, as they bustled about with dripping hats and greatcoats. Malcolm waited his turn, then followed the others into the parlour.

"Here," the attorney said, pushing a glass into his hand. "I sent Bird out to buy a couple of decent bottles this morning. There are pastries and meat on the sideboard, too."

Malcolm shook his head. He had long since lost his appetite for wine, and never wished to regain it.

"I insist. You will need something to fortify you before... well, it would be best."

For the first time, Malcolm felt a flicker of interest. Before what... the reading of the will? He had no expectations there. Great-uncle Zachariah had a son, after all, and although he had been a ne'er-do-well and a common thief in his youth, no doubt he was a respectable burgher now, and would inherit the house and whatever money had been hoarded away. Not much, he supposed, for the old fellow had never splashed it around.

He took the glass of wine, pretended to take a sip and then ambled over to the sideboard. Tucking the glass behind a bowl of fruit, he found himself a plate and loaded it with as much as it would hold. He might have forsworn intoxicating drink, but food was always acceptable.

"Well, Gage! No doubt we will see more of you now," Monk said, clapping him on the back so hard that Malcolm almost choked on the meat ball he was eating. "Another of your talks to the Society would be well received."

Swallowing hastily, Malcolm said, "I cannot say when I shall next be in Oxford, sir."

"Now, now, no need to pretend, is there? Surely the house will be yours, and you will be settled here."

"My great-uncle has a son," he said stiffly.

"Fell out, I thought. The boy was worthless and Zachariah cut him off without a penny, so I heard."

"You are misinformed, sir. When Kenneth came out of prison the last time, my great-uncle paid his passage to India and set him up in business out there. He long since forgave him for his youthful follies."

Monk's bushy eyebrows rose in surprise, but he made no further comment, and Malcolm retreated to a quiet corner to eat in peace, and consider that odd quirk of his great-uncle's character. For a man who never attended church, and had told his servants never to allow a man of the cloth across the threshold, he had held to remarkably Christian principles.

Forgiveness, he had always said, was the mark of civilisation, above any other virtue. But they had never seen eye to eye on that subject and never would, and eventually they had spoken of it no more.

After a while, Mr Colville called the company through to the drawing room for the reading of the will. Two rows of chairs were set out, but Malcolm sat on the window seat, a little apart. The gentlemen took the front row, and behind them Mrs Staines, the manservants and the wizened old gardener, stiff in his Sunday best, who was older than his master but still put in six full days of work every week, and would no doubt continue to do so until he dropped down dead in the asparagus bed.

The attorney sat behind the mahogany card table. If the old man had left Malcolm anything, and surely he must have done, for he would not have been invited else, he hoped it would be that elegant little table, with its interchangeable tops inlaid with mother-of-pearl to mark out chess or backgammon or cribbage boards. Today it was the plain baize, with Colville's papers laid in a neat pile.

The reading began. The small bequests came first — to the servants, to several charitable institutions, to the Society. A bursary to the college, to support a promising local boy. Then an odd one — *'To my son, Kenneth Gage, last known address Madras, India, my watch, engraved with my name, given to me by my father, but only on the condition that he comes to collect it himself. If he should be dead, then to his heir, if any, with the same condition. If the watch is unclaimed on the fifth anniversary of my death, then it may be given to whoever resides at Maitland House or otherwise at the discretion of my executors.'*

Malcolm had to smile at the old boy's eccentricity. Would anyone travel all the way from India to claim a watch? It seemed unlikely. But when did he lose touch with Kenneth? Quite some time ago, perhaps, for he had not mentioned him for years.

Mr Colville removed his spectacles. "The remainder of the will concerns only Mr Malcolm Gage, and Mr Monk and I, as executors, are agreed that no other person needs to be privy to the contents at this time."

That was unexpected. As everyone shuffled out except Colville and Monk, Malcolm weighed up the possibilities. The house... yes, it must be the house and whatever money the old fellow had. But there was some catch, he knew it. Colville's manner beforehand, suggesting he fortify himself... yes, there must be a condition. Marriage, perhaps, for his great-uncle had been nagging him on that score for years. Or was it more complicated than that? Had his great-uncle left other illegitimate children, besides Kenneth? He was a secretive old buzzard, so anything was possible. But he had left Malcolm *something*, that much was plain. Something to lift him out of this dreadful grinding poverty. A bubble of hope arose inside him.

"Will you not come a little closer, Mr Gage?" Colville said, gesturing towards the now empty seats in the front row.

Reluctantly, Malcolm lounged across the room and took one of the front seats, arms folded and legs stretched out before him.

Colville looked pained at such casualness, but he replaced his spectacles and picked up his papers again. But then he laid them down, and removed the spectacles.

"Mr Gage, I would ask that you listen carefully to the entirety of what follows and not... hmm, not arrive at any precipitate conclusions. The requirements are complicated, and I must insist that you hear the *whole* of your great-uncle's dispositions. Then we may discuss the matter."

"You terrify me, Colville," Malcolm said, amused. "What can possibly be so dire in a will? I presume that there are some devious conditions, but what is that to me? Either I will accept them or I will not. Let me hear the worst."

"But you will not... storm out? Or anything of that nature?"

"I will make every effort not to do so."

Colville stared at him for a moment, as if trying to assess the likelihood that he would or would not. Eventually, with a sigh, he replaced his spectacles, and began to read.

"'To my dear great-nephew, Malcolm Augustus Gage, formerly of Lower Maeswood Grove in the county of Shropshire, and lately master at Harrow School, in the county of Middlesex, I make the following stipulation, that he should make arrangements with his brother, Laurence Adolphus Gage of the said—"

Malcolm jumped to his feet, fists clenched, boiling with rage.

"'—Lower Maeswood Grove...' Do please resume your seat, Mr Gage. There is a great deal more, and it is very much to your advantage."

Yes, he should hear it all, every last miserable word of his great-uncle's betrayal. *Then* he would walk out. Slowly he sat.

"'...of the said Lower Maeswood Grove, to instruct his son Edward Henry Gage of the same place of residence such that the said Edward Henry Gage shall be admitted to the Society of Gentleman Linguists of Oxford, this task to be accomplished within three months of its commencement and in such a manner that the said Malcolm Augustus Gage resides at all times under the same roof as the said Laurence Adolphus Gage. If the task

thus described is successful and the said Edward Henry Gage is admitted to the said Society within one year of my death, I bequeath to the said Malcolm Augustus Gage my dwellinghouse, known as Maitland House, together with all my household goods furniture plate linen china and personal effects of whatever sort such as may be found within the said dwellinghouse, for his own absolute use and benefit together with nine tenths of all monies held and invested on my behalf by Fletcher and Parsons of Oxford, and the said Edward Henry Gage shall receive the remaining one tenth part of all the monies so described. If the task thus described is not accomplished successfully, the said house and all monies shall be disposed of in charitable bequests at the discretion of my executors.'"

The silence was absolute. Malcolm sat unmoving. A house... nine tenths of the money, which must be worth a few hundred, at least. Independence, the life of a gentleman... he would never be poor again. He should have howled with rage, but oddly he was now calm. Icy calm. The slimy, devious, scheming, *treacherous* old devil.

"Do you understand, Mr Gage?"

Oh, he understood, all right. He understood perfectly.

"It is a considerable sum," the attorney said, in a wheedling tone. "Above five and twenty thousand for you and almost three thousand for the boy, even after the other bequests. An income of twelve or thirteen hundred a year."

So much! That was a shock. The sly old fellow had been hoarding his money then, for he had never spent so much. He had written several books, of course, or perhaps those ships he liked to invest in had been more profitable than he had suspected. Malcolm would have been a wealthy man...

"It is only three months, Mr Gage, and the boy is very able, by all accounts. It should not be a difficult task, and you would have your house and a good income. Enough to live on quite comfortably."

Another silence.

"Is it so impossible to spend three months under your brother's roof?" Monk said. "Come, Gage, what do you say?"

Malcolm rose, looking down on the two men disdainfully.

"No." He turned and walked towards the door.

"Mr Gage, I think you should—"

"No. A thousand times no. *Never."*

He left the room, shutting the door quietly behind him, and went to sit in his room until the dinner hour. Colville left him in peace. They were bound to dine together, for that, too, had been decreed by the dead man, but then Colville would leave and Malcolm would be alone again, as he had been, in truth, for almost half his life.

~~~~~

MAY

The morning had been a rather more enjoyable one than many. A dull Greek lesson had devolved into a long discussion of the Peloponnesian War, with particular reference to the Megarian decrees, which led him to the astonishing but inescapable conclusion that one or two of the scholars had a modicum of intelligence between their ears after all.

One of the porters was awaiting him as he left the room. He gave the discreet cough which all the porters used when they were required to address a master.
~~~~~

"Dr Butler respectfully requests your presence, sir."

Malcolm grunted an acknowledgement, and made his way directly to the head master's office. As soon as he entered, he groaned aloud, for there was Colville sitting in front of Butler's desk, half-smiling in a rueful manner.

"What the *devil* are you doing here?" Malcolm said, too annoyed to moderate his language. "As if it were not enough to torment me with your letters, now you must approach me here?"

"Do sit down, Gage," Butler said in pleasant tones. "You are such a great, tall fellow, and you make me nervous looming over us in that glowering way."

Heaving a disgusted sigh, Malcolm took the chair beside Colville.

"I was not aware of the existence of your brother, Gage," Butler said. "He is older than you, I take it?" Malcolm nodded. "So he got the estate. Was that what the quarrel was about — the inheritance?"

"Good God, no! As if I cared about that!"

"What then? Was it a long time ago?"

Reluctantly, Malcolm said, "Sixteen years."

"Then it must have been a serious matter, I surmise. Not some trivial boys' tiff."

"Not trivial, no," Malcolm conceded. Then, because Butler looked at him expectantly, he added, "A woman. He stole her from me, and then he *killed* her."

"No, no, no," Colville said, in some agitation. "Such intemperate language, Mr Gage. Your great-uncle told me all about it when he drew up his will. They both wished to marry the same lady, Dr Butler, and Mr Laurence Gage was the one who carried off the prize, so to speak. And later, she died in childbed. A great tragedy, but hardly worth sustaining a feud for so many years, I should have thought."

"You know *nothing* about it!" Malcolm said savagely. "She was forced into it! She—" He stopped abruptly. "The details do not matter, but there was no honour in my brother, that is all you need to know. The rift is as much his doing as mine. He would no more welcome me back in his life than I would wish it."

"Now there you are wrong," Colville said triumphantly. "I was obliged to write to him, you know, to apprise him of the terms of Mr Zachariah Gage's will, and he responded with the utmost civility. Let me read you some of it, for it was quite lengthy. Let me see... ah, yes. *'You may be sure that I will place no obstacle in the way of the proceeding, given the benefit to my son.'* There, you see! He places no obstacle in the way."

It was hardly a resounding welcome, however, but it mattered not a whit. "Irrelevant, since I have no intention of complying with these outrageous terms. If I wish to quarrel with my brother, then I shall do so, and no effort of Great-uncle Zachariah will prevail upon me to change my mind."

"Then let me see if my effort will meet with better success," Butler said placidly. "You are relieved of your post here, Gage. If, in the fullness of time, you return here having attempted your appointed task and assure me as a gentleman that you used your best endeavours, I will offer you your position again. Otherwise, I am afraid I cannot employ a man who displays such a grim example of implacable resentment to the boys. I have never concerned myself with your sense of morality, nor worried that you were not in Holy Orders like the other masters, but I cannot condone such an unchristian attitude. Attempt to overcome it and you may return here, but otherwise my doors are closed to you. You may stay here tonight and leave tomorrow."

Malcolm rose and walked out of the room, but it took every ounce of effort not to slam the door behind him.

2: An Unexpected Arrival

Nothing looked the same. He had known where he was as soon as the cart passed the Woollercott road, as the open fields gave way to the boundary wall of the Hall on one side and the woods on the other, but it looked oddly different from his memories. The wall was lower, and the woods less forbidding than he remembered. There was a house tucked away in the trees — he had forgotten all about that. But the entrance to the Hall and the lodge were the same, and then, almost before he was aware, the gates of Lower Maeswood Grove came into view.

"Stop! Stop! I will get down here."

Obediently the carter drew to a halt, as Malcolm threw his portmanteau into the road and jumped down himself. With a wave, the fellow moved off into the village, half hidden by a cloud of dust. Malcolm coughed his way through it to the gates... no, there were no gates any more, just the stone gateposts topped with the lions, each with its paw resting on a stone ball. That at least had not changed.

The drive was longer than he remembered, the avenue of elderly trees replaced by rounded shrubs with glossy leaves. There was the house, just as it had always been, although the imposing arched wall partly surrounding the carriage circle was new. He strode across the gravel, his boots crunching, and jumped up the steps to the front door, knocking and then ringing. The door bell clanged more loudly than he remembered. Perhaps that was new, too.

The front door creaked open and an unfamiliar face gazed out. Even the butler was new, then. "Yes?"

"Good day to you." And then, because it seemed foolish to announce himself at the door of his old home, he simply walked past the butler and into the hall. That at least had not changed. The colours were different, perhaps, but the familiar pilasters, the deep windows and the decorated ceiling were just as they had always been. He laughed in delight, transported back in a moment to his childhood.

"The master is not here at present," the butler said in repressive tones. "Would you perhaps care to leave your card... or make an appointment?"

Malcolm laughed again. No, he would not care to leave his card! He would certainly not make an appointment, like a provincial attorney. "Who *is* at home?" he said cheerfully, dropping his portmanteau and wandering about the room, gazing at the pictures. Most were new to him.

"Only the ladies. Perhaps you would care to return when the master is at home." There was a definite frostiness in his manner now, but he was still held back by uncertainty. The shabby coat and dilapidated portmanteau suggested the man of business — attorney or land agent, perhaps — but he did not dare offend one who, to judge by the luggage, might be an honoured if unexpected guest.

"You must be new here," Malcolm said. "What is your name?"

The man drew himself up to his full height, although he still had to look up to Malcolm. "I have been employed in this house for thirty-seven years," he said with dignity. "My name is Skeates, and if you would care to—"

"Good God, not William Skeates? Well, I never! You were the under-footman when I left, and now you are butler. Well, well, well."

Skeates' face changed in an instant, his jaw dropping open. Before he could speak, a female voice was heard.

"What is it, Skeates?"

Malcolm stared at the woman who entered the hall. Unlike Skeates, he was in no doubt of her identity. The plain gown, the sharp tone of voice and suspiciously narrowed eyes were as familiar to him as her features, although the intervening years had not been kind to her. The last vestiges of her youthful bloom had been lost to advancing age, and deep frown lines marred her forehead, but she was still undeniably his sister.

"Well, Vi, how are you?"

She stared at him, and then, as realisation dawned, the blood drained from her face and her eyes opened wide. She covered her mouth with her hands, gazing unblinking at him.

Abruptly, with a small squeak of distress, she collapsed into a deep swoon, crumpling unchecked to the floor.

There was a stunned silence, then Skeates rushed forward, pushing Malcolm aside. "John! *John!*" he yelled, as he knelt beside Viola's prone form. "Here at once! *At once!*"

Running feet, shocked gasps. Faces appearing from the inner lobby, the service stairs, the library. People crouching over Viola, barking orders, someone running to fetch the physician.

Malcolm backed away from the confusion. What a damnably silly woman she was sometimes! She must have known he might turn up on the doorstep one day, given the terms of the will. A bubble of guilt rose inside him. He should have warned her. She had always been a bit hen-witted, so he should have— But it was too late now. So many things were too late.

A burning desire to be somewhere, *anywhere,* else propelled him through the open door to the library, a haven of peacefulness. Gently he pushed the door to, and gazed around him. This room, as least, looked unchanged. Every inch of wall was filled with a glass-fronted bookcase, and every bookcase was full to overflowing, books piled on top of other books, not a crevice left free.

In front of the fire still sat the four armchairs where Malcolm, Laurence, Selena and their father had habitually sat after dinner reading in companionable silence. Occasionally, one or other of them would recite a puzzling passage aloud and they would all try to understand it, tossing ideas back and forth like shuttlecocks. The rest of the family had liked to sit in a chattery group in the drawing room, but in the library for most of the evening the only sound was the slow ticking of the clock. It was still there, too, but it no longer ticked. The hands had stopped at seven minutes to twelve.

Above the mantel was the portrait. It had always been called that, not the family portrait or the Brookes, after the artist, although since he was neither famous nor particularly talented, perhaps his name was best forgotten. But there they all were, captured for ever in swirling oils not long after Viola's eighteenth birthday, when she and Selena had just come out and Mama had realised, in a moment of terror, that they would soon marry and the family would be broken apart. Mama sat on a chair, with

Father standing behind her, one hand on her shoulder. Around them, the children stood, the three girls at one side, Laurence on the other and Malcolm, all of ten years old, sitting at Mama's feet, grinning.

He smiled, remembering those happy days, before Ursula and Selena had married and Viola had gone to be a companion to Aunt Millicent. Before Father had had his apoplexy and Mama had faded away from grief. Most of all, before Catherine. Before Laurence had betrayed his own brother and stolen her away and driven a wedge between them too great to ever—

"You are not welcome here."

Malcolm jumped, then spun round. A boy, no more than — no, he knew his age to a nicety. He was twelve years old, dressed in a coat finer than Malcolm's own and a neatly tied neckcloth.

"That is true," Malcolm said. "Nevertheless, I have as much right to be here as you have."

The boy raised his chin defiantly, but perhaps he did not dare to contradict him directly, for he said, "You are not a good person, and we do not want you here, making trouble."

"True again, and bravely spoken, my young infantryman. You are defending your domain like the good soldier you are."

"You are sneering at me," the boy said.

"Not at all, I assure you. Your father is from home, so you are taking his place to repel the intruder. That is admirable. However, I have his permission to be here."

"I do not believe you."

"Nevertheless, it is true, Edward."

"You know my name, but you do not tell me yours."

"I believe you could guess it, if you were to consider the matter. There cannot be many people who could cause your aunt to faint clean away without a word spoken."

Without a second's hesitation, the boy said, "You are Uncle Malcolm, but you should have introduced yourself, you know. It is uncivil not to. And you should have let us know you were coming. That was uncivil, too."

He knew that, of course, but it was humiliating to have it pointed out by a boy of twelve. He chose to make light of it. He had no wish to antagonise the boy, after all. "Now where would be the fun in that? I wanted to surprise you, but you do not seem pleased to meet your long-lost uncle."

The boy raised disdainful eyebrows. "Some surprises are pleasant and some are not, and since you have made Aunt Viola ill, this is not at all pleasant. It is quite horrid, in fact, and I wish you will go away at once!"

A gentler voice spoke. "He is family, Edward. How do you do, Uncle. I am Henrietta. Your niece," she added, a little uncertainly. She was tall for her age and well-formed, the perfect little lady in a white muslin gown with a delicate silver cross at her throat.

He smiled, and bowed to her. "I am delighted to make your acquaintance, niece. You must be fifteen now, I believe?" She nodded. "How is your Aunt Viola? I did not mean to frighten her so badly."

"She is a little better already. Dr Beasley has been sent for, and her maid is with her. Are you staying here? I will need to inform Mrs Blenkinsop and Mrs Rogers, if so."

If Edward was taking his father's rôle in the encounter, Henrietta was taking her mother's... or her aunt's, perhaps, as the principal female of the family.

"There are rooms at the Boar's Head," Edward said quickly.

"I am obliged to stay under this roof, I am afraid," Malcolm said.

"Why?" he said, eyes narrowing.

"He is *family*, Edward," Henrietta said again.

"That does not mean—"

"Family," she said firmly. "I shall go and find Mrs Blenkinsop, Uncle Malcolm."

When she had gone, Malcolm wandered about the room, opening one bookcase after another, hauling out a random book or two, then thrusting them back in increasing irritation. "These are years old. Where does your father keep the new ones, eh?"

"In the study," he said, watching Malcolm through unblinking blue eyes.

A jolt of recognition — *Catherine's eyes.* Or were they? Surely her eyes had been almost grey, not this clear blue.

Frowning, he marched through the connecting door to the study. Now this room was different! In his father's day, it had been little used, kept ready for a secretary, empty and cold, the furniture regimented around the walls. Now it was a cosy place, with comfortable chairs scattered about, a working table strewn with open books and two walls filled with new bookshelves.

Malcolm picked up some of the books on the table — Theocritus, Homer, Plutarch, Eratosthenes, Julius Caesar. An atlas of the ancient world lay open at the map of Greece. He laughed, turning to Edward, who had followed him into the room.

In Greek, he said, "These are yours, my boy?"

He responded the same way. "They are."

Then, in Latin, he said, "What think you of the Alexandrine War?"

In the same manner, Edward said, "All Caesar's works are interesting. I prefer the Gallic Wars."

Malcolm laughed again. The boy was good! In English, he said, "What other languages do you speak?"

"French and Italian."

"Nothing else?"

He shook his head, with a slight frown.

"What would you like to learn?" When there was no answer, he went on, "I can offer Hebrew, Russian, German, Old English... well, maybe not. That would be a stretch for both of us, probably. Oh, Spanish, too, but for some reason I never got round to Portuguese. I have a smattering of Polish, and some Turkish, but nothing suitable for polite company. What would interest you most?"

"You want to teach me?" Edward said, his expression now thoroughly confused.

"Well, of course, that is the whole point of— Oh, did your father not tell you? That is why I am here — to make sure you are fluent in five languages. Since you only have four at present, that means learning a new one."

His face lit up. "Truly? You are not just funning, are you? Because that would be cruel."

"Truly," Malcolm said, chuckling at the eagerness in his face.

"And you will not shout at me... or throw things?"

Malcolm's eyebrows rose. "Does your father do so?"

"Oh... no, it was Mr Hawksbee, my tutor for a while. He was horrid. He had huge bushy eyebrows, like giant caterpillars, and he called me *'little boy'* in a nasty, hard voice and... I did not like him at all. Papa sent him away when he shook me so hard he bruised my arms."

Malcolm heart ached for the boy, who spoke so matter-of-factly of what must have been a terrible time. "Well, I have no caterpillar eyebrows," he said, eventually. "Ah, Henrietta... and Mrs Blenkinsop, or Mary the under-housemaid, as you were in my day."

The housekeeper went pink. "Well, fancy you remembering me from all those years ago, Mr Malcolm. How lovely to see you again, sir. There will be such a celebration, I'll warrant."

"Well... possibly," he said. "As to that, I cannot say. My brother knows of my reasons for being here, but he may not be very happy about it."

"He is to teach me a new language," Edward said happily. "Any one I like. He knows a great many different ones."

"Aye, he was always so clever, Mr Malcolm was," the housekeeper said. "I've put you in the blue room, sir. Becky's just seeing to it now. Is that all your luggage, just that one portmanteau?"

"There will be another box coming, once I know what books I will need."

"Books!" she said, smiling at him. "You always cared more for your books than your clothes. Will you go to your room now, sir?"

"I will find myself a book to read first, thank you, Mary... Mrs Blenkinsop."

"Very well, sir. Miss Henrietta and Master Edward will entertain you, and there is Madeira, sherry and Canary on the sideboard there. Shall I send in some food for you?"

"Thank you, I should like something to eat. Is my sister recovered? May I see her?"

"She's gone to her room to rest, and Dr Beasley's with her just now, but I'll let her know you were asking after her."

For a while, Malcolm examined the books on the shelves, creating a haphazardly balanced pile of interesting ones. Edward followed him around, saying, "What does Russian sound like? What about German?" and Malcolm obligingly translated a few sentences from whatever book he had in his hand. Laurence's tastes had grown soft with the years, he thought. There was nothing challenging on his shelves, merely some traditional philosophy, estate management works, even novels, for heaven's sake! What sort of man read novels? And sermons. Far, far too many sermons, but that had always been one of the differences between them, that Malcolm had always doubted God and Laurence never had.

The food arrived, and Malcolm settled at the table to eat. Edward sat down beside him, nibbling at this and that from the tray unselfconsciously. Somehow it seemed quite natural for them to fall to talking of the Peloponnesian War, which Malcolm had been discussing only two days before with boys not much older than Edward, who had not a tenth of his lively intelligence.

Henrietta returned to show him to his room before they had even got far into Attica, and it was not a surprise when Edward followed them, still rattling away in Greek. Henrietta understood it too, for she made one or two remarks in the language, and Malcolm found himself delighted with both of them. They were true Gages with such a facility in languages, and although he had not expected it, he was pleased that Henrietta, too, was receiving a broad education and not confining herself to needlework and watercolours.

The blue room had been called the south-eastern apartment once, an oppressively old-fashioned room that had been reserved for important guests. Aunt Millicent had favoured it, he recalled, a lady who liked everything just so, and not a thing must be changed from one visit to the next. Now it was done up in pretty blue-flowered wallpaper above the dado, with the panels a pale gold and expensive Turkish rugs on the floor. The bed was already made up, a bath sat beside the fire awaiting hot water, and a footman was arranging his few clothes in the press.

Malcolm pulled off his boots, and sat on the edge of the bed, as Edward plumped himself down on the floor and continued the conversation without missing a beat. Henrietta, like a good housewife, checked that everything was as it should be before pulling a chair nearer the bed to listen.

They were still thus when a delicate tap on the door was swiftly followed by Viola's anxious face. "May I come in? Do you have everything you need, brother?"

"Vi!" Malcolm cried, leaping to his feet and rushing across the room to wrap her in such a tight embrace that she squeaked in protest. "Are you feeling better? How infamous of me to startle you so, but how missish of you to swoon away like a chit of a girl."

"Oh, Malcolm, why did you not let us know you were coming? After all these years, to simply turn up on the doorstep, like that. It was the utmost shock to me! I could scarce believe my eyes. But look at you, so thin and drawn. We shall have to feed you up a bit. Mrs Rogers is preparing a good dinner for you. You will stay for a while, I hope? You will not rush away just yet, will you? We have so much to talk about."

"I shall be here for three months, Vi. Surely you knew that? Laurence knows all about it."

"Laurence knew you were coming? But he said not a word... he has not mentioned you since— He has not said anything to me. Henrietta, Edward, did your father tell you anything of this?"

Edward shook his head, and Henrietta said quietly, "Nothing, Aunt."

"Teasing man! Such wonderful news that you are reconciled at last, and yet to keep it from us, but then his head is in the clouds at the moment, so perhaps it is not so surprising. He is— Yes, Mrs Blenkinsop, what is it?"

The housekeeper shook where she stood, her face a picture of embarrassment. "I'm so sorry, madam, but the master is home and—" She shot a sideways glance at Malcolm. "He said... his instructions are that Mr Malcolm is to have a room on the nursery floor... in the night nursery, to be precise. He said that he may use the day nursery for his... his project, and he is to have all his meals there and not to come downstairs. He said—" She paused, wringing her hands helplessly. “He said he doesn’t never want to see Mr Malcolm, not at all, not even on the stairs. He’s to use the service stairs. He said so, madam, I swear he did, so please don’t be cross with me!”

Viola had gone so pale that he was afraid she would faint away again, but Malcolm saw the funny side. “Well, he is putting me back in the nursery where he thinks I belong, no doubt.” He laughed. “Cheer up, Vi. This room is far too grand for me anyway. I shall be perfectly comfortable in the nursery, and you may tell my brother that I have no wish ever to see him, either. There is no reconciliation between us, and never will be.”

3: A Late Breakfast

Malcolm stayed up half the night reading, skipping from one book to the next like a bee after nectar. Even so, he woke at his usual time, the habit of many years impossible to shake off. But today there were no morning prayers to be endured, no boys waiting for their lessons, no discipline to be meted out. Today he was free from all that. He still had a monumental task to accomplish, but the boy was quick, there was no doubt about that, and he would be a pleasure to teach, whatever the outcome. And while he taught him, there would be the familiar comforts of his old home, plenty of books to read and perhaps a horse to ride, occasionally. Such a treat *that* would be.

He jumped out of bed and strode across to the window for his morning gratitudes. Pulling the pendant from beneath his nightshirt, he closed his eyes. "I am grateful for a bright, clear day that lifts my spirits. I am grateful for the substantial breakfast I shall soon be enjoying. I am grateful for surviving the mail coach unscathed." He kissed the pendant, and tucked it back inside his nightshirt.

From the window, he looked out over lawns towards the shrubbery, grown rather wild in the sixteen years since he had last seen it. It was not much of a garden, just a few formal beds around the terrace and dull, straight paths to nowhere. Much of the park had been abandoned to nature years ago. Apart from the avenue, nothing much had changed.

As he watched, a figure emerged from the basement door three floors below him, five dogs bounding about him. Even from far above, he recognised Laurence's rather squat frame as he strode across the lawn and then disappeared into the shrubbery. Had he grown old, as Viola had? He walked with energy, certainly. Laurence had always been happier on his own two feet, rather than riding. The two of them had walked for miles when they were boys, exploring the park and then further afield.

A wash of yearning for those companionable days caught Malcolm by surprise. He suppressed it ruthlessly, determined not to drop his guard just because he was forced to live in his old home for a few weeks. Three months, that was all he had to endure, and then he could leave and never see his brother again. He would not surrender. He would never surrender. Honour demanded it.

He returned to his books. At least he would have a decent supply of reading material during his stay at the Grove. Not as extensive as at Harrow, but still, he would be able to occupy his spare time when he was not with the boy.

"Beg pardon, sir. I did knock, but there was no answer."

Malcolm looked up in surprise to see a footman standing in the doorway holding a coat. "Oh… I am dead to the world when I am reading," he said. "What are you doing with my coat?"

"I made a few repairs, sir," he said, placing it tenderly in the press. "What would you like me to lay out for you this morning?"

"Are you are trying to valet me? I can manage perfectly well for myself, you know."

"To judge by the state of the clothes you arrived in, I beg leave to differ, sir."

Malcolm laughed. "If you had spent a whole night on the mail coach, you would look a trifle rumpled, too, I wager. What is your name, my outspoken fellow?"

"John, sir."

"Very well, John, you may clean and mend my clothes but I shall shave and dress myself."

"Very good, sir. I shall return with your washing water. Should you like some chocolate, sir?"

Chocolate! Another part of his childhood that he had imagined gone for ever. "No, I will have coffee with my breakfast."

John bowed and withdrew, and Malcolm returned to his books.

Breakfast was late, of course, for the family would take priority. That brought another unwelcome wave of envy. Once he had been part of the family, too, wrapped in the gentle blanket of shared meals and shared experiences, surrounded by people who *cared* about him. No, he would not be maudlin, or he would be undone. He still had enough anger to sustain him through his ordeal.

The day nursery had been newly scoured, to judge from the overpowering smell of beeswax and raised dust. He waited there for his breakfast to arrive, flicking through the books on the shelves, spinning the globe and setting the rocking horse in motion. He brought his books through, and settled down on a wooden chair at the table to read while he waited. His stomach was growling by the time John had laboured up three flights of stairs with the tray. He should have asked for chocolate after all. At least it would have staved off the hunger pangs. Still, there was more than enough to satisfy his appetite.

He had barely begun when two heads peeped round the door. "Come in," he said, mumbling through a mouthful of mutton chop. "No point loitering out there."

In they came, Edward in a different coat, and Henrietta in pale blue today, wearing the same silver cross. There was something about her face, the soft curve of her cheek and her gentle expression, that put him in mind of Catherine, but the memory skittered away like a frightened mouse.

Behind them, twittering in dismay, came Viola, with her severely plain gown and her neat little spinster's cap. When had she started to wear a cap? But then she was six and forty now, a confirmed old maid.

"Oh dear, oh dear! My poor brother, how are you? I hope you managed some repose and will not think too badly of Laurence. Have you only just received your breakfast? I will have a word with Mrs Blenkinsop to make sure you are seen to earlier, for I would not wish you to think—" She stopped going pink. "I hope you do not suppose that *I*—"

"No, no," he said quickly. "My quarrel is only with Laurence, and his with me. I do not blame you in the least."

The children looked uncomfortable at this talk of adult quarrels, and Henrietta said brightly, "Shall we come back when you have finished eating, Uncle Malcolm?"

He smiled at her, and she visibly relaxed. "No, why ever should you do that? I am used to company while I eat, usually a great deal of company, but you will have to provide the conversation. Henrietta, you may begin. Tell me three interesting things about yourself."

"There is nothing interesting to tell," she said. "I am a very ordinary person."

"Rubbish!" he said. "Everyone has something extraordinary about them. I have seen it a score of times at the school. A boy will arrive who looks and sounds and behaves exactly like his peers in every respect, and yet when one begins to know him, one discovers that he can shoot the pips out of a card at twenty feet, or he knows every battle of the Civil War by heart, or he can list forty-seven different kinds of beetle found in his home county, and describe the distinguishing features of each, and he is not ordinary in the least."

"But those are boys," she said, with such heart-breaking sincerity that he threw down his knife and fork in despair.

"Girls do extraordinary things too, just as much as boys," he said firmly. "You speak Greek, for a start. That is definitely not ordinary. I expect you play and sing, too, and sew and paint and make reticules and net purses and—"

"But everyone does that, and I cannot do any of it well, not as well as Mama did. I think that I shall be a good dancer, one day, for I love to dance. Sometimes when there is no one about I go into the Roman Saloon and hum the music and dance just for myself."

"Ah, but that is wonderful!" he cried. "I can imagine the scene... it should be by moonlight, to capture the moment in its full glory, and there you would be, your arms aloft, your skirts swirling about you, your feet as light as thistledown."

She put her hand to her mouth to cover her smiles of delight, but her eyes were on fire.

"Well, I think that is silly," Edward said stoutly. "To be dancing all by yourself... what is the point of that?"

"You have no soul, Edward," Malcolm said, mournfully. "Take no notice, Henrietta." But she had lapsed into embarrassed silence and he could not get another word out of her.

"Henrietta, take the tray down to the kitchen," Viola said, in her usual abrupt manner.

"Yes, Aunt."

"Edward, there is paper here and ink, but no pens. Go and fetch a box of quills from the study."

"Yes, Aunt."

"Cross with me, Vi?" Malcolm said, amused, when the children had left.

She sighed. "You have lost none of your charm, Malcolm, and not even I am immune to it, but Laurence will not thank you for filling Henrietta's head with nonsense."

"Is it nonsense? To suggest to her that she is worth every bit as much as a man? Women are beaten down and suppressed in this world, Vi, and taught to do only as they are told and never think for themselves. It is despicable!"

Her eyes widened at his vehemence, but she answered him calmly. "Henrietta is an heiress, Malcolm. She has her mother's entire fortune as her dowry, so when she comes out, she will be snapped up at once and will become a wife and mother. That is her destiny. You do her no favours by encouraging her to think herself special."

"But she *is* special!" Malcolm cried. "Everyone is special in some way, and it would be obscene, Vi, to toss her into the arms of some cold-eyed fortune hunter. Surely Laurence would not—"

He stopped, recalling that his brother had once been the cold-eyed fortune hunter himself, and Catherine the heiress who had been tossed into his arms against her will. Yes, perhaps he would not hesitate to do the same to his daughter, and there was nothing anyone could do to prevent it. He shivered.

Quickly, he went on, "Oh, let us not fall out over it. After all, it is nothing to me what she does with her life, and perhaps she wishes for nothing more than to be a wife and mother."

"Of course she does, for every woman wishes that, Malcolm."

"*Every* woman, Vi?"

She pursed he lips and said firmly, "Every woman. What else is there for her to do except to be a drain on her family, and eke out her life as a kind of glorified servant, of no consequence to anyone?"

There was an edge of bitterness in her tone that took him by surprise. He had always taken his sister for one of life's natural spinsters, and her letters to him, written on the first Sunday of every month without fail, had never given the least hint of dissatisfaction with her rôle, quite the reverse. But the children returned at that moment and there was no opportunity to enquire further.

"So, shall we discuss what language you are to learn?" Malcolm said to Edward.

"Russian," he said at once.

"Why so?"

"I like Tsar Alexander. He stands up to Bonaparte."

Malcolm considered that. "It helps that he is a long way from Paris. It would be quite a task to conquer Russia, would you not agree?"

"Bonaparte will never conquer Russia," Edward said instantly. "The Tsar has a massive army, and the spirit of the Russian people will never be subdued."

"Yes, but—" Malcolm stopped, seeing the blank expression on Vi's face. "We can discuss this later, in Russian. Your father has explained what you have to do?"

"He said that I must be accepted into a society and there will be an examination. I like examinations."

"You will not like this one," Malcolm said. "To be accepted into the Society of Gentleman Linguists, you must demonstrate fluency in five languages. This is tested by examination by a panel of five members of the Society, each fluent in one of your chosen languages. Each one will address you in his own language and you must respond in kind."

"That sounds easy enough," Edward said.

"At first, they will address you one by one, and allow you time to consider your response, but gradually they will speed up and begin to talk across each other and you will be expected to keep up, to switch languages at will, to continue to respond coherently and not to panic, freeze or scream, which I assure you, you will feel like doing. This whole process may take up to an hour in the great hall of one or other of the colleges and in front of the entire membership of the Society, at present almost forty persons. If you succeed, you will be the youngest person granted admittance by five years."

Edward stared at him, his face white. "You think I will fail," he said flatly.

"No, I think you will succeed, but I do not wish you to have unrealistic expectations, or to approach the examination in an overly confident frame of mind. You may know your languages intimately, but the examination is a test also of your fortitude and your mental agility."

"Why do you think I can succeed?"

"Because Great-uncle Zachariah would not have proposed such an ordeal if he had not thought you capable of it, and because I am to teach you. I have many faults, Edward, but I am a very good teacher, and I shall have you speaking Russian like a peasant inside three months, I guarantee it."

"I do not want to speak like a peasant," the boy said indignantly. "I want to speak like the Tsar."

"Ah. Well, I think you will find that His Imperial Majesty generally speaks French."

"French! How disloyal of him to speak the language of the enemy," he said disgustedly.

Henrietta laughed, and again Malcolm caught a tantalising glimpse of her mother. "Do you want to change your mind and learn German instead?" she said teasingly.

Edward answered her seriously. "No, I cannot like the Germans."

"Do you know any?" Malcolm said mildly.

"Well, no, and I am sure they are perfectly pleasant people when one meets them, but the language is... harsh-sounding. I will learn Russian, even if I can only talk to peasants."

"So what happens next?" Viola said. "Shall you begin at once? What do you require?"

"Only my books from Harrow. I shall write to have them sent to me, and to the Society to inform them of our little enterprise, so that they may arrange a date for the examination. Then we shall begin with Russian, but we shall have to practise your other languages, too, so that you will be prepared. But I fear that nothing can prepare you for the examination itself."

"Could we not try, though?" Henrietta said. "If we have five people to speak the languages, we might give Edward a little taste of what he will face. We have no great hall, but the saloon is large and our friends will make up an audience."

"That is an excellent idea," Malcolm said, much struck. "But who might be able to help? Henrietta, you speak Greek."

"Not very well," she said hastily.

"Viola, you used to speak French."

"Not for years, Malcolm. I should hesitate to try to teach Edward anything, but there is a native Frenchwoman at the Dower House at present, lady's maid to Mrs Middlehope. She is *very* French, for she speaks no English at all, although she understands it very well."

"Excellent. A native speaker will be perfect."

"Lots of people speak Latin," Henrietta said. "Mr Truman, the parson, might help out. And Miss Winslade from the Manor speaks Italian."

"Good grief, is she not married yet? I daresay Laurence will not mind if I borrow a horse to call upon her."

"Oh, I am sure he will not... that would be perfectly in order, I am sure," Viola said, wringing her hands anxiously. "He can have not the least objection."

"Will you ask him? I can always write to Susannah, if need be, but I should like to speak to the squire, and the boy, too. What was his name? Henry, that was it. He must be four and twenty by now. How did he turn out?"

"Oh... you know how young men of that age can be," Viola said vaguely. "There is no harm in him, of course, but he does not seem *steady*, somehow. He will settle down when he marries, I feel certain."

"So that is Latin and Italian," Malcolm said, not feeling that settling down to marriage was a fruitful topic of conversation. "And what about Greek?"

He knew the answer before the words left his mouth. The three exchanged glances.

"Papa is the only other fluent Greek speaker," Edward said.

There was a long silence.

"Well, you will just have to ask him," Malcolm said. "If he refuses, then I shall take both Russian and Greek."

"I will ask," Edward said. "I am sure he will want to help."

Malcolm could not be so optimistic. If Laurence would not even meet him, how likely was he to participate in a mock examination? But if he would not, it was not in anyone's power to make him.

Dispatching the ladies to do whatever it was that occupied their morning hours, Malcolm dashed off his letters, while teaching Edward his first Russian words. Pen... paper... table... chair... window... teacher... student... smile. This last Edward obtained from his teacher by dragging the corners of his mouth into an exaggerated grin with his fingers.

His light-heartedness boosted Malcolm's spirits, too. They had a challenging few weeks before them, but the boy was not one to be downcast by the difficulties, and he seemed unconcerned by the enmity between his father and uncle.

The letters written, they must be taken at once to the post, and Edward agreed to accompany him, the better to add to his vocabulary. They crept down the back stairs like thieves, then out of the boot room door and round the house to the lane. The Glebe was empty, the grass tall.

"Does the parson keep no cattle?" Malcolm asked.

"No."

"How strange. I never knew a parson yet who made no use of his Glebe. Even if he does not care to pasture his own cattle, he might rent it out for a few pounds a year."

"Mr Truman is rich."

"Ah. Well, that would account for it. But in that case, we need not scruple to use it as a short cut."

He strode away across the field, and was halfway to the village before he remembered Edward's shorter legs and slowed with an apologetic smile.

The letters deposited at the Boar's Head to await the mail carrier, they were walking past the shop when Edward cried out,

"There is Marie. The French lady. You can ask her if she will help. *Marie! Bonjour, Mademoiselle!"*

A young woman just leaving the bakery, head down, looked up with a mischievous smile. "Good day to you, Master Edward," she said in French with a strong Parisian accent. "How are you today?"

"I am well, thank you, Mademoiselle," he answered. "Come and meet my uncle." Obediently she walked towards them. "This is my father's brother, Malcolm Gage. He is a teacher at Harrow School, but he is here to teach me Russian. Uncle, this is Mademoiselle Marie Fournier."

"Enchanted to meet you, Mademoiselle," Malcolm said, executing his bow.

She curtsied demurely, but there was so much impishness in her face that he almost laughed out loud. Here was an unusual lady's maid indeed! She was far too pretty to be a servant, that was his first thought. His second was that although her pelisse and bonnet were unassuming, there was a certain style about them that would not have been out of place on her mistress. French style, of course. They had a natural flair for the modish.

Malcolm explained the matter to her, and she agreed at once to help. "My mistress is away at present so I am quite at leisure," she said. "Send word to me at the Dower House whenever you need me."

They parted on the most amicable terms, and Malcolm walked back to the Grove in silent contemplation of dark eyes, dark curls and a charmingly heart-shaped face. There was something about her that struck him forcibly, but he could not for the life of him work out what it was.

4: Bluebells

'13th May. Another dull day. How I am to get through the time until Madam returns is beyond me. I have finished reworking the sleeves on the jade green muslin which I hope will please Madam better than the last effort. I still have the new riding habit to finish, and I have enough material for one more nightgown, but after that I shall return to my lace at last. I am not sure what to make with it — perhaps a collar, although Madam is not one for frilly furbelows. I cannot understand why she buys so much lace, except to help the women who make it. It would suit Miss Beasley best. She is such a mouse of a creature, but she would look so well with a little more colour to her gown and a bit of good lace to trim it. I did have one interesting encounter today, with Mr Malcolm Gage, as handsome a man as ever breathed and with a smile to break hearts wherever he goes, although the frayed neckcloth irritated me beyond endurance. He must be very poor, I suppose, and he cannot help the worn coat, but why he could not borrow linen from his brother I cannot see. He is here to tutor the Gage boy in five languages and I am to help with his French. I could not refuse, of course, but it is concerning all the same. Mr Malcolm has penetrating eyes that seem to bore into me, so that I quake inwardly, quite certain that he sees all the way to my soul. Still, an hour with young Master Gage now and then is no great

trial. Ben is to make poulet à la duchesse for us tonight, and Mr Gage's gamekeeper has promised us plover's eggs, which I shall look forward to with great delight. It is a great deal better than mutton stew. Five hundred and sixty seven.'

~~~~~

The next day was Sunday, which Malcolm passed in blissful non-attendance at church, sneaking down to the library and study to top up his supply of books while the family was dutifully praying, and spending the rest of the day reading.

On Monday morning, Edward took Malcolm to visit Mr Truman, the clergyman, to see if he could be induced to help out with the Latin. Their knock on the door was answered by a very smart footman, and they were shown into a lavishly appointed parlour, gleaming with polished mahogany and silver candelabra, a plush rug on the floor and several good paintings on the walls. Edward had been quite right, then, when he had said that the parson was rich. The place had been comfortable enough when the Cokelys had lived there, for the living was a good one, but this was a gentleman's home.

Truman himself was a handsome man, and he knew it, too. There was a preening, self-satisfied air about him that Malcolm disliked on sight. He was affable enough, however, and readily agreed to lend his good offices to the enterprise.

"He sounds an eccentric gentleman, this Mr Zachariah Gage," he said, with his perpetual smile. "Such odd terms to put in his will! But there will be some benefit to you, Edward? There is an inheritance at stake for you?"

"Mostly for Uncle Malcolm, but I shall have one tenth of the money. Uncle Malcolm will get the rest, and the house, of course."
~~~~~

"How marvellous for you, and naturally I wish to play my part in such a worthy cause. It is a valuable property, I take it? A large estate?"

"Not large," Malcolm said, not liking the intrusive questioning.

"Well worth having, I am sure," the clergyman said smoothly.

"It is by no means certain, however," Malcolm said repressively. "Edward must be fluent in all five languages and satisfy the examiners of that. It is not at all easy."

"I shall do my best, Uncle Malcolm," the boy said, looking up at him with those guileless blue eyes.

Malcolm smiled down at him. "Of course you will, but it will not be the end of the world if you do not succeed."

Returning to the Grove, they spent an hour on the Russian alphabet, as Edward learnt to read and write the few words he already knew. Malcolm steadily added to his vocabulary, speaking to him always in Russian. When Edward was summoned to his father's study for his mathematics lesson, Malcolm took the opportunity to call at the Manor to see Susannah Winslade. Viola had confirmed that Laurence had no objection to him borrowing a horse so he took himself down to the stables.

There was no one about, so he wandered from stall to stall, inspecting the beasts. Most were exactly as he expected, solid, worthy animals perfectly capable of pulling the coach or hacking about the countryside with an undemanding rider. One horse, however, was very different, a magnificent grey who whickered imperiously at him as he stroked the velvety nose.

"Well, my fine fellow, my brother's taste is vastly improved if he rides the likes of you. But he is busy just now and I have need of you. Would you like to take me to Cloverstone Manor? It is not far, but distant enough for you to stretch those elegant legs of yours."

The horse snuffled his hand, which he took for assent, and in a very few minutes he had him saddled and ready, and was trotting happily down the drive. At the road he paused to look at the Dower House directly opposite, where the pretty little French maid lived. To one side of the house, beside the stable block, a man and a woman stood chatting, perhaps a maid and groom. Not Marie, though. Even at this distance he could tell that this girl did not have Marie's trim figure. She had made quite an impression on him, the little Frenchwoman, for him to notice such a detail.

Malcolm set the horse in motion again for a short way, then turned in through the open gates of Maeswood Hall. Just beyond the lodge was a riding track that skirted the whole perimeter of the park, and he was able to give his fine mount his head for two miles or more, until he came to the gate that gave access to farmland, then across the river and on to the Manor.

He was detained some time at the stables, for the two elderly grooms sweeping the yard recognised him and exclaimed so loudly that they brought another three running, and then the wives of the older two, all of whom wanted to know all about him and what had brought him back to the Grove. It was some time before their pleasure and good wishes had died down enough for him to get away. If only his own brother could be half so welcoming! But then he would be obliged to be civil to him in return, which would be an offence against his sense of justice.

In days of old, Malcolm had come and gone from the Manor by the stable door, but today he went politely round to the front door and sounded the knocker. It was a fine old house in the Jacobean style, although sadly dilapidated. Leaking drain pipes, peeling paint and the occasional missing pane of glass stuffed with rags spoke of years of neglect. Only the stables seemed to be well cared for.

The elderly retainer who opened the door did not blink when Malcolm gave his name. The fellow shuffled off to see if Miss Winslade was receiving, while Malcolm paced about the Great Hall in increasing impatience. She was indeed receiving, it appeared, and Malcolm was led through endless corridors and rooms and up two flights of stairs to a small room with large windows, filled with a cool light.

"Mr Gage, madam."

She was at her easel, paintbrush in hand, but turned to greet him with a smile, which was quickly replaced by confusion. "Oh, but you are *not* Mr Gage... wait... it is not... can you possibly be *Malcolm?* Oh, good gracious! Binns, run and fetch my father at once, and Mr Henry, if they can be found. Tell them that Mr Malcolm Gage is here. Mr *Malcolm*, mind."

The butler left at the same dawdling pace, and Malcolm could not help laughing. "It is a trifle optimistic to tell the poor man to run, Susannah. But how are you? All grown up, I see."

She was indeed grown up, the stout little girl of ten blossoming into a well-proportioned young lady of six and twenty. There was no disguising the plainness of her features, and nor did she attempt to, for her hair was drawn into a severe knot on the top of her head, not a tendril escaping to soften her face. But her grey eyes were alight with intelligence, and her smile was sweetness itself.

"I am very well, Malcolm. You do not mind, I hope, if I work on my painting as we talk, for my bluebells will wilt if I leave them and then I shall be undone."

"You capture them very well," Malcolm said, admiring the delicate colouring of the painting. "You have a light hand with a brush. Why do you have Latin written at the top here?"

"It is the proper name of the plant — *'Hyacinthoides non-scripta'*. I like to give each plant its correct name."

"What is wrong with calling them bluebells? Everybody knows them as such."

"Except that if you visit Scotland, you would find a very different plant under that name, and the red campion, for instance, is also known as adder's flower, Robin Hood or cuckoo flower. It is better to have a single name that defines each plant uniquely. But tell me how you are, Malcolm, and what brings you back after so many years. Have you and Laurence finally set aside your differences?"

"Not quite," he said, explaining about the will and its peculiar terms. "Will you help? You are fluent in Italian, I am told."

"I am, although I have had little enough practice lately, apart from the occasional song after dinner. I will look out my books, for I would love to help if I can. What a wonderful thing for you, and for Edward too. Who else will be involved in your little scheme?"

"Marie Fournier for French, and Mr Truman for Latin." A hesitation. "I would hope that Laurence will help with the Greek."

She wiped her brush and picked up another. "I do not pretend to know all the circumstances of your dispute with Laurence. All I know is that it concerned his wife, but Catherine Gage has been dead for many years now. Surely it is time to set your grievances aside? I hate to see a family torn asunder."

Malcolm hardly knew what to say to this direct attack. "It is a matter of honour," he managed eventually.

"Ah, masculine honour. And a large dose of pride, I daresay. Well, it is your own affair. There. I have captured the essence of the bloom, I feel. The rest may be added later." She laid down her brush. "Let me clean up a little, and then we may go downstairs and I can receive you properly in the drawing room, as you deserve."

The drawing room had an air of expectancy, with Madeira laid out ready and platters of pastries and tarts filled with strawberry preserve and lemon cakes, appearing so soon that they must have been sitting in an ante-room ready to be summoned. Malcolm refused the Madeira but made great inroads on the edibles, while Susannah told him all about her step-mother's ill-health and the children's progress and her brother's new hunter that was his pride and joy. She asked nothing about Malcolm, but then very likely she already knew the whole of his miserable existence from Viola. There were no secrets when one had a sister like Viola.

Then a surprise. The elderly butler returned and announced in portentous tones, "Miss Saxby and Miss... um... um... Saxby, madam."

Susannah jumped up with an unladylike squeal of delight. "Cass! Agnes! How lovely to see you out and about at last."

Cass Saxby was a pleasant-faced girl of Susannah's age, with a pronounced limp resulting from a childhood illness. Agnes had been barely out of leading strings when Malcolm had last seen her. She must be... he calculated swiftly, and reckoned her age at around twenty years. They wore black, but relieved with a little grey and white. Of course, Lord Saxby had died suddenly in the winter, and the heir, too. Lord, what was the boy's name?

When Malcolm had been introduced, and the two ladies had expressed suitable astonishment at his reappearance, he murmured politely, "May I offer my condolences for the unexpected death of your father... and your brother."

Cass made an unexceptionable response, and the conversation moved swiftly on to the subject of Great-uncle Zachariah's will, as Susannah recounted all she knew of it to Cass. Agnes, however, was silent, staring at him as if mesmerised, her cheeks a little pink. Cass was no beauty, but Agnes was undoubtedly the plainest young woman he had ever seen. Perhaps in her middle years she would make a formidable dowager, but as a girl in her first bloom she was downright ugly, there was no other word for it.

She had taken a seat directly opposite him, from where she gazed at him unswervingly as he continued to eat. After a while, she crossed the room to sit beside him on the sofa.

"Is there a Mrs Gage?" she said.

His eyebrows rose. "There is not."

"So you are not married?"

"No."

"Ah." She smiled at him, and he had a strange sinking feeling in the pit of his stomach. Being a younger son and one without a glittering career to bolster his fortunes, he had never been the object of marriage-minded young ladies, but he had a strong suspicion that he was about to become so. She went on, "Do you need any help with your project? I should be very happy to help out in any way." There was an unnerving eagerness in her manner.

"I should be glad of your help if you can speak Latin, Greek, French, Italian or Russian fluently," he said.

Her face fell. "I speak a little French and Italian, but I would not say I am fluent," she said. "Perhaps I could prepare pens for you, or… or something of the sort."

"Most of the lessons will be spoken not written," he said.

"Then you must come for dinner," she said brightly. "Mama is about to begin inviting a few guests for dinner, close friends only just at present, but I am sure you would fall into that category."

"I am not here to undertake social engagements," he said.

"Oh, but everyone must eat their dinner," she said. "You may as well eat at the Hall as at the Grove."

He gave up the effort to deter her and as soon as was decent, he made his departure. Neither the squire nor Henry had made an appearance. The grey was impatient to be on his way, and Malcolm let him make his own pace. Lord, the joy of a fine horse beneath him and the ground disappearing under his hooves! How many years was it since he had ridden anything beyond a slug of a hack, and that but seldom?

In no time, the beast was trotting into the stable yard at the Grove, although Malcolm could tell he was lively enough for many more miles.

"Thank you, my fine fellow," he murmured as he slid from the saddle, and led the horse into the stables.

Two figures rushed at him agitatedly, one an anxious-looking groom, and the other a very familiar face, despite the rage infusing it. Even after sixteen years, there was no mistaking his brother.

"What the *devil* do you think you are doing?" he yelled, in a very un-Laurence-like manner. "Let go of Gaius Valerius at once!"

He should have been outraged by such an uncouth reception, but somehow it just made him want to laugh. Laurence was half a head shorter than he was, and not stout exactly, but certainly solidly built, and just at that moment he looked as ridiculous as a turkey cock in full display. Malcolm contented himself with saying, "Oh, is that his name? How fitting!"

"What are you doing riding him? You had no right, none at all!"

Malcolm's eyebrows lifted, but he responded mildly, "You said I might borrow one of your horses, brother."

"Yes, one of *mine*, but not Louisa's."

"Louisa? Who is Louisa?"

"Louisa Middlehope. From the Dower House. My future wife. Do not *dare* to touch her horse again, do you hear, or you will be out of here so fast you will not know what happened."

"Your future wife? You are to marry again?" Malcolm said, feeling abruptly as if he had been punched in the gut.

"I am. Not that it is any concern of yours. Good God, Malcolm, just keep out of my way, will you?"

"Well, I am trying," Malcolm muttered as Laurence stalked off, hands still clenched into fists.

The groom was engaged in feeling over the horse's legs, but he looked up with an amused grin. "Brothers, eh? Who'd have 'em?"

That brought a reluctant bark of laughter from Malcolm. "I have not harmed Gaius Valerius, you know. I had not the least idea to whom he belonged, although I confess I was surprised to find such a fine mount in Laurence's stable. He is not noted for his horsemanship."

The groom chuckled. "True enough. I'd never let *him* near Gaius, but I could see at a glance you know one end of a horse from the other."

"Well, thank you for the compliment!" he said wryly. "What is your name, my man?"

"Spencer, sir. Gaius is my special charge, and there's only me and the mistress ever ridden him, till today."

"Tell me about your mistress, since I know nothing about her, except that she has excellent taste in horses, and must be a fine rider."

Spencer nodded. "Aye, she is that. She's the widow of Mr Edward Middlehope of Roseacre in County Durham. He were heir to a baron, Lord Mountsea, but Mr Edward died first so the title went to the younger brother."

"Has she children?"

"No."

"Is she pretty?"

"Hmm." A long pause. "She's a fine lady," he said eventually.

Malcolm laughed, and supposed he would have to make his own judgement when he met her. "She is from home at the moment, I understand?"

"Aye, sir, gone back to Roseacre for her books. She's mortal fond of those books. She'll be back in a week or two."

"I look forward to meeting her," he said, rather grimly. And that was true enough. He would be very interested indeed to meet the woman who was to succeed the incomparable Catherine Haywood as wife to Laurence.

How could he do it? After tasting paradise, how could he so lower his sights as to marry a widow from County Durham? It was unfathomable.

And more to the point, why on earth was Laurence so angry with him? *'Just keep out of my way,'* he had said, for all the world as if he were the injured party, not Malcolm. That, too, was unfathomable.

5: Lobster And Cheesecake

"Come, Vi, you must tell me the truth," Malcolm said. "What bee is in Laurence's bonnet? Why does he hold me in such dislike? I am the injured party here, after all."

"Oh yes, indeed you were most grievously injured. Most certainly you were. There is no doubt about that, no doubt at all, and so I have always said. Have I not always said so? Laurence did not quite behave as he ought, but then the estate... and poor Papa... and Mama in such a dreadful state..."

She lapsed into a distressed silence, twisting her hands together convulsively. Edward had been called to his father's study for his lesson in mathematics, and Viola had crept up to the nursery with a plate of apricot pastries for Malcolm. Since she had disturbed his hour of solitude with his books, he could not resist trying to tease the truth out of her.

"But why is he so angry with me now?" Malcolm said.

"I cannot tell you, for Laurence is hardly rational on the subject. You will have to ask him yourself."

"And how am I supposed to do that when he will not even see me?" he asked in reasonable tones, but she only twittered ever more anxiously.

"It is not right!" she burst out. "Brothers should not be at war like this. It is a dreadful thing for all the family. Such a bad example to the children. They go to church on Sunday and Mr Truman preaches about charity and forgiveness and turning the other cheek, and Laurence comes home and ignores the presence of his own brother in his house. It is not right."

"And you are caught in the middle of it all, eh? Poor Vi! We are wicked to distress you so. Let us talk of other matters. You may tell me about Louisa Middlehope, if you will, or is that a secret, too?"

"Oh! Oh, yes, *dear* Louisa! So happy for them both."

"You like her, then?" he said, reaching for his third, or perhaps fourth, apricot pastry.

"How could I not when dear Laurence is so besotted? I confess I *was* a tiny bit suspicious of her motives at first, but she is such a wealthy woman that there can be no objection, not the least in the world. She would have been a baroness if her husband had but lived a few months more. Such a tragedy. And no children, after twelve years. Such a dreadful pity, to be barren. How desolate she must feel inside at failing in her primary duty, but she never shows it, not in the least. She is always so cheerful and gracious, and very stylish. I have ordered a new bonnet for the wedding and Louisa was most helpful in choosing a style. Most helpful."

Malcolm decided that he was not going to get anything sensible out of Viola, so he gave it up. Anyone who judged a woman by her taste in hats was not someone with whom he could find common ground.

Moments after Viola had left, a delicate knock at the door brought him another visitor, one to raise a smile from any man.

"Bonjour, mademoiselle."

"Bonjour, monsieur." She set a cloth-covered basket on the table, chattering away prettily in French. "I bring you some gifts from Monsieur Chambers, the artist who rules the kitchen at the Dower House. I report to him how thin and ill you look, and his heart is greatly moved. Here, you see? Some fish in the shell, three creams of some kind and these little cakes of cheese and almonds. For your supper, perhaps."

"Everyone wishes to feed me," Malcolm said, laughing. "Thank Monsieur Chambers very kindly for all of this, if you please. Oh, lobster! That looks delicious. Tell him I shall enjoy it very much. There is an apricot pastry left. Would you like it?"

"I think you need it more than I do, monsieur. I am excessively well fed at the Dower House."

"On lobster and cheesecake? Your mistress is generous."

"She is very kind, yes," Marie said.

"So she does not beat you when you fail to starch her collars correctly, or remove a stain?"

Marie raised one delicately arched eyebrow. "But no, for I never do so. I am a most superior lady's maid, me. Every stain is taken away, every tear made invisible and every lace fichu as white as snow, although not starched. A lady does not wear the shirt collar stiff like a man, no. Everything about her must be soft and flowing and so, so feminine. You understand?"

Malcolm was enchanted. There was a pertness about her that was perhaps unbecoming in a lady's maid, but she had the most mischievous mouth he had ever seen, curling up at the sides even in repose as if she were perpetually about to break into laughter. And her eyes... as dark and lustrous as a glossy conker.

When she smiled up at him in that mesmerising way, her head tipped to one side like a little bird and her gaze holding his, he felt something melt inside. It was as if he had known her for ever.

"Do you like being a lady's maid?"

"But yes, certainly. It is a very respectable position, and the work is not arduous. I consider myself fortunate to have such a good place."

"Are you all alone in the world, or do you have family still in France?"

Was there a slight hesitation before she answered? A sore subject, perhaps. "I have no family in France, and I prefer to be alone, monsieur. Some people are naturally alone, and need no one else."

Some people are naturally alone... That was very true, and Malcolm himself was of their number. He had much in common with the petite lady's maid, and his heart turned over in sympathy. They were so much alike. No wonder he felt this strange affinity for her.

"Did you learn your trade in Paris?" he said, for the sake of keeping the conversation going.

Her eyes clouded momentarily, and he cursed himself for breaking the spell, but after a moment, she said smoothly, "Paris? But no. I am from Dijon, but I learnt my trade, as you say it, here in England. Where is young Edward? Is he ill, or has he been sent to his room in disgrace?"

"Neither. He is with his father doing his sums like a good student. He will be back soon. Would you like to stay and test him on his French? You need only chat to him about everyday things for now. We will become more ambitious and hurl philosophical questions at him later."

She agreed to it, removing her bonnet and gloves, but it was not long before Edward bounced into the room, and learnt the good news that he was to practise his French. Malcolm took no part in the conversation, so he had the pleasure of listening to Marie's musical voice as she chattered away to Edward. They talked of nothing very much — Laurence's forthcoming wedding, the people they had met at church on Sunday, the physician's odd turn on Saturday night and what might be the matter with him — but it was delightful to listen to Marie's dulcet tones, and watch the animation on her so-expressive face.

Malcolm felt curiously light-headed, as if he had been cut free of his mooring and was about to float away somewhere. It was the oddest feeling. What could it possibly mean? His gaze was drawn to Marie's lips as she spoke, to the shapely lips that curled up ready to smile, even in repose. Those smiling lips, the heart-shaped face, the eyes, clear and bright.

It was unfathomable, for was not his love for Catherine eternal and all-encompassing? There was no room in his heart for any other woman, even one so delightful as Marie. Or was there? Catherine was gone beyond his reach, but Marie was here now, alive and enchanting and free, and he responded to her, just as he had once responded to Catherine. Then he had known that his future wife was before him. And now...?

Something inside him shifted, filling him with a yearning for the settled married life he had been denied once before. Then he knew his destiny — he would marry Mademoiselle Marie Fournier, and they would live in Great-uncle Zachariah's house in Oxford and be blissfully happy. This could be accomplished only if Edward managed to succeed in his task, of course, but there were three months yet before the boy would be put to the test, and he was clever enough to do it, without doubt. And then Malcolm would have his house, and he and Marie could go to the parson and have the banns heard, and then—

No. That was wrong. Marie was French and must therefore be Catholic. Yet she attended the church in the village. How very odd.

That brought him back to earth with a crash. Viola had described her as *very* French, speaking no English, and perhaps she had arrived on the shores of Britain after the troubles in her native country, but it would be unlike a Frenchwoman to surrender her faith. Yet seemingly she had. And that was definitely not a Dijon accent. Now that he was alerted to the oddity, he listened more attentively to the conversation, and began to spot one or two places where her phrasing sounded odd to his ears. Could it be a local dialect? Definitely odd.

They were interrupted by Viola. "So sorry to disturb you and pray forgive the intrusion but Kidwell is asking if you want your usual lesson today, Edward, since the weather is so settled. He has Little Star ready for you if you should wish it, and if your uncle can spare you, of course. I did not quite know what you wish to do about such matters, Malcolm, and now I see that Miss Fournier is here so you may not want to—"

"Non, madame," Marie said. "It is not important. Edward, ride the horse if it pleases you. We can practice French another time."

How interesting. A woman who spoke no English, yet could disentangle Viola's jumble of verbiage and deduce that she referred to a horse, even though the word *'cheval'* had not been mentioned. How very, very interesting.

Edward looked at Malcolm. "Should I, sir? I do not wish to waste time that could be spent learning a language."

"It is also important to allow your brain to cool down after a period of intense thinking," Malcolm said, with a smile. "If you would like to go, then by all means do so. The air and exercise will do you good."

He looked relieved, and happily went away with Viola. Marie rose, and reached for her bonnet and gloves.

"Stay a moment, *mademoiselle."*

"Oui, monsieur. Certainement."

"Speak to me in English. I know you can, for you understand it perfectly."

"Mais non, monsieur. I understand everything, but the sounds are too difficult to say."

"Nonsense." Her eyes opened wide at his brusqueness, but he continued relentlessly. "You are not French at all, are you? Does it increase your value as a maid to pretend to be French? But who are you, madam? I assure you I mean you no harm, but I need to know your true name."

Her face was pale, but she answered composedly. "Truly I am French, monsieur, I assure you. I come from Dijon."

"What street?" He still spoke in English.

She licked her lips. "Near the *Rue de Paris."*

"Then you must know my friends who live on the *Rue de Tivoli*, the Bridgers. Do you know them?"

"Non, monsieur. Your friends are rich. I am poor. Truly, you must believe me."

Malcolm shook his head, smiling at her, and watching her wary expression soften. "There is no *Rue de Tivoli* in Dijon. I do indeed have friends in the town, you see. I think you are English. You are certainly not Catholic, that much is certain, for no good Catholic would attend divine service in a Protestant church. Tell me your name. That is all I want to know."

Now her high forehead with its little ring of curls drew into a frown. *"Pourquoi?"*

"Because I am going to marry you, and I can only do that if I know your real name," he said evenly.

Her jaw dropped, and then she burst into a rather strained laugh. "You are mad!"

Still laughing, she swept up her bonnet and gloves and left him alone in the nursery.

~~~~~

'16th May. Mr Malcolm Gage suspects. He does not yet know anything, but he told me to my face that he believes I am English and he wants to know my name. And then, if you please, he told me that he is going to marry me! No proposal, no mention of love, and I have met him precisely twice, but he has decided that he will marry me. He is utterly insane. It is a great pity, of course, for he is so handsome and quite charming, and when he smiles— but that is foolish and I must not follow that train of thought. He is not for me, and I must do nothing to put myself at risk of discovery. I shall smile sweetly and keep him on leading strings until he loses interest or leaves. He and his brother hate each other, so sooner or later there will be an explosion and he will leave. I am very glad I have trusted no one over the years, for there is no possibility that he can find out anything about me. I am quite safe. Five hundred and sixty four.'
~~~~~

~~~~~

Boredom sucked at Marie's spirits. If only Madam would come back and give her something to do! She was very thankful not to have suffered the endless days in the swaying carriage on the long journey north, for travelling always made her so ill, but it was a challenge to fill the long hours without real employment. She had used up all the supplies of fabric she had on hand, so she could not hide away in the unused parlour with her sewing. Impossible, too, to stay in the Dower House with the other servants coming and going all the time. They were accustomed to the idea that she spoke no English and asked her no questions, but still they were always there, watching her.

The one disadvantage to speaking no English was that she could not ask any questions herself. If she wished to know what was going on, she had to go to Mr Timpson's shop and lurk behind the sacks of rice, listening to the gossip. Whatever was happening in Great Maeswood, or further afield, the news would be brought first to Timpson's and thence disseminated all over the village. Not a horse could lose a shoe or a young lady gaze bashfully at a young man but Mrs Timpson would know it, and thus every gossip for miles around.

Mostly Marie went there for amusement, to hear the latest titbits and laugh at her fellows, but now she stood in grave need of information. She had to know more of Malcolm Gage. Her stomach lurched with fear when she thought of him. She reassured herself that he could not possibly find out who she was, for she had left no clues anywhere, but still the thought was terrifying. Was he serious in wanting to marry her? If so, he was fit only for the asylum. But all she knew of him was that he was clever enough to speak many languages and that he had quarrelled with his brother, a quarrel maintained over many
~~~~~

years. And that he was handsome, of course, with the sweetest, most enticing smile that made her want to like him, very much. But that was irrelevant.

Now she needed far more information about him. She needed to know what sort of man he was, and why he had sustained so long a feud with his brother. So on the day after the non-proposal, she walked down to Timpson's and wandered about the shop. The advantage of a village shop was that it sold absolutely everything. Its principal function was as a grocery, but Mr Timpson sold all manner of other goods besides, many of which were of interest to Marie. At different times he offered ribbons, buttons, gloves, laces, wool and thread for tatting or embroidery, hair pins, stays, feathers and silk flowers, mirrors and combs, beads and spangles and much more. Every time she went, there was some new thing to be seen, and occasionally strips of lace or swansdown or velvet, which Marie could not afford but liked to see and to touch. Today there was a whole box of oddments of fabric, for making handkerchiefs or fichus or trimmings, and Marie settled contentedly to rifle through them all, obscured by a pile of tea chests from the other customers.

At first she thought there would be nothing to be learnt that day, for the talk was all of Dr Beasley, who had suffered a seizure a few days earlier and was confined to his bed as a result.

"He is talking about retiring from his medical practice altogether." That was Miss Gage's distinctive twitter. "I have just come from the Villa, and Miss Beasley told me so herself."

"Poor Dr Beasley!" came Mrs Timpson's louder voice. "And Miss Beasley had to call out Mr Edser to attend to him — an apothecary looking after a trained physician! But Mr Edser is very good. He fixed up Tilly's ear last year, if you remember, Miss Gage. Very dependable."

"Oh yes, indeed, I have nothing to say about Mr Edser except... well, that business with Miss Agnes."

"Oh yes," Mrs Timpson said sympathetically. "Poor Mr Edser. Broken hearted, he were, and still has hopes, but she only has eyes for a certain person now, I hear tell. But we'll say nothing of that, eh, Miss Gage?"

"Oh certainly, for I *cannot* see that Malcolm will ever be inclined to marry. He is quite a settled bachelor now, I believe."

"We thought that of Mr Laurence, too," Mrs Timpson said, chuckling. "That were a surprise, eh? So maybe your Mr Malcolm will be drawn in by Miss Agnes, bless her. Poor mite, for she's nothing to look at and deserves a good husband more than most. And she's very clever, Miss Agnes is, so she'd be a good match for Mr Malcolm, I reckon. Just the tea today, then, Miss Gage? I should have the lemons in tomorrow without fail. Shall I send a box along for you?"

When she had gone, another voice spoke up. "Mr Malcolm a settled bachelor, is he?" That was Mrs Preece, the smith's wife. "That's one way to describe 'im."

"Now then, Kitty! His heart was broke all those years ago, and he's never forgot her, and who would, lovely lady that she was?"

"It's not natural, bearing a grudge all these years. Just because 'is brother married the lady 'e'd set his 'eart on, is no reason to tear the family apart. 'E should learn to turn the other cheek, like the Good Lord said. Oh 'eavens! 'Ere 'e is now. I'd best be off. Good day to you, Fanny. Good day, Bill."

Well, that was interesting. So that was the cause of the breach between the brothers. They had both wanted the same woman, but the older brother had married her and the younger had gone off in a decades-long huff. And had the lady been given any say in the matter? Had she happily married the man of her choice, or had the poor girl been cajoled and threatened and pressed to marry the more suitable older brother, the heir to a great estate?

She shivered.

6: An Invitation To Dinner

At first, the shop looked empty. Malcolm nodded to Mr and Mrs Timpson, and went straight past the groceries to what he thought of as the odds and ends section, the corner of the shop holding a multitude of strange goods, a place where almost anything may be found.

Rounding a stack of tea chests, he found a familiar heart-shaped face, topped with the most fetching little velvet hat.

"Bonjour, mademoiselle." He swept off his hat and made her a sweeping bow, and she blushed very prettily as she curtsied.

"Bonjour, monsieur. Bonjour, Eduard."

"We are here to practise some Russian," he went on in French. "I say the word in Russian and Edward points to it, and then makes up a sentence with it."

"That is an unusual way to learn," she said. "Generally one learns from books."

"My books have not yet arrived, so we must improvise." Then, picking up a square of fabric from a box, he said in Russian, "Edward, what is this?" The boy shook his head. "Cloth. This is cloth."

"What did you say to him?" she said in French.

"I told him it is cloth."

"Cloth? But no. It is a fichu, like so." She held it in front of her gown, then at her hem. "Or a flounce, thus. Or a handkerchief. Or a cap," placing it on top of her hat.

Laughing, Malcolm gave the Russian word for each, then said in French, "I stand corrected, mademoiselle, and bow to your superiority. I apologise for my lack of insight into the possibilities, but being a mere man hampers me."

Seeming rather flustered, she made some reply and took her leave. Malcolm went to the window to watch her walk away down the road. She was so neat and precise in her movements. Her walk was upright and confident, and she neither strode away with indelicate haste nor dawdled lazily. She was a woman who knew her own worth, just like Catherine had been.

"Pretty lady," Edward said in Russian.

"Yes, she is."

"You like pretty lady."

"Every man likes a pretty lady. You will like pretty ladies, too, when you are older."

Edward puzzled over the intricacies of the sentence before hesitantly repeating it back.

They passed a pleasant half hour in the shop, bought a pound of sugared almonds before they left — "We have to buy *something,"* Edward whispered — and then ambled back through the village, chewing contentedly. Edward recited the name of every object he saw, moving or stationary, greeted every passerby in impeccable Russian and needed no more than the occasional correction from Malcolm as they walked.

This left Malcolm's mind free to consider the more interesting question of Mademoiselle Marie Fournier, the pretty lady who was naturally alone yet always seemed pleased to see him. Who was she? Not a jumped up housemaid, that much was certain. Lady's maids often started life as something lowly and were trained up, and Marie said she had learnt her trade in England, but how would a housemaid learn French, and with a perfect Parisian accent, too. She had denied any origins in Paris, yet she had acquired that distinctive accent from somewhere. Not from Dijon! Her mother, perhaps? That was a possibility.

As soon as they turned into the Grove's drive, they could see bustle about the stables, and the coach house doors standing wide.

"Visitors!" Edward cried, reverting excitedly to English. He ran on ahead round the corner of the house to the front door, bouncing happily back before Malcolm, even with his long legs, was halfway up the drive.

"This is famous!" Edward yelled to him. "It is Aunt Ursula and Aunt Selena come to stay. They are such fun!"

Malcolm gave a resigned sigh. "I will be in the nursery if anyone wants me," he said glumly, but Edward had already gone.

He crept into the house by way of the boot room, and up the back stairs to the nursery, where he tossed aside his greatcoat and cast himself on the bed, wreathed in gloom. It was bad enough to have Viola twittering over him like a demented sparrow, but now he would have to put up with the combined sympathy and reproach of Ursula and Selena too. No man should have three sisters older than he was, for it was at least two too many.

The sugared almonds were still in his pocket, so he retrieved them, picked up the topmost book on his pile and crunched his way through several chapters while he waited. And waited.

It was a full hour before they came, a tentative knock on the door followed by two lace-capped heads already showing quite a lot of grey. But they were all of them older now. He had been two and twenty when he had left this house, and now he was eight and thirty, descending rapidly into his middle years, still solitary, still hurt, still *angry*.

"Oh, there you are, Malcolm!"

"Goodness, how thin you are, brother!"

"But you are well? You look well otherwise, apart from not eating properly."

"What a strange start this is, on Great-uncle Zachariah's part."

"But then he was always eccentric, was he not, sister?"

"Quite an original! But you have made a beginning already. Edward was gabbling away in Russian. Such a clever boy!"

Malcolm let them run on uninterrupted. It was only when Ursula said, "You may tell us all about it at dinner," that he felt obliged to intervene.

"Not at dinner. I am banned from good society… from all society, in fact. I eat up here."

The sisters exchanged glances. "That you shall not," Selena said, in her no-nonsense way. "You will dine with the family tonight. We will tell Laurence."

"He has given me very explicit instructions," Malcolm said firmly. "I will only agree to it if I have an invitation from Laurence himself — in writing."

It was a further two hours, and perilously close to the hour to dress for dinner, before John arrived, note in hand. "From Mr Gage, sir," he said, blank-faced.

'Please join us for dinner tonight and every night,' the note said, in Ursula's floridly feminine hand. Below, in a different hand, it was signed, *'Laurence'.*

Malcolm laughed. "What did they have to do to get him to agree to this?" he murmured.

"I couldn't possibly say, sir," John said, grinning, "but the fires of Hell came into it, and a great many verses of the Bible, especially the parable of the prodigal son. And then they cried."

"That would do it," Malcolm said, shaking his head. "No man can withstand tears. Well, if I must, I must."

He descended by way of the back stairs, just in case of unexpected encounters, and slipped into the drawing room at the very last minute. It was more crowded than he had expected. He saw Laurence at once, his unsmiling face glaring at him from the far side of the room. He had worn better than Viola, at least. Perhaps he was a little rounder about the middle, but it was slight and he still had all his hair and not a single grey amongst the brown. He could say nothing about his teeth until he bared them, either in a smile or a snarl. Frankly, the latter seemed far more likely. Henrietta looked nervous, her gaze flicking from father to uncle and back again. Edward grinned and waved cheerfully at him. Three unknown gentlemen watched his entrance with interest.

For a moment Malcolm was taken aback, quite unprepared for guests. Was Laurence so afraid of a confrontation that he needed some neutral forces between the two opposing camps? But then his sisters rose and surrounded him in a defensive cloud of lace and expensive perfume and waving feathers, and gently steered him into the room.

It was Viola who took charge. "Do come and meet everyone, Malcolm. This is Mr Willerton-Forbes. His father is the Earl of Morpeth, you know. Captain Edgerton is from the East India Company Army, but he has left off his sword and pistols for the evening. And last but by no means least..." She tittered a little at her jest, her cheeks pink. "Mr Chandry. He is from Cornwall. My other brother, gentlemen."

The four bowed politely to each other. Two of the three men were just a little younger than Malcolm, dressed in forbiddingly fashionable London style. Chandry was the youngest, probably not yet thirty, with the sort of carelessly handsome features and roguish smile that no doubt melted female hearts. He had certainly melted Viola's.

They were gentlemen, however, and therefore too polite to ask all the burning questions that must buzz around their heads at the reappearance of the long-lost brother after so many years, so the conversation was bland. They had not progressed much beyond the state of the roads and means of travel — "The mail coach! You brave man," the captain said feelingly — when Skeates announced dinner.

Malcolm sat as far as he could from his scowling brother, which put him beside a jumpy Viola and opposite Captain Edgerton. Viola could always be depended upon to propel the conversation onwards, filling the tiniest void with trivial chitter-chatter, whether the other party be willing or no, and as it happened Malcolm was not at all willing. Fortunately, Captain Edgerton was sharp-witted, and whenever Viola addressed a question to Malcolm, he jumped in himself with some nonsensical anecdote, of which he appeared to have an inexhaustible supply. Since he also kept Henrietta entertained on his other side, Malcolm gave him full credit for his deftness, and managed to chew his way through the meal without uttering a word.

When the ladies and Edward had retired to the drawing room, Willerton-Forbes and Chandry moved nearer to Laurence, but Malcolm stayed where he was, and Edgerton kept his seat, too. A conveniently placed epergne gave Malcolm some relief from his brother's glowering countenance, emboldening him to say to Edgerton, "So what brings a captain of the East India Company Army to this quiet backwater of Shropshire?"

Edgerton lowered his voice to a dramatic whisper. "Murder! A long-dead body in the Dower House wine cellar, to be precise."

Malcolm raised an eyebrow in surprise. "You were involved with the body in the basement, were you? But that was months ago."

"True, but it takes time to investigate such matters thoroughly, and the final pieces of the puzzle were only put in place last week. A most enjoyable puzzle, I might add. That is my business now, solving murders and other mysteries where the magistrates are stumped."

"Is there much call for such a service?" Malcolm said.

"You would be surprised, sir. It is not merely the solving of a crime that we undertake, for any half-competent Bow Street Runner may do as much, but when persons of quality are concerned in the matter, there is a great need for discretion."

"Keeping everything quiet, I suppose."

"Ah, you are cynical, Mr Gage. Sometimes that is the case, but generally the difference lies in the approach. Many of the higher ranks of society view Bow Street Runners and thief-takers as little better than criminals themselves — low men without manners or morals. They object in the strongest terms to interrogation by such men. Willerton-Forbes, on the other hand, may go anywhere and mingle with the lords and ladies and gentlefolk. He has only to mention his father the earl and doors open for him and the grandest duchess will talk freely to him. Chandry and I are not quite so elevated, but we can pass muster in drawing rooms, and we may also mix rather freely with the lower ranks. It gives us an edge, you see, over more conventional forms of investigation, and we are quite clever enough to challenge the most devious of miscreants. At least, Willerton-Forbes is. He is a lawyer, so his brain is honed to the sharpness of a sword. We are quite the best investigators of crime in the land, in my perfectly humble opinion."

Malcolm could not but be amused by such hubris, and since Edgerton was quite aware of his conceit it was impossible to dislike him.

When the gentlemen re-joined the ladies in the drawing room, Henrietta was playing a pretty little French song. When she had finished, she came over to him and said, *"Avez-vous aimé la musique, mon oncle?" Do you like the music, Uncle?*

"Tu joues très bien du pianoforte." You play the pianoforte very well.

"Merci beaucoup. Je joue tous les jours." Thank you. I play every day.

The card tables were being put out and she was called away to make up a four, but Malcolm sat as if struck by lightning. For his niece, taught at home by a governess or perhaps by Laurence, he could not say, had a perfect Parisian accent. That was, naturally, the way all gently-born girls were taught to speak the language. Henrietta sounded exactly like Marie. The conclusion was inescapable. Marie was not merely some low-born child who had clawed her way up to the level of a lady's maid. Someone had seen to it that she was properly educated, at a halfway decent school. Not gentry, perhaps, but more likely from the respectable merchant or shopkeeper class.

With the arrival of Selena and Ursula, there were enough players for two whist tables, leaving Malcolm and Edward to play backgammon in Russian in a corner. When the ladies retired to bed, scooping up the long-forgotten Edward along the way — "Heavens, child, what are you doing still up at this hour?" — the other four men merged onto one table, and Malcolm took the opportunity to leave too. But he did not go to bed. Instead, he concealed himself behind the voluminous curtains in the empty saloon and waited.

He could not say how long he stayed there, for the clocks had stopped chiming the hours, but eventually he was rewarded. The men drifted out of the drawing room into the saloon, moving slowly, still chatting away loudly. Laurence went up the spiral staircase, but the other three ambled through the ante-room towards the main staircase. As soon as they were out of sight, Malcolm raced for the service stairs, and was concealed behind another curtain before the three had reached the head of the stair. There they paused, still talking, although more quietly now, before parting for the night.

Here Malcolm was lucky, for Willerton-Forbes and Chandry went one way and Edgerton the other. Malcolm had taken the precaution of removing his shoes, so he crept silently from his hiding place and followed Edgerton's candle down the darkened corridor. He could tell to which room they were heading, so he stopped.

At once Edgerton stopped, too, turning towards him. "Did you wish to speak to me, Mr Gage?" he said pleasantly.

Malcolm laughed. "There is no fooling you, is there, Captain?"

"I should certainly hope I would not be taken in by such a simple trick," he said easily, and in the flickering candlelight his teeth gleamed as he smiled broadly. "Come in, and you may tell me why you are creeping about the house in your stockinged feet."

Like the south-eastern apartment, this room had been redecorated, and now sported a boldly striped wallpaper above pale panels and a matched set of modern furniture. A couple of small but well-executed paintings hung on one wall.

"Does it look different?" the captain said. "The late Mrs Gage had the whole house redone from top to bottom, seemingly." But not the library, oddly. That was still just as it was. The captain went on, "She had exquisite taste, if I may say so."

"In interior design, perhaps," Malcolm said sourly.

"But not in husbands, eh?" Edgerton chuckled, walking across the room to a sideboard laden with decanters. "But then women are entirely unaccountable. Who knows what goes on in their heads? Please have a seat. I shall not offer you a glass of your brother's excellent Cognac, Gage, since I noticed you drank nothing at dinner, but you will not mind if I do, I am sure. Your brother may have a long memory for perceived insults, but he keeps a magnificent cellar and it would be churlish not to take advantage of it."

"And why he should perceive *any* insult is the mystery of it," Malcolm burst out. "I am the aggrieved party in this case."

"He won the lady, it is true, but... is there some other matter between you?"

"How could there be? We were the best of friends until we went to Bath and he stole Catherine away from me." There was the familiar stab of pain to accompany his words, the anger rising up inside him. Damn Laurence for all eternity!

"Do you wish me to talk to Mr Gage about the matter?" Edgerton said politely. "To find out how he imagines you to have injured him, or perhaps to intercede on your behalf?"

"No, no. That is between Laurence and me, and I care nothing for his good opinion. I shall do what I can to get Edward his inheritance, but beyond that I want no more to do with this family."

Even as he spoke the words, he knew them to be untrue. For months after the breach he had waited for a sign from Laurence, an olive branch extended to him, but there had been nothing. Just a letter to inform him that the marriage had taken place, but no hint of an apology. Not that he would have forgiven Laurence, but he should have shown some contrition, and for him to portray himself now as the affronted party was beyond anything!

But that was not his concern now. "It is another matter upon which I seek your counsel."

"By all means. What is your difficulty?"

Malcolm looked at him thoughtfully. "It is important that this not be widely known."

"You may depend upon my absolute discretion," Edgerton said. "I give you my word of honour as a gentleman. Whatever you say will not leave this room, unless you permit it."

"Very well then. Are you acquainted with Mademoiselle Marie Fournier?"

"Mrs Middlehope's French lady's maid? Indeed. A very charming and pretty young person."

"She is not French."

Edgerton's eyebrows rose a shade, but he said evenly, "It is not uncommon for a maid to claim a more exotic background to increase her value to an employer."

"That was what I thought at first, too," Malcolm said eagerly, "but it is not so. She speaks French too well to be some jumped-up ragamuffin. Not perfectly, mind you, but she has been well taught, and she has a Parisian accent, just like Henrietta."

Edgerton understood, a flicker of interest in his eyes. "You think she is gentry?"

"Not gentry, for what lady would so demean herself as to seek employment as a maid? But respectable, certainly. I asked her what her real name is, but she would not tell me and why hide it?"

"She has some reason to remain anonymous," Edgerton said, leaning forward in excitement. "And you wish to know the truth, before your brother introduces this secretive person into his household. If she means mischief, it is better to discover it at once."

That was not at all the reason for Malcolm's interest, but as an excuse for probing Marie's background it would serve as well as any other.

"Can you find out her real name?" he said.

"It would be foolish of me to make rash promises of that nature, but you may be assured that I shall do everything in my power to find it out," Edgerton said. "I shall have to take my colleagues into my confidence on the matter, but their discretion is absolute."

"I... am not sure that I can pay your fees just at present," Malcolm said uncertainly. "If I manage to obtain this inheritance—"

"There is no need to worry about that," Edgerton said, with an airy wave of the hand. "It is a small matter to undertake, and will serve to repay your brother for his most generous hospitality." He raised his brandy glass with a rueful smile. "It will be a pleasure to uncover Mademoiselle's little secrets, and if we find there is nothing of great moment there, why then she may go about her business without ever knowing what we have been about. But if, on the other hand, we discover anything underhand, the full force of the law will be brought to bear, you may be sure."

"The full force of the law?" Malcolm said, suddenly anxious. That was not at all what he had in mind!

Edgerton gave him a long look, then said carefully, "Naturally, we will use the utmost discretion in deciding what the law needs to know about the matter, Mr Gage."

And with that Malcolm had to be satisfied, but he began to wonder if he had done Marie a great wrong in unleashing Captain Edgerton and his colleagues. Perhaps he should just have kept silent.

7: Lower Maeswood

"I am grateful for this fine view over the gardens, wearing all their myriad spring greens. I am grateful for my sisters' concern for me, in coming here to see me. I am grateful for Marie, whose sweet face and impish smile lift my spirits."

Malcolm kissed the pendant and tucked it away inside his shirt with a smile of his own. Every thought of Marie made him smile! In a strange way, she reminded him of Catherine. Not in appearance or mannerisms — Catherine had been so composed and serene, with her cool blonde beauty and her demureness, whereas Marie had not struck him as demure in the least, and her dark colouring was nothing like Catherine. But he felt the same pull towards her, the same joy in her company, the same desire to make her his for ever. How strange!

Noises from the day nursery next door alerted him. Doors opening and closing, chairs scraped across the wooden floor, and then female voices. He sighed. The trouble with sisters, especially when they were older than he was, was that they could not be deterred from interfering. They called it 'helping', but in truth it was nothing short of interference, and they all interfered in different ways — Viola by sheer bossiness and fussing, Ursula by talking at him relentlessly and Selena by organising. Yes, all that furniture being shifted around could only be Selena. She would have a Plan for his lessons with Edward. Selena always had a Plan.

He chose not to rush, merely returning to his bed with a book, and even when John arrived with his washing water, he did not stir. Let them wait!

"Your chocolate, sir," John murmured. "I have pressed your coat and made another repair to the left sleeve, which I believe you will find a great improvement."

"Did I ask for chocolate?"

"No, sir, but Mrs Pibworth thought you might like it. Shall I remove it, sir?"

"Oh well, I may as well drink it, since you have brought it."

John smiled. "Mrs Malling has found one or two items of gentlemen's clothing which Mr Gage no longer requires. Should you like me to alter them to suit you, sir? Just to have a spare or two in case you go out in the rain."

Malcolm laughed. "Lord, these meddlesome sisters of mine! But if Laurence has no objection to the ladies rooting round in his wardrobe and depriving him of his least regarded clothes, I have no objection to wearing them. They will be finer than anything I can afford."

"Mr Gage's tailor is an excellent fellow, whose work is said to be comparable with anything from London. Although having seen the quality of Mr Willerton-Forbes' attire, sir, I can't entirely agree with that."

"He is quite a dandy, indeed, and the good captain not greatly less so. I suppose their valets are starchy fellows, eh? Do they have one apiece?"

"Only two valets, sir. Mr Leach, who does for Mr Willerton-Forbes, is a little grand, it is true, but Mr Neate seems a most agreeable sort of person, not in the least starchy. He doesn't reject my offers of help, at any rate. I am at rather a loose end now that Mr Gage has employed a *proper* valet."

"A proper valet? Are you not a proper valet?"

John gave a tight smile. "I'm just a footman, sir, but I've looked after Mr Gage's clothes for six years now and he's never made any complaint. But now he's engaged some sharp fellow from London who thinks himself very grand indeed. Mr Lockyer looked after the heir to a viscountcy before he came here, and thinks he's quite gone down in the world. There, sir. That's your clothes for this morning laid out for you. Should you like me to assist you today?"

"John, you are a fine fellow and an excellent valet, I am sure, but I have managed without for sixteen years, so I believe I can contrive to dress myself without your assistance."

John chuckled, and said, "As you please, sir. Just ring if you need anything at all."

Malcolm finished his chapter while sipping his chocolate, then washed, shaved and dressed without haste. He was just knotting his neckcloth when there was a brisk knock on the door.

"Enter!"

It was Selena, naturally. "Are you decent? Oh good, because your breakfast is in the day nursery and I have a few ideas to put to you while you eat."

The day nursery had been transformed. The table had been turned round, all the chairs shifted and several new paintings adorned the walls, showing scenes of pastoral tranquillity, stormy cliffs or bustling towns.

"For vocabulary," Selena said brightly. "We used these as girls when we learnt our languages."

Viola and Henrietta were kneeling on the floor engaged in sorting through books on the low shelves, while Ursula arranged slates, paper and ink neatly on the table. Edward, looking bemused, was idly nibbling at a bun from Malcolm's breakfast tray.

"That is mine, you horrible child," he said in Russian, smiling at him.

Edward grinned back. "You have… much," he said. "Some for me also."

"Selena, you have precisely ten minutes to explain your ideas to me, and then Edward and I must get down to business. We cannot waste a moment."

"Ah. Well… I am afraid we must deprive you of him for today. He is to go to Shrewsbury to be fitted for a new coat, for all his old ones are too short in the sleeve now, since he refuses to stop growing, the obstinate boy!" She laughed indulgently.

"You are going to take him away for the whole day?" Malcolm said, dismayed.

"Only for a few hours. We will be back by two… or perhaps three. He must look presentable for this examination, you know, brother, and Laurence's tailor is very slow. It would not do to delay. We shall obtain linen for shirts and so forth while we are there, so that Mrs Irvine may be working on those while the coats are made. It will do him good to have a day away from his lessons for a change. Now, here are my plans for your lessons. Just suggestions, of course, but with children it is essential to keep to a proper routine, do you not agree? Now on Mondays…"

Malcolm let the words flow over him, stolidly eating his way through everything on the tray that Edward had left to him, and making no comment. At the end of it, he accepted Selena's notes with a smile and tucked them away in a pocket, knowing that he would never look at them again.

"Thank you for your efforts, sister. Enjoy your day out, Edward, and I shall see you again at two… or perhaps three."

"You could come with us," he said, with an optimistic tone to his voice. "I should like to order a new coat in Russian."

That made Malcolm laugh out loud, while his sisters tut-tutted and watched him anxiously. They did not want him to go, that much was clear, and perhaps it was better not to walk about the streets of Shrewsbury where there would inevitably be acquaintances to be bumped into and awkward introductions to be made, and no end of difficult questions or embarrassed silences.

"Better if I do not," Malcolm said, "but while we wait for the carriage to be brought round I shall teach you how to order your coat in Russian."

They had half an hour, that was all, before John came up to whisk Edward away and Malcolm found himself unexpectedly free for the day. He did not have to consider what to do, however, for he had only one object in mind. Shrugging himself into his greatcoat, he went down the service stairs and out by the boot room, his long legs striding down the drive, across the road and up to the Dower House, a little buzz of pleasure warming him inside. He would see her again! For the whole day! It was so deliciously unexpected, and that was surely the best kind of occasion.

There was no point in knocking on the front door, for with the mistress away, very likely no one would answer. Instead he walked round the house to the kitchen door. Inside, the first person he saw was the roguish Mr Chandry, deep in conversation with a maid, who was giggling and blushing furiously. Chandry nodded to Malcolm, not in the least discomposed.

"Good day to you, Mr Gage," he said. "Are you looking for someone?"

"For Mademoiselle Fournier."

"Ah. Then your business is similar to mine." He grinned wolfishly. "Nellie, where is Marie?"

"She'll be in the parlour, sir, with her sewing. That's where she'll be. I'll show you."

She led the way up the service stairs from the basement to the ground floor, and thence to a room near the front door. Chandry followed them, Malcolm noticed, torn between disapproval and admiration for his talents with females. Malcolm had never had that easy way of it, making them giggle and look coy. Not that he had ever tried flirting, but he was tolerably certain that he could not do it and would not much care for any woman who expected it of him.

Marie sat at a table liberally spread with squares of material, a sewing box beside her. She looked round in surprise as the three of them poured into the room.

"Gentl'man to see you, Mam'selle," Nellie said, bobbing a curtsy to her.

"Thank you, Nellie," Malcolm said firmly, holding the door open for her. She left but Chandry lingered. Malcolm raised an eyebrow and with a soft chuckle Chandry sauntered out.

Then they were alone.

~~~~~

Marie carefully secured her needle and laid down her sewing, looking up at him expectantly. He was well worth gazing at, she could not deny. She could not remember ever seeing a handsomer man, and imposingly tall, too. He made her feel as dainty as a fairy. The intensity of his gaze made her feel something else, too, something she had not felt for years, not since she became a lady's maid. Feminine, perhaps. Pretty. Desirable. He saw her as a woman. There was a danger in that, naturally. Any man who saw past the outward appearance of the lady's maid to the person inside was a threat to her. She must be very cautious.

Just now he was frowning. "Is Chandry often here?" he said in French.

"Sometimes. He is trouble, that one," Marie said. "Nellie should be careful. How may I help you, Monsieur Gage?"

He smiled at her, and she was bathed in warmth, just as if the sun had come out. "I find myself with an unexpected free day," he said. "Since I know your days are mostly free also, I thought we might enjoy our free time together. Would you like to go for a walk?"

A walk! What did that mean? "Where will we walk to?"

"To Lower Maeswood, to see the *jacinthes des bois*."

She frowned, struggling to recognise the expression.
~~~~~

In English, he said, "Bluebells. They are at their finest just now."

"Jacinthes des bois," she repeated thoughtfully.

He chuckled knowingly, and she cursed herself for the slip. He had already guessed that French was not her native language, but there was no point in reminding him of it.

Should she go? It could be dangerous, as any outing might be for a woman alone with a man, but if he raised the question of marriage again or became amorous she would have an opportunity to deter him more forcefully than before, when he had taken her quite by surprise. Besides, his French was excellent and she could learn from him, so that her time spent with Edward would not be so taxing. That first hour of conversation had made her head ache abominably! "Very well. I will fetch my bonnet and spencer."

She returned swiftly and they walked down the drive, across the road and into a lane that passed between the boundary wall of the Grove and the parsonage grounds. Mr Gage talked in fluent French as they went, telling her something of the history of the church and the village generally, but she was not required to give more than the briefest answer, which was lucky for he rattled away almost faster than she could keep up.

From time to time he slipped in a question. How long had she worked for Mrs Middlehope? What was the lady's previous home like? She could answer those. Where had she worked before that? What did her father do to earn his keep? And that was where Marie's answers stopped. She was willing enough to talk about Mrs Middlehope and Roseacre, but she deftly turned aside any query related to her life before that.

Instead she turned the questions on him, and like all men, he never minded talking about himself. As they walked through dappled shade and into sunshine again beneath the brilliant spring greens of ancient, sprawling oaks, it all came tumbling out. His childhood in Shrewsbury, his arrival at the Grove as a boy of eight, the long exploratory rambles with Laurence — he could not hide the closeness between them in those years, two brothers as inseparable as twins.

"Why do you now hate him so much?" Marie said gently, hoping the soft French words masked the harshness of the question.

"Why should I not hate him?" he growled. "He has given me every reason, after what he has done to me. Hate him? Yes, I hate and despise him, and it would suit me very well never to see him again. After these three months are over, I shall go to Oxford and he and all my sisters will be gone from my life."

He had stopped dead, hands clenched into fists as if he wanted to beat his brother's face to pulp by thought alone. He looked so angry! Gently, she laid a hand on his arm and his face softened. They walked on again.

"What did he do?" she said.

"He stole my betrothed away from me." This time he seemed calmer.

That was a surprise! "You were betrothed? That is very bad, perhaps, but the lady had a choice, I presume?"

"Laurence and her witch of a mother dragooned her into it. She was a gentle creature, so good and obedient, she would have done what she was told."

"Then she deserved what happened to her," Marie said crisply. "A woman who marries where she is told is a foolish mouse. Oh look! Bluebells!" *Jacinthes des bois.* Hyacinths of the woods. Such an apt name! There was a poetry in the French language that English lacked. To describe those delicate blooms merely as blue bells was depressingly prosaic.

The woods were covered with a carpet of hazy blue, their delicate scent floating in the air. For a while they were silent, walking slowly as they admired the beauty of the scene. A romantic man would have picked a bouquet for her, but Mr Gage was not a romantic, it seemed, for he did no such thing.

They emerged from the woods into a small village, no more than a hamlet, with neither church nor mill nor smithy to be seen, just a few cottages with chickens scratching in the dirt and a cluster of geese. Several goats grazed in a small paddock.

"Lower Maeswood," he said. "All of this belongs to the Grove estate."

"To your brother," she said mischievously, and then was consumed with guilt for reminding him.

Surprisingly, he seemed unconcerned. "Yes, to my brother. It is all his." There was no hint of anger or jealousy in his manner, and that was to his credit, that he did not begrudge his brother his birth right. It was not money or position he craved, only the lady. She was long dead yet she still lay between the two brothers, as impenetrable a barrier as a wall.

Mr Gage was instantly recognised by the villagers and a great number of them came out to greet him, those who were not away at their work. There were cries of delight and smiles and hands pulling both of them to the largest dwelling. Then they were seated on benches outside the cottage, tankards of foaming ale pressed into their hands and platters of bread and cheese passed about, while the villagers clustered around and threw questions at them.

Marie had supposed that Mr Gage would be the principal focus for their curiosity, but they seemed already to know the reason for his precipitate return to Shropshire. Instead their attention was on Marie, for they had seen her at church but never had the opportunity to talk to her. They hurled question after question at her which Mr Gage, with laughing eyes, translated into French. He then obligingly translated the answer back into English for them.

At least, that was how it must have looked to the villagers. In fact, their exchanges were far more complicated than that.

"Ask the lady how she came to England. Did she have an exciting escape from France?" one of them said.

In French, Mr Gage said, "Shall I tell them you were smuggled out of the Bastille at dead of night, and shipped across the Channel in an empty wine barrel?"

"In France, no wine barrel stays empty long enough for an escape plan. The usual way is to pay for passage on the packet ship."

Smoothly, he said in English, "She was saved from the guillotine by a distant cousin who smuggled her to the coast disguised as a boy and helped her to stow away on a merchant ship."

The audience eyed her with wonder, and she was hard put to it not to laugh out loud. It was wicked of him to tell such bouncers, but it was done in so charming a manner that it was impossible to be cross with him.

Eventually the villagers were drawn back to their chores, and Marie and Mr Gage were able to begin the walk back to Great Maeswood, passing into deeper woods with no bluebells. The shade was welcome now that the sun was reaching its zenith, but it was not the heat that made Marie's head ache. So much French, combined with the need to watch every word against revealing too much, was stretching her ingenuity, so she was relieved that Mr Gage expected no conversation from her now. Instead, he hummed gently as they walked and then began to sing little nonsense songs — English ones, mainly, but some in French, one in Italian and a couple in languages she could not identify. He had a rather fine baritone which would have been better employed raised in song at St Ann's on Sundays, but it was both restful and amusing to hear it turned instead to chanting silly rhymes. She smiled, and then more broadly, and eventually, as the words became sillier and sillier, she laughed out loud.

"Ah, much better," he said in English, turning to her with a smile of his own. He had such a warm smile, that made his eyes light up with a merry glow. "You looked so tired for a while, but I prefer to see you happy."

In French she said, "The beer has certainly made *you* happy, monsieur."

"Not the beer," he said, again in English. "It is your company that makes me happy. I shall not be able to escape during the morning hours again, but may I come to see you in the evenings?"

She stopped, her insides twisting suddenly. Now was the moment. "No, monsieur, you may not."

A little frown crossed his face. "Why not, *ma chérie?*"

My darling? That made her heart race. Such a treacherous organ, the heart. "It is impossible, this... this friendship."

"Is it?" he said, still talking in English. "I rather thought you liked me, at least a little. Was I wrong about that?"

"It does not matter. I am a lady's maid, you are a gentleman and—"

"I am a *teacher*," he said in fierce French. "I was not born to that rôle, just as you were not born to the life you now lead, but we are not unequal in rank, not at this moment. If I succeed in my task with Edward, then I shall again be a gentleman, and as my wife you will be a lady."

'You were not born to the life you now lead.' For an instant, terror gripped her so hard that she panicked.

"No!" she cried, and in her distress the word came out in English. Correcting her mistake quickly, she went on, *"Non, monsieur.* I shall never marry you. I shall never marry anyone. I am content with my life just as it is, and I beg you will leave me alone."

"Ah, you reverted to English for an instant there," he said smugly. "I am making progress."

Deliberately she calmed herself, and said more temperately, "I ask you, monsieur, not to torment me. It will do you no good, for my mind is quite made up. I implore you as a gentleman to leave me in peace."

Then she strode away, her heart hammering. Would he acquiesce or would he persist in harassing her? Please God let him leave her alone! He could have no idea how much it mattered.

8: A Pleasant Evening

Malcolm watched Marie go in surprise. How could she simply dismiss him in that abrupt way, as if he cared nothing for her? It was unaccountable. Yet she wanted him to leave her alone — asked it of him as a gentleman, and he must abide by her wishes. And perhaps it was for the best. Unless Edward managed to succeed in his examination, and that was very far from certain, Malcolm had nothing to offer Marie. As a schoolmaster, he could certainly not afford to take a wife, even if it were permitted. No, he must say nothing more of marriage to her. But surely he could still see her sometimes? At church, or accidentally in the shop. She would not mind that, would she?

Within moments she was out of sight, a bend in the path and a clump of brambles rendering her invisible, but he could still hear her — the crunching of dry leaves underfoot, the occasional twig snapping or a bird flying off, shrieking. But gradually all sounds died away, and still he stood motionless, perplexed.

Recollecting himself, he strode after her and his long legs soon saw her ahead of him, still doggedly moving forward, but more circumspectly now, dodging around grasping bramble tendrils or wading slowly through bracken. Once she had to scramble over the trunk of a fallen tree. Gradually, as she slowed and then stopped, he caught up with her.

"This is hard work," she said in French, and she looked so forlorn that he wanted to take her in his arms and comfort her.

In English, he said gently, "There is a gate just a little way ahead that will allow us back into the grounds of the Grove. Let me show you."

He hopped over a fallen tree and marched off down the overgrown path, but when he turned to check that she was following, he saw her still standing uncertainly the other side of the tree.

"What is the matter?"

Mutely she gestured at the tree.

"What? Oh... do you want a hand?" He went back, hopped back over the tree trunk and unceremoniously put his hands on her waist and swung her over the obstacle.

She gave a little shriek which almost at once turned into a giggle. *"Merci, monsieur,"* she said demurely, slightly pink about the cheeks. "I am not attired for such conditions."

He looked her up and down, noting the thin leather of her half-boots and the delicate muslin gown, which her spencer did nothing to protect. "True. Next time, you should wear something more practical."

"There will be no next time," she said, eyes flashing.

He was dismayed, but he said nothing, hoping with all his heart that she was wrong about that.

A little way further on, a side path branched off, even more overgrown, but within a very short time they were opening the wooden gate in the wall and entering the better tamed grounds of the Grove. A weedy path led towards the distant house, the chimneys just visible above the shrubbery surrounding it. The path was wide enough to walk side by side, and Malcolm began to sing again, in the hope of reactivating that delightful smile. But a turn of the path brought them to the old fountain, long since dried up, and on the rusty old bench opposite, Laurence sat, reading a letter and smiling to himself.

There was no avoiding the encounter. Laurence looked up and saw them approaching. The smile instantly became a frown. Marie dipped a curtsy and murmured, *"Bonjour, Monsieur Gage."* Malcolm nodded briefly to his brother, but dared not speak. It was for Laurence to speak if he wished it, but he merely glared at them, his eyes flicking from one to the other.

Then they were past him and into the main part of the gardens, rather better tended, and within a few minutes they had reached the house, and she turned to make her farewells.

"Au revoir, Monsieur Gage, et merci."

In English, he said, "I shall escort you back to the Dower House, mademoiselle."

"Non. There is no need."

And with a quick curtsy she hastened away down the drive. Malcolm stood and watched her go with some regret. Two hours, perhaps, that was all, and her company had been every bit as delightful as he had anticipated, but she had said she would not marry him, and that was unexpected. She did not mean it, of course, for how could any woman prefer to be a lady's maid, at the beck and call of a temperamental mistress, when she could be a wife and mistress of her own establishment? It was too ridiculous. She could not possibly be in earnest. Could she?

As he stood, lost in thought, he heard quick steps on the gravel behind him. Laurence, his face stormy.

"What the *devil* do you think you are about?"

"I beg your pardon?"

"Do not pretend to misunderstand! Whatever you are up to with Mademoiselle Fournier, I give you fair warning, brother, if you harm one hair of her head you will answer to me. She is Louisa's maid and I am responsible for her welfare while Louisa is away, so if you think to play your games with her, you had best think again."

"Games? What are you talking about? I mean her no harm, I assure you."

"No harm!" he said contemptuously. "You had better not, that is all." He stabbed Malcolm furiously in the chest. "Leave her alone, that is all. You will not play your tricks on *her*, I shall see to that."

So saying, he stormed away across the carriage circle, took the steps to the front door two at a time and disappeared inside the house. Malcolm was left angry, mystified and resentful, all at once.

~~~~~

Once again Malcolm was expected to appear in the drawing room at the appointed hour before dinner. He looked a little more stylish tonight in a cast-off coat and waistcoat of Laurence's, his neckcloth starched to board-like rigidity by the over-enthusiastic John.

"You are turning me into a dandy, John," he grumbled, gazing at his reflection in the looking glass. "Did you ever see
~~~~~

such an absurd figure? I feel like a bird all trussed up ready for the spit."

"You look very well, sir," John said, brushing a last imaginary speck of lint from Malcolm's shoulders. "If I may say so, you are admirably proportioned for the current fashions, and this style of coat shows you off to great advantage."

"Ha! You flatterer, you. Well, I shall do. Is it time? I had better go down, I suppose. Good night, John. Enjoy your evening."

"I shall wait for you tonight, sir. You will need a hand out of this coat."

"Hmm... You think I will tear the seams, and cause you a great deal of repair work, do you? Very well, since it is not my coat you may wait up for me."

The drawing room was full. Ursula and Selena were determined to entertain all their acquaintances during their stay at the Grove, and tonight's contingent was the local aristocracy from Maeswood Hall. Lady Saxby was not yet fifty, the remains of her delicate beauty enhanced by a fragile air and drooping fronds of lace on her mourning gown. She had all four daughters with her. Malcolm had seen Cass and Agnes, the two eldest, but not the two youngest. They had been mere babies when Malcolm had left Shropshire, and were now grown women. Flora, at eighteen, had inherited all her mother's looks, while Honora at sixteen was also a very pretty girl. The two sons from Lady Saxby's first marriage, Jeffrey and Timothy Rycroft, last seen as grubby boys, were now just the sort of strutting, handsome young men that Malcolm despised, and was turning out by the score at Harrow.

He was unnoticed tonight, lurking in his corner quietly, watching the smiling faces and listening to the chatter. Beside the door, the men's deep voices rumbled to each other in one group. Near the fire, the older ladies talked in low, desultory murmurs. Over by the window, the young ladies had their heads together, whispering away and interrupting each other excitedly. Henrietta was in this latter group, the youngest of them, but taking full part in the chatter. Edward had been banished to the nursery wing for the evening, and Malcolm sincerely wished that he could be there with him, the two of them eating their dinner from trays and talking in Russian.

His tranquillity could not last, and it was Agnes Saxby who spotted him first and made straight for him. "Mr Gage! How lovely to see you again. How are you? And how is your work with Edward coming along? Are you making progress? Such a difficult challenge, but you are so clever that I have no doubt you will succeed. So many languages! I am attempting to improve my Italian but it is so hard to practice from books. How lucky Edward is to have you to teach him. Is he an apt pupil? I am sure he is and will do splendidly in this examination."

"You have greater confidence than I do," he murmured when she finally drew breath.

"Oh *no*, I am sure that— Ah, we are going through. Perhaps...?"

She gazed up at him expectantly, one hand hopefully raised ready to be placed on his arm. He bowed his head, half in acknowledgement and half in defeat, and offered his arm to escort her through to the dining room, knowing perfectly well that he would now have her company for the duration of the meal. She was a pleasant enough girl, but he had no wish to give her any encouragement when his heart was already bestowed.

He could not miss the irony of his situation — two women, the one he wanted who would have nothing to do with him, and the one who pursued him relentlessly despite his lack of interest.

Agnes was pleasant enough company, and once her initial gushing had expended itself, she proved to be a thoughtful girl, not unintelligent, and widely read. It seemed that the proper guidance in her reading had been lacking, however, for he found her opinions not always well formed. She was equally willing to listen to his views as to advance her own, and so, after a few trials of other subjects, they settled to a deep and satisfying discussion of *Othello*, which occupied them for most of the meal.

When the ladies withdrew, most of the gentlemen gathered around Laurence but as before, Malcolm kept his seat at the far end of the table. Again, Captain Edgerton joined him.

"You are quite wrong, you know," he said conversationally. "Everything that happens is Iago's fault. Othello is not to be blamed."

"No, no!" Malcolm cried. "Is Othello to be credited with no free will? Is he naught but a—? Oh, you are roasting me, Captain. Were we talking so loudly as to disturb the far end of the table?"

Edgerton chuckled. "I have excellent ears, Mr Gage, and you and Miss Agnes sounded so engrossed in your conversation that I envied you. So many young ladies have neither interest nor ability in such discussions. You do realise, of course, that the lady is only interested in the Moor of Venice as a means of leading you to the altar?"

"I... suspected something of the sort," Malcolm said slowly. "I am not much of a catch for a baron's daughter, though. Her mother would not encourage her to dangle after a schoolmaster, surely?"

"A schoolmaster who may very well soon come into a handsome inheritance, if the scheme with Master Edward comes to fruition, and you are a gentleman by birth, after all."

Malcolm sighed. "Then I know not how to discourage her, and that is the truth. What can I do to escape an unwanted entanglement?"

"Avoid her company, Mr Gage."

"How can I when she attaches herself to me like a leech? I do not dislike Miss Agnes, and she is better company than many, but she is a very determined lady."

"Yes, there was no avoiding her company at dinner," the captain said thoughtfully, rolling a walnut between his fingers. "You have done your duty by her now, however, and may look elsewhere without guilt. Do you play chess, Mr Gage?"

"I do."

The captain smiled. "I suspected as much. Very well, then, I challenge you to a game when we re-join the ladies. If Miss Agnes comes to watch us play, as she very well might, I undertake to entertain her on your behalf."

"That is uncommonly generous of you, sir."

"All part of the service," he said, grinning. "Your brother wines and dines us so splendidly that I like to repay him in whatever little ways I can find. But you must promise to be gentle with me at the chessboard, and not have me checkmated in five moves, as I suspect you could do very easily, for I shall take it very ill, I assure you."

"I make it a rule to play with the utmost circumspection against an opponent who carries both sword and pistols, and presumably knows how to use them," Malcolm said solemnly.

"Ah, if only everyone were so sensible," the captain said with a sigh.

~~~~~

Malcolm rested his forehead against the rain-spattered window. "I am grateful for my walk through the bluebells yesterday with Marie. I am grateful for an excellent dinner last night. I am grateful for Edgerton's good nature in diverting the attention of Agnes Saxby."

With a sigh, he kissed the pendant and tucked it inside his nightshirt. A tap on the door startled him, for it was not yet time for John to put in an appearance.

"Enter."

Captain Edgerton's head appeared round the door. "If you care to join me in the day nursery, Mr Gage, I have something to show you."

Throwing on his ancient robe, Malcolm followed him through.

The captain's eyes gleamed with excitement. "There!" he said, laying two opened letters on the table. "Read those."

Malcolm picked up the first, dated five years earlier.

'To Mrs Edward Middlehope, Roseacre, County Durham. Madam, I have by good fortune this very day found a young person who meets your requirements in every particular. She is but eighteen years old, but has spent three years in her previous employment from which she has a very good reference. She is French, so she has exactly that style that is so important in one engaged in assisting the toilette of a lady of quality. Although she speaks no English, she understands the language perfectly, and is well able to take instruction, as I have this day determined for
~~~~~

myself. She is not in the least 'starchy', as per your explicit request, and therefore I commend her to you, and highly recommend that you do not delay a decision, since a person of such outstanding quality is not often to be found. I await your early response. Miss Frances Hurley, Proprietrix, Hurley's Register of Domestic Servants of Distinction, Oxford Street, London.'

The second letter was even more surprising.

'Welby Hall, Northamptonshire. To whom it may concern. Mademoiselle Marie Fournier has been in my employ for three years, under my instruction, and is now competent in every aspect of the duties of a lady's maid. She can clean, repair and alter clothes, has full knowledge of a range of methods for the removal of stains, can dress hair in all the latest modes, and has a keen eye for colours and styles. She is, in addition, efficient, honest and trustworthy, and I have never had cause to censure her for any matter. I only relinquish her services because she wishes to move on now that she is fully trained, but I shall be extremely sorry to lose her. Lady Julia Stapleton.'

"How on earth did you obtain these?" Malcolm said in astonishment.

"You really should not enquire," Edgerton said, grinning.

"I beg to differ," Malcolm said. "I cannot see that these could have come into your hands by any honest method."

Edgerton rubbed his nose ruefully. "Which is precisely why you should not enquire."

"Captain, I asked you to find out something about Marie, but I did not intend you to... well, I suppose you must have broken into the Dower House and rifled through Mrs Middlehope's papers, and if you are about to be dragged off to gaol I should like to take my share of the responsibility for your burglary."

"No, no! There will be no dragging off, I assure you. Do you truly wish to know how it was done? Well, then I shall tell you, but you must not tell a soul. In such cases, discretion must be absolute."

"Of course."

"My young colleague Michael Chandry has certain characteristics that make him very useful to our enterprise, one of which is that he appears, for some incomprehensible reason, to be irresistible to the female sex. He made an assignation with Nellie from the Boar's Head, who has been working temporarily at the Dower House as a replacement for Sarah the housemaid, who has gone north with her mistress."

"Why?" Malcolm said.

"Why did he make an assignation?"

"No, why did she take a housemaid with her?"

"Oh, I see. To act as lady's maid. Mademoiselle Fournier suffers severely when travelling by carriage, so as a kindness Mrs Middlehope left her here and took Sarah instead. Anyway, Michael arranged for Nellie to leave the garden door unlocked in the drawing room. He slipped in for his assignation, and our very talented James Neate slipped in behind him and went to Mrs Middlehope's study. Michael had asked Nellie to show him around, so he knew where the room was. There James picked the lock on the davenport and found these papers. You see? You would have been much better off not knowing anything about it."

"That is appalling!" Malcolm said. "So Mr Chandry seduced the maid and Neate became a burglar, just so that I could learn that Marie knows how to remove stains. I never intended such consequences."

"Oh, I know. You thought we would ask a few questions and you would find out all about Mademoiselle Marie. Well, we asked questions, Mr Gage, and do you know what we discovered? Absolutely nothing. No one knows a thing about her. She has no close friends. She speaks to no one. She neither sends nor receives letters. She is a mystery. But now we have a crucial piece of information."

"Do we?"

"We have a name and address. Lady Julia Stapleton of Welby Hall, Northamptonshire. She engaged Marie and trained her up, so she must know where she came from. She was fifteen when she first went to Welby Hall, and did not appear out of nowhere."

"Ah. Of course. So... should we write to Lady Julia to ask for more information?"

Edgerton grinned widely. "Now, where would be the fun in that? She will have ample time to consider her reply and to compose something suitably unhelpful. No, far better to confront her. I like to see a person's eyes, Mr Gage. That is the way to know what is in their hearts."

"You are proposing to go to Northamptonshire?" Malcolm said, startled. "I cannot afford to pay for such a trip."

"You need not worry about that," Edgerton said airily. "We are all agreed that the mystery is an intriguing one, so we shall let Chandry loose with his skill with cards. He is a very talented young man, if one does not look too closely at his methods. We must trace your young lady back to her origins, one step at a time. I shall go to Welby Hall and find out where she came from before that. Then I shall go to that place, and ask again. And sooner or later, we will find a Miss Jane Smith, a wheelwright's daughter, who thought to better herself. Or something of the sort, anyway."

"A parson's daughter," Malcolm put in. "That is my guess. A parson who married a French woman."

"Very possible. I will take a fair copy of each of these letters, and then Michael will make another assignation with the obliging Nellie and James will return the originals and leave everything just as it was. No one will ever know, I assure you. And if you are worried about Nellie's reputation, you need have no concerns on that score. She fell from grace several years ago, and is well paid for her good nature."

"Ah. That is a different matter," Malcolm said. "I do not suppose Mr Chandry suffered too greatly for his part in this enterprise, either."

The captain chuckled. "Indeed. He and James had a very pleasant evening, in their different ways, as we shall enjoy a pleasant trip to Northamptonshire. An interesting county to visit, I am sure. For what is it noted?"

"Hmm... shoes?"

Edgerton laughed. "I shall look it up. I do not think I have ever been there before. What fun this is! How glad I am that you set this particular hare running, Mr Gage."

9: A New Bonnet

'Friday 19th May. A day free of Mr Malcolm Gage. I was afraid that he would turn up on the doorstep every five minutes but either he is fully occupied at the Grove or I have done enough to deter him, for I have not seen any sign of him today. I shall make sure I am not available if he calls again, but beyond that I can do no more. We are bound to meet sometime, for I cannot hide for ever, and why should I? I cannot imagine what about me draws his notice. Has he no pride, to be pursuing a mere servant? But I am determined not to make every day's diary entry about him. There is much else to report, not least that Ben is now fixed at the Grove to cook the dinners there, for they have guests every night and must have vermicelli soup, chicken à la reine and sturgeon à la broche with a Madeira sauce. No boiled chicken for them! They are to have suckling pig tomorrow, if you please, while we are left to the tender mercy of Tilly and her sister, and spit-roasted mutton. It is always mutton. But tomorrow will be a good day. Tilly and I are to go to Shrewsbury for the day with her father, he to replenish the stocks for the shop, Tilly to buy boots and I to wander around the shops in a delirious haze, and perhaps buy a paper of pins. Five hundred and sixty one.'

~~~~~
~~~~~

Malcolm began to see real progress with Edward. He came straight to the day nursery each morning as soon as he was dressed, and if Malcolm was not there he settled down to read one of the books that had now arrived from Harrow. He rode for an hour each morning, and spent another hour with one or other of his other language tutors, and the occasional lesson in mathematics with Laurence, but otherwise he was alone with Malcolm all day, speaking nothing but Russian. With his quickness of mind, he could not fail to reach a degree of fluency.

Selena, with her usual efficiency, had organised the rota for the other four language tutors. Marie's day was Tuesday, but Malcolm had a niggling fear that she would decide not to come rather than meet him. The fear lurked at the back of his mind, unsettling him. His days were so fully occupied that he had but little opportunity to see her, but that one hour a week was a sweet delight to be anticipated. By Saturday, two days after their walk amongst the bluebells, he determined to see her and understand her mind. And perhaps, his heart whispered, she had softened towards him just a little.

Accordingly, when Edward went for his riding lesson, Malcolm marched across to the Dower House, and asked for her at the kitchen door.

Nellie answered his knock, wiping floury hands on a cloth.

"Mam'selle's not 'ere," she said discouragingly.

"Have you been told to say so, Nellie?"

"No!" she said indignantly. "Tis true! She went off wi' Tilly and Mr Timpson first thing, and won't be back 'til late. Gone to Shrewsbury, they 'ave."

Disconsolately he ambled back down the drive and began walking along the road towards the village. One of the first houses he came to was Bramble Cottage, where he saw Lucy Cokely, gardening trowel in hand, talking to Mr Truman over the low hedge that fringed the property.

"Oh, Malcolm!" she cried, her thin features lighting up at the sight of him. "I am so glad to see you. Why have you not called on us, such old friends as we are? But I expect you are very busy. We have heard all about your great endeavour with Master Edward. Mr Truman, are you acquainted with Mr Malcolm Gage?"

"As I am also to be a part of the great endeavour, I have had the pleasure of meeting Mr Gage," the clergyman said, doffing his hat and making a rather elegant bow. "Although not in church, I regret to say."

Malcolm had no hat to doff, having forgotten it, but he bowed politely. "God and I have been at odds for some years," he said amiably. "We have agreed that we are best kept apart."

"That is a pity," Truman said. "Divine service is not merely good for a man's spiritual welfare, it is also a way of uniting the community."

"Oh yes, one meets all one's friends there," Lucy said. "We miss your voice in the hymns, Malcolm. He has such a fine singing voice, Mr Truman, quite beautiful."

"Then I regret your absence even more, Mr Gage. However, I will not tease you about it. That is not my way, to be unduly censorious of my parishioners' foibles. The gentlest of hints, that is all, if one or other of my flock has strayed from the path of righteousness."

There was a smugness to his manner that irritated Malcolm intensely. By what right did he sit in judgement on his fellow men, and pronounce them righteous or not? But then logic reasserted itself, and he supposed that it was his job, after all. It was in the nature of a clergyman to be disapproving.

Lucy laughed. "You are a most understanding parson, Mr Truman, and far more the gentleman than Mr Lancaster, who came in after poor Papa died. He was very odd in his habits. Malcolm, have you time to go in and have a word with Mama? She would love to see you. She is not what she was… her mind is not sharp any more, but when I told her you had come home, she perked up wonderfully and was perfectly lucid for fully half an hour. She is in the window there, you see? The front door is open."

Come home. It was hardly that. A temporary and most unwelcome visit, on all sides. But he merely smiled and said that of course he would love to see Mrs Cokely. He looked up at the cottage and there she was, a diminutive figure in black with a snowy lace cap. She waved as he looked, and he waved back cheerfully, making his way through the gate and up the lavender-edged path to the front door.

He had fond memories of the Cokelys, who had been mainstays of the parish long before he had even been born. They had been genuinely good people, always helping, and certainly never censorious. The whole village had grieved when Dr Cokely had been struck down, some twenty years ago now. Mrs Cokely and her daughter had moved into the tiny cottage opposite their former home at the parsonage, and Lucy had been obliged to make hats to earn a little extra money.

Mrs Cokely sat in a chair placed in the bay window, so that she could see everyone who passed by. She turned to face

Malcolm as he entered the parlour, weaving his way through the hat stands and tables that dotted the room.

"How are you, Mrs Cokely? Do you remember me?"

"Of course I remember you, Malcolm Gage! I well remember you falling out of that tree house. Your brother had more sense than to climb up there, but you — you always had to have a go." She chuckled, and waved him to a chair beside her. "Sit down and let me look at you. Well, what a fine young man you are now. Do you still have that bad-tempered black horse of yours, the one that bites all the grooms?"

"That was years ago, Mrs Cokely," he said, laughing. Twenty years ago... no, more than that, and he had fallen out of the tree house — or rather, fallen through it, for the wood was rotten — at the age of eight. But old ones lived in the past, so he patted her mittened hand genially. "You are looking very well. Does Lucy look after you?"

"Oh, Lucy is a good girl, always was, although she never gives me partridge any more. I do like a bit of partridge. And how is your dear mother? She had a cold last week. Is she feeling better?"

No point telling her that she had been dead for fourteen years. "She is perfectly well now, Mrs Cokely."

Just then, Mr Truman bade farewell to Lucy, and with a wave crossed the road to enter the parsonage directly opposite.

"Parson into the parsonage, three minutes after noon." She tapped a clock on the table beside her with a pencil and scribbled something in a notebook.

Amused, Malcolm said, "You have a fine view of the parsonage from here, and what a grand sight it is, with the fellow strutting about like a lord."

"He is a bad man," Mrs Cokely hissed, her eyes narrowed.

"Mr Truman? Now what have you got against him? I should dearly like to know."

"He is a very bad man," was all she said, then abruptly, "Mrs Burrows going towards the lodge carrying a covered basket, six minutes after noon." Again she tapped the clock and wrote something down.

"Would you like some tea, Malcolm?" Lucy said, shutting the door behind her as she entered from the tiny vestibule. "I can spare some for you, and Mama will be glad of a cup, too."

Malcolm went through with her to the kitchen at the back of the house, filling the kettle and hanging it over the fire as Lucy bustled about fetching cups and unlocking the tea caddy, and then fetching a plate with a quarter of a cake from the pantry.

"Here, cut yourself a slice. You need fattening up."

He cut a thin slice and demolished it in two bites, then took the plate back to the pantry. It was their supper, he guessed, and if he left it on the table he might absentmindedly eat it all.

"How did you find Mama?" Lucy said. "Did she know you at all?"

"She did, although she asked after Beast of Night — do you remember him? Poor creature must have gone to the knacker years ago. Oh, and she asked if Mother's cold was better." Lucy laughed, and he went on, "She also said that the so elegant Mr Truman is a bad man."

Lucy lifted her eyes heavenwards. “I cannot guess what bee she has in her bonnet, but she has taken him quite in dislike, although I confess that he has not quite won me over, either. He is very popular amongst the young ladies of the parish, but I do not like him dangling after the Saxby girls, as he does. It seems a little ambitious for a parson, who is only a parson’s son himself, after all.”

“Is it Flora he has his eye on?” Malcolm said. “She is the pretty one, if I recall.”

“Not her, no. He seemed to be keen on Agnes first, but then Lord Saxby died and the three younger girls got very little and Cass Saxby inherited a fortune from her mother. After that he seemed to like Cass better.”

“Maybe he thinks Cass would make a better parson’s wife,” Malcolm suggested.

“I might believe that if he were a better parson himself,” Lucy said tartly. “Oh, he performs the offices with a flourish on Sundays, but the rest of the week he is very much a gentleman of leisure. He neglects his glebe, and he neglects his parish duties, too. He has not once come to see Mama, and she would love to have him say a few prayers over her, for she cannot get across to the church any more. The parlour and her bedroom next door, that is her world now, and even getting from one to the other taxes her. But he never comes, despite my hints. There now, the kettle is boiling.”

While she fussed around measuring the tea leaves, he said gently, “How are you managing, Lucy?”

“Oh, we get by,” she said with a slightly forced smile. “With Mama’s little annuity and what I can make from the bonnets, we do well enough. The squire is very good to us, sending us fish and game and surplus fruit from the hothouses, and Laurence, too."

"Nothing from the Hall?"

"Not of that kind, no, but Cass Saxby brings baskets of things from time to time. Potted meat and bottled fruit, that sort of thing. Butter and cheese, which we cannot make ourselves any more. There now! Let us take the tray through to the parlour, and we can have a comfortable coze."

Malcolm stayed for half an hour, but before he left he paid for a bonnet to be sent to Marie — "Just put a note in saying *'From a well wisher'*" — and then walked briskly down to Timpson's shop and paid for a pound of tea to be added to the Cokelys next order. He might not have much money, but he had more than Lucy Cokely and her mother.

~~~~~

Sunday brought Marie a surprise, for Mr Malcolm Gage was in church. He had not been there the previous week, and she had discovered from her lurkings in Mr Timpson's shop that he was an habitual non-attender, except for weddings and funerals. Nevertheless, there he was. She had not been aware of him at first, for she sat in Madam's pew near the front, but when the hymn started, there was no mistaking his fine baritone from somewhere behind her.

When she went outside, he was loitering beside one of the yews and wearing rather a fine coat. His brother's most likely, for his usual coat did not fit him half so well.

He smiled when he saw her wearing her new bonnet, and walked boldly across the wide path to intercept her.

"Mademoiselle Fournier."
~~~~~

"Monsieur Gage." He bowed, she curtsied, then she fell silent. Let him speak, if he would, for there was no polite way to avoid the encounter. Nor did she wish to, she realised. Just three days since she had last seen him, and yet she had missed him. How odd.

"I just wished to ascertain that you are still available for Tuesday's French lesson with Edward," he said in English.

"Oui, monsieur. Why do you speak English?"

"So that everyone who overhears knows that our conversation is innocuous." Then he went on smoothly, "I wish to trick you into speaking English too."

That made her laugh out loud, but whether at his audacity or his honesty she could not say. Even so, his smile was friendly and his eyes rested on her with such warmth that she could not dislike him. No, she definitely could not dislike him.

"May I escort you home, mademoiselle?"

Was he wooing her formally? This was a very public meeting and he must be aware of what would be said of them. Or perhaps he did not care. Somehow, that thought pleased her.

He offered his arm and after only a moment's hesitation, she took it, eyes demurely downcast. How hard it was to rebuff him! But deep inside she knew that she did not want to. He was her only friend, and no matter how dangerous that friendship was, she could not quite give it up.

She smiled and nodded at a few acquaintances, and some stared with open curiosity. Agnes Saxby watched them pass by, her expression hard to read. Disappointment, perhaps. Did she truly have hopes of Malcolm for herself? But she said nothing. No one ever spoke to Marie. The servants and working people spoke no French, and the gentry would not make conversation with a servant. Except for Malcolm. He was different from the rest.

"Thank you for the bonnet, monsieur," she murmured as they passed through the lych gate.

"You guessed it was from me?"

"Who else would send me a bonnet, monsieur?"

"You look very well in it. Do you like it? Lucy chose it. She said the style would suit the shape of your face."

"It is beautiful, but sadly it does not go with my pelisse. I shall make one to match it."

"A new pelisse? You can make such a thing? You have clever fingers, mademoiselle."

They walked slowly, the warmth of the sun gentle and comforting, not yet at summer strength. Most of the crowds outside the church had drifted away in the other direction, so they were almost alone. It felt intimate, almost as if they were married, to walk side by side in that way, going home from church together.

Impulsively she said, "Will you come in for breakfast, Monsieur Gage? If you do not object to sitting with the servants."

"I am a servant of sorts myself," he said, smiling at her.

Her heart would be under better regulation if he would only refrain from smiling at her in that oh-so-intimate way. She laughed, and they went into the house side by side.

~~~~~

Malcolm was quietly pleased with his progress. Far from refusing to see him again, Marie had willingly accepted his
~~~~~

company and had even invited him to join the other Dower House servants for breakfast. Perhaps this would be the first of many breakfasts together. How delightful she was, especially when she blushed and lowered her head in that enchanting way. Although it must be confessed that she was equally delightful when she was upbraiding him, eyes flashing and chest heaving with indignation. She was uniformly delightful, that was all there was to it.

Ben Chambers, the expensive man-cook of Laurence's betrothed, was already in the kitchen, his apron on, frying chops and eggs on one griddle and potato cakes on another, and sliding a tray of buns into the oven. Gradually the household drifted in from church — William, the footman, Nellie, the housemaid, Tilly, the general maid and Spencer, the groom.

"Morning, Mr Gage," Spencer said easily, not at all put out at finding him there.

"I thought you would be at the Grove," Malcolm said. "Gaius Valerius is there, after all."

"Oh, I live there now, but the food's better here," he said with a grin. "We'll all be there soon enough. When are they getting married, do you know?"

"No idea," Malcolm said. "I am not in my brother's confidence on the matter."

Spencer laughed at that. "Aye, I daresay. He's still not speaking to you, then? Whatever did you do to upset him?"

Tilly looked at them with horrified eyes. "Hush, Spence!"

Malcolm smiled. "I have no idea what *I* did to *him*. I know perfectly well what he did to me, but I shall not speak of it."

The door opened again and Mr Neate, the lock-picking valet, came in, clutching a sketchbook.

"Oh, Mr Neate, will you do me?" Nellie said eagerly. "You did Mr Chambers on Friday and Tilly yesterday, so it must be my turn."

"I should like to capture Mademoiselle in her Sunday finery, especially the very fetching new bonnet," Neate said, "but I can stay long enough to attempt you too, Nellie. I have left you until last because you have such a complicated face."

"Ooh, complicated! How exactly?"

Neate talked and ate as he drew, filling Nellie's head with what sounded like nonsense, sketching furiously and stopping now and then to take a bite of food. When he had finished drawing Marie, he started on Nellie's likeness, making a great show of exclaiming over mistakes and rubbing them out, so that Nellie was visibly preening herself on her complicated features.

Malcolm sipped his coffee and watched the performance, amused. He had no idea what Neate was up to, but he was deft with both pencil and words, and it was entertaining to observe.

The two walked back to the Grove together, coats buttoned tightly against the cool breeze that had arisen.

"So what was all that about?" Malcolm said quietly. "Complicated face indeed!"

"Oh, just keeping her sweet," Neate said. "I have achieved my objective, however."

"Which was what precisely? If it is not a great secret."

"I have a likeness of Mademoiselle Fournier. Tomorrow Edgerton, Chandry and I depart for Northamptonshire, and a drawing of the lady may jog a few memories."

"Ah. Then I wish you luck," Malcolm said.

"Luck does not enter into it," Neate said complacently. "Planning and preparation, that is the key. If Mademoiselle's secret lies in that county, then we shall discover it, you may be sure."

10: Hopes And Wishes

Monday was the final evening before Selena and Ursula returned to their homes, so there was another formal dinner to endure. The guests of honour were Squire Winslade and his son and daughter. Malcolm had seen Susannah since his return, for she was helping Edward's Italian, but he had not seen the squire or Henry. Now he found his hand being vigorously shaken and his back heartily thumped.

"How are you, boy, how are you?" the squire said. "Goodness, what an age it is since you were last here. How wonderful to have you home again, where you belong. So you have given up this schoolmaster folly, I take it? You will stay here in the bosom of your family, like a sensible fellow?"

"I am only here to fulfil the terms of my Great-uncle's will, sir. I shall be gone again in August."

"Ah well, ah well," the squire said vaguely.

The squire was as fine a dandy as any seen in London, his shirt points almost high enough to put out an eye, and Malcolm felt like a country bumpkin by comparison. Henry was the very opposite of his father, looking as if he had dressed all by guess, and with the sort of young man's swagger that reminded Malcolm of Lady Saxby's two sons.

The Beasleys were there, too, Dr Beasley as the focus of everyone's attention after his seizure a week earlier. This was his first venture from home, and although he smiled and told everyone that of course he was fine and there was nothing to concern anyone, he looked pale and his hands shook a little as he grasped the glass of sherry Laurence thrust into his hand.

Malcolm retreated to his corner, watching it all. The Andersons were the most amusing arrival, for when they saw him they were so clearly torn between the propriety of greeting with civility a member of the family, and the equal propriety of not antagonising the host by acknowledging him. In the end they nodded to Malcolm with stiff smiles and moved on as swiftly as decorum would allow.

It was Miss Beasley who sought him out in his corner, standing silently beside him for some minutes, her untouched sherry glass in her hand.

Her silence was restful, but since they were the only two not speaking, he was eventually drawn to say, "Is he truly recovered or is it all bravado, Phyllida?"

"Oh, bravado," she said in her soft voice, so low she was almost inaudible. "It is his heart, you see. Fatally weakened. He could have another attack at any time and then... But if he rests..."

He followed her anxious eyes to where Dr Beasley stood, swaying slightly but smiling and nodding to the squire, who was holding forth in loud, arm-waving fashion.

"He would be better sitting down," Malcolm said.

"Oh yes! But will he listen? Men can be so stubborn."

"He will take notice of a lady, however," Malcolm said firmly. He weaved his way through the groups standing about the drawing room, ignoring Laurence's frown, until he found Ursula. "Can you persuade Roland to sit down?" he whispered in her ear.

She nodded, and he made his way back to Phyllida Beasley. By the time he reached her, Ursula and Selena had already swept in and claimed Roland, the three settling on a sofa together.

"Thank you!" Phyllida said, eyes shining. "He is not quite accustomed to his own weakness as yet, but he has accepted that things must change. He can no longer go on as before."

"Will he truly give up the practice? That will be a blow to the village."

"Not entirely," she said, smiling a little. "He will remain as coroner, for he loves that work too much to relinquish it, but he will take on a partner to ride out in the middle of the night to difficult births or fevers, and manage the Market Clunbury consulting. He has already written to his colleagues at Edinburgh for a recommendation."

"Ah, that will be a relief. Edser is a very good sort of fellow, no doubt, but there are times when only a qualified physician will do."

"Mr Edser is an excellent apothecary and surgeon," she murmured. "Malcolm..." She stopped, looking at him uncertainly.

"What is it? We are old friends, Phyllida, so you need not hesitate to say what is in your mind."

"I saw you walking home from church with Mrs Middlehope's maid," she said in a rush, going rather pink. "Are you courting her? She is such a sweet, quiet little thing, and it would be so romantic, with her not speaking a word of English and you the only person who can talk to her. I tried, you know, when she first came here, but my French is so basic and I think she could not understand me."

"Did no one else try to talk to her?" Malcolm said, frowning. "Most people have some French, after all."

"Oh, but none of the servants do, and most people of our class would not think of it, but I came upon her one day in Mr Timpson's shop — practically smashed into her — and so I said a few words to her, apologising and so on, but she just smiled and ran away. Do you get on well with her? I should so like to see you happy, Malcolm."

"You are a romantic, Phyllida," he said, gruffly, but he was rather touched, all the same.

~~~~~

'Northampton, 24th May. Sir, I have called at Welby Hall, and have been received by the Countess of Bradcaster, only to be informed that her sister-in-law the Lady Julia Stapleton is now the Lady Julia Welles and resides in Sussex. I have been given her direction, so I shall proceed there forthwith. However, the countess assures me that Lady Julia never employed a French maid, and has had the same lady's maid since she first put up her hair some ten years ago. My colleagues Neate and Chandry will continue their investigations here in Northamptonshire, for it seems likely that Mademoiselle Fournier originated from these parts, or she would not have known anything of Lady Julia otherwise. I am still optimistic that our mission will see a successful conclusion. Yours ever hopeful, Michael Edgerton.'

~~~~~

Tuesday saw the departure of Selena and Ursula, but Malcolm could not be downcast, for it was the day that Marie was to come to test Edward's French. A whole hour of Marie! She came laden with another basket of treats from the Dower House kitchen, which he received with gratitude, but he was unreasonably disappointed to see that she wore one of her old bonnets instead of the new one. However, there was no opportunity to ask her about it because Edward was already chattering away to her.

Malcolm made no pretence to occupy himself with a book. Instead he sat opposite Marie at the table, leaning back in his chair, gazing at her face and listening to the musical tones of her voice. He had tried asking her direct questions about herself, without the least success, but there was much that could be learnt simply by watching and listening. He set himself to analyse her accent first, and now he detected something beneath the Parisian accent. Southern English, he thought, although he could not say more than that. It might even be Northamptonshire. Her father was perhaps a clergyman or provincial attorney, and her mother might truly have been French, for how else could she have learnt the language? No village school had taught her so well. Only the best schools could impart such a clear accent.

Twice he caught her in a tiny slip, nothing that Edward noticed, but to Malcolm, who had talked to many *emigré* French, such mistakes jarred. He said nothing, however, storing them away as evidence.

She had brought some stitchery to occupy her hands, as if she could not bear to sit and talk and do nothing. Not a lady, then! A lady might make a pretence of sewing, but in his experience the needle would always be set aside when there was conversation to be had. He had never thought it likely that she was of his own class, for what lady would so demean herself by becoming a servant, no matter how desperate she may be? Now the practical nature of her occupation — she was darning a stocking — confirmed it. A sensible girl of the middle class, then.

That did not deter him. He might have been born a gentleman, but he had earned his own bread for sixteen years now, and in the lowly profession of schoolmaster. What did rank matter anyway? When one was in love, it was utterly irrelevant. It had not mattered when he had wanted to marry Catherine, who was above his touch by any rational measure, and it would not matter with Marie, either. She was his, of that he was certain. As to why he was so certain, it was a question he could not answer, but nevertheless she was his destiny, even if she did not yet know it.

After a while, he noticed that she was speaking less, and the stocking was abandoned. Once she sighed, and when she raised one hand to her temple, he said gently in French, "Are you tired, mademoiselle?"

She nodded. "A little."

"Edward, your French lesson is over. Do you wish to demonstrate your ability with mathematics to your father?"

With a grin, Edward dashed from the room and Marie sat back in her chair with a sigh, of relief, he suspected. Now Malcolm was alone with her, but he had learnt his lesson from their walk through the bluebells. He would not talk to her of marriage or destiny, in case she ran away from him again. He would not let her run away! No, he would be very careful not to frighten her.

"Would you like some tea?" he said.

"Thank you, that would be pleasant, monsieur."

He rang the bell, then unpacked the basket of treats from the Dower House kitchen, falling on a plum cake with a little cry of joy. "Your Mr Chambers is a treasure," he mumbled through his first mouthful. "Would you like some?"

But she only shook her head, with a wry smile on her face. "You are hungry, monsieur."

"I am always hungry."

John arrived, rather out of breath from the number of stairs he had been obliged to climb to answer the bell, and Malcolm ordered the tea. Then he settled down in earnest to the plum cake. After his third slice he reluctantly pushed it aside, for if he left it within reach he might eat the whole of it and have nothing left to sustain him through his night-time reading session.

Marie had closed her eyes, and he had no wish to disturb her by trying to talk. He began to hum, very softly at first, a lullaby to help her rest. She smiled, although her eyes stayed closed. It was pleasant to sit thus, humming gently and watching Marie smiling, even if she was not exactly smiling at him. She was content to be in his company, and that was progress.

So he hummed, and she rested her eyes, and he was able to watch her as much as he wished, and at that moment it was all he wanted in the world. Marie was not so responsive as Catherine, and had never looked at him with eyes dewy with love, or rested her hand on his arm with a whispered, *'Oh yes, sir! You are quite right, sir.'* No, Marie had not fallen into his arms — not yet. She would one day, of that he was sure, but until then he would wait and watch and hum lullabies to her. He would woo her, as she deserved, and the thought pleased him.

How strange and unaccountable love was. He would have said that he was a man of rational thought, whose head ruled firmly over his heart. He could be reckless, sometimes, and careless of his own safety, but he was never foolish, he hoped. Yet twice in his life he had fallen instantly in love, and with a certainty and steadiness of purpose that was undeniable. Just as his love for Catherine had sustained him through many dark years, so he was utterly confident that this new love would last for a lifetime. There was not the smallest sliver of doubt in his mind. And this time, he had no rival to fight off, so he could be circumspect and pursue his suit slowly.

At length the tea arrived in a little procession, John and Mrs Blenkinsop bearing the trays of tea things and an array of pastries and biscuits, with Skeates to supervise the placement of each item. The butler, at least, knew what was due to a son of the house, banished to the nursery though he might be. With the slightest movement of a finger, he directed John to clean up the plum cake crumbs liberally scattered around Malcolm's part of the table.

"Will you pour?" Malcolm said to Marie, when they were alone again.

"You are too grand to pour your own tea, I suppose?" she said archly.

"No, merely too incompetent. I never know quite how much tea to add or how long to leave it to steep. A lady seems born knowing such arcane mysteries."

A little frown flickered across her forehead at the word 'arcane'. *Ésotérique.* That was not in her French vocabulary. Or perhaps he spoke more quickly than she did. Yes, that was true. She spoke clearly, without the elision of words that happened with a native speaker, or one fluent in the language. Schoolroom French. He wondered that he had never noticed it before.

She poured, they drank. Malcolm unthinkingly cut himself another slice of plum cake.

Marie set her cup down with a sigh. "That is much better. Tea is so refreshing. More?"

"Just a little to warm it up. It cools so quickly in these silly thin cups."

"*Silly thin cups?* This is Crown Derby, and very beautiful."

"Is it? I know nothing of such matters."

But Marie did, and that was interesting. She immediately shot a few rungs higher on the social scale. A family that could afford Crown Derby china was not the impoverished background he had envisaged, yet there she was darning stockings. She was a mystery and no mistake. But whatever her history, Captain Edgerton would find it out, of that he was certain. And once he knew who the lady was, then he could woo her in earnest, and win her heart.

~~~~~

Malcolm had supposed that once his sisters had left, he could quietly disappear back to the nursery each evening, but John arrived promptly at the dressing hour with freshly starched neckcloths draped over his arm.

"Must I?" Malcolm said despairingly. "I am sure I am not wanted."

"Miss Gage's orders, sir, and Mrs Rogers has been told to cook for five."

Five! Even the genial Captain Edgerton and his colleagues were not there to provide a buffer of civility between the two brothers. Fortunately, Laurence was taken up with the two
~~~~~

children and Viola filled any awkward gaps with a ceaseless stream of inanities. Somehow the dinner was got through, and afterwards guests arrived for a card party and Malcolm was able to slip away.

But on Thursday, there was an addition to the family gathering. As soon as Malcolm sidled into the drawing room, he could not help but notice her. She wore a silk gown the colour of the sea in a sandy bay, deep and vivid, that shimmered as she moved. The contrast with Viola's drab, dark gown and Henrietta's white could not be greater. The gown was cut to reveal smooth white shoulders below a rather ordinary face which gazed at him unsmilingly, her expression an exact mirror of Laurence's. Disapproving, that was it.

"Oh, Malcolm, there you are," Viola twittered. "Do come and meet dear Louisa, who has just returned to us from the north. Louisa, may I present to you my other brother, Malcolm. This is Mrs Middlehope, who is to become our sister."

Malcolm bowed politely as she made him a small curtsy.

"How do you do, Mr Gage," she murmured, her voice icy.

She was not at all what he had expected. He had supposed her to be of Laurence's own age, a frumpy matron descending rapidly into old age, but this elegant creature must be ten years his junior, at least, and as comfortable an armful of womanly charms as he had ever seen. But her disdain goaded him into provocation.

"A pleasure to make your acquaintance, ma'am," he said. "But I knew I would like you the moment I rode Gaius Valerius. I must always approve the owner of such a splendid mount."

Her eyes narrowed in anger. *"You rode Gaius Valerius?* Laurence, what are you about to permit such a thing?"

"I did not permit it," Laurence growled.

"Then how dared you, sir? How *dared* you?" She quivered with anger, but Malcolm was not intimidated by her fury.

"He gave me permission to borrow a horse, so I did," Malcolm said urbanely. "How was I to know?"

"Well, you know now," she snapped, "and if you have any understanding of Laurence, you would have realised he would not ride such a horse."

"Oh, I know it. I could hardly believe my luck to find such a mettlesome creature in the stable amongst so many fat slugs."

"And he accepted you?" she said suspiciously. "He did not toss you into a hedge?"

"Not at all," Malcolm said. "We did not go far, only to Cloverstone Manor, but he was able to stretch his legs a little on the ride through the Hall grounds. A magnificent animal, ma'am."

"He is wonderful, is he not?" she said, breaking into a sudden smile. "My father-in-law bought him for me, and my brother-in-law very kindly allowed me to keep him."

"I wish I had such generous relations," he said with genuine feeling, and she laughed, lighting up her rather undistinguished features into something approaching beauty. For an instant, Malcolm saw just what attracted his brother to this stylish widow. She was the very antithesis of Catherine's cool, composed beauty. Watching her at dinner, a glass of wine in her hand, deep in animated conversation with Laurence, her whole body alive as she talked, he understood completely. And he saw in Laurence's face the deep happiness that could only come from overwhelming love.

It was hard not to feel bitter at the sight. Was it not enough for Laurence to have enjoyed seven years of bliss with Catherine? It would be enough for most men, and it would have been enough for Malcolm. Yet now Laurence was embarking on a second round of marital happiness. Why was he so lucky when Malcolm had not had the joy of even one great love?

Was it so much to ask that he might be allowed to love and to be loved in return just once in his life?

11: Secrets And Lies

'Thursday 25th May. Madam is back and all is well. She has her books again, and I have work enough to keep me busy for a month, for Sarah has done nothing about Madam's clothes except to help her in and out of them. There are stains and dirt and tears and I know not what. However, Madam managed a trip into Durham city and has brought a dozen or more lengths of fine material and all manner of trimmings to keep my needle busy. I am to make her up a wedding gown, if you please, and a new ball gown for the celebrations. Best of all, we are to take Mr Gage's carriage into Shrewsbury for even more shopping, so I shall be able to buy some material to make a pelisse to match my new bonnet. It should be silk, but I cannot afford that, so I will have to settle for something plainer, which is a great pity, for I have never had so fine a bonnet before. Miss Cokely is very clever. I daresay I should not have accepted it, but I am not a lady and need not take account of the genteel proprieties. If a gentleman gives me a bonnet, and a very fetching one at that, and asks nothing in return, then I do not see why I should refuse. He is kind, Mr Malcolm, and does not press himself upon me as some men do. Just because I am a maid, they think I am nobody, and unworthy of any respect, but he is not like that at all. He treats me like a lady, and that makes him a true gentleman. A slightly rum one, to

be sure, but very agreeable to be with. Five hundred and fifty five.'

~~~~~

The next morning, Viola accompanied Malcolm's breakfast tray, and as soon as John had left, she sat down, wringing her hands fretfully and said, "Brother, I hope you will not take umbrage at dear Louisa's manner towards you when you were first introduced last night. She is normally the most affable and agreeable company, but... well, I daresay she feels that her loyalty is towards Laurence now, and she must display some coolness towards you for his sake. It is so unlike her! She practically hissed at you! I declare I went hot and cold."

"It is not of the least consequence, Vi," he said. "I care nothing for her good opinion."

"But it is so uncomfortable, to have this... this chill in the air. Laurence is bad enough, but I had so hoped that dear Louisa's return would soften him towards you, and I *cannot* understand why he is so implacable about it. After all, it was a great many years ago now, and surely whatever imagined slight still irks him could be forgiven now, in Christian charity."

"You do not know what he holds against me, then?" he said curiously. "After all, I was the one wronged by him, and it is a mystery to me what injury he thinks he has suffered."

"Exactly, but he will not speak of it. I should tell you, brother, that Ursula and Selena told him in no uncertain terms that he should reconcile with you, for the good of the family and his own immortal soul. I should never have dared to tell dear Laurence what he should do — goodness, the head of the family! How impertinent of me *that* would be. He must be the best judge of his own behaviour and what is proper in the case, and he
~~~~~

knows all the circumstances, as perhaps we do not, for we were not witness to the events in Bath and... well, to be honest, Malcolm dear, and do not bite my head off, but we have heard only your side of the story, and Laurence may see everything entirely differently. As he does, of course. So I have never ventured to... but Ursula and Selena did not scruple to tell him exactly what they thought and what he should do. They argued the case most convincingly, in my opinion. But he was adamant, utterly unmoved by their reasoning."

"Did he give any explanation for his refusal?"

"No, none. He said it was a matter of honour between the two of you, and that what you had done was entirely unforgivable. And that is what terrifies me, brother, for as Christians we must always forgive, must we not? Even you, who— But the less said of that, the better. Laurence, at least, has always been a good Christian, in every other way but this he is a good, kind, generous man, perfectly tolerant of other men's foibles, but in this he is implacable and I could not bear him to go to meet his Maker with hate in his heart. I could not bear it!" She ended on a rising wail, tears trickling down her worn cheeks.

Malcolm moved round the table to sit beside her, one arm around her thin shoulders. "There, there, Vi. You must not upset yourself over two foolish men fighting like cockerels in the farmyard. We are not worth it, you know. Neither of us is worth a single tear, and if you had a husband and children of your own to occupy your thoughts, as you should, you would not be so overset by our foolishness. Why did you never marry, Vi? Did no one ever take your fancy?"

"Oh... oh yes, there were one or two, but none who ever took a fancy to me." She went a little pink as she spoke.

"I never understood why you went to Aunt Millicent," he said abruptly. "That was a waste, to shutter yourself away with that crotchety old woman when you were still young."

"Oh, but I could not stay... not after—"

"Not after what, Vi?"

She pleated her skirt anxiously, head lowered. "Not after... after Ursula fell in love with John Malling. He was supposed to be for me, you see. The son of friends of Mama's, the heir to a good estate, very eligible, and I was the eldest, so he was invited to stay and... and Ursula fell in love with him and that was that. He felt obliged to marry her, you see. Mama said—" She stopped, heaved a great breath, then straightened her back. "Mama said that it was all right because he was intended to marry one of us and it made no difference to him which one, and I was a good girl who would not make a fuss. And I did not, naturally, but I thought it best to... to go away."

"Maybe you should have made a fuss," Malcolm said.

"Oh *no!* One must not fall out with a sister over such a matter, and Ursula was in such a glow of happiness that no one could wish to deny her everything she desired. And they have been very happy together, so that is the greatest comfort, and Aunt Millicent was very kind... on the whole... and of course I have been useful to Laurence, and Louisa says I may stay on here and be useful to her, for she is not very housewifely, so you see, my life has not been wasted at all, not in the least. I do so like to be *useful.* Do you see?"

Malcolm saw very clearly. Poor Viola! There was no comfort he could offer, not to a woman of six and forty whose only chance of happiness had been snatched from her, but he understood her very well. After all, he had done much the same when Catherine had been snatched from him — he had run away to hide and lick his wounds and heal, if he could. But perhaps there was no healing from such an injury, one must only endure it as best one could. So he hugged her, and shared his coffee with her, and a Bath bun, and let her chatter away until she was quite composed again.

Later that morning, Malcolm dispatched Edward to his mathematics lesson, the last remaining part of his education not related to language. Edward would quite happily have spent all day rattling away in a foreign tongue, but Malcolm insisted he take an hour a day to ride and an hour to study some other subject to rest his brain.

It also gave Malcolm time to rest his own brain from the relentless force of Edward's enquiring mind, a quiet hour to pick up a book or to think his own thoughts. Today he was most in need of a book, for his thoughts were melancholy. He had been obliged to dig deep to find the morning's gratitudes, for he was still consumed with envy for his brother's good fortune. Laurence had all the luck and Malcolm had none. What was the point to his miserable existence? He had no money, no home, no family beyond the casual interest of his sisters, to whom he was no more than an irritating loose thread to be stitched back into the warp and weft of the Gage clan. Perhaps they would prefer it if he died, so that they could file him tidily away at last. There was no one who *truly* cared what became of him, and he was not at all sure whether he cared much himself.

The one woman he had loved, with whom he could have been happy, had married his brother and he had survived on pure anger since then. Now he could not even summon the energy to be angry with Laurence any longer. Catherine had gone to her grave years since, and that was the end of it. Once he had been able to conjure her face effortlessly in his mind, but now the image was hazy. Fair hair curled around her face, a slender frame, the delicate hands... but her eyes, her mouth, her nose? He could not remember. He caught echoes of her in Henrietta and Edward, but that was all a mirage. He was a fool to think he could recapture the past. It was gone for ever. Everything was gone.

He fetched the plum cake to nibble, picked up a book at random and began to read. He had not turned the page more than twice before there was a knock on the door.

“Ah, there you are. May I come in?”

Mrs Middlehope, of all people.

“Of course,” he said, rising politely.

“You may tell me to go to the devil, if you wish,” she said conversationally. “I would, if I were you, after my treatment of you last night. I am not usually quite so snappish, and I apologise profusely.”

Malcolm gave a bark of laughter. “Heavens, ma’am, if I owned a horse like Gaius Valerius and some stranger decided to hack about the countryside on him, I would have knocked his head off. The apology must be mine, I fancy.”

“You did not know, and besides, it was Spencer’s fault, he has admitted it. He was supposed to be in the stables that afternoon, but he had gone off on business of his own, about which he is very coy, I might add, so I suppose it is strictly male business. However it came about, he left Gaius unattended and I cannot blame you for preferring him above Laurence’s dreadful hacks. But that is not why I sought you out in your lair. This came from the Hall this morning.”

She placed an invitation card on the table.

'Lady Saxby requests the pleasure of the company of Mr Malcolm Gage at Maeswood Hall to dine on Saturday 27th May at 7 o'clock. Carriages at midnight.'

"We are all invited, Laurence, Viola, Henrietta and me, so if you wish to go, we will use the travelling carriage. What do you say, Mr Gage?"

He sighed. "I did not come here to be scampering about to evening engagements. If you are all out, Edward and I can eat together, and advance his language skills." And perhaps, he thought, he might go for a walk after dinner and might happen to be passing the Dower House and might call upon Marie. And here perhaps was an opportunity to find out more about her. "What do you know of Marie's history?"

"Marie? My maid? Nothing at all. What is your interest there, Mr Gage? She is a very pretty girl, I grant you, but I shall take strong exception to any attempt to detach her from my employment."

He considered for a moment the idea of enlisting Mrs Middlehope to his cause, for she could certainly help him on the road to matrimony if she wished. Almost instantly, he dismissed the thought. Although they had reached a degree of *rapprochement*, it was fragile and not to be depended upon.

Cautiously, he said, "She interests me, that is all. You know nothing of her family, or her previous employment?"

"Of her family, not a thing. My French is deplorable, and she speaks no English, so she has never told me anything about herself. I had a very good reference from her previous employer. Other than that, I know nothing at all about her, except that she is an excellent lady's maid and I should be loath to lose her. Two weeks without her has only increased my good opinion of her abilities. Beyond that, I cannot help you. What are you reading?" She picked up his book. "*The Lake of Killarney.* I have not read this one. What think you of Porter?"

And somehow they fell into a discussion of poetry, and time and the plum cake disappeared, and Malcolm began to understand just what his brother saw in this unusual widow, beyond the smiles and the curves. Somewhere a clock chimed and she jumped up with a guilty expression.

"I must go. Laurence will be wondering what has become of me."

"Does he know you are consorting with the enemy?"

She laughed. "Oh yes. We talked at length about you last night, and we are agreed that his quarrel with you is not mine, and therefore you are not *my* enemy, Mr Gage."

"But you see, I do not understand why I am *his* enemy, either," Malcolm said, aware that he sounded resentful. "I am the aggrieved party, after all. What have I ever done to him?"

She went very still, her eyes widening. "You know perfectly well what you have done."

"I do not," he said shortly. "No action of mine has ever harmed him, ever."

"If you will forgive me for saying so, that is a somewhat disingenuous remark."

"It is the truth. He stole Catherine from me, after all, and nothing I did hindered him. He destroyed my chance of happiness, and I was powerless to prevent it. Why should he hate me so? What possible reason can he have?"

"Perhaps the fact that you enticed his wife into an adulterous liaison," she said, her voice as cold as ice.

Malcolm felt as if he had been punched in the gut. He could barely breathe, cold fires shivering through him.

"What?" he croaked.

"Did you think he knew nothing of it?" she said. "You are mistaken, Mr Gage. Your betrayal shocked Laurence to his core, and hurt him deeply."

"A liaison? Whatever gave him that idea?" He jumped to his feet, too agitated to sit still. "He truly believes that I did such a thing?"

"He knows it, Mr Gage. You cannot deny it."

"*Devil* take him!"

He spun on his heel and tore from the room, down two flights of stairs and into the library. It was empty. Swearing under his breath, he flung open the door to the study. Three surprised faces looked up at him, Laurence, Henrietta, Edward, seated round the table.

"You two - out!" he said to the children, as they jumped to their feet.

"No, stay," Laurence barked at them.

"Out!" He held the door open for them, and they scuttled out, Henrietta curious, Edward frightened. "Now, brother, you can tell me—"

"Get out, Malcolm, for God's sake!"

"—what the *devil* you mean by telling your future wife that I had an affair with Catherine."

"Why should I not tell her? It is the truth, after all."

"It is a damned lie, do you hear! A complete and utter falsehood!"

"Stop yelling," Laurence said. "And stop compounding your guilt. I know what happened, brother, and no denial of yours, however vehement, will change that."

Mrs Middlehope arrived, rather out of breathe. "Please do not quarrel," she said.

The brothers glared at each other, and Malcolm wondered briefly if Laurence was going to hit him. They had almost come to blows in Bath, yet somehow they had avoided it. But now...

"He is the one quarrelling," Laurence said. "He always makes a melodrama of everything."

"A melodrama? When you accuse me of the most heinous of crimes? And it is all a fiction, and why you would do—"

"Fiction! Ha! Stop lying, you devil!"

"—such a thing... Good God, Laurence, what must I do to convince you? There is not a word of truth in it, I swear it by the shards of the old tree house!"

Laurence gave a harsh crack of laughter. "The shards of the old tree house? Good grief, Mal, what are you, eight years old?"

"If I swore on the Holy Bible you would hardly believe me, I daresay, but it is the absolute truth. I never laid eyes on Catherine after that last day in Bath, not once, and certainly never did... what you are suggesting, *never.* I fought for her openly, like an honest man, and I would never dishonour her or you in so underhand a manner. I cannot imagine why you would even think it of me, or of her."

"Because she wrote of it in her diary," Laurence said quietly.

For the second time, Malcolm felt as if he had been punched. "Her *diary?* But… it is not true. Why would she put lies in her diary? I cannot believe this."

Another crack of laughter. "Now you know how I feel," Laurence said. "Give it up, Mal. You are caught in a lie, and had best admit it at once."

"But I am *not* lying. Where is this liaison supposed to have been conducted? Did she come to Harrow? Or to Oxford? Because those are the only places I have been for the last sixteen years."

The anger deepened on Laurence's face. "You came *here*. You seduced her here, in the gardens."

"But I have not been here," Malcolm said, bewildered. "She must have invented all this. It is so peculiar. Why would she do such a thing?"

"She would not, of course," Laurence said crisply. "Which is why your lies are so offensive, brother. Oh, get out of my sight! Let me see no more of you. Do what you have to with Edward, but then take your miserable self out of our lives for ever."

Malcolm stumbled out of the room, through the office and along the passage to the inner hall, hardly aware of where he was going, only knowing that he had to get away from Laurence to somewhere quiet, somewhere where he could think and try to make sense of the nonsensical things his brother had said. Worse than nonsensical — impossible! And yet Laurence believed the lies.

He stopped abruptly with a gasp. There she was on the wall, a huge portrait of her head and shoulders, the blonde hair artfully arranged in stiff curls, the gown elaborately trimmed with an abundance of lace, jewels everywhere. He barely recognised her. The eyes were bluer than he remembered, the mouth smaller, the nose sharper. And the smile — no, this was not the soft, gentle Catherine he remembered. This was another woman entirely, a woman glorying in the trappings of the married state, triumphant and gloating. Look at me, the portrait seemed to say, look how rich I am, how beautiful, how unattainable. *Look at me.*

Malcolm turned and ran for the service stairs.

12: The Old Tree House

Marie decided to wear the new bonnet again for church, even without the matching pelisse. She told herself it was only because it was by far the most fetching bonnet she possessed, but deep inside she knew that she wore it for Malcolm, especially after last night. They had had such a lovely evening! He had brought Edward to the Dower House with him, and they had sat in the servants' hall playing vingt-et-un for fish, and working their way steadily through a whole tray of shortbread until Madam had returned from the Hall and everyone had had to jump about.

Yet it was so dangerous! He had stopped asking questions about her family and where she had come from, which was a great relief, but there was still a danger in his company, and perhaps more so in the sort of rambunctious game they had played last night. Usually she would sit in a corner with her sewing, listening to the others talking and joking, but never part of their circle, and they never tried to draw her in. But Malcolm had not allowed her to sit apart. He had chosen the game because of its French name, and taught the rest of them some other French numbers too, and then carefully explained the rules to Marie. She had felt obliged to play too, since he had gone to so much trouble, and it was touching to see the pleasure in the others' faces.

"It's lovely to see her joining in," Sarah said.

William had added, "You'll have to come more often, Mr Gage, so Marie can join in more of our silly games. It's not right for her to be kept out of it just because we can't talk to each other."

It was the greatest fun with everyone getting boisterous and yelling a bit. Marie had got swept up in the excitement, too, calling out *'Buy!'* or *'Twist!'* or *'Stick!'* with the best of them. And sometimes she had forgotten that the words were supposed to be new to her, and had just shouted them out without hesitating or stumbling or putting on a French accent. Once when that happened, she caught Malcolm's eye and he smiled at her so knowingly that she blushed scarlet and was very, very cautious for the rest of the game.

"I will see you at St Ann's tomorrow," he had said as he left, smiling in a way that made her melt inwardly. It was quite ridiculous at her age, to be so susceptible to a handsome face and broad shoulders and a certain warmth in a man's eyes. She was not fifteen any more, blushing and stammering when the curate spoke to her. Yet she could not deny that she was drawn to Malcolm, and there was no point in pretending. She should not encourage him, she knew that perfectly well, but it was hardly encouragement to meet him at church, was it? Or to wear the bonnet he had given her? Was it?

He was not there when she first arrived at church, but she turned round once or twice, surreptitiously, as everyone was settling in their pews, and there he was, visible from a great distance by his imposing height. He saw her looking and smiled widely, which of course made her blush. Quickly she turned her eyes downwards, glad that Madam was not yet in her seat to notice.

After the service, Marie was not surprised to find Malcolm outside the church doors for her.

"Do you want to come back for breakfast?" she said hopefully.

He replied in English. "Do you have to go back to the Dower House? It is such a lovely day — we could pick up some food at the Grove and go for a picnic." A small hesitation, then he said, "I should like to talk to you, if I may."

His face was serious, but there was nothing of the lover in his manner. Somehow, she trusted him. *"Oui, monsieur."* Besides, Ben was at the Grove today, so there was only Tilly to cook the Dower House breakfast. A picnic with Malcolm was far more enticing.

She waited outside the servants' entrance at the Grove while he went into the kitchen to find food for them, emerging with a cloth-covered basket. They set off through the grounds of the estate, soon plunging into a tangle of overgrown shrubbery and then into woodland proper, the canopy dense at this time of year, providing a pleasant shade.

He said little as they walked, merely to advise her of a muddy patch or stray bramble, offering a hand across fallen branches or rocky patches. Eventually they emerged in a sunny clearing, dominated by one massive old oak tree.

"The old tree house." He spoke in English, pointing upwards through the branches to where a few fractured planks still clung to their position. "There is not much of it left, now," he said, laughing. "It was here when we arrived, and I climbed up at once and fell straight back down again. The wood was rotten, you see. I was all for repairing it, but Mother was not and so it was never done. But this was still our favourite place when we were boys. Laurence and I came here all the time, but we never climbed the tree again. Not that one, anyway." He sighed. "Ah well. That was a long time ago."

He spread his coat for her to sit on, and then unpacked the basket — half a pie, some chicken legs, bread and cheese, cake and a flask of something, with a wine glass.

"Only one glass?" she said.

"I never drink wine these days," he said, "but I thought you may like some. It is the good stuff, not the watered down travesty you probably get in the servants' hall, if you get wine at all. What will you eat? Try the pie. Mrs Rogers makes a lovely pigeon pie."

She tossed aside her bonnet and gloves, trying a little of everything and sipping the wine, for it was such a treat, smooth and fruity, warming her inside as the sun warmed her face. Women spent so much time indoors, or close-bonneted against the complexion-ruining rays, yet she loved the feel of it on her skin, reminding her of her childhood freedom. Happier times.

Malcolm sprawled out on the rough grass beside her, heedless of the risk of green stains on his breeches. When she had eaten her fill, she shifted so that her back was against the rough trunk of the oak tree, the wine glass in her hand. She could not see his face, for his head was turned away from her, and she wondered whether he were falling asleep in the sun.

"You wished to talk to me, monsieur?" she said.

He turned to face her, and then abruptly sat up, legs crossed. "I should like to do so, if you do not object." She made no response, so he went on, "I must speak in English, I think, so that you will understand everything fully. Something has occurred which is very strange. I do not understand it, and it has been rolling about in my head for two days now and I need to... unburden myself of it. I do not expect you to advise me, or say anything at all if you wish not to, only to listen. Do you understand?"

She nodded, puzzled but also flattered that he saw her as a friend to whom he could talk... unburden himself.

"You are aware that my brother and I fell out years ago over a woman — Catherine Haywood. A great heiress, from her father's wool trade, but also a great beauty. I loved her, but *he* married her... and that is perhaps all that needs to be said of the business. Laurence and I parted in great anger — mostly on my side, it must be said. He was angry with me at first for trying to interfere in his plans to secure her fortune for himself, for the estate was in desperate straits, but once he had accomplished that... once he and her mother had browbeaten her... well, that is all water under the bridge now. He was cold towards me, I raged at him but he was unmoved. I left him to savour his success and went to my sisters for a while, but I could not trespass on their kindness for long and naturally I could not go home... not when *she* would be there. So I went to Oxford, and took up my old lodgings that I had left only weeks before and settled down to drink myself into oblivion."

He sighed, wrapping his arms around his knees. "That was a bad time. Not that I remember much of it, for I was thoroughly jug-bitten. Luckily for me, Great-uncle Zachariah dragged me out of there by the ear, took me home with him and sobered me up.

Then he found me work at Harrow, and I cannot imagine how many favours he had to call in to do it, for I was not at all qualified for the position. Not ordained, you see. But I had the requisite Greek and Latin, and could pass muster in historical matters, so off to school I went. And there I stayed, Michaelmas, Hilary, Easter, Trinity, Michaelmas, Hilary, Easter, Trinity, year after year, the vacations spent in Oxford with Great-uncle Zachariah. I never returned to Shropshire, never saw Laurence, never saw Catherine. My sisters, occasionally, when they came up to London, but Laurence and Catherine — never.

"And now I discover that Laurence believes I conducted some kind of secret liaison with Catherine, here, in these very woods. Somehow I tooled up here from Middlesex or Oxfordshire in my free time, in my curricle and pair no doubt, quite the gentleman of leisure, and seduced his virtuous wife, and he cannot forgive me for it. Well, who could blame him? I would not forgive a brother who seduced my wife, either. Except that it never happened. None of it is true, yet he believes it, and why? Because she wrote of it in her diary."

He stopped, rocking slightly in distress. Marie said nothing, as perplexed as he must be. How was it possible? Yet she did not for a moment doubt him. There was sincerity in every word, in the bewilderment in his face, in the whiteness of his knuckles as he clasped his knees to his chest. He was not angry, just confused.

"Why would anyone do that?" he said, lifting his distraught face to Marie. "Why would she write such things in her diary — her private diary, for heaven's sake? Why would any sane person lie to her own diary? It makes no sense! It makes not a scrap of sense, but she did and Laurence believes it and hates me for it... for something that *never happened!*"

He fell silent, shaking his head in disbelief.

Marie closed her eyes, considering all he had said. Somewhere in the branches far above them a bird warbled, its melodious tune filling the air. A slight breeze set the branches soughing softly. A bee hummed in a sunny patch of clover. Such a peaceful spot, with its gentle summer sounds and the smells of bruised grass and wild garlic, the sun warm on her face. It was so like home, or home as it had once been, that she was momentarily awash with grief for her lost childhood. She had been so happy, for a while, until she had grown up and everything had changed. Being a grown-up was a miserable business, for her and for Malcolm too, evidently. How old had he been when he had fallen out with his brother? Twenty-one? Twenty-two? Young, in love, desperate. Her heart ached for him.

She understood the enormity of his story, the compliment he paid her by trusting her with his confidences. It seemed to her that she must show him that she understood, and trusted him in equal measure. So when she spoke, it was in English.

"A diary is a strange device," she began, and at the sound of her voice, his head shot up, a delighted smile on his face. She went on, "To the world, we appear as we wish to be seen. We each wear a mask to disguise our true natures, so you show the world the mask of stoical schoolmaster with no pretensions. And I — I wear the mask of a French lady's maid. But inside... ah, inside we are both different, you and I. Inside we are both in great pain, hurt and unhappy and terrified of the future."

He opened his mouth as if to speak, then closed it again and merely nodded.

She continued, "Catherine wore a mask, too. I can say that without any fear of contradiction, for everyone does. I do not know her, so I can only guess what she was like from the tiny droplets of information I have gleaned as I loiter behind the rice sacks in Mr Timpson's shop, or sit sewing in my corner in the servants' hall. She wore the mask of a contented wife and mother, but she enjoyed society more than the company of her family, it is said. Balls, routs, card parties — anywhere she could dress in her finest gowns and jewels and be a queen for a few hours. She liked to be a queen, so people say, and be courted and admired and have men fawning over her. That was her public life. But in her diary — why would she lie to her own diary? Because even in such a private place, she was wearing a mask. The gentle flirtations of her public appearances became, in the secrecy of her diary, something much more torrid. I suspect her life as Mrs Laurence Gage was very dull. He is not an imaginative man, I think, your brother. He likes a quiet life buried in the country, with his dogs and his guns and his card parties with friends twice a week. For a woman who only comes alive in company, and especially admiring male company, such a life must have been a torment to her. Perhaps she felt drawn to men other than her husband and, fearing that she would act upon it, she chose instead to do so in a safe way, within the covers of her diary. Or perhaps real life did not supply enough of the admiration she craved, so her imagination filled the need. But it was *you* of whom she dreamed between the covers of her diary."

Not her dull husband. Not her many admirers. She dreamed of Malcolm, her passionate suitor, the man she could never have.

"Laurence himself always said he was the dull one," Malcolm mused. "That was one of the reasons why I never imagined Catherine would accept him. What a life she must have had! If, as you surmise, she wanted to be admired and received no such admiration at home, then—"

"Oh no," she said. "Everything I have heard suggests that your brother adored her, right from the start. He was utterly distraught when she died, and there were concerns for his sanity. That is why there was such surprise when he took up with Madam, for they never thought he would marry again, and she is very different from Catherine, by all accounts."

"That she is," he said, with a bark of laughter. "Catherine was a princess, so beautiful and serene, but this woman is merely ordinary." A princess? So he had thought when he had first known her, a shy slip of a girl, radiant and glowing with love for him. But the Catherine in the portrait was a different creature, not shy at all, but very sure of herself, proud and queenly. But not in the least ordinary, as Mrs Middlehope was.

Marie laughed. "Madam is far from ordinary. Not a princess, I will grant you that, nor beautiful either, but she is a lovely, warm creature and she deserves a bit of happiness. I will not have a word said against her."

"You are commendably loyal," he said.

"I must be, or she will turn me off without a reference and then where would I be?" she said demurely.

He laughed, and then to her surprise he grasped her hand and lifted it to his lips. Oh, the warmth of lips pressed against her skin! How she had missed the touch of another human. Ever since Mama had died, she had been so utterly alone... until now. Now she had a friend, and perhaps something more than a friend. He had said no more about marriage, and perhaps he had changed his mind about that, but surely he was a friend, someone upon whom she might depend.

"Ah, you are so good, Marie," he said, his eyes filled with warmth. "You lift my spirits, do you know that? You make the world seem a better, happier place. Thank you for speaking to me in English." And then he kissed her hand again.

For a moment, terror gripped her. Please, let him not kiss her mouth, let him not turn into a lover, for she was not sure she could resist him, and she must, at all costs she must. But he let go of her hand, laughing, and sprawled out on his back, looking up at her with teasing eyes, almost as if he knew her thoughts.

"You will not tell anyone that I speak English?" she said, when her heart had slowed to a more normal rate. "You must not tell, Malcolm. It is very important."

He sat up again, serious now. "You need not worry about that."

But she did, of course. How could she not? One careless word could destroy everything.

13: An Apology

JUNE

It was Tuesday and Malcolm was impatiently awaiting Marie's arrival when Captain Edgerton returned from his travels to Northamptonshire and Sussex. He strode into the day nursery, still wearing his greatcoat and sword.

"Ah, you are hard at work, I see," he said, beaming at Malcolm and Edward. "I shall talk to you later, Mr Gage, if I may."

"If you wait but a few minutes, Mademoiselle Fournier will be here to brush up Edward's French, and we may talk then."

"An excellent idea," he said, removing both coat and sword, before taking a seat.

"Why does he always have a... oh, what is the word? The sharp thing like a big knife?" Edward said in Russian.

"Sword. That is a sword, and he has it because he is a soldier."

"He is not in the army now," Edward said, quite reasonably.

"A soldier never quite lays down his arms," Malcolm said. "Who knows when we may have cause to be grateful for his skills." Then, in English, "We are speaking of your sword, Captain, a fascinating device to a boy of twelve."

"To some of us, it never loses its fascination," the captain said, grinning wolfishly. "Guns, too, it has to be said. But do not let me disturb your lesson."

In no more than ten minutes, Marie appeared with her basket of delights from the Dower House kitchen. Malcolm explained that he needed to talk to the captain, and was rather pleased to see the slight hint of disappointment on her face. He took Edgerton to an unused bedroom nearby, ghostly with holland covers shrouding the furniture. Sitting on the window seat, he gestured to Edgerton to tell his tale.

"Lady Julia Welles received me most graciously," he said. "There was no difficulty in obtaining an audience with her, she was perfectly affable and showed no sign of alarm or anxiety. She read the reference, and then told me plainly that she had never written it and had no knowledge of Marie Fournier."

"That is disappointing," Malcolm said. "But that must mean that Marie wrote the reference herself."

"That is one possibility," Edgerton said. "That was, in fact, my first thought in the matter. But fortunately I had the company of Mr Willerton-Forbes on the journey from London, and his devious lawyer's mind suggested other possibilities. One is that some other person wrote the letter for Marie, using Lady Julia's name. However, Pettigrew is inclined to discount this as unlikely. He feels it complicates things rather too much."

"But there are other possibilities?" Malcolm said.

"Just one — that Lady Julia is lying. And that is far more interesting, would you not agree?"

"Why would she lie?" Malcolm said. At first sight, it was implausible that an earl's daughter would lie about so trivial a matter, but now that he was aware that Catherine had lied even in the secrecy of her own diary, he must consider the female sex capable of anything.

"As to that, we can only speculate," Edgerton said. "However, it would suggest some underhand dealings, so we shall investigate further until we have uncovered the truth."

"Hmm. I am not sure if it would be right to pursue the matter," Malcolm said, frowning. "Marie told me that it is important that no one suspects that she is not French, and if she either wrote the reference herself or Lady Julia wrote it and is willing to lie about it... well, there must be a good reason for it."

"I agree with almost every word," Edgerton said with a grin. "That there is a reason, I accept unreservedly, but it does not necessarily follow that the reason must be a good one, and if Mademoiselle is bent on mischief, then—"

"No," Malcolm said, quietly but firmly. "She has been in Mrs Middlehope's employ for five years now, and has done nothing except be a very efficient lady's maid. There is no cause to suspect that will change. I am sorry now that I ever asked you to look into it. There is no harm done, fortunately, and there is no need to investigate any further."

"It shall be as you wish, Mr Gage," Edgerton said easily. "I shall at once recall Neate and Chandry from Northamptonshire and we can return to our enquiries regarding Dilys Hughes, a junior housemaid at the Hall, who left on the common stage one morning twenty-nine years ago, arrived in Shrewsbury and then vanished."

"Housemaids disappear all the time," Malcolm said, amused. "Why is this one so interesting?"

"She is a loose thread, Mr Gage, and I do so dislike a loose thread. It is unlikely that we shall find her after all this time, but one must do one's best, and unless something more interesting offers itself for our investigative talents, Miss Hughes will have to do."

~~~~~

When Edward had gone for his daily ride, Malcolm took a book to the window seat, and stretched out his legs, gazing longingly out of the window at the clear summer skies and the myriad greens of the woods. How he wished he could ride, too, and clear his head with a fast gallop but there was only one beast capable of pleasing him, and he was forbidden. After the glory of Gaius Valerius, he could not bear to hack about on one of Laurence's docile mounts.

The book stayed unopened in his lap. Today he was not minded to read, for a stray thought was running round in his head like a squirrel in the attic, and he needed to catch it and drag it into the open air to be examined.

When he had talked to Marie on Sunday, he had been so pleased that she was speaking English at last, that she *trusted* him, that he had taken little heed of her words. But ever since then, the conviction had been growing in his mind that he had done his brother a great injustice. *'Laurence adored her, right from the start,'* she had said. Had he? He had seemed quite composed when he was with her, not like Malcolm, who could not suppress his joy in her presence. But then Laurence was never demonstrative. When Father had suffered his apoplexy, and the rest of the family had fallen into a maelstrom of despair,
~~~~~

Laurence had quietly taken on the management of the estate, without fuss. When it became obvious the coffers were empty, he had set about a scheme to replenish them. Malcolm would not have known what to do, but Laurence quietly got on and did it, without the least complaint, and Malcolm had always assumed the lack of emotion meant that he felt none. Now he wondered if he had entirely misread his brother.

Marie had said, *'He was utterly distraught when she died.'* He recalled Viola's tear-spattered letters from those dreadful days, telling of how grief-stricken Laurence was, but he had disregarded it as just Viola's way. She was one of life's hand-wringers, to whom every little trouble was a crisis of insurmountable proportions. Ursula and Selena had written in more moderate terms of visiting to console Laurence, to help with the children, to comfort his loneliness. It could not compare, of course, with Malcolm's own grief, or so he had thought. It had not occurred to him that Laurence could feel one tenth of his own pain at Catherine's death.

It was as if the earth were sliding away from under him, the solid ground of his convictions giving way to an extraordinary state of uncertainty. For sixteen years he had been unshakably confident of the rightness of his position. He had loved Catherine, as she had loved him, but Laurence had cared only for her money. Now even that surety was slipping away.

How terrible it would be if he had misjudged him. Would he have felt differently if he had known that Laurence loved Catherine just as passionately as he did? Impossible to say for sure, but he liked to think that he would. He might not have been happy to lose her, but it would have been a comfort to know that she was held in affection, and not viewed merely as the means of restoring the Gage fortune.

He had reached this uncomfortable point in his musings when the door opened and the man himself looked into the day nursery.

"May I... may I come in?"

Astonishingly, Malcolm saw the same chagrined expression on Laurence's face that he felt sure was on his own. "Of course," he said, sliding his legs round to stand up.

"I thought you might be out in the fresh air — riding, or some such. You should get away from your books for a while," he said hesitantly, one hand rubbing against his breeches.

"Your stable is a collection of slugs, any one of whom would be a penance to ride. There is only one horse worth riding and he is forbidden me."

"Ah... yes, well... best not to ride Gaius Valerius or there would be the devil to pay," Laurence said, tugging at one ear. Was he nervous? How strange. "I owe you an apology," he said abruptly.

"Oh." Malcolm was too startled to formulate a more sensible response.

"You were quite right. It was all lies. In Catherine's diary."

"Oh," Malcolm said again. "What was it that convinced you?"

"I looked at the dates," he said, wrapping his arms around himself, "and I could see that it would have been in the middle of the Hilary term, so you would have been at Harrow. Also, the day when... when it supposedly happened, it was March and there was snow on the ground, and I do not for one moment believe that you and Catherine were rolling about in the snow. *You* might well have done, for you are quite mad enough for anything, but she hated snow and mud and dirt of every kind, and I cannot for the life of me understand why I did not see that at once. I apologise unreservedly for doubting you, Mal. You were always honest — too honest, sometimes — and I should have remembered that. Can you ever forgive me?"

Malcolm opened his mouth to say "Oh" again, then snapped it shut. He was beginning to sound moronic. He knew he ought to say something conciliatory at this point, but all he could grasp was the least salient point. "How did you know there was snow on the ground?"

Laurence grunted with what might have been laughter. "I asked Vi. She keeps a diary too, but she records all the trivia of the day — including the weather. It was an unseasonably cold March that year, seemingly."

Malcolm could hardly get his mind to accept it. One question was still swirling round in his head, and so he blurted, "Did you love her? Marie says that is what everyone says of you."

"*Marie* says? You have discussed our private affairs with Marie Fournier, have you?" Abruptly, the anger was back.

"She is my friend, and I trust her," Malcolm said simply. "I needed to talk to someone about all this, and I have no other friends."

"Damnation, Mal, you must have more suitable confidantes than a simple lady's maid! Your sisters, if no one else. But at least the chit will not spread the tale about, since she speaks no English."

Now it was Malcolm's turn to be angry. The chit, indeed! A simple lady's maid! As if she were not a wonderful, rational, feeling person. He ground his teeth in frustration at the insult, but he did not want to discuss Marie, so he said, "*Did* you love her?"

Laurence rubbed his face tiredly. "Catherine? Oh yes, I loved her, for what it was worth, but you knew that, surely? I told you many times, I am certain of it. At least... I think I did. But she never loved me. She loved *you*, Mal. Her diary is full of her feelings for you."

"Is it?" he said gloomily. "But if she can lie so abominably about this... this *liaison*, how is any of it to be believed? If she had truly loved me she would never have married you."

With a wry smile, Laurence said, "I never understood why she married me, to be truthful. I was very grateful, but it always felt like something incomprehensibly miraculous, a shaft of sunlight in the midst of grey cloud. You have always been the handsome, lively, interesting one. I am a very dull dog by comparison."

Malcolm laughed at his downcast face. "You are the sensible one, Laurie. I was always the idiotic, reckless one."

Laurence rubbed his face again. "This would be so much easier if we could have a drink together. Do you never drink, or is it just my claret you dislike?"

Malcolm laughed. "I dare not! After you married Catherine, I fetched up in Oxford at my old lodgings and there seemed to be nothing more interesting in my life than the bottom of a bottle. I do not trust myself with it."

"Damnation, Mal!" Laurence said, his voice unsteady. Abruptly he rose and strode to the window where Malcolm still stood, throwing his arms around him. "We should not quarrel, brother. I hate this *stupid* feud — *hate* it! Can we be friends again? Please?"

"With all my heart," Malcolm said, hugging him back, his throat unexpectedly tight.

"Thank God!" Laurence said, releasing him as suddenly as he had embraced him. "But even if you can withstand the temptation, I must have a drink. Come down to the study with me. Edward is riding and Henrietta is out paying calls with Viola, so we shall be alone."

"Mrs Middlehope is not here?" Malcolm said, as they made their way downstairs.

Laurence chuckled. "She is at home looking out some books for me. She brought two carriages entirely filled with books, can you believe it? We are to convert the South Saloon to a library for her, to accommodate them all."

"However has she acquired so many?"

"Her parents' collection, plus her own purchases. She has some fine works amongst them, books I have wanted to read for years, but have never been able to afford. Books are so damnably expensive."

In the study, Laurence poured himself a large glass of something or other — brandy, by the colour — and waved him to a chair beside the fire. It was too warm for it to be lit, so there was an embroidered fire screen in front of it, covered with winding vines and trumpet-shaped blooms, with birds peeping through the leaves. In the lower corners, almost hidden by denser foliage, a fox and a cat lurked, waiting for the opportunity for a meal. Malcolm realised there were many such screens about the house, and cushions and footstools, too, all with the same fine embroidery, and often with a little story to them. Not his sisters' creation, that much was certain, and surely not Henrietta's either, for he had seen her labouring to hem a handkerchief in the evenings. There was only one conclusion.

"This is Catherine's work."

"It is." Laurence's face clouded inexplicably. "She was always embroidering, stitching away all evening when we were at home." He sounded almost bitter, which was a puzzle. Then, bizarrely, he went on, "Did you ever talk to her? I mean, about books or art or the world? Did you discuss things more interesting than the weather?"

"Of course we discussed things," Malcolm said, and then was immediately assailed by doubt. "At least… I talked and she listened."

"Exactly!" Laurence said, sounding pleased.

"But it is the same thing… no, I suppose it is not. Actually, now that I think about it, she said very little, except *'Yes, Malcolm'* or *'No, Malcolm'* or *'Gracious, Malcolm'* and then she would blush prettily."

He could not help comparing the silently blushing Catherine with Marie, who had listened without judgement to his rantings beneath the old tree house, and had then calmly and sensibly given him her opinion. In French she was reticent, for her mastery of the language was too shaky for serious debate, but in English she was as rational as anyone could be.

"*You* should have married her, not me," Laurence said fiercely, swirling the brandy in its glass. "*You* would have made her happy, as I could not. It is obvious now that she always loved you, and regretted losing you."

A spike of pure pain deep in his chest almost stopped Malcolm from breathing. "Oh, a fine time to tell me *that!*" he cried, not bothering to modify his tone. He jumped to his feet, and prowled about the room, arms waving. "Good God, Laurence, is that supposed to help somehow? Am I supposed to be grateful to you for realising that you stole her unjustly? Are you finally apologising for it?"

Laurence was on his feet, too, the brandy set aside. "Stole her? I did no such thing! We agreed that we would leave the decision to her, remember? I asked her, she accepted me and that is all there is to it. I have never, and will never, apologise for that, for I have done nothing which deserves an apology. The choice was entirely hers, Mal, *entirely* hers. Whatever you may choose to believe, she accepted me freely."

"You *forced* her to do it, you and that evil mother of hers."

Laurence groaned. "No one forced her. How can anyone force a woman to marry against her will? One would have to question the understanding of such a woman. If she had truly wanted you and yet married me instead, that would be absurd beyond permission. Whatever her feelings, she *chose* me."

Malcolm was about to contest the point vigorously when he remembered Marie's words. *'A woman who marries where she is told is a foolish mouse.'* There was something to that, and Catherine had never struck him as a foolish mouse. Demure, perhaps, and outwardly meek, but when he had talked of elopement, her eyes had shone and she had said, *'Oh yes! Yes, Malcolm! If it must be so, it must.'* She had known precisely what she was doing.

"Marie said that, too. That she deserved her fate, if she allowed herself to be persuaded into an unwanted marriage."

Laurence's face reddened and his hands clenched into fists. "Oh, *Marie said,* did she? What is between you and Marie, anyway? You had better leave her alone, Mal, because Louisa would not like it if you hurt her."

"*Louisa* would not like it?" he echoed, anger boiling up inside. How dared he speak so to him? As if he cared tuppence for Marie, when she was life itself to Malcolm. Insufferable man! "Who cares what Louisa likes? She is nothing to me! What about what Marie likes? What about what *I* like? Have you thought about that, brother? Have you ever thought about me at all?"

"Have *you* ever thought about anyone else?" Laurence growled, and made for the door. Handle in hand, he stopped, and turned again, looking suddenly tired. "Damnation, Mal, this is not working. We were very peaceful here until you arrived, and now we are at each other's throats every five minutes. Three months of this will be the death of me — or of you, maybe. I will not have you disrupting us a moment longer. This arrangement is at an end. I want you out of the house by the end of the day."

"What about Edward? His inheritance?"

"I will make sure he gets the money that would have been his."

"But what am I to do? Where am I to go?"

"You can go to the devil for all I care." So saying, he stamped out of the room.

14: A Falling Out

Malcolm paced back and forth across the room, too angry to be still. The insolence of his own brother! For all his grand words about apologies and forgiveness, he was just as intolerant as ever… could still see no other view but his own. Where was his sense of honour, to agree to allow him to teach Edward, and then renege on their agreement? There was no justice in it.

And what in God's name was he to do? He could not go back to Harrow, for Butler would not accept him unless he had tried his best to succeed in the task set him, and he was tolerably sure that quarrelling with his brother would hardly meet that standard. He had acquaintances in Oxford who would house him until he could find employment, or his sisters would take him in, if he could only get there. He was not even sure that he had enough money left for the common stage.

Then there was Marie. He would never see her sweet face again, with that mouth that seemed always on the verge of smiling. Such a mischievous smile! If he had had the rest of his three months, perhaps he could have persuaded her to look on him more favourably. But it did no good to think about that, for now he had no hope of ever winning her. Now he had no home, no work, no money and no prospect of ever obtaining any. His rage abated as suddenly as it had appeared, to be replaced with cold fear. What the *devil* was he to do?

He heaved a despairing sigh, and cast himself into Laurence's chair, one leg over the arm, wreathed in gloom. It had been a mistake to come back to Shropshire, he could see that now. Curse Great-uncle Zachariah for his foolish meddling! They had all gone on perfectly well as they were, and apart from a bit of agonising from Viola in her monthly letters, they had been quite content. All this dragging up the past did no one any good, disrupting them all. If the old fellow had left matters in more orderly fashion, Malcolm would at that moment be living as a gentleman in Oxford, and not on the verge of destitution. What on earth was he to do?

On the table beside him, mere inches from his hand, rested Laurence's brandy glass, the barely-touched contents calling to him. For almost sixteen years, he had not drunk any alcoholic liquor, not so much as a glass of wine with a meal, nothing but small beer, when there was no tea or coffee or fresh water to be had. For sixteen years he had been strong, his resolution fuelled by his anger and his certainty of himself as the injured party. But now his anger was no more than burning embers. He could not sustain it in the face of the truth — that Catherine had made him believe she had loved him, and perhaps had even believed it herself, but she had calculatedly chosen Laurence. She had wanted the house, the estate, the position in society that only the eldest son could give her. And Laurence had loved her devotedly, that could not be denied. All Malcolm's resentment of his brother's success was foolishly misplaced. They could have been friends all these years, as they should have been — as they once were.

All his anger was gone, and there was nothing left but misery and hopelessness. He reached for the brandy glass and drank.

The aroma hit his nose first, and then the taste of it exploded in his mouth. Warm, smooth, pungent — he swallowed, and it burned all the way down. He took another sip, rolling the liquid around in his mouth to intensify the flavour before he swallowed, then again. He sat back in the chair, closing his eyes, cradling the glass in his hand. How many times had he and Laurence sat together of an evening, often with Father, sharing a bottle of something or other, talking over the day's events, discussing an interesting book or the progress of a new horse? Happier times! If only he could go back to those days of easy camaraderie...

But he could not. The past was gone. That boyhood friendship was gone, Catherine was gone, Marie would soon be gone, everything was gone. He was finished.

He picked up the brandy glass, and after a moment's thought the decanter too, and went to his room to pack.

~~~~~

The movement of the carriage was soothing. It was not a new or even a well-sprung carriage, but it was comfortable and for the moment that was all Marie asked. Mr Gage's fat horses proceeded at a measured pace and the road to Shrewsbury was smooth, so they were not unduly jolted, and the journey was short enough that even Marie could not feel more than mildly queasy. Madam was silent, gazing out of the window and not even pretending to read the book she held in her lap. She had been unusually quiet for a few days now, and Marie knew precisely why. Well, that little difficulty was easily resolved.
~~~~~

It pleased her not to have to listen to Madam, or attempt to talk to her. Instead, she could ponder her own little problem, a problem with broad shoulders and intense blue eyes and hair that flopped over his forehead in a way that made the desire to push it back almost irresistible. He had lovely hair, she decided, dark but not too dark, and disordered in a way that was entirely natural, the result of running his fingers through it when he was talking excitedly. She wondered what it would feel like to run *her* fingers through his hair — silky and soft and very, very pleasurable.

But that was not really to the point. The question that had been bubbling in her mind for two days now, ever since they had talked under the oak tree on Sunday, was whether Malcolm might be the way to resolve her problem once and for all. It was possible... truly it was possible, and then she could stop pretending and be herself again. But she would have to tell him everything, and that was so dangerous. Could she trust him? She believed she could, for he had kept the secret of her not being French, but even so, it was the most tremendous risk.

They came into the outskirts of Shrewsbury and turned into the yard of the Talbot, where Mr Gage's carriage was recognised and they were greeted with a bustle of respectful attention from the ostlers. Having secured a private parlour for their use, Madam proceeded down the street, with Marie and William, the footman, trailing in her wake.

It was not until the third drapery that Marie found precisely what she wanted. It was not silk, of course, for she could not possibly afford such a thing, but a very pretty muslin, eminently suitable for summer wear and the exact colour she wanted. She had carefully detached a short length of the ribbon from the bonnet to take with her so that she could match the colour.

Taking it to the counter, she said, "Price, *s'il vous plaît ?"*

The superior woman behind the counter looked her up and down. "Two shillings a yard."

Marie put on her most disdainful expression. *"Oh, non, non, non, madame."*

"Hmpf. One and sixpence."

Marie raised her eyebrows and tipped her head expectantly.

"Oh, very well. One and fourpence, since your mistress is buying so much and *she* is not quibbling over the price."

"Elle peut se permettre de payer vos prix scandaleux." She can afford to pay your outrageous prices.

The length of fabric was wrapped and paid for before Madam had made half her choices. They made their way back to the Talbot, where Marie accompanied Madam to the parlour and William, after depositing their numerous parcels, went off with a relieved air to the common room.

A knock on the door heralded not the expected coffee and a cold collation, but Captain Edgerton.

"Good morning, ma'am," the captain said. "We saw your carriage in the yard. Is there any service we may render you while we are in town?"

"Nothing, unless you wish to share the claret I have ordered," Madam said with a smile. "What brings you here today, Captain? Still looking for missing housemaids?"

"Just one housemaid, who stays resolutely missing, despite our best endeavours," he said, coming fully into the room and bowing with his usual flourish. Such a funny little man! Yet for all his flamboyance and swaggering about with a sword, Marie suspected that he would be formidable in a fight.

A troop of servants arrived with food and drink. Madam and the captain broached the wine, and Marie poured herself some coffee and filled a plate with cold meat and pastries, listening quietly and unnoticed to the conversation.

"Are you quite sure the girl reached Shrewsbury?" Madam said, once she had drunk deeply of the wine and settled back in her chair.

"Quite sure," the captain said. "We have two servants who worked with her at the Hall who saw her board the coach in Great Maeswood, and we have the guard who remembers her boarding and who saw her alight in Shrewsbury in the Raven's yard. He was rather sweet on her, so his memory can be depended upon. He says that she collected her two portmanteaux and set off down the High Street, as if she knew precisely where she was going. But after that... nothing. There is no record of her in any of the hotels or inns, although to be honest their records are not very complete. Her name is not in either of the two employment registers in existence at the time. The workhouse, which has very complete records, has no Dilys Hughes listed. No one remembers a girl of that description."

"It was twenty-nine years ago," Madam said in amused tones. "Do you truly expect anyone to remember a passing housemaid after such a time? If it were twenty-nine *days* ago, I should be astonished if anyone remembered her."

"So should I, for there was nothing at all to distinguish her from any other housemaid. However, we have many other lines of enquiry to pursue. We are presently engaged in looking through the parish records for a marriage that might have taken place shortly after her arrival here, or a baptism some six or seven months later. Parsons are very accurate about records, luckily. Once we have exhausted the churches here in Shrewsbury, we will move out into those parishes nearby. She cannot have gone far, I believe, not on foot and burdened with two bags. We are very thorough, Mrs Middlehope."

Marie shivered. Thorough indeed! Relentless and merciless, like the hounds in pursuit of a fox. It was fortunate indeed that Captain Edgerton and his friends had not been set to find her own secrets, for she was very afraid that there would be no hiding place from them.

~~~~~

Malcolm packed as much as he could into his battered old portmanteau. He had extra clothes now, for Laurence would not miss a few unwanted garments, but they were too fine for normal wear, so they could be sent on in the box. He tossed them onto the bed, then began gathering up all the scattered books. They went onto the bed, too. After each armful, he took another gulp of brandy. He was beginning to feel pleasantly warm and mellow. The world was definitely a less hostile place when viewed through the bottom of a glass. He refilled it from the decanter and went back to the day nursery for more books.

Edward was there, gazing with puzzled eyes at the disordered shelves. "What is happening?"

"I am leaving," Malcolm said shortly. Then, seeing dismay on the boy's face, he went on, "Your father is throwing me out."

"Did I do something wrong? Am I not working hard enough?"
~~~~~

"No, no, no! It is nothing you have done, I swear. It is my fault — we quarrelled and he wants me out of the house today, that is all."

"Can I come with you? I can carry on learning, and—"

"That is not possible," Malcolm said gently. "The terms of the will state that I must stay under this roof for the whole three months leading up to the examination. Once I leave, it is over. I am sorry, Edward, truly I am."

Without a word, the boy spun on his heel and left the room. Malcolm shrugged miserably. That was the end of it, then. Not so much as a hug to see him off. He would have liked a hug, or at least a handshake. *Something.*

He had gathered all the books together into a great mountain on the bed, retrieved his box from the box room and begun to fill it when John came in at a rush.

"Is it true? You're leaving, sir? Oh… it *is* true. Sir! Do you need a valet, sir? Will you take me with you? Please?"

Malcolm sat back on his heels, astonished, trying not to laugh. "Are you mad? The only respectable clothes I possess are my brother's cast-offs, and I cannot afford to buy more."

"Oh, not yet, sir, but when you inherit your property in Oxford, you'll want—"

"That will never be, John, I am sorry to say. Once I leave this house, the property in Oxford is lost to me, and it was always an outside chance, after all."

"Oh." John flopped onto a corner of the bed, causing a little landslide of books to the floor. "I'm very sorry, sir. You've been such a pleasure to dress. You look well in everything you wear, and it would have been… ah, well."

He sounded so despondent, that Malcolm said, "You should sign up for one of these employment registers as a valet. You could find yourself a good position, I am sure."

"Not as good as serving you, sir," he said dejectedly. "As least I can help you to pack. All of this is going in the box, is it? I'll have it sent on to Harrow by the next carrier."

"Not Harrow. My position there is no longer available." The books would have to go back eventually, for they belonged in the library there, but not yet. He could not bear to part with them just yet. How was he to manage without books?

"So where will you go, sir? To the school at Shrewsbury? I daresay they'd give you a place, since you went there yourself."

"Shrewsbury…" Malcolm said thoughtfully. It might answer. He was known there, and his reputation was such that they would not ask for references. It was nearer, too, so would cost less to get there, and the bank manager knew him, and might lend him a few pounds until he had an income again. And there was a library there. Yes, it was a good plan, and perhaps he could still see Marie occasionally. He slapped that thought down instantly. There was no point even considering it. A schoolmaster on a salary of fifty guineas a year could not support a wife, even if it were permitted. "Shrewsbury it is," he said firmly. "I shall send for my box when I am settled. Good bye, John, and if ever I find myself in need of a valet, I shall send word to you."

"Thank you, sir. Good luck and God speed, sir."

They shook hands, Malcolm took up his greatcoat, hat and portmanteau, and headed for the back stairs.

~~~~~
~~~~~

The drive home from Shrewsbury was miserable, for the roads became steadily worse, the ruts deep and jarring. Marie's stomach was beginning to rebel when they turned into the drive of the Dower House.

"There we are, home again," Madam said, with her friendly smile. "You will feel much better now."

She went straight into the house, leaving Marie to help William with all the parcels. They had barely begun unloading — heavens, how much had Madam bought? — when running feet on the gravel made them look up. It was Spencer, running full pelt up the drive.

"What's happened, Spence?" William said.

"There's been some kind of dust-up at the Grove. Mr Malcolm's down at the Boar's Head this very minute taking a room for the night, and he's to go on to Shrewsbury tomorrow. *'I thought you were here till August,'* John Brownsmith said, quite pointedly, and you'll never guess what Mr Malcolm said! *'No, that's all over.'* And John said, *'But you'll be back, won't you?'* and he says, *'No, never. I'm not wanted there.'* And then he said he was going to find work in Shrewsbury. Have you ever heard the like? He must have properly fallen out with his brother this time."

Marie froze. Malcolm leaving? Going away without seeing her? When she had thought she had two more months of his company. He could not leave without a word, surely he could not! She had to see him, to say goodbye at least.

"*Marie!* Come on, bestir yourself, girl," William said, dumping a pile of packages into her arms. "I must go and tell the mistress."

She struggled up the steps into the house, as William rushed ahead to impart the portentous news.

"Going to Shrewsbury?" Madam said in astonished tones.

"I thought you would wish to know at once, madam."

"Thank you, William, you did quite right. Heavens! I wonder what has happened? I had better get over to the Grove and find out. I should change first, but Laurence will not mind all my dirt. Marie, I shall leave you to unpack everything. Be very careful with the Chinese silk. I shall be back in time to dress for dinner. The sea green, I think, and the emerald pendant and combs. Help me on with this bonnet again, will you?"

Marie unpacked as quickly as she could, placing each length of India muslin or cambric or lustring in a box layered with plain cotton strips. Then the ribbons and buttons and combs and silk flowers had to be found homes. Gloves and stockings and slippers and a big roll of linen for undergarments. Finally, there was Marie's own parcel to be secreted away in her room. Then and only then dared she slip out of the house and walk briskly along the road to the inn.

Where would he be? In his bedchamber, or a private parlour? Although he did not seem like the sort of man who would take a private parlour. She saw John Brownsmith, the innkeeper, disappearing through a door.

"Excuse-moi! Où est Monsieur Gage?"

"Mr Malcolm? He's in the common room. COMMON ROOM." He pointed, and she murmured her thanks. The common room! That was rather public, but it could not be helped. She had to see him before he left for ever, she *had* to.

She walked down the corridor towards the low murmur of voices, pushed open the door, carefully looked around. Where was he? Not by the counter where the beer was dispensed. Wherever was he? There he was!

He sat at a table not far away, a tankard of ale in front of him and several used plates, as if he had eaten a hearty dinner. And he was smiling... *laughing.*

The reason for it was not hard to detect, for sitting across the table from him, her dark head close to his, was an unknown woman. She was talking animatedly, one hand waving, while the other rested on the table. And Malcolm was smiling widely at her, nodding at her, amusement written all over his face, engrossed in her words. He was holding her hand.

Marie turned and fled.

15: Matters Of Honour

Malcolm had packed in such haste that he had forgotten to bring even a single book. Not that he could have settled to read if he had, but perhaps later, in the desperate hours of darkness, it would help. For now, he sat on the creaking bed listening to the sounds drifting up from the common room below — a low rumble of voices, an occasional burst of laughter or Brownsmith the innkeeper yelling at someone. His wife, most likely. From the yard outside came the pungent aroma of horses, and sometimes a soft whinny from within the stables. Someone in steel-tipped boots clinked across the cobbles and a door creaked open, then creaked closed again. On the road outside, female voices chattered as they bustled home to prepare dinner for their menfolk.

He had eaten early so that he would be able to walk down to the Dower House later, at a hour when Mrs Middlehope would be at the Grove with Laurence and Marie would be free to talk to him. He had to see her to say good bye — after all that had passed between them, he could not simply disappear without explanation. He needed one more memory of her lovely face and those great, dark eyes to sustain him through the lonely years ahead. And one more favour he would ask of her.

Eventually it was time, and he was lucky, for there were few people about now to delay him. He strode down the street, waving to Mrs Cokely as he passed Bramble Cottage, and then up the short drive to the Dower House.

"She's not here," Tilly said, wiping her hands on her apron, when he asked for Marie at the kitchen door. "She went out after she'd dressed the mistress for the evening, and she's not come back and we've started dinner without her." She gazed up at him with anxious eyes. "I hope she's all right."

"Does she often go out unexpectedly like this and miss meals?"

"No, never, sir. She's not one for wandering."

"Tell her I will call again in the morning," he said frowning.

Where the devil had she gone? Perhaps she was at the Grove with her mistress, but then the servants would have known that. She had no friends in the village and no means of transport, unless she found a lift from a passing farmer, and why on earth would she? If she had left with luggage, Tilly would have known it, and if she had not, she would return in her own good time, and there was nothing to be done about it.

He set off down the drive again to walk back to the inn.

~~~~~

Marie had no idea where she was walking. No, that was not true, for her steps had led her to the lane where she had walked with Malcolm that first time, when he had taken her to see the bluebells and told all sorts of tall tales to the villagers and called her *'ma chérie'*. Such a lovely day, almost as lovely as the picnic, when he had told her all that troubled him and she had trusted him enough to speak to him in English. She had not intentionally
~~~~~

walked that way, and perhaps it was a bad idea to increase her pain with such memories, but there was a bittersweet pleasure there, too.

Such a fool she had been! No man was trustworthy — she had known that for years, and had kept herself safely hidden away from temptation, but he had weaselled his way into her affections, and it turned out he was a devious, two-faced scoundrel, just like all the rest. Why was she crying? She never cried! How idiotic it was to shed tears over such a rogue. She would *not* cry! But somehow the tears kept coming and no amount of scolding deterred them.

Who was she, the woman he had been smiling at with such gladness? No one from the village, she was sure of that. Great Maeswood had been her home for three months now, and she had surely seen everyone at least once, and none of them had boasted such black hair, or such smooth, dark skin. That hand resting in Malcolm's — his large and pale, and hers slender and dark. Who on earth could she be, this stranger who had captured his heart?

It was only when she heard voices ahead of her that she realised she was almost upon the village of Lower Maeswood, where she might be recognised after the day of the bluebells. Instantly she wheeled round, wiping her wet cheeks on her sleeve, and set about the return walk.

~~~~~

Malcolm strode down the Dower House drive, head down, lost in thought. Where had Marie gone, and why? Would he have time to see her in the morning? What time did the mail cart pass through anyway? He could not afford to miss it and lose a day, but he had to see Marie before he left.
~~~~~

He was so unaware of his surroundings that he swung around the gatepost and crashed — oof! — into a solid form, which swore at him roundly.

"What the *devil* are you doing, Mal? I have been all over the village looking for you, and dinner has had to be put back and it is all wildly inconvenient."

Laurence.

Malcolm frowned, trying to make sense of it. "Why?" was the only question that sprang to his mind.

"Because Viola is having the vapours, Henrietta is weeping incessantly and my son — *my own son* — tells me that I have agreed to this arrangement and it is dishonourable of me as a gentleman not to adhere to it, that is why. Dishonourable! As a gentleman! And the tears of the women! It is more than a man can bear, I assure you."

He looked so indignant that a bubble of laughter rose in Malcolm and would not be suppressed. "Edward said that? You have given him the soundest of principles, then, and you should be proud of him, brother." He laughed again. "Dishonourable! I should love to have seen that."

"It is not funny! But you will have to return to the house, or I shall have no peace."

Malcolm laughed again, and shook his head, half in disbelief. "And what says Mrs Middlehope to this melodrama?"

Laurence's face softened at once. "Ah, Louisa is composed and reasonable, as always. She is equal to anything, although..." He rubbed his nose sheepishly. "She tells me that two grown men should be able to coexist under the same roof without falling into conflict, and I suppose she has a point. Will you come back?"

Thank God! "I should be very happy to do so, and promise I will keep out of your way as much as I possibly can."

Malcolm had no intention of telling Laurence just how much of a relief it was. For two or three hours he had been entirely destitute, with neither home nor income, and a rapidly dwindling supply of coins in his purse. Now at least he would have a chance to win his inheritance, and if he failed he would have his position at Harrow to fall back upon. He was saved by the tears of the ladies and the honour of the gentlemen, and he must never, ever allow his stupid temper to jeopardise his future again.

He would have gone back to the inn to collect his things, but Laurence would not have it — "We will send John to collect everything" — and so he was steered across the road. And there at the entrance to the lane beside the gateposts, half hidden by foliage and as still as a statue, was Marie, gazing pale-faced at him. His breath caught in his throat.

"I... I must talk to her," he muttered, not taking his eyes from that still form.

"What about dinner? Viola will want you to eat with us."

"Tell her I am indisposed... delayed... a tray in my room... anything you like," he said distractedly.

Laurence sighed theatrically, but made no other protest and went on briskly towards the house. Then there was only Marie. She had not moved an inch, reminding him of a hind peeping out of the forest, quivering and ready to run away at the least unwary movement. He must not startle her! Slowly, so very slowly, he moved across the road and she stood motionless, watching him. Her face — dear God, her face! She looked as if she had stared at death itself, there was so much grief written there, and were there traces of tears on her cheeks?

"Marie?" he said softly as he drew near. "What is it? What has happened?" And then, a sudden thought, both terrifying and exhilarating — was she distraught because he was going away? "Did you hear that I was leaving? But I am to stay after all."

Her face changed not one iota. Still she stared at him, those great dark eyes still filled with tears. So it was not that. His spirits sank again instantly.

"Have you been crying?"

She looked down, then, embarrassed or ashamed, perhaps. He was so close to her, only a few feet away and still she gave no sign of moving. He knew he should stay back... not press her too closely, but he could not bear to see her distress. So he walked right up to her and cupped her face in his hands, softly wiping away the remains of the tears on her cheeks with his thumbs. She looked up at him then, eyes brimming with unshed tears, and stepped wordlessly towards him, to sob quietly on his chest. He wrapped his arms around her and held her tight, as tight as if she were rightfully his, and rocked her very gently.

"Hush, *ma chérie.* Hush, sweet one, everything is all right. I am here now. Ssh, my darling."

Gradually she quieted in his embrace, not moving, allowing herself to be held, to be comforted. Still he rocked her, murmuring into the softness of the close-fitting felt cap she wore. A small feather adorning it tickled his nose. He wished he could remove the cap altogether, and bury his face in her hair, feeling the gentle touch of those soft curls. He wished he could turn her face up to his and taste the salty sweetness of her lips. He wished... oh, he wished a thousand jumbled thoughts as he whispered to her.

On another day, perhaps even an hour ago, he would have done it. He would have kissed her and shown her how much he cared for her. Not now. He could not do it. He was newly chastened by his brush with disaster, and somewhere at the back of his mind was the thought of Edward, sternly telling his father that his actions were dishonourable. What would he make of a man who took advantage of a lady's distress to press his suit upon her? So he held her, and did nothing more, despite his own longing. One day he would kiss her. One day, when Edward had succeeded and Malcolm was a gentleman of means, he would kiss her and beg her to marry him. Until then, he would wait. He must, for he had nothing to offer her.

He had no idea how long they stood thus, his arms around her, but eventually she shifted slightly and he loosened his hold. She stepped back, looked him straight in the eye and said, "Who is she?"

His head was so full of Marie that he could only stare at her, bemused. "Who is whom?"

"The woman you were with at the inn. In the common room. You were holding her hand."

Slowly, he dragged his mind back an hour. "Oh... that woman. A cousin."

"She is no cousin!"

"What? Oh, you mean the dark complexion? She is, I assure you. Wait... she is a *second* cousin. You know of my Great-uncle Zachariah, who set up this foolish business with Edward? He had a son, illegitimate but always acknowledged. Kenneth. He was an utter rogue, in and out of prison, and eventually he was packed off to India to straighten himself out. I am not sure whether he ever did or not, but he married out there and Charu is his daughter. When Kenneth died a few years ago, she came to England. She saw a notice in the newspaper that Zachariah had left a watch to Kenneth, or his heir, so she went to Oxford to claim it, the attorney told her about her family here, and she came to find us. It was quite by chance that we met at the inn. Oh Lord, I forgot to tell Laurence about it. Well, no matter, it will be a surprise to him."

Her face had lightened a little. Was she... could it be possible that she was jealous? Just a little bit? His spirits soared. Now that would be something! It would mean that she cared for him... that she felt he was hers, in some indefinable way. Which he was, of course. There was not the slightest doubt lingering in his mind. He loved her, beyond all question.

"A cousin," she said slowly.

She was speaking in English, he realised. He smiled. "I like it when you talk to me in English," he said, raising a flicker of a smile from her. "It means there is no pretence between us. Total honesty."

The smile vanished. "Not completely," she said crisply. "I have not told you anything about myself, nor will I. And now I must get back to the Dower House. Good evening, Mr Gage."

He watched her walk swiftly away from him and cursed himself for an utter fool. But he had time now. He had two months. He would come about.

~~~~~

'2nd June. What a day! It began splendidly enough with our outing to Shrewsbury. Mr Gage's carriage is old fashioned but very comfortable inside, and fortunately for me his horses are so sluggish that even my rebellious stomach lasted the full distance
~~~~~

in each direction. I managed to find the perfect fabric for my pelisse to match Malcolm's bonnet, which was something of a miracle in so small a town. Only three linen draperies worthy of the name, and I hunted down my quarry in the third. There are not many occasions on which I miss London shops, but this was one of them. Almost any drapery in Oxford Street would have had a better selection. However, I have found something, so I am not displeased with Shrewsbury. Unfortunately, my pelisse will have to wait, for Madam found something, too, or rather a great many somethings to add to the mountain she brought back from Durham, which it will be my task to turn into a flattering wardrobe for her wedding. That may become problematic before too long. The sooner she marries, the better. The second half of the day was more trying, for Malcolm and his brother quarrelled again and he was banished from the house. Then, when I went to the inn to find him, he was hand in hand with a woman I had never seen before! A servant, I guessed her to be from her clothes, but it turns out she is a distant cousin of some sort. I do not know what to make of it, or of myself. I was angry with him, I think, for I supposed he had made a fool of me and I do <u>not</u> like the feeling. Even now, I am not sure that he has not, for no matter how much he murmurs endearments into my ears, he has not mentioned marriage again. If he should do so, I am very much minded to accept him, for it would solve all my problems. But perhaps he no longer has any thought of it, and unless he speaks, there is nothing I can do. Except to think of him constantly, of course, and be jealous of every other woman he looks at. How pathetic I am. Five hundred and forty nine.'

~~~~~

If Malcolm had been hoping to slip back into the Grove unnoticed and enjoy a restful evening, he was speedily disabused of the
~~~~~

notion. Edward bounced into the day nursery first, beaming from ear to ear, and pumping his hand in a very manly way. Then Henrietta, hurling herself at him and hugging him fiercely. Viola came too, weeping a little, and mumbling, "So glad… so very glad… so upsetting… family… very bad… such a relief!" And finally, Mrs Middlehope arrived, a twinkle in her eye, to assure him that Laurence was very happy to have him home again, which Malcolm doubted, and that everyone hoped he would dine with them every night in future.

Then she tipped her head on one side and said, "What is between you and Marie?"

It was on the tip of his tongue to tell her to mind her own business, but he was trying to guard his temper so he bit the words back. Marie was her employee so her welfare very much was her business. "Nothing dishonourable, ma'am."

Her eyebrows rose. "Anything honourable? Such as marriage?"

Malcolm hardly knew how to answer such a direct question. Honestly, he decided. They were alone and there was little point in prevarication. He still had Laurence's brandy at hand, so he took as sip as he composed his thoughts. "When I first met Marie, I felt as if I recognised her — as if she were a kindred spirit. I thought perhaps she reminded me of Catherine Haywood, but now that I have seen Catherine's portrait, I do not see any likeness at all. But for a while I was sure that we were destined to be together, just as I felt with Catherine. I even told Marie that I intended to marry her. Since then… let us say merely that reality has an irritating way of reasserting itself. It has been borne in upon me, and forcibly so in the last few hours, that I have no money, no home and just at this present no employment either. I have a thread of a chance of an independent income, but it depends entirely on a boy of twelve. Sturdy and unafraid as he is, resting my entire future happiness on his shoulders is too great a burden, I feel. So I have… drawn back from any talk of marriage. If ever I am so fortunate as to come into my inheritance, I should certainly wish to pay my addresses to Marie."

"To a lady's maid?"

"To a most superior lady's maid," he said solemnly. "She told me so herself, so it must be true."

Mrs Middlehope chuckled. "Indeed it is. In fact, I may never find another so good. But does she return your regard?"

A difficult question to answer. Her tears that afternoon suggested *something* but he hardly knew what, and her abrupt departure was discouraging. "I cannot say, ma'am. The signs are… confusing."

She laughed outright at that. "Very well, I shall not tease you about it, Mr Gage. It would be a wondrous great match for her, so for her sake I wish you every success, even though for my own comfort I would very much like to keep her. And now I had better go downstairs again before Laurence starts a search for me. You *will* dine with us tomorrow, will you not?"

He murmured something non-committal, which brought on the twinkling eyes again. However much he might wish to, it was hard to dislike such a sensible woman. She was a very good match for Laurence.

Malcolm had not been alone for long when a small procession arrived from the kitchen, headed by Ben Chambers himself, bearing his dinner. His *second* dinner.

"I've brought you a couple of ducklings in a Madeira sauce and some plovers' eggs, since there wasn't enough of them for the dinner table," he said cheerfully. "And a few other odds and ends. You must be hungry."

He was, in fact, for he had eaten little at the inn. Anything would be better than the grey slop he had been served there.

The very last to arrive, not long before midnight, were Captain Edgerton and Mr Willerton-Forbes.

"We were just off to bed and thought to see if you were still up," Edgerton said.

"When I get reading I hardly notice the time," Malcolm said, laying down his book, and deftly trimming the guttering candles with his fingers. "How are you, Willerton-Forbes? Did you have a good journey from London?"

"Oh, tolerable, tolerable, thank you, sir, and I am perfectly well now that I have got the difficult interview with Lady Saxby out of the way. I was charged with informing her that all the lines of descent from the Third Baron are now extinct and so it will be necessary to go back to the Second Baron to find the new Lord Saxby. A most disagreeable business, with so much uncertainty hanging over the family."

"Indeed. Are you optimistic, sir?"

"Oh, certainly. The Second Baron had four sons and the First Baron seven, so there will be an heir to be discovered somewhere, to be sure. But how are you, Mr Gage? There has been some turbulence, I hear, but all is well now, I trust? Excellent, excellent. And Michael has some news for you, should you wish to hear it."

"Oh?"

Edgerton, normally the most imperturbable of men, looked somewhat embarrassed. "This is rather awkward, I fear, Gage.

You charged me with discovering, if possible, the true name of Mademoiselle Fournier, and subsequently you decided not to pursue the matter, as is your right, of course. However, while I was away in Sussex to find Lady Julia Welles and travelling hither and yon, my esteemed colleagues Neate and Chandry were left behind in Northampton. They had a full week there before your change of heart and—"

"You know her name!" Malcolm cried.

"I had a letter from them today. They have found several people who recognised the sketch of Mademoiselle that James drew. We have a name but—"

"If you now prefer not to know," Willerton-Forbes put in smoothly, "we shall say not another word about it. Our discretion is absolute."

"Who is she?" Malcolm said eagerly. "I must know!"

Edgerton and Willerton-Forbes exchanged glances.

"Are you quite sure?" Edgerton said.

"Quite. Tell me!"

"Marie Fournier is the Lady Mary Fallon, only daughter of the Earl of Neston, of Springwell Place, Northamptonshire."

16: A New Cousin

Whatever Malcolm had expected to hear, that was not it. The daughter of an *earl?* Masquerading as a lady's maid? Impossible! How? And more to the point, why? It was so incredible that he could scarcely take it in.

"Are you sure?" he said, his voice hoarse.

"Quite sure," Edgerton said gently. "Neate showed the drawing to numerous people who all identified her immediately. There is not the least doubt."

"But why? And how? An earl's daughter acting as a lady's maid? But *why?"*

Edgerton chuckled. "Quite so. Unfortunately, only the lady herself can answer such a question. However, I will tell you all that Neate has gleaned about the family. Lord Neston is a man of around fifty years, highly regarded locally, a good landlord, a benefactor to numerous local charitable establishments and a deeply religious man. His wife was a Winfell, related to the Duke of Dunmorton. They mostly lived apart, but not for any reason other than temperament. She loved London and the gaiety of the social whirl, and he is a country man, happiest in his own territory. No one has a bad word to say for either of them. She died about ten years ago, leaving two children, Lady Mary, and a son, Viscount Hedlund, just two years of age at the time. A number of eligible ladies have fluttered their fans in Lord Neston's direction, to no avail. He remains faithful to his late wife. Lord Hedlund lives with his father, under the care of various tutors. His father dotes on him, and the boy wants for nothing."

"A paragon, indeed," Malcolm said. "Does he have a flaw?"

"None that Neate could find. Bear in mind he has talked not only to Neston's servants, who will naturally be loyal in the presence of strangers, but to his tenants and provisioners, and various people in the neighbourhood who owe him no allegiance. He seems to be a genuinely good man."

"And what do all these people have to say of the Lady Mary? If she and Marie are one and the same, then how is her disappearance explained?"

"Lady Mary, it is said, was deeply grieved when her mother died. She was thirteen at the time, an impressionable age, and as she grew towards womanhood, her father felt increasingly unable to offer her the guidance she would need. At the age of seventeen, therefore, she was sent to live with her aunt in Scotland, and has not been seen since."

Malcolm pondered that, which seemed to raise as many questions as it answered. Edgerton watched him, a little smile on his lips.

"Before her mother died, did Lady Mary live with her in London?" he said eventually.

Edgerton's smile broadened. "An excellent question. There were brief visits once or twice a year, but not enough to account for an excess of grief. Lady Mary never lived anywhere but with her father at Springwell Place, under the care of a governess, who seemingly spoke very good French, no doubt with a Parisian accent."

"What happened to the governess?"

"She was not required in Scotland, and so was sent away."

"And Lady Mary never visited from Scotland? What about friends — did she ever write to them?"

"More excellent questions. She has never visited, nor has anyone ever gone north to visit her. And her friends — who included the Lady Julia Stapleton, who before her marriage lived just a few miles from Springwell Place — have heard nothing from her, as far as Neate was able to determine. The generally accepted story is that Lady Mary's melancholy grew to such an extent that she was unequal to society, and is being cared for in seclusion. Lord Neston is so grieved by it that he becomes visibly distressed at any mention of her. There is one other question you should ask, Gage."

"What is that?"

"The dates. Lady Mary Fallon left her home six years ago. Marie Fournier obtained a reference from Lady Julia five years ago."

"So what happened in the intervening year?" Malcolm cried. "Where was she? Was she ever with the aunt in Scotland? Did she run away?"

"Precisely so," Edgerton said, grinning outright now. "Intriguing, is it not? But now *I* have a question for *you*. Do you wish us to investigate further? The indefatigable Neate and Chandry are quite prepared to toil up to the wilds of Scotland if you wish it, for they have a direction for the aunt, but this is your enquiry and so we await your further instructions. If you still wish us to call off the hunt, we will of course do so."

Malcolm took a long draught of brandy. "Yes, call it off," he said sombrely. "Let Mr Neate and Mr Chandry pursue some other business. We can guess what they might find in Scotland, after all. Marie must have had good reason to leave her home, and whatever it was, it is not our concern. She is free and happy, and even if the work she does is beneath her, she enjoys it. Let us leave her and her past in peace."

~~~~~

Miss Charu Gage, the unsuspected second cousin of the family, sent a brief note of introduction to Laurence, and was duly summoned to the Grove to meet the family. Malcolm was summoned, too, amused to find himself acknowledged as a part of the family again, even if only for the length of a morning call.

She was a little more formally dressed than when Malcolm had met her in the common room at the inn. Then she had looked like a servant, albeit a superior one, in a plain gown of some dark-coloured cotton. Now, she wore a pale muslin gown and spencer with some pretensions to fashion, and her shiny black hair was hidden under a neat bonnet.

"What a lovely house!" she cried, as soon as she had crossed the threshold. "So magnificent! It looks so plain from the outside — large, of course, but a very simple, symmetrical design and quite unadorned. But the interior is so lovely. How old is it?"

"It was begun almost two hundred years ago," Viola said. "The architect was—"

"Two hundred! Goodness me, and has it been altered much? Oh, this room is lovely, too. What do you call this?"
~~~~~

"The Roman Saloon, because—"

"The busts around the walls, of course. Are they all emperors? Which one is Caesar?"

"All of them," muttered Laurence.

"Lovely! What a charming tiled floor! And the ceiling..." She craned her neck to gaze upwards. "So clever, the way the clouds are painted. Just like being outdoors."

"Do have a seat, Cousin," Viola said firmly, gesturing to a chair.

"Oh yes, thank you so much. Shall I sit here? How kind of you to receive me so graciously, when you know nothing of me, a complete stranger."

The rest of them sat too, Laurence in the matching chair to the visitor, and Viola, Henrietta and Edward perched on a sofa. Skeates hovered while John passed around glasses and plates and cups of tea. Malcolm, aware that he was only there by courtesy and not desire, leaned against one side of the mantel, trying to be inconspicuous. Although the visitor was politely addressed by her baptismal name of Cornelia, Malcolm preferred her Indian name, Charu. It seemed to suit her.

While the servants were still in the room, the talk was the usual polite chit chat, about India and Charu's father — no one asked about her mother — and how she had come to find them. Charu rattled away inexhaustibly on the subject of India, a seemingly random collection of odd facts held together with fascinating little stories of the country's inhabitants, both British and native. Malcolm amused himself by watching Viola's stupefaction at this onslaught. Then Charu hopped to London, and how she had seen the notice in the newspaper of her inheritance. She showed them Great-uncle Zachariah's watch, and told how pleased the attorney was that she had come to collect it. Malcolm could imagine Colville beaming with pleasure, another file closed, the ribbons tied and consigned to the archives.

As soon as Skeates and John had vanished, she turned to Laurence and said, "Do you want to see my papers?"

"Your papers?" Laurence said.

"Everything that proves I am who I say I am. I do not expect you to acknowledge me without some proof, Mr Gage. I have the record of my baptism, and letters from the Governor-General and the bishop, and one from my present parson asserting my good character. Also, you must not imagine that I mean to impose on you, for nothing could be further from my thoughts. I have worked in a drapery on Oxford Street for several years now. I do so love my work! So many wonderful fabrics — marcella, cashmere, paduasoy, taffeta, shagreen, nankeen, tussore silk, calamanco... I love the *feel* of them. And all the lovely muslins. Madras muslin, that is my favourite, I think... or perhaps organdie. Mmm, this is such a delicious apricot tart — lovely!"

"Will you have another, Cousin?" Henrietta said politely, jumping up to fetch the plate.

"Ooh, lovely! Thank you so much. Anyway, if you are agreeable, Mr Gage, I should like to find employment near here, so that I may visit you occasionally. You are my only family now, you see. Of course, I shall quite understand if you do not wish to accept me as a part of your family, for the connection is most tenuous, and it is a great shock to you, naturally. Goodness, so delicious," she said, biting into the tart.

There was a silence so deep one might drop a pebble into it and never hear it hit the bottom. Her accent was good, and although there was a slight hint of her Indian upbringing, there was no sense that she might not belong in any drawing room in England. A more fashionable lady might look down on Charu's simple style of dress, but her deportment and manners were the equal of anybody. On the other hand, no lady would admit a shop worker to her acquaintance. Malcolm waited, amused and intrigued, to see how Laurence would deal with her painfully honest approach.

"My dear Cousin Cornelia," he began.

"I prefer my mother's name for me. She called me Charu, which is a Hindi word meaning beautiful or graceful or pure — or all three. A great deal to live up to, is it not? Rather a challenge, but something to aspire to, I feel." She smiled, and Malcolm was struck with her air of assurance. She was not at all intimidated by the elevated society in which she now found herself.

"Then I shall call you Charu, too," Laurence said, smiling back at her. "Charu, you are family, and therefore you are *always* welcome in this house." He flicked a sideways glance at Malcolm. "I hope you will stay with us until you have decided what you wish to do."

Viola said nothing, but she twisted her handkerchief nervously in her hands and her smile was rather forced.

It was Henrietta who jumped up, and hugged her father. "Oh, I was so hoping you would say that, Papa! I am so looking forward to getting to know you, Cousin Charu. You must tell me more about India."

"And will you teach me Hindi?" Edward said eagerly. "I know nothing except European languages, and I should think it is very different. Will you? Please?"

"Haan," she said. "That means yes, Cousin Edward."

"But not until your Russian lessons are complete," Laurence said firmly. "He has an examination to prepare for in August, Charu, and it is very important that he does not get distracted. Henrietta, will you talk to Mrs Blenkinsop about preparing a room for Charu? Edward, you might like to take Charu to meet Captain Edgerton. He is in the library at this present. The captain was in the East India Company Army for a number of years, Charu."

The children disappeared excitedly with Charu, leaving only Laurence, Viola and Malcolm.

"I know what you are going to say, Viola," Laurence said. "A complete stranger turns up on the doorstep claiming cousinship, and you do not like me taking her in without a second thought. Am I correct?"

"We know nothing about her," Viola whispered. "She could be an utter fraud."

"Who will murder us in our beds, no doubt, and steal the silver. Bear in mind that she has already been to Oxford and seen Great-uncle Zachariah's attorney, who examined every document she carries very carefully."

"You do not know that," she said, less confidently.

"But I do. Colville wrote to me several days ago to advise me of it, and that she would very likely make an approach. I assumed she would write from London, but since she is here I shall not turn her away. I would have invited her anyway. She is *family,* Vi."

Viola gave a little moan. "She works in a *shop*, Laurence! A drapery!"

"And Malcolm is a humble teacher, who is not one whit less a member of this family. Come, Vi, I look to you to set the example and welcome Charu to Great Maeswood and introduce her to all our acquaintances."

"No," she said quietly, her lips compressed. "This is your house, Laurence, and you may invite whomsoever you wish to stay here, but I will *not* introduce a shop girl to my friends and it is unreasonable of you to expect it of me."

So saying, she made a dignified exit.

"She has a point," Malcolm said.

"True," Laurence said. "But what else am I to do with the girl? I cannot refuse to receive a cousin, no matter how lowly, and I will not house her in the attics with the servants. She is a guest in my house and as such she will expect to be entertained."

"She is a sensible girl, and I am sure she will not put herself forward in company. There is no need to mention the drapery on Oxford Street, is there? I have to admit, your generosity surprised me. There is not one man in a thousand who would so overlook her humble origins. Her father was not even a legitimate son, after all. You could have refused her."

"That is Viola's fault," Laurence said with a frown. "I should have brushed her off when I received her letter this morning, except that Viola had that awful pursed-up look on her face, where she looks like a prune, and I suppose I did it to spite her. I try to pretend that I have grown into some sort of — not wisdom, precisely, for that would be too much to hope for, but a degree of maturity, and then I do this. Do we ever grow out of such foolishness?"

"Why would we want to?" Malcolm said, with a lift of one shoulder. "Imagine how boring life would be if we were always sensible and rational."

Laurence gave a bark of laughter. "It is an odd thing, brother, but today I am quite in charity with you. Tomorrow I shall no doubt want to punch you on the nose again."

"Why wait until tomorrow?" Malcolm said, and they both laughed.

For a brief moment, the years rolled away and they were fast friends again, just two young men facing the world together, united and indivisible. Or so they had thought. Until Catherine. If only they had never met her.

"What would you have done, if I had married her and not you?" Malcolm said impulsively, and then instantly wished he had not as Laurence's face darkened.

"What good does it do to wallow in the past? What happened, happened and that is all there is to it. You were always too inclined to bear grudges, Mal. Let it go, for pity's sake."

So saying, he stamped out of the room, and Malcolm was left to rue his own stupidity, and resolve for the thousandth time to learn to mind his tongue.

17: After Church

Marie received a short note from Malcolm asking her to participate in a mock examination for Edward. He had obtained Madam's permission in advance, he said, so he hoped to see her promptly at noon on Friday. This was a very public trial for her, since she would have to expose her rather limited French to general scrutiny. Who else would be there? And would they be as fluent in French as Malcolm? Was she about to be unmasked once and for all? But she had agreed to it and she could not back out now, however terrifying the prospect of exposure.

She considered carefully what she might wear, and eventually decided that she ought to acknowledge the importance of the occasion by wearing her Sunday clothes, which meant her new bonnet and pelisse. This was not, of course, anything to do with the fact that Malcolm had given her the bonnet. No, these were merely the newest and smartest of her garments, she told herself firmly, and she almost believed it. It was unfortunate that the pelisse was not yet finished — in fact, she had only just cut out the pieces — but by sewing long into the night she managed to get it made up to her satisfaction without delaying the progress of Madam's nuptial wardrobe.

On the appointed day, she arrived promptly, finding herself in the wake of a stream of other callers making their way up the Grove's drive by carriage, on horseback or on foot. Half the village had been invited for the occasion, it seemed, which made her very glad that she had taken so much care over her appearance. It did not make her any less nervous, but it gave her a little more confidence to know that she looked her best.

She followed the flow of people across the entrance hall, through an inner lobby lined with portraits, on to an ante-room with deep windows overlooking tranquil courtyards on either side, and thence to a very grand saloon. It was a large square room with a patterned tile floor that must have been forty feet wide and just as tall, with a balcony above around all four sides. Four massive chandeliers dangled from an exquisitely painted ceiling. She smiled in appreciation at such grandeur.

Malcolm's head was visible above the crowds, and he soon spotted her, smiled widely and made his way through the throng to her side, rather as if he were wading through deep water.

"Bonjour, mademoiselle! How beautiful you look in your new bonnet and pelisse."

She blushed like an ingenue at the compliment, and could only murmur, *"Bonjour, monsieur,"* as she curtsied.

"Will you take your seat?"

He led her across the room, past several rows of chairs and then to a long table with five more chairs. On the table in front of each chair was a silver spoon. Marie sat as he directed her, at one end of the table. Two seats away Miss Winslade nodded to her politely, then Mr Truman, the parson, took the seat beyond her. Gradually the seats behind them began to fill up as the audience took their places. Mr Laurence Gage sat down next to Marie, scowling. He looked fearsomely cross, curtly muttering, *"Bonjour, mademoiselle.* Good day, Susannah. Truman."

In front of them, Malcolm was talking to Edward, who looked terrified, as well he might. To be tested publicly in one language was surely ordeal enough, but five at once was inconceivable. It would be every bit as much of an ordeal for her, too, if he only knew it.

Eventually, Edward took the lonely chair that faced the table of inquisitors and the audience behind. Henrietta sat at one end of the long table, in charge of the egg-timer and bell to time their sessions. Malcolm stood beside Edward and held up his hands for silence.

"Lady Saxby, Squire, ladies and gentlemen, thank you all for coming today. We are here to familiarise Edward with the challenge he will face in August, when he will be required to demonstrate his fluency in five languages simultaneously. Here we have his five examiners, Miss Winslade for Italian, Mademoiselle Fournier for French, Mr Truman for Latin, Edward's father for Greek and myself for Russian. Our time-keeper and adjudicator is Miss Henrietta Gage. The examination will proceed thus — each of the examiners will speak to Edward for five minutes in his or her designated language, asking him questions, which may be on any subject of the examiner's choice. Edward must reply in the same language. When each has—"

Susannah raised her hand. "What if he does not know the answer?"

"Then he must say so, with a correctly formulated sentence. It is his language skills which are under test, not his knowledge or opinions. When each of us has had a five minute session, we move on to a fifteen minute session where we each take turns to ask a question, but quickly, so that Edward must switch rapidly from one language to another. The final fifteen minute session is known as the battle. Any of us may ask a question at any time, in any order, even simultaneously. If you have a skill in one of the other languages, you may use that as well. Whenever you ask a question during the battle, you hold up your spoon, and only lower it when Edward has answered you in the correct language. Is that clear?"

They all nodded, for he had already explained the rules to them beforehand.

"Edward, are you quite ready?" Gamely, he nodded. "Very well. I shall take the first session, and we will move down the table in order. Henrietta, you may ring the bell."

The first sessions were easy, gentle and slow, and Edward answered everything without difficulty. Marie was the last to speak, so she had time to prepare herself, and consider the questions she might ask. She could see that Edward was quite comfortable now, his voice strong and confident. One question of hers about the weather made him laugh, and she guessed that he had been asked the same question already. The second session was more exciting, for the questions came more quickly, and Marie's turn came round so fast that she had to exert herself to think up another question in time. Fortunately for her, Edward's answers were simple and did not stretch her vocabulary.

And then the 'battle' began. At first they were quite gentle with Edward, not speaking over each other and giving him time to answer, but gradually Malcolm began to push harder. He started hurling questions at the same time as another questioner, and then he changed languages. Twice he spoke in French, and once she thought it was Greek. Faster and faster he went, hopping from language to language, as Edward's face strained in concentration, but always keeping up. Susannah fell silent first, then Mr Truman. Marie struggled for a while before ceding the field, awed by the virtuosity on display. Mr Gage kept up with Malcolm the longest, but eventually it was just the two of them, Malcolm and Edward, back and forth, as quick as lightning, every question a different language.

Then Edward cried out in English, “Hey! That is not fair! I do not even know that language.”

Malcolm laughed out loud. “It is Turkish, and well done. Keep going. *As-tu un—”*

The bell rang. It was over. The audience broke into applause, and Edward leaned back in his chair in relief, and Marie was scarcely less relieved. It was over, and her schoolroom knowledge of French had not been exposed. Only Malcolm had ever found her out.

Malcolm jumped up. “Refreshments in the Roman Saloon, everyone.”

Marie leaned back in her chair and stretched out her arms, aching from tension. There was a general murmur of voices and scraping of chairs as people began to move about.

Beside her, Mr Gage threw down his spoon with a clang.

“Papa! Did you enjoy that?” Edward cried, beaming at him. “Uncle Malcolm is so clever, is he not?”

“Oh, yes, quite the star performer!” he said with a scowl. But then his face softened. “He always was incredibly clever, and you take after him, Edward. You acquitted yourself very well. Whatever happens at your examination, I am very proud of you.”

~~~~~
~~~~~

Sunday saw Malcolm at church again. Truman's sermon, inspired no doubt by Edward, was on the subject of endeavour and hard work and resolution, and he expounded at such length that Malcolm, having been up half the night reading, almost fell asleep. Only one thing kept him awake, and that was the sight of Marie's neat little bonnet in the pew immediately in front of him. He had been persuaded by the combined arguments, and a few tears, of Viola and Henrietta to share the Gage pew. Laurence said nothing, naturally, his expression inscrutable, so Malcolm had reluctantly agreed to it. Now he was positioned immediately behind the Dower House pew, and so he sat no more than two feet away from that delectable bonnet and the even more delectable wearer of it.

Lady Mary Fallon, he reminded himself. The daughter of an earl. Even if they had met under the most conventional of circumstances, their eyes meeting over the teacups in a drawing room, or dancing the cotillion in a ballroom, he could never, ever aspire to her hand. No wonder she had told him so forcefully that she would never marry him. Of course she would not! She knew her proper place in society, and while she may masquerade as a lady's maid for now, she could never be anything other than a peer's daughter. She was entirely beyond his reach.

However that may be, when he wandered outside after the service, Edward chattering in Russian beside him, Marie sought him out. The three of them left the crowds congregating outside the church and set off amicably together down the road, the language having switched effortlessly to French. He was so delighted with her ease in his company that he scarcely noticed the post-chaise and pair pulled up at the side of the road ahead of them. The chaise door was open, with a man of respectable mien lounging there. The postilion had dismounted and was examining the hoof of the nearside horse.

"Is there a problem?" Malcolm said politely. "There is an inn a little further down the road if you need to change horses." The postilion grunted unenthusiastically, so he added, "I have some expertise myself. May I have a look?"

The man looked up with an odd sort of grin on his face, standing aside so that Malcolm could kneel beside the horse. Then, inexplicably, he kicked Malcolm hard in the chest.

An explosion of pain took his breath away. It was almost as startling as the time he was thrown from his horse, when he had been quite unable to move for several minutes, but this — why would the fellow attack him? Even through the haze of agony, he tried to make sense of it, and failed utterly. He dropped like a stone, curled up in torment in the dirt, quite unable to move or to avoid the next kick.

It never came. Instead there were yells, and a brief scream — Marie! What were they doing to her? Then more yells, a door slamming and the horses starting into motion. He opened his eyes, to the sight of the carriage disappearing at speed down the road, dust clouding behind it. With a massive effort, he summoned the strength to roll over. All he saw was Edward, hauling himself out of the dirt, tears rolling down his cheeks.

"They took Marie!" he cried, his voice high with distress. *"They took Marie!"*

~~~~~

For an instant, Marie was too shocked to protest. One moment her gaze was focused on Malcolm kneeling beside the horse, the next moment he had gone flying. The man lounging at his ease
~~~~~

beside the open door of the carriage sprang into action, pushing Edward aside and grabbing her arm so hard she cried out in pain. Then she was bundled into the carriage, the man climbed in beside her and in moments they were in motion.

"What are you doing? Let me out of here! Stop this carriage at once — *at once*, do you hear?"

"Shut your mouth," the man said, his accent rough and harsh. He took her arm and shook her hard. A boy of twelve or fourteen on the opposite seat gazed at them with terrified eyes.

"Let me go, you beast!" She tried to push him away, but within the confines of the carriage, there was no room. She wriggled instead, clawing at his hand tight on her arm, wrestling free herself from that painful grip. "Let *go* of me!"

"Shut up, damn you!"

He tried to grab hold of her other arm, and for a fleeting moment he loosened his grip on the other arm, so that she was briefly able to tear herself free, flying across the carriage to land half on the floor and half across the knees of the boy.

With a growl, the man seized her hair, ripping the bonnet from her head, and dragged her back towards him, spun her round and slapped her so hard that her head crashed against something hard and she fell to the floor again. She cried out, but was too stunned to move. He hauled her back onto the seat and pinioned her wrists painfully tightly.

"Rope!" he yelled.

The boy scrabbled about and then Marie was aware of her hands being bound. The man pulled out a knife to cut the ends of the rope, then waved the knife in front of her face. "You see this?

Just you remember it and give me no trouble, and there'll be no need for me to hurt you, understand?"

She nodded.

"Good. So shut your mouth and sit still until we get there."

Then he pulled a piece of rough sacking over her head and the world went dark.

Until we get there? Where exactly was 'there'? But she did not need to wonder 'who'. She knew exactly who was behind this, and why, too, and she was reasonably confident the knife would not be used. She was no use to anyone dead or injured. But still, her prospects were dire. There would be no possibility of escape, not this time. She had to get away, she *had* to! Think, Mary, think...

With seeming obedience she sat quietly, aware of the dull ache in her arms from being manhandled, the chafing of the rope bonds on her wrists, the throbbing on one side of her face. The sacking tickling her cheeks smelled strongly of chicken. There was a strong aroma of unwashed skin emanating from the man.

She could hear, too. The steady clop of the horses was reassuring. Two horses only, and not the fastest in the world. Not as slow as Mr Gage's slugs, which were overfed and underused, but plodding. These two were probably hired, and the rather shabby carriage too. That was a mistake, she felt. Four good horses would have been much more sensible. It was possible to catch a hired post-chaise and pair.

Malcolm... Her heart flip-flopped in fear. Was he still lying motionless in the dirt at the side of the road? Perhaps he was even dead! No, no, she must not think of that, but he was injured, perhaps, unable to help her. There was only Edward. He had merely been pushed aside but he could have hit his head... Optimism, Mary, never assume the worst. They had not been the only ones ambling away from the church. Someone would have seen something, someone would find Malcolm and Edward, they would tell what they had seen and then someone would come after her.

But there was so little time... Where would they change horses? Market Clunbury, probably. They might even have a faster carriage waiting, and then she would be whisked away and that would be the end of it. Market Clunbury was only seven miles away. At this pace, they would reach it in under an hour... perhaps only three quarters of an hour. Could the pursuit catch up in so short a time? How long would it take to hitch the horses to the carriage— No, any pursuers would ride. That would be quicker. But the time to work out what had happened, to get to the stables, to saddle horses... it might not be enough. She must be ready whenever they changed horses — to run, to scream for help, anything. The man would not use the knife... would he?

The carriage lurched over a bump in the road and she felt the familiar nausea rising up to distract her from all rational thought. She had never been more frustrated by her dreadful weakness. She squeezed her eyes tight closed but a single tear escaped and burned its despairing way down her cheek.

18: The Hero

Slowly, groaning through the pain, Malcolm crawled onto his hands and knees, struggling to catch his breath. Edward grabbed hold of one arm and helped him to his feet, still doubled over with the pain.

"You... all right?" Malcolm croaked.

"Yes. They pushed me over, that is all. Who are they?"

"Unimportant." A long rasping breath. "Find... Captain... Edgerton. Tell him. *Run.*"

Edward ran. Malcolm forced himself to... not run, he was not capable of that, but to walk... to stagger, perhaps, in the direction of the Grove. He knew exactly what had to be done. The kidnappers had but two horses to their chaise, so they could be caught, but only by the fastest horse. And he knew precisely where to find it.

Gradually, as his legs discovered that they still worked and his lungs reluctantly began to cooperate, he picked up speed until he was shambling and then actually running, albeit still bent over. In through the gates of the Grove, then up the drive. Surely the drive was longer than it had ever been! Why was it so far to the stables?

There at last was the yard, and he ran into the stable building, grabbed saddle and harness, and carried them to the stall where Gaius Valerius eyed him with imperial haughtiness. But he whickered softly when Malcolm spoke to him and stood still to be saddled. He was almost finished when he was startled by a yell.

"Hoy! What are you doing? Leave that horse alone!"

It was Spencer, every inch the outraged groom defending his mistress's property.

"Marie has been kidnapped," Malcolm said tersely. "Only one horse can catch her."

So saying, he vaulted into the saddle, clenching his teeth through the pain, and pointed Gaius at the door. Spencer jumped aside, and Gaius shot out of the stable as if he had been fired from a gun. Down the drive, onto the road, then a little more circumspectly through the village, the road still thronged with churchgoers. Only when the way was clear did he give the horse his head and settle into a steady gallop.

At first the road was straight and well-maintained, and Gaius stretched his magnificent legs. Three miles on, they came to Astley Cloverstone, with not a soul in sight, as the inhabitants were all still making their way back from the Great Maeswood church. But Malcolm did not need any help to work out which way the chaise had gone, for the dust was still settling on the road to Market Clunbury. Riding a touch more slowly through the village to avoid the geese near the pond, he was able to speed up again as he passed beyond the final straggle of cottages. Another mile passed by. The road wound about more now, but surely he must be closing on the chaise, for the churned up dust swirled around him.

There it was!

Not two hundred yards ahead of him, the back of the chaise was visible through the dust. It was driving steadily, but Gaius Valerius was much faster, and in no time Malcolm found himself behind the carriage, then alongside and then pulling ahead, level with the horses.

The postilion saw him, his eyes wide. He whipped up the horses, but Gaius easily matched their pace, and Malcolm snatched the whip and tossed it over the hedge. Then he reached for reins. The postilion tried to shove him aside, and for a moment as they tussled the horses veered about and Malcolm experienced a moment of pure terror as he envisaged Marie hurled into a ditch and broken to pieces. Desperately the postilion tried to push him away, but Malcolm was fuelled by fear as much as anger. He stabbed a quick punch to the postilion's jaw, and as soon as his hold loosened, grabbed the reins, forcing the horses to slacken their pace. Gradually the equipage came to a halt, half slewed across the road, the postilion hanging partly off his mount.

In one fluid motion, Malcolm slid from Gaius' back, hauled the postilion to the ground and hurled him into the hedge.

"Hoy, what are you—?"

A face at the open carriage door. In two long strides, Malcolm reached him, picked him up by the lapels, dragged him to the road and executed a hard punch to the jaw. The fellow dropped to the ground and lay unmoving.

Malcolm had just turned to the carriage again when there was a huge bang, followed by a muffled scream. Gaius startled, then shot away down the road. If Malcolm had been angry before, now he was filled with a burning rage. A white face peered out of the carriage, no more than a boy, a pistol in his hand. With a yell of rage, Malcolm snatched the pistol and lobbed it over the hedge. Then the boy, squeaking with fear, was dragged out and put into the dirt with his fellows by a sharp right hander.

Silence. The boy and the two men lay motionless. Malcolm's heart was racing, but there was no time to catch his breath. He looked inside the carriage.

Marie was huddled against the far wall, sacking over her head, her hands tied.

"Marie? Are you all right?"

"Malcolm?" Her voice was barely audible.

Gently he pushed the sacking from her head, and pulled out his pocket knife to cut her bonds. She gazed at him, her face so white and tear-streaked that his heart turned over. But it was imperative to escape before the three kidnappers came to themselves again, and his horse was gone.

"Quickly!" he said, reaching a hand help her out of the carriage. She had not taken three steps before she swayed and would have fallen. Without a thought, he scooped her up, with an exclamation as his injured ribs protested, and set off at a run down the road towards Astley Cloverstone. It could not be more than a mile away, and once there, they could go into the Cross Keys to be safe.

He had barely rounded the first corner, when rapid hoof beats alerted him to an approaching rider. Almost at once, the horse was upon them, pulling up sharply in a spray of dirt and gravel. It was Spencer, who must have saddled up and ridden after them at once.

"Sir! And Marie! Are you uninjured? I heard a gunshot."

"No injuries, thank God, but Gaius took off towards Market Clunbury."

"I'll go after him," Spencer said.

He would have ridden on at once, but Malcolm yelled, "No! There are three men there. I knocked them out, but probably not for long and they may have more pistols."

"You knocked out three men? Single handed? While they were shooting at you?" Spencer said, laughing. "Well, what a story! But you must get Marie to safety. Here, you take Old Billy here, and I'll walk back."

Malcolm had no fault to find with this plan. It was the work of a moment to lift Marie onto Old Billy's back, and mount himself. With a hasty word of thanks to Spencer, they rode away from him.

Old Billy was not the equal of Gaius Valerius, and was carrying two riders besides, so his pace was somewhat more sedate, ambling along as if he were out for a gentle afternoon hack through the fields. Malcolm hardly noticed. He had Marie resting snugly in his arms, she was safe and unharmed, and he was so exhilarated at his successful rescue that he began humming softly. Marie looked up at him and smiled, then snuggled more comfortably against him.

More help arrived, in the very welcome person of Captain Edgerton, Mr Neate and Mr Chandry, riding hard.

"Are we redundant, Gage?" Edgerton called out, pulling up alongside. "You seem to have managed the business perfectly well without us."

"Nevertheless, I am very glad to see your sword, Captain, and I hope your pockets are hiding a pistol or two. There are three men lying in the dirt about a mile east of here, but they may be awake by now, and they may have more than the single pistol they fired at me, so have a care. You will see Spencer on foot somewhere nearby, for I lost my own horse and have borrowed his."

"You lost Gaius Valerius?" Chandry said, eyebrows lifting.

"Misplaced, merely. He ran off when the pistol discharged."

"We will find him," Edgerton said cheerfully. "First the three in the dirt, then the horse. You two go home, and leave the mopping up operations to us."

Malcolm was very happy to follow these instructions. As they made their way back to Great Maeswood, two more parties of rescuers passed by, the Rycroft brothers from the Hall with several grooms, and a group from the inn. Malcolm sent them onwards, although he doubted Captain Edgerton needed any help.

As they approached the first cottages of Great Maeswood, he became aware that Marie was gazing fixedly at him, her dark eyes intense. He could see now the beginnings of a bruise down one side of her face.

"They hurt you," he said softly, the horse halting as the reins slackened.

"I struggled a bit. It was an accident. I lost the bonnet you gave me."

"Never mind that. I will buy you another one." Gently, he ran one finger down her face. "But are you all right otherwise?"

"I am now," she said, and her smile made his breath catch in his throat. "My hero. Malcolm..."

Oh, the thrill of hearing her say his name! And there was no false French any more. She was using her true voice.

"Malcolm, you once said that you wanted to marry me. Did you mean that?"

He felt as if he were melting inside, turning to blancmange. No words came, so he nodded.

"Then let us do that," she said. "As soon as possible."

If only it could be so! But she was distressed from her narrow escape and looking on him with desperate eyes as a protector, and besides, she was still an earl's daughter and out of his reach.

"We will talk about this later," he said, his voice sounding harsh to his ears. "Not here. Not now."

He urged the horse into motion. There were few people about the village, but on the road between the Grove and the Dower House stood two slender figures.

"You rescued her!" cried Henrietta, rushing out to meet the approaching horse.

"Where is Gaius Valerius?" Edward said.

"He ran away when a gun went off."

They both gasped in a most satisfactory way, turning to run alongside. "There was shooting?" Henrietta said. "How exciting!"

"Was anyone injured?" Edward said.

"No one was hurt and it was not exciting at the time, I assure you." Malcolm allowed the horse to slow to a walk. "I cannot let you go back to the Dower House," he said to Marie. "I cannot protect you there. You will stay at the Grove. Edward, will you run ahead and tell Mrs Blenkinsop to prepare a guest bedroom for Mademoiselle Fournier. A proper bedroom, mind, not in the attics."

They both ran off, and Marie raised her eyebrows. "A proper bedroom?"

"I am not having you banished to the attics like a servant," he said firmly.

She digested that for a moment as the horse plodded slowly up the drive. "Why do you not want to marry me, Malcolm?" she burst out, gazing at him with her clear eyes.

"I *do*, but—" How could he explain, without revealing that he had set Captain Edgerton to investigate her origins? "Later, when you have had time to recover from your ordeal."

"Kiss me."

"What?" The horse came to a complete stop.

"I need you to kiss me."

Malcolm scoured his mind, but was unable in that moment to come up with a single convincing reason why he should not do as she asked. Or perhaps he did not want to refuse her, not when she was nestled there in his arms, as if she belonged there... belonged to *him*. So he hugged her a little closer, and gently pressed his lips to hers.

He began by intending it to be the world's most restrained, unloverlike kiss, and indeed it started so, as chaste as ever a kiss could be. But somehow it was impossible to keep to that objective. He could not quite bring himself to move apart from her, so sweet and gently yielding as she was, and so the kiss went on longer and longer. Nor did she show any sign of wishing to end it. Somehow, his free hand was behind her head, pulling her towards him, and one of her arms was around his neck. If his rational mind had been anywhere in the vicinity, it would surely have decided that this was the most magnificently ardent kiss he had ever enjoyed. But his rational mind was nowhere to be found and some force far less rational and yet more powerful held sway.

"Je t'aime, ma chérie," he murmured, his lips lifting from hers by a fraction of an inch. *"Je t'aime, mon doux ange."* And then she drew him back into that ocean of never-ending sweetness, so deep that he thought he would drown.

Hoof beats approaching on the drive brought them back to reality with a start. It was Spencer, riding Gaius Valerius. He hailed them cheerfully. "The captain has everything in hand. Lord, he's a handy man to have around in a crisis, isn't he? Do you want to hop off at the house, and I'll see to these two fellows. Extra oats for both of them tonight."

There was quite a little crowd gathered on the steps to greet them. Marie was whisked away by Viola, Henrietta and Mrs Middlehope, and Edward and Mr Willerton-Forbes shepherded Malcolm into the dining-room, where a wide-eyed John was busy laying out dishes on the burners. Charu crept into the room behind them.

"We waited breakfast for you," Edward said, adding wistfully, "I suppose we ought to wait for the others."

"Who knows when they will be back," Malcolm said, sniffing the tempting aromas hungrily. "Besides, those of us who have been pushed into the dirt this morning, and in my case been shot at, need to restore our equilibrium somewhat, and nothing does that quite like a… what is under that lid, John?"

"Mutton chops, sir, and kidneys here."

"Excellent! Very fortifying, mutton chops and kidneys. Mr Willerton-Forbes, will you join us?"

"Only if you tell me every detail of your exciting adventures, Mr Gage." His eyes gleamed with excitement. "Especially the part where you were shot at."

So Malcolm ate and talked, and the others ate and listened, and they passed a very agreeable half hour, the audience gasping and sighing and exclaiming at all the proper places. There is nothing more exciting than the retelling of a difficult and dangerous enterprise which has been satisfactorily concluded without harm. However alarming it might have been at the time, however terrified the participants were, they will always be revered when the stirring tale is recounted to a rapt audience.

Malcolm had indeed suffered a moment or two of terror, but he had been so fired by rage that he had not once stopped to consider the consequences of his actions. Had the kidnappers been better prepared, he would have been the one in the ditch, probably with a bullet in him, and that would not have been of the slightest use to Marie. He should have waited for Captain Edgerton. Even now he went hot and cold at the thought of what might have become of her. Anger and sheer luck had got them through it. Still, it was very pleasant to hear himself praised for his rashness.

"A heroic rescue, Mr Gage," Willerton-Forbes said, sipping his coffee. "I commend you."

"Anyone would have done the same," Malcolm murmured.

"Indeed not," Willerton-Forbes said. "I should certainly not have been brave enough."

"Nor I," Edward said. "Papa was brave, though, for he was ready to go after you, but then Mrs Middlehope suggested he ride for the squire instead. She said that Captain Edgerton was sure to capture the bad people and so he would have need of the magistrate."

It turned out that Mrs Middlehope was quite right, for within the hour the captain and a now large group of rescuers returned in the best of humours, with three men under close guard. The Rycroft brothers took them off to the Hall, to lock them away in a large store room until the squire had seen them.

"I doubt we will get anything useful out of them," Edgerton said, as the long-suffering John replenished the chafing dishes in the dining room. "Not local, and very close-lipped, the three of them, even the boy. The squire is not the man to lean on them hard enough to make them squeal."

"So we will never know what they planned to do with Marie," Malcolm said gloomily, absentmindedly helping himself to another Bath bun. "How can we be sure there will not be another attempt?"

"We cannot," Edgerton said shortly. "But I daresay the lady herself could shed some light on the matter, if she chose."

That made sense. Whatever drove Marie to leave her home and pose as a lady's maid under a false name, it was clear that she wanted to hide from something — or some one. If that person found out where she lived... Yes, it might very well be connected to Marie's former life. Yet if so, why would it happen now, after five perfectly tranquil years? But he knew the answer to that. He had sent Captain Edgerton and his friends off to

Northamptonshire and stirred things up, and somehow they had led the kidnappers here, to Shropshire.

"Even if she knows the reason for it, she might not tell us," Malcolm said. "She is very reticent."

"She would not tell me, but she might very well tell *you* something of it," Edgerton said. "At the very least, if today's events are likely to recur, we can help her to find another refuge. Will you make sure she knows that? We are entirely at her disposal if she feels the need for protection, or any assistance at all. It is most disturbing to have young ladies snatched up in an English village, and on a Sunday, too. It is outrageous!"

Malcolm could entirely agree that it was disturbing. *If today's events are likely to recur…*

Next time, they might not get off so lightly. Next time Marie might disappear for good. He shivered.

19: Revelations

Viola bustled in, saw Malcolm and started. "Heavens, Malcolm, are you still eating breakfast?"

"What else is there to do on a Sunday?" he said mildly.

"I have been looking all over the house for you, and it is most inconvenient to be trailing up and down stairs after you, I assure you, and the servants all at sixes and sevens and no one to send, so I have had to go myself, and you have been here all the time. It is most thoughtless of you."

Malcolm opened his mouth to protest, then thought better of it. There was no remonstrating with Viola in this mood. "I am at your disposal, Vi."

"Laurence is back," she said abruptly. "He is in the study with Fournier. You are needed to translate."

"I shall go to Mademoiselle Fournier at once," he said, fighting against his rising temper. Fournier! How tempting it was to point out to Viola that Mademoiselle Fournier was in fact the Lady Mary Fallon, and then watch her fall over herself to fawn on Marie. But she would never change, he supposed. To Viola, women who worked as lady's maids or in drapery shops were to be despised, and the aristocracy was to be revered, and that was all there was to it.

He went out into the South Saloon, already smelling of freshly cut wood in preparation for the construction of Mrs Middlehope's library. Viola followed him out, plucking at his sleeve agitatedly.

"What is it, Vi?" he said gently. Poor Viola, she hated this disruption so much.

"Is it not a huge coincidence?" she hissed in his ear, although there was no one else in the room. "This mysterious *cousin* appears out of nowhere and the next thing there are lady's maids being snatched off the streets and who knows what going on. I knew Laurence should have refused to acknowledge her, I knew it!"

Was that possible? He had left Charu in the dining room, watching them in silence over the rim of her coffee cup, her dark eyes calm and thoughtful, with no sign of unease at the strangeness of it all. Perhaps, as a stranger, she felt remote from the crises of her distant kin, or perhaps there was something more to it? No, surely not. How could Charu have any connection to Marie? This could only be because Malcolm had stirred things up in Northamptonshire. How he wished he had left well alone!

The dining room door opened again and Captain Edgerton appeared, followed by Chandry and Willerton-Forbes.

"Do you mind if we accompany you?" the captain said. "I believe Chandry may have some relevant information arising from our recent journey. If you permit, Gage."

"What does it have to do with Malcolm?" Viola said sharply.

Malcolm understood. "Yes, we must tell Mademoiselle what we have done. The time for secrecy is past."

"What *have* you done?" Viola said querulously. "What is going on, Malcolm?"

For answer he opened the door at the far end of the South Saloon, which led directly into the study. Inside, Marie and Mrs Middlehope sat decorously on either end of a sofa, while Laurence prowled restlessly about the room.

"About time! Where the devil have you been hiding, brother?"

"Oh, not hiding, Laurence," Viola cried in alarm. "He was in the dining room, and not the least idea he was wanted. I am certain he would have come at once if he had known you wished to speak to him, for he would—"

"Yes, yes, never mind that," Laurence said. "What is going on, Mal?"

"It is hardly Malcolm's fault," Viola said. "He cannot be blamed for—"

"Well, whose, then?"

"This new cousin of ours, who—"

"Nonsense! How could she have anything to do with it?"

Malcolm ignored them. His eyes were fixed on Marie, who watched him with a steady gaze, and a little smile on her lips. He crossed the room and knelt at her feet, taking her hand in his. It was such a tiny hand, her fingers slender and white against his rougher skin.

In French he said, "How are you? Are you well?"

"Perfectly well. And you?"

Et tu... she used the intimate form. He smiled, then nodded, momentarily unable to speak. It was the first time she had ever addressed him thus, a moment to be treasured.

"Will you not join us on the sofa, Mr Gage? The floor is so uncomfortable, is it not?" That was Mrs Middlehope, her voice amused.

He chuckled and rose to sit between them, although without relinquishing Marie's hand. Captain Edgerton held a seat for Viola, and Laurence sat too, still glowering at Malcolm. The captain retreated to stand beside Chandry and Willerton-Forbes near the door.

"I am rather afraid that this is, in fact, my fault," Malcolm said. "I was curious about Marie, and she would tell me nothing about herself, so I asked Captain Edgerton to see if he could find out about her. It is very possible that his investigations have, in some manner, caused someone to seek out Marie."

The captain coughed apologetically. "Unfortunately, I believe that to be true. It seems that in the course of our investigations, Mr Chandry may have been a trifle indiscreet while talking to someone, and thus caused that person to learn where Mademoiselle Fournier currently resides. He is a ramshackle sapskull, and I shall deal with him later, but first let me apologise without reservation for his stupidity, Mademoiselle, and offer our services in any way possible to protect you from further harassment."

Chandry looked suitably abashed. Malcolm could guess how it had happened. No doubt he had bedded some chambermaid to gain information, and had been bamboozled himself.

Viola twittered vaguely in distress, probably not fully understanding all the implications of this discreet summary, but Laurence frowned.

"Yes, but why?" he snapped. "Why would anyone want to kidnap a lady's maid?"

"As to that, I cannot say," the captain said smoothly.

"It hardly matters why," Malcolm said. "The imperative now is to ensure that Marie is kept safe."

"But how is that to be done without knowing the reason for it?" Laurence said. "We cannot protect her from an unknown enemy."

"It seems to me that there is a great deal about Marie that is unknown," Mrs Middlehope said pointedly.

Marie squeezed Malcolm's hand a little, although whether for her own comfort or his was hard to say. "You are quite right. I owe you an apology, Mrs Middlehope," she said.

"You speak English!" Mrs Middlehope cried.

"I do. I am not French and speak it poorly, and it is only because your grasp of the language is so tenuous that you have not discovered it long since. Malcolm knew almost at once." She paused, then said quietly, "I am Lady Mary Fallon, and my father is the Earl of Neston, of Northamptonshire."

Viola squeaked, and Mrs Middlehope's jaw dropped.

"Good God!" Laurence said. "Then why on earth did you become a lady's maid?"

"To hide from my father, who wished me to marry a friend of his, and would not take no for an answer. He locked me up to force me into it, but I ran away and here I am."

She spoke so matter-of-factly, so *bravely,* but Malcolm's heart was wrung. He could not bear to think of her caged like a songbird, with her father pushing her towards an unwanted match. And so clever, to manage to run away, to conceal herself as a French maid, to hide for five full years with no one suspecting a thing. Until he came along and blew apart her secret.

"That is despicable!" Mrs Middlehope said. "To use such extreme means... was he quite horrid, this man he wanted you to marry?"

"Not horrid, exactly, but my father's age... a man I regarded as I might an uncle. I certainly did not want to marry him."

"Quite right, my dear, quite right," Viola said, moving in sympathy to a chair closer to Marie. "One should never be *forced* to wed, for that is most disagreeable, however much one wishes to oblige one's father and be a dutiful daughter. Was he a man of consequence, this suitor? A man of rank?"

"He is a baron," Marie said. "Lord Purval, of Oxfordshire."

"Oh, a *baron!* Goodness! And yet you disliked him. Such a pity, although perhaps as an *earl's* daughter, your father might have done a little better for you."

"That is hardly to the point, Vi," Laurence said acidly. "Purval is a respectable man and would doubtless be a good match for anyone, but no father should press his daughter to marry against her will."

"Do you know him, Mr Gage?" Marie said, suddenly alert.

"Certainly. He was a good friend to the late Lord Saxby, and has often stayed at Maeswood Hall. A pleasant enough man and very wealthy, but he has never married, I believe, so it was quite a compliment that he held you in high regard, Lady Mary."

"I daresay," she said. "Is he indeed wealthy? I never knew that, for he lives rather quietly, without much show. All his energies go to improve his house and the pleasure grounds. Strachan Park is all he cares about."

"He gave the impression of wealth," Laurence said. "I have seen him lose thousands at the card table without turning a hair. However, that is not relevant now. The question is how Lady Mary is to be kept safe now that her location is known."

"We can help with that," Captain Edgerton said at once. "A safe haven, with suitable protection. I have some ideas already."

"If legal steps are in order, you may call upon my services," Willerton-Forbes said.

"I have a better plan," Marie said crisply. "The only protection I need against my father's scheme is a husband. I am going to marry Malcolm."

There was a very long silence, broken eventually by Viola clapping her hands excitedly. "Oh, how romantic! A whirlwind courtship indeed, and what could be more appropriate for a lady in trouble than a gentleman to take care of her."

"Really, Vi!" Laurence said in exasperated tones. "Appropriate, indeed!"

Malcolm's heart seemed to have stopped beating. He was barely aware of the voices in the room, although Mrs Middlehope was laughing, he thought, and Captain Edgerton and his cronies were murmuring together. His eyes were fixed on Marie's pale face, those dark eyes and the rather disordered curls which framed them.

"I believe you are supposed to say something at this point," she said to him, her head teasingly tipped to one side. "You might speak of honour and gratitude, if you wish. Or you might say that you are obliged to me, but you have no thought of matrimony at present."

"I think..." he said, his eyes never leaving hers, "I... I should like to speak to Marie alone, if all of you would not mind."

Still chuckling, Mrs Middlehope led the others out of the room. The door clicked shut and silence fell.

Malcolm lifted the tiny hand that still lay entwined in his and kissed it, then gently turned it over to kiss the palm.

"That is not a refusal, then?" she said, her voice full of laughter.

"I cannot marry you... not yet," he whispered. "I have no more than twenty pounds in the world, and my prospects are very uncertain. In August, if Edward succeeds—"

"No, it must be now," she said gently. "Papa sent those men – or perhaps Lord Purval. Whoever it was, he knows where I am, and even if I run away and hide again, he has a place to start looking. It is too dangerous. Only a husband can protect me now, and I know you love me and wish to marry me, Malcolm, for you have told me so. Marry me and keep me safe."

"I cannot ask you to live in abject poverty, and—"

She shook her head. "I am doing the asking, remember, and abject poverty is not part of our future. I have money of my own, or at least it will be mine when I marry or reach the age of twenty-five. I have been counting the days, I assure you! Five hundred and forty four days until I turn twenty-five, or a lot less, if you will marry me. Then I shall have the money that is mine."

"Enough money to live on?"

"A competence. Enough, if we are not extravagant. Malcolm... why do you hesitate?"

"Why do you *not?* For years now, we have both stayed hidden away from the world, and that strategy has kept you safe and me sane. Now we are recklessly throwing that away. If we marry, it must be done under your proper name and it will be a public event, known to the whole world, reported in the newspapers and talked about everywhere. It is madness! I have always been the reckless one of the family, and for you I would dare anything if it involved only myself, but to do this — to make a public show, to throw away any possibility of hiding — to allow your father to hunt you down—"

"He wants me to marry Lord Purval. Once that is impossible, he will be unable to press me any longer. Neither of them can press me. I shall be free. They will not harm me, Malcolm."

"Can you be sure of that? These men injured you, after all."

"It was an accident. My father would not harm me, never, nor Lord Purval. The sooner we marry, the sooner I shall be safe."

"You cannot be sure of that, and on what basis do we risk so much? How can you trust me so easily? We have known each other for precisely three weeks, and met no more than half a dozen times. What do you know of me, or I of you, that would make a rational foundation for a lifetime together?"

"I know that you *see* me!" she cried with passion. "No one else does, for in five years not a single person saw beneath the façade of the servant to the person hiding behind it — not until you came along. It was not just my French mistakes that you noticed — you saw *me*, the real me hiding inside, and you drew me into the sunlight. Your eyes see right into my soul, Malcolm. Even knowing me to be a fraud, you never judged me or turned away from me, and you opened your heart to me and shared your deepest fears. You are my friend, and you will never betray me, as my father did. I am safe with you. Please... keep me safe. Protect me."

Her eyes glittered with unshed tears, mesmerising him. "I will... I will..." he murmured. How could he deny her anything she wanted? Impulsiveness had always been his downfall, but even knowing that, he could not gainsay her.

"Good. Then you must go to the bishop and get a licence, so we can be married at once."

"A licence? *At once?* But I cannot go to Lichfield, licence or no. I have to stay here or forfeit this contest of Edward's. We must abide by the exact terms of the will."

"Oh." Her brow furrowed. "What precisely does it say? Do you have a copy of it?"

"The will? No. Are you looking for a way around it? Laurence might know what it says."

She got up, and walked across to the door to the South Saloon, throwing it open to reveal the others still deep in conversation. Malcolm followed her, bemused but also intrigued by this new, decisive Marie.

"Mr Gage, do you have a copy of the Oxford gentleman's will?" she said.

Laurence gaped at her. "Great-uncle Zachariah's will? Whatever do you need that for?"

"I have a copy," Willerton-Forbes said. They all turned to him in astonishment. "I was interested and it is public information," he said apologetically. "A most original will to add to my collection of unusual legal documents. What do you wish to know, my lady?"

"Malcolm needs to go to Lichfield to procure a marriage licence, but he tells me he must stay here under the terms of the will. Is that so?"

"Not quite," Willerton-Forbes said, beaming. "It is a particularly nice point, and one of the many little details which makes this such a fascinating document. He and his brother must stay *under the same roof* for the three months required before the examination, but the particular roof is not specified."

Marie laughed. "Perfect! Then you must go to Lichfield with Malcolm, Mr Gage. You need to go anyway, so it will be very convenient."

"I... why do I need to go?" Laurence said, looking bewildered.

"To get your own licence, of course."

"No, no, no," Viola said. "Laurence and dear Louisa are to be married by banns, and there is to be a celebration ball and all manner of delights beforehand. It is all arranged. One cannot rush these things."

"Wedding first, ball later," Marie said firmly. "It will be for the best, would you not agree, Mrs Middlehope?"

"But her wedding clothes will not be ready!" Viola protested. "A lady cannot be married without her wedding clothes. It is most unseemly. Louisa, you will not agree to this, surely?"

Mrs Middlehope had gone rather pink, but she said brightly, "There is no point in waiting, is there?"

"Louisa..." Laurence began.

"We can discuss it later — in private," she said firmly.

"But—"

"Later."

Captain Edgerton said smoothly, "I shall go and see if there is any coffee left in the dining room. Michael? Pettigrew? Are you coming?"

Chandry looked as if he might protest, but Edgerton grabbed him firmly by the elbow and steered him away, Willerton-Forbes in his wake.

"What is going on?" Laurence said petulantly. "What is so secret that it can only be discussed in private? I do so *hate* to be the last one to know."

Mrs Middlehope ushered them all back into the study. "Well, thank you for that, Marie, but I suppose one can never keep secrets from one's lady's maid. To be frank, I preferred the discreet Marie Fournier to the rather forthright Lady Mary Fallon, but I daresay honesty is for the best. Sit down, everyone, for I have shocking news for you. Well, it shocked *me,* I can tell you. After twelve years of marriage without the least sign of a child, I now find that I am... not barren after all."

There was a silence so still that the sound of a horse clip-clopping down the road could be clearly heard.

Then Malcolm laughed. "You old devil, Laurence!"

Laurence let out a startled huff of breath. "Good God! I never supposed... it never occurred to me..."

"Nor I," Mrs Middlehope said, with a quick laugh. "Are you pleased?"

"Of course, but... "

Viola emitted a great wail of anguish. "Oh Laurence! How *could* you!" In a flurry of tears, she dashed from the room, the lappets of her cap flying.

"Oh dear," Mrs Middlehope said. "Laurence?"

His face had creased into a worried frown. "Oh, it is wonderful news, naturally." Yet he still looked horribly glum.

"What is it, my love?" she said gently.

He looked at her with anguish in his eyes. "Catherine *died* in childbed, Louisa. I thought you, at least, would be spared that. I thought we were safe."

20: Lichfield

The journey to Lichfield was slow, very slow. It was a distance of under fifty miles by road, but it took them all day, owing to Laurence's sluggish team and the need to stop every two or three miles for Marie to cast up her accounts into the ditch. Malcolm had found it impossible to leave her behind.

"I shall not know a moment's peace," he had said.

"How protective you are, future husband," she had said, with laughter in her eyes. "Captain Edgerton will guard me, and you have my word that I shall stay safely in the house."

But he could not be convinced, and in the end his wishes had prevailed. Then Edward had insisted on being of the party, to work on his Russian, and Mrs Middlehope had said that if they were all to go jauntering about the country and having adventures, she would come too. By the time Captain Edgerton and Chandry had appointed themselves as armed guards to the company, the expedition had become rather larger than anticipated.

They left Viola in something of a state, pained to the core by the discovery that Laurence and Louisa had anticipated their wedding vows, and distracted by the presence of Charu in the house. Laurence had dithered about going to Lichfield at all, but Mrs Middlehope, in her calm way, had said, "Henrietta will take care of the house. She is a sensible girl."

And so they had left, and a strange journey it was, too, with the constant stops and starts for poor Marie. Mrs Middlehope read placidly the whole way. Laurence pretended to read, while fretting over the multitude of disasters that could befall them. And Edward learnt to say *'Marie is vomiting'* in nine different languages.

It was fortunate that Edward was there to provide some occupation for Malcolm's mind, for otherwise his thoughts would have skittered about alarmingly. He had not been so agitated for years. Naturally he was happy to be on the brink of matrimony with Marie — more than happy, delirious with joy. And yet, his delight was tempered with the fear that he was nothing more than a convenient way to solve her dilemma. She would marry and be free of the importuning of her father once and for all, but when that was done, and they were irrevocably wed, what then? Would she begin to regret her impulsiveness, and wish that she had waited for her twenty-fifth birthday after all? For she had spoken no words of love to him. Her manner had been briskly business-like, and he was very much afraid that her kisses were more for his benefit than hers. She had kissed him to ensure that he could not refuse her, and it was a dispiriting thought.

When they reached Lichfield, they stopped at the first coaching inn they saw, since none of them knew of a better place.

"You will have to use your correct name," Malcolm said to Marie in an undertone as they turned into the yard. "It will look quite odd otherwise, since we must obtain a licence in that name."

"I know," she said. "The time for secrecy is past, I think. I am so glad to stop moving. It will be bliss to lie down and not be swayed about constantly."

"Ma pauvre chérie," he murmured, kissing her forehead. "You will have all day tomorrow to recover."

"I shall be better directly," she said with a wan attempt at a smile. "Once all motion ceases I quickly revive, and then I shall be starving, so be sure to order a good dinner for us."

Laurence took charge of arranging matters at the inn with a quiet confidence that Malcolm could only envy. He had never quite had that way of speaking that commanded instant respect without once raising his voice.

"Have you a chamber already prepared?" Laurence said to the innkeeper. "Lady Mary suffers from the movement of the carriage and must rest at once."

"Of course, sir! Our best room will be prepared in a trice. Carrie! Show her ladyship to the big room at the back. A very quiet room, sir, no noise from the street or yard. Some tea for her ladyship? Or something a little more sustaining? A jug of claret or port, perhaps?"

"Tea would be just the thing," Marie said, as she turned to follow the maid.

"Tea for her ladyship, then, and the claret for the rest of us in the parlour, in the bottle, if you have it. And brandy. Dinner for seven in one hour."

"Of course, sir, of course. Are you here to view our beautiful city, sir? The cathedral is surely the finest in England. No other has three steeples, I believe, and there are many fine monuments within. As for churches—"

"I am sure they are splendid, but we are here on a matter of personal business with the bishop."

"Aaah!" the innkeeper said, eyeing them up expertly. "A licence, eh? If it would suit you, sir, I can have Bob run round to the Deanery at once to make an appointment for you for tomorrow."

Laurence allowed that this would indeed suit him, and they were conducted without further delay to a neat little parlour overlooking both the street and the yard. While Edward gazed out of the window, chattering in Russian to Malcolm, a little stream of servants darted in and out with an array of bottles and glasses, and then platters of bread, ham and cheese, and little cakes.

"Ooh, what kind of cakes are these?" Edward said excitedly, breaking into English to address the elderly serving maid.

"Lemon, sir," she said.

"Quite my favourite. Thank you very much."

She bobbed him a curtsy, muttering as she left the room, "Well now, but he speaks good English for a foreigner."

Malcolm was absurdly pleased that Edward passed for a native Russian speaker, even to so undiscriminating a person as a maid at an inn.

"We are very well attended to here, thanks to Marie," Mrs Middlehope said, with her easy laugh. "How useful she is, and yet how lowering to be outranked by one's lady's maid. Now I shall have to find another, and she will not be half so efficient as Marie. I am very cross with you, Mr Gage."

"You do not expect me to apologise, I trust?" Malcolm said, amused.

"Naturally I do, but I have been expecting something of the sort from the day she fetched up on my doorstep. She is by far too pretty to be a maid. I shall make sure my next maid is exceedingly plain, and then she will stay with me for ever."

Captain Edgerton appeared briefly to inform them that the carriage and horses had been safely stowed, and disappeared again to loiter in the common room with Chandry. Laurence refreshed himself with a glass of claret, and then another, before saying, "Shall we stretch our legs a little? Stroll about the town? We have time before dinner, I fancy."

Mrs Middlehope jumped up with alacrity, and Edward pleaded to go, too.

"Yes, do go," Malcolm said. "I shall stay here in case Marie wants anything."

As soon as they had gone, he left the parlour, and asked directions of a passing manservant to Marie's room. Her name alone was enough to achieve his objective. He tapped on the door, and it was opened by a fierce looking elderly woman in an old-fashioned mob cap.

"Yes?" she said, with unpromising sternness.

"I wondered how Lady Mary is?" he said.

"She be resting."

"May I see her?"

"No visitors." She folded her arms across her ample chest and glared at him, as if defying him to object.

He gave it up, and went down to the common room to find Captain Edgerton, who was sitting in a corner with a bowl of something unappetising in front of him. "I am forbidden from seeing my betrothed," Malcolm said gloomily. "There is a dragon guarding her door. Whatever are you eating?"

"Beef stew, allegedly, although I take leave to doubt it," the captain said, lifting a spoonful of brown slop and letting it fall again. "Stew, definitely, but the beef is very questionable. I thought to have something to put me on, for the parlour dinner is bound to be served late, but it was a mistake, I feel. I must apologise for the dragon, but one cannot be too careful. She is the innkeeper's mother-in-law, and he assures me that she can curdle milk at twenty paces, and will see off any potential miscreant in a heartbeat."

"I believe it, but you cannot expect trouble here, surely? The men who attempted to kidnap Marie are safely locked away in Shrewsbury."

"I expect trouble everywhere, Mr Gage," the captain said cheerfully. "Usually I am disappointed, but I should very much hate to be caught off guard. Someone wishes to remove the Lady Mary from her friends and I shall not allow that to happen."

~~~~~

As the captain had anticipated, dinner was late to reach the parlour, but fortunately it was a great improvement on the beef stew. Since Marie had recovered enough to eat heartily and the wine was surprisingly good, the meal passed off in great contentment to all parties. There was whist afterwards, and backgammon in Russian for Malcolm and Edward, with Marie watching, and Malcolm could not remember a more enjoyable evening. He was not much given to introspection, but for that one night he understood his own mind very clearly. He was in the same room as Laurence, and there was no discord between them. He also had Marie with him, openly using her own name,
~~~~~

with no more secrecy. The world was in harmony, and it felt good.

The ladies and Edward retired to their beds early, and Captain Edgerton and Chandry went off to *'patrol the camp and secure the perimeter'*, as the captain put it, leaving Malcolm alone with his brother. Laurence seemed abstracted, sitting with a glass of brandy at his elbow, lost in his own thoughts. Malcolm picked up a book to read, but it was hard to concentrate. Every time he glanced down the table, he saw his brother's glum expression and it wrung his heart.

Eventually he closed the book, found an unused glass and walked to the other end of the table.

"Do you want to talk about it?" he said, filling Laurence's glass and then his own.

Laurence shook his head, then said with a lift of the eyebrows at the brandy, "Am I leading you into bad habits?"

"I am learning, rather belatedly, to trust myself with drink. To my great surprise, I am capable of moderation."

His brother laughed at that. "You never did anything by halves, did you? I always envied you that intensity, did you know? I wished I had a little of it myself, but I was always too timid."

"Or sensible, perhaps."

He shrugged, with a little smile. "There is a lot to be said for hurling oneself into life with complete abandon."

"And I would say there is much to be said for restraint. Perhaps I am growing up at last, and not before time."

Finally, Laurence laughed. "Who wants to grow up? Not I! Do you ever wish we could go back to the days of our youth, with none of the burdens of responsibility pressing down on us? Before Father had his apoplexy and Mother declined — when we were free."

"Every day for sixteen years," Malcolm said at once.

"Yet you never wrote... never tried to heal the breach," Laurence said querulously. "I never understood that. You could have come back at any time, surely you knew that?"

For an instant, anger boiled up in Malcolm. "*You* never tried, either!" he snapped. Even a few days ago, he would have allowed his rage to ride him, but something in him had shifted, and the anger died away as abruptly as it had arisen. He let out a long, slow breath. "I wanted to write to you, but I had no idea what to say. There seemed to be no way to approach the matter that would not seem suspiciously like grovelling, and my pride precluded that. So I let my anger bubble away to sustain my righteous indignation."

"Lord, what a pair we are," Laurence said. "I was no more inclined to grovel than you, and if you resented me for marrying Catherine, I felt *guilty*, undeserving wretch that I was. You were always the golden son of the family, and I could never quite believe my luck, that she chose me over you. Of course, I now know that she chose the Grove, rather than me, but at the time it felt like something of a miracle. To be honest, I was terrified that if you came back into our lives, she would see what she was missing. It seemed better to let things lie. Even after she died, I never quite knew what to say to you. Now Louisa would say—"

He broke off and took a long draught of brandy, then lapsed into silence.

Louisa... that was what was on his mind. The prospect of losing another wife in childbed.

"It must have been hideous," Malcolm said slowly. "When Catherine died in that way, I mean. I cannot imagine what it must have been like for you." Laurence's head came up with a flash of fire in his eyes, and Malcolm wondered if he was making a dreadful mistake to even mention the subject. But it was too late now.

"It *was* hideous," Laurence said in a low voice. "The worst kind of nightmare for any husband to endure. I had sooner have been dead myself than that, far sooner. And now... damnation! I thought we were safe from that possibility, at least! Twelve years married with no child, and after one night with me, lo and behold — she is pregnant. God, it is hot in here!" He tore at his neckcloth, unwinding it from his neck and hurling it onto the table in disgust.

"Oh good, I have been longing to do that," Malcolm said, ripping off his own neckcloth. Or Laurence's, if he were being honest. John had surreptitiously replaced his own frayed ones.

Laurence laughed. "Shall we get bosky? Just like the old days, eh?" Then, eyes narrowing, he said, "What is that around your neck?"

"My pendant."

"Is it... good God, it is hair, is it not? Catherine's? No one else had such golden hair." Malcolm nodded, and Laurence went on, "Then... if she gave you a lock of her hair... you were *engaged* to her!"

"That was my understanding, yes. I talked of marriage and she never discouraged the idea, but I never asked her directly, openly. It was just assumed, I suppose. At least, *I* assumed it. Seemingly I was mistaken."

"The deceitful little hussy!" Laurence said indignantly. "To lead us *both* on in that despicable way is beyond anything, and if I had not been so angry with you, if I had listened to you—"

"That ship sailed a long time ago," Malcolm said ruefully. "I am done with being angry about Catherine."

"And I am done with being angry with *you,"* Laurence said more temperately. "To tell the truth, my real anger was against her — my perfect wife, who not only despised me, she hated her own children. Hard to believe, is it not? Ever since I read those diaries, I have been boiling with rage, and I took it out on you. Can you forgive me, brother?"

Malcolm's throat was tight, so he merely hugged Laurence.

"We must never let anything come between us again," Laurence said.

"Not a woman, anyway, for we each have our own," Malcolm said, laughing suddenly. "We both have the most wonderful future to look forward to." Laurence winced. "Yes, I know you are terrified, but you must not let that cloud your happiness, brother. Enjoy your newfound love, and do not let fear sour your joy."

"Easy to say," Laurence said, but his expression seemed a little lighter than it had been.

Malcolm could do no more. Only time would settle the matter once and for all.

~~~~~

Marie slept badly, her truckle bed still swaying about in her dreams. Across the room, she could hear the gentle breathing of Mrs Middlehope. Or Louisa, as she supposed she must eventually
~~~~~

call her, since they were very soon to be sisters. For the moment, however, they kept to their previous rôles of mistress and maid.

The gentlemen left early for their appointment with the bishop's officials, and there was no sign of Captain Edgerton or Mr Chandry, so the two ladies and Edward enjoyed a leisurely breakfast.

"I suppose we ought to visit the cathedral," Mrs Middlehope said. "It is a fine building, by all accounts, and Viola will want to hear all about it, I am sure."

"Do we go for Miss Gage's benefit or our own?" Marie said.

"Both," Mrs Middlehope said promptly. "We shall be thought people of no intellect or sense if we visit a cathedral city without bringing back any report of its finest edifice, and whatever we tell Viola will be relayed to everyone in three villages without the least effort on our part. She will be suitably grateful to us for offering her the opportunity to do so. Thus you see there are benefits to all parties."

"Do you want to go?"

"Not really, for it is bound to be exhausting. These great buildings always are. Nevertheless, I feel it is expected of us."

"Why not merely buy a guide book and learn the description from that?" Marie said. "Miss Gage will be just as happy, and if anyone asks awkward questions, we may say that it was too magnificent for words. I am sure it is true, after all."

Mrs Middlehope laughed. "How very appealing! Yet I do feel we should make the effort."

"Very well, then, let us walk to the cathedral and buy the guidebook there. After all, there is bound to be a stall selling a pamphlet on the history or some such. Thus armed, we need not walk around it and may repair back to the inn for the remainder of the day. Or do a little shopping, perhaps."

"Do you know, you are far more interesting when you speak English. Quite subversive, in point of fact. Were you like this in French, too?"

"One may have a great deal of fun in a foreign language," Marie said solemnly, winking at Edward. "Is it not so, Master Gage?"

Edward grinned. "Yes, but it would be very bad to say rude things about people when they cannot understand."

"Quite right, Edward," Mrs Middlehope said briskly, but with amusement gleaming in her eyes. "Shall we get ready to go out?"

The streets were crowded with people, for it was market day, they discovered. Nevertheless, they ploughed onwards, achieving their object and agreeing with the small booklet they found for sale that the cathedral was indeed one of the wonders of England, and they were very glad that they had seen it. They turned their steps towards the town again with rather more enthusiasm, and followed the throng to the market square, where all manner of delights enticed the eye, the ear and, less pleasantly, the nose.

"So many pigs," Marie muttered, holding her gloved hand across her mouth.

"If one wanted a basket, one might have any shape or size one desired," Mrs Middlehope said. "Edward, is there anything of interest, or shall we—?"

A great shout rent the air, followed almost instantly by a very loud crack. Marie spun round in alarm, just as a man crashed heavily against her, stumbled half to the ground, then with a grunt staggered off into the crowd.

"Careful!" Edward yelled at him. "Hoy, what are you doing?"

Someone screamed, several people yelled. A man ran past, then another. People turned, stared, gasped.

Marie stood transfixed, disbelieving. There was only pain, sudden pain. What was happening? With a strange kind of slowness, she fell to her knees and then to her side, watching a rivulet of blood flowing onto the cobbles.

21: Blood And Brandy

Feet. So many feet, in stained boots or buckled shoes, some with pattens against the mud. Crowds of skirts and smocks and torn trousers closing in around her. Screaming very close by, so close it hurt her ears. The cobbles were cold and hard beneath her cheek.

"Move back! Give her air!"

That was Mrs Middlehope, her aristocratic voice making them shuffle back a little way.

"A physician! Someone go for a physician — at once!"

Now she was on her knees beside Marie, gently rolling her onto her back, pressing firmly against her side. A spike of intense pain made Marie gasp and writhe.

"Ah! There we are. Just lie still, Marie. Nothing too drastic, I believe. We shall have you patched up in no time."

Then arms lifted her unresisting and she was borne away. Mr Chandry, she saw. Where had he come from? Mrs Middlehope ran alongside, struggling to keep up with his long stride.

"Wait, wait! Marie, can you hold this just here, like this? Press hard. Good girl. Carry on, Mr Chandry."

The crowds parted for them, and she was carried away from the market, around the corner into the main street, still busy but people stepped aside for them. Then they were at the inn, rushing inside, more horrified faces milling around her, but she could not think about them. The pain! What had happened? She had just been standing there, watching the pigs, a man had fallen against her and then the pain in her side had started.

She had been stabbed. It was the only thing she could think of to account for it. That man had crashed into her, drunk, presumably, and he must have had a knife in his hand. Perhaps he had hoped to rob her, to cut her reticule from her wrist, but something had startled him and he had stabbed her ribs instead. But the pressure helped. Mrs Middlehope had given her some cloth to hold against her side — a folded handkerchief, most likely. It was helping. And she was not insensible. Her legs had given way, more in surprise than anything else, but otherwise she felt quite calm.

Mr Chandry carried her upstairs, puffing a little. "I can walk," she murmured guiltily.

"Nonsense," he said, with a little smile. In truth, she was quite relieved to be carried, for she was by no means certain that her legs would support her.

Mrs Middlehope directed Mr Chandry to the bedchamber, where he laid Marie gently on the bed.

"No, no," she said. "That is my bed, over there, the low bed."

"This will do very well," Mrs Middlehope said. "Have you a pocket knife on your person, Mr Chandry?"

"Naturally."

A little trail of concerned people followed them, lurking around the door — the innkeeper, several inn servants, a farmer from the market, and a couple of housewives with baskets over their arms.

"Thank you, everyone, but we can manage now," Mrs Middlehope said briskly. Then, to the innkeeper, "Not you, my good sir. We need a physician, at once, or a surgeon. The best Lichfield can supply. Also, we shall need hot water, clean cloths and brandy. And send the Mr Gages up as soon as they return from the bishop's offices."

"Yes, madam. At once, madam."

He scurried away, the ogling onlookers drifted away too, and Mr Chandry shut the door on them. "Tell me what you wish me to do next, ma'am," he said.

"Nothing for the moment, except to be on hand to protect Marie," she said, bending over the bed, and lifting the folded handkerchief, making Marie wince again. "Anyone beyond our own party who enters this chamber must be considered suspect from now on."

"Exactly so. The window... Captain Edgerton would tell me to check the window, I am certain."

He crossed the room and threw open the casement, peering down and around, before closing it and restlessly prowling around the room, checking inside closets and even under the bed, while Mrs Middlehope began to cut away Marie's blood-soaked gown around the wound.

"I was very fond of this gown," Marie said.

Mrs Middlehope smiled. "You have been rolling about in the debris from the market, and to judge by the smell, even your skills could not make it wearable again. Mr Chandry, in the second drawer down, you will find a supply of fresh handkerchiefs."

"I shall never get the blood out of them," Marie said, making the others laugh.

"You'll do well enough," Mr Chandry said, bringing a neat pile of folded handkerchiefs. "Thought we'd lost you for a minute there, but you ladies have some spirit, both of you. There's nothing untoward in the room, and it would take a good long ladder to reach the casement, so I'll patrol the corridor and keep the riff-raff away."

"Be sure to come in when the maids or the doctor arrive," Mrs Middlehope said. "We must not take the slightest chance now."

"I'll do that," he said. The door closed behind him with a soft snick.

"You cannot truly believe me to be in any danger, surely," Marie said. "It was just some drunken fool or an inept thief— was it not?"

Mrs Middlehope looked up from her work mopping up the wound, her expression unusually serious. "All I know is that if Captain Edgerton had not been following us, and had not cried a warning, and had not fired a pistol into the air, you would in all probability be dead by now. You moved, the knife nicked you, no more than that, and the miscreant ran off, knowing that he had been spotted. Captain Edgerton and Edward ran after him. You are lucky to be alive."

Marie lay back in silence, pondering this new information, but she could make nothing of it. The kidnap attempt she could understand, for surely that was her father or Lord Purval trying to recover her and continue pressing her to marry, but neither of them would ever set a knife-wielding madman loose on her. It must surely be an accident, a mistake.

The servants came in and out, bringing water, cloths and the brandy, which Marie discovered was more for Mrs Middlehope's benefit than hers.

"You have merely been spiked with a knife and carried home, whereas I have suffered the great shock seeing these dreadful events unfold. It is far worse to watch another person bleeding, I assure you," she said, as she poured a generous measure of restorative liquid into a glass. "If you are very good, and the physician approves, you may have a sip later."

The physician was a silver-haired man who tended Marie's wound and bandaged her with reassuring competence. He teased her gently about the incident in a way that made it seem like the merest mischance that could happen to anyone, and not at all the consequence of a murderer on the loose. He approved the idea of brandy at once.

"Do you live far from here?" he said when he had finished, sitting on the bottom of the bed in relaxed fashion, and sipping a glass of brandy himself. "You should go home as soon as may be."

"A day's drive, and we planned to return tomorrow anyway," Mrs Middlehope said. "We cannot stay longer, however much Marie might wish it."

"Ah, you love our fair city too much to leave it, is that it?" the doctor said, his eyes twinkling at her. "Perfectly understandable."

"Any city has the great advantage over a carriage in staying still at all times," Marie said. "I love to travel, but my stomach does not."

"Is that so? I have the remedy for such a difficulty, dear lady. Brandy, that is the answer."

"You recommend brandy for everything," Marie said, laughing.

"For most things, certainly, and perhaps in many cases it does not so much cure the complaint as cause the sufferer to forget that he has a complaint at all. But for the sickness caused by motion, brandy truly cures it. Half a glass before departure, and you will feel perfectly well for the whole day."

Marie nodded and made some non-committal remark, unconvinced. Carriage sickness was her curse in life, and it was not the worst thing that could happen to her.

~~~~~

Malcolm and Laurence returned triumphant from the cathedral close, marriage licences in their pockets and no awkward questions asked. Seemingly it was commonplace amongst those *'of your position in society'* to apply for a common licence and avoid the delay of calling the banns, according to the very superior dean or canon or whatever he was who had attended to them. Laurence had been terrified that he would have to explain to pious churchmen his reasons for marrying with urgency, and Malcolm's reason was not a great deal better. *'Because my bride may be kidnapped again'* was liable to raise some intrusive
~~~~~

questioning. But no questions were asked and the licences were treated as an everyday piece of business.

Their euphoria evaporated the instant they entered the inn, when they were accosted by half a dozen voices at once, including a couple of complete strangers, with a jumbled story that seemed to involve pigs, knives, a gunshot and a chase through town. Only one phrase made any sort of sense to Malcolm — *'Lady Mary was carried home injured'*. He listened to no more, and fled up the stairs two at a time, up and up, and along the narrow corridor, practically crashing into the solid form of Michael Chandry.

"Let me past!"

"She is perfectly well," Chandry said, holding him off with casual ease. "A very minor injury. The doctor is with her just now."

The door opened, and Louisa's head appeared. "Ah, Malcolm, there you are. Come in."

Marie was propped up on the bed wrapped in a shawl, a little pale, a glass of something amber in her hand. She gave him a tremulous smile as he crossed the room and perched on the edge of the bed.

"Ma chérie? Are you all right?"

"Oh, yes. Nothing but a scratch. Did you get it?"

"What? Oh... yes, I got it. But what happened?"

Louisa intervened. "We will discuss it all in exhaustive detail once Captain Edgerton returns, for I confess I do not fully understand it myself. Marie is well, however, as you see. I shall just see the doctor out, and then we can go down to the parlour."

The door opened, she ushered out an older gentleman Malcolm had hardly noticed and then he was alone with Marie.

"You had no trouble getting it?" she said eagerly. "May I see it?"

Willingly he handed over the licence, and she smiled as she read it. "Good. So we can marry as soon as we like. Can it be done here and now? Today?"

"No, you would need a special licence for that. A common licence merely allows us to marry without any reading of the banns, but it must be done in our regular parish church. See this part here? It specifies the parish. We shall go back to Great Maeswood tomorrow and Truman can marry us the day after that."

She looked pleasingly disappointed, but he was sure that was to put herself out of reach of her father and not from romantic ardour. How he longed for a little ardour from her! Catherine had looked at him with adoration in her eyes, and even though he could no longer be sure of her sincerity, she had acted the part with conviction. But Marie made no such pretence. She was excited to be marrying, but not to be marrying *him.* Not a single word of love had crossed her lips.

Louisa returned moments later. "The captain is back, and Edward too. Marie, are you well enough to join us in the parlour? There will be more space there for all of us."

Captain Edgerton was grim-faced. "We lost the fellow, despite our best endeavours, eh, Edward? We nearly had him at one point, but he ducked down a busy back lane, and I was never able to get a clear shot at him. But you are not seriously injured, Lady Mary? That is the greatest relief. He followed you almost all the way from the inn to the cathedral and back, but he kept some distance behind you so I was not alarmed. It was only when you mingled with the greater crowds in the market square that he closed in on you, and when I saw the knife, I tried my best to alert you."

"And probably saved my life," Marie said. "You have my sincerest thanks, Captain, and Edward too, for so bravely giving chase."

"He is as game as you like, with never a thought for himself," the captain said, patting the boy on the shoulder, as proudly as if Edward had been his own son. "It was probably just as well for the villain that Edward never caught up with him, for I never saw anyone look so fierce."

"He hurt Marie!" Edward said indignantly. "He should not be allowed to get away with it. But I got a good look at him, and I would know him and his yellow hair anywhere."

"Did you see him at all, Lady Mary?" Edgerton said. "I should be interested to know if you recognised him."

"It all happened too quickly for me to see what happened."

"Ah. A pity, because I am certain he will be from Northamptonshire, like the three we captured on Sunday. They have the same way of talking as the people we met in that county recently."

"You think my *father* sent him?" Marie said sharply.

"Do you not? Who else could be responsible?"

"My father would never, ever try to harm me," Marie said with some heat. "He has not always treated me as he should, but he has never used physical assault against me. He has the gentlest nature and abhors violence of every kind."

"Yet he tried to coerce you to marry against your will," Malcolm cried, outraged. "He locked you up for a whole year — is that not a form of violence, too?"

"He never *hurt* me!" she cried. "Nor could this be Lord Purval's doing, for he wished to marry me, and murder hardly advances that object. But if it is not Papa or Lord Purval, who else could it be?"

There was a long silence.

"Perhaps it is time we heard the complete story of the marriage your father proposed for you, and your imprisonment, Lady Mary," Captain Edgerton said. "You have been admirably discreet, but I cannot feel, under the present circumstances, that there is any need to conceal the full details from us. Your life may depend upon it."

She lifted her chin, and for a moment Malcolm thought she might protest, but then she glanced towards him and her expression softened. "I suppose I owe you the whole sorry tale," she said, with a hint of a smile. "Very well, then. Lord Purval and my father met at Eton and have been friends ever since. Strachan Park, his family's estate, is barely a day's drive away, so we have been often staying there and he with us. He has never married, although he teased that he would have married Mama if Papa had not got there first, but I do not know whether that is true or just his little jest. He is an amiable man and I like him well enough as a friend of Papa's but no more than that. After Mama died, he seemed to visit more often and then, when I turned sixteen…"

She paused, her expression troubled, and reached absently for Malcolm's hand. His spirits soared at this instinctive gesture of need.

"Lord Purval came to my birthday celebrations," she went on, "and after he had left, Papa told me that he wished to marry me. I cannot tell you how shocked I was, for he had never said or done anything — not the least hint — that he held me in any affection beyond that of his friend's daughter. For myself, I had never viewed him in that light at all, and so I told Papa. He was by far too old for me, and much as I respected him, I could never feel for him that regard which a wife should have for the partner of her life and the father of her children. Papa told me that it was quite all right, that he had been surprised himself by such an application from his old friend and he would explain my feelings to Lord Purval himself. He even joked about it, saying that Lord Purval loved Strachan Park too much to have any affection to spare for a wife."

She fell silent for a moment, but her hand still rested in Malcolm's and he gloried in even so small a gesture. The others waited until Marie felt ready to continue.

"On my seventeenth birthday, he came again and this time he spoke to me himself. He told me that my father had approved his suit, and surely I wished to do my duty and be an obedient daughter. You may imagine how I answered *that.* I went straight to Papa, but this time he told me to accept Lord Purval. It was a good match, he said, and he wished to see me settled with a good man who would cherish me as I deserved. I told him that I would choose my own husband, and when I went to London to be presented by Mama's sisters, I would have a far wider choice of potential husbands than a man in his forties, however respectable he might be. And then Papa said—"

She broke off, her breathing rapid, and she clutched Malcolm's hand painfully tightly. "I beg your pardon... it is difficult..."

"Take your time, *ma chérie,*" he said gently. "Will you take some wine? Should I send for coffee?"

She laughed, and shook her head. "The physician has been plying me with brandy, so I need nothing more. But I must tell you the rest of my tale, for now I come to the part that mystifies me. Papa told me that he wished me to marry Lord Purval, that it was a matter of family honour that I do so, and he would not ask it of me were it not imperative."

"Family honour!" Malcolm said. "I cannot imagine what matter of honour would be so important that it would require you to marry."

"Nor could I, and Papa would not tell me. He gave me a week to consider Lord Purval's offer, and when I still refused, he drove me to a remote part of the estate where there is an ancient tower. There I was imprisoned in the topmost room, with two elderly servants my only attendants. My governess and personal maid were forbidden me. Papa told me that I would not leave that room until I were wed to Lord Purval. I told him that I would never leave it, in that case. And there he left me, and thereafter he was my only visitor. He came often, so I was not starved of rational company. I was not permitted to write or receive letters, but I was allowed books and the materials to make my own clothes, an occupation I have always enjoyed and which proved fortuitous. From each length of material, I cut away small strips and stitched them together to make a long rope. It took me a full year to be sure I had a length sufficient to reach the ground from the window. Then I walked ten miles to my friend Julia, who gave me money and a reference as a French lady's maid, and got me a seat on the mail coach to London. The rest I believe you know."

"Indeed we do," Captain Edgerton said, leaning back in his chair. "That is most interesting."

"But it invites the obvious question," Malcolm said. "Why would Lord Neston insist on this marriage? What is this matter of family honour that is so imperative that he would lock up his daughter and even try to kill her?"

"With respect, Mr Gage," Edgerton said, "I believe you are conflating two different questions. The family honour is one question, and it was so important to Lord Neston that he kept his daughter under confinement for a whole year, involving a great deal of deception. But if we accept Lady Mary's evaluation of her father's character, and she must know him better than anyone else, he would not harm her. Lord Purval would hardly do so, since it would destroy his hopes of marriage."

"Then who tried to kill her today?" Malcolm said.

"A good question, and this is the one that exercises my mind. Two days ago, three men tried to kidnap the Lady Mary, and those we must presume were sent by either Lord Neston or Lord Purval, continuing the effort to force her to marry according to their wishes. But today an attempt was made on her life. What has occurred in the intervening two days? Only that she is now set on marrying elsewhere, and as soon as may be. Someone does not want that marriage to take place. So the question *I* would ask of you, Lady Mary, is this — who stands to gain by your death at this precise moment? What happens to your inheritance if you should die *before* you marry?"

Her eyes opened wide. "It would revert to my father. If I die unwed, my father would take it all."

"Then I believe we have our answer," Captain Edgerton said grimly.

22: A Marriage Is Arranged

Marie could hardly breathe. Was it possible that her father had sent a man to *kill* her, purely to keep her inheritance for himself?

"No," she said slowly. "My father did not send that man. His fortune is large enough that my modest inheritance is nothing to him." No one spoke. Malcolm still held her hand, his face as anguished as her own must be, and in the others she saw only sympathy. "No," she said more firmly. "This is not my father's doing. The kidnapping, perhaps, but not this — not a knife-wielding madman. He would never do such a thing, and yet..." They all waited, watching her expectantly. "The answers lie with him, I cannot deny. Whatever brought this man to Lichfield, whoever it is who wishes me dead, my father is at the centre of it." To Malcolm she said, "We must go to Northamptonshire at once. We must confront him."

"No, no, no!" Captain Edgerton said in alarm. "Forgive me, my lady, but I must vehemently disagree with you and I am sure Mr Gage will take my side in this matter. Of paramount importance now is the need to protect you from further attack. You have seen for yourself how difficult that is to achieve in a town where we are all strangers. Anyone we meet may be an enemy, or even if otherwise friendly, may be receptive to a few coins from a passing stranger for information or assistance. The chamber maid could be the means of revealing which room is yours. One of the ostlers might be persuaded to leave a door unlocked at night. You would never be safe."

"We could stay at Springwell Place," she said. "As a member of the family—"

"Even worse!" the captain said. "Consider, my lady, that your father is the person at the heart of this conundrum. Would you put yourself willingly in his power, surround yourself with *his* loyal servants? Mr Gage, I implore you, please convince Lady Mary not to take such a terrible risk."

"I agree," Malcolm said slowly. "It would be too dangerous. Even if Lord Neston means Marie no harm, someone close to him may. But how else might we proceed?"

"We must all return to Great Maeswood as soon as may be," Captain Edgerton said. "You must marry Lady Mary, and then she should write to her father informing him of her marriage, and inviting him to visit her there."

"What is the advantage of that?" Marie said. "There will still be a confrontation."

"True, but it will be in the Gages' household and in the village where they are known and respected. Every single person in Great Maeswood is loyal to the family and to you as a known and valued member of the community. No stranger can stay at the Boar's Head without the Brownsmiths knowing it, and informing us, if we ask it of them. No one can ask odd questions without it being reported to Mrs Timpson at the shop and thence to every part of the village. There you will be safe and protected and your father, if he comes or sends another in his place, will be the outsider. I can protect you there as I cannot in Northamptonshire. Do you see?"

Marie nodded slowly, calmed by his certainty. "And I would be married."

"Exactly so. You would have a husband to protect you in law."

"Then let us do that," she said briskly.

~~~~~

'It is settled. He has the licence, we are to return to Great Maeswood tomorrow and marry there on Thursday. I shall be Lady Mary Gage and even my father can do nothing about it. He will be mine, my husband, my darling, my love, my world. I want nothing but him. I am a greedy creature, and cannot get enough of him. Ever since he kissed me, I need him so much it is like a pain inside me. When he looks at me in that intense way he has, I feel so exposed, like a snail without its shell, and yet it is not an uncomfortable feeling, not with him. It is hard to believe that my life has changed so abruptly again. When we wed, I shall have known him for not quite a month, and loved him for precisely three weeks. Madness, he called it, and so it is — complete insanity! Yet I have never been more sure of anything in my life. Just as I knew that I did <u>not</u> wish to marry Lord Purval, so I know with absolute surety that I very much want to marry Malcolm Gage. My dearest Malcolm, who tells me he loves me but only when I force him to kiss me. Does he truly love me, or was his interest never more than a momentary attraction that has now faded? It is selfish of me, but I truly do not care. He has agreed to
~~~~~

marry me, and that is all I ask of him. I will make very sure he has no cause to regret it. ~~Five hundred and~~ Oh joy! I no longer need to count the days until my birthday, for I shall be free a lot sooner. Two days.'

~~~~~

Malcolm was surprised to find the journey home a great deal more pleasant than he had expected. Marie was quiet, as on the outward journey, and Laurence and Louisa were engrossed in their books, so Malcolm and Edward chatted in Russian and occasionally, for variety, in one of the other languages. After a while, he began to anticipate the first halt for Marie's stomach. Instead, to his great surprise, she fell asleep on his shoulder.

When they stopped for horses, she stirred, and he said, "Are you all right?"

She chuckled. "Perfectly. A little sleepy, that is all, but no nausea. Do you want to know why?"

"I want to know," Edward said at once, sitting up a little straighter, his eyes alive with interest.

"Brandy," she said. "The physician who attended me yesterday recommended half a glass of brandy before departure." She raised her hand to hide a yawn. "It seems to be working."

"I suppose being bosky is preferable to the alternative," Malcolm said. "However, if you begin singing bawdy songs, I might change my mind."

"Marie will not know any rude songs," Edward said. "She is a lady!"
~~~~~

Marie laughed. “I have heard one or two. You would be surprised what people will say when they imagine they cannot be understood.”

“But you understand English perfectly,” Edward said. “Even when you were being French, you understood.”

“Indeed, but people hear the French and make assumptions.”

“They underestimated you,” Malcolm said, with just a touch of smugness. “As your father did.”

She nodded, but a shadow passed across her face at the mention of her father, and Malcolm cursed his ineptness. Naturally she was worrying about what her father would do when he heard the news of their marriage.

Their marriage! As always, a delicious shiver of anticipation ran through him at the thought. She would be his wife! And, just as always, the very next feeling was fear. They knew so little about each other and a lifetime was a very long time to endure if they turned out not to be suited. And the biggest question of all — did she care for him, truly care, or was he just a quick way out of her hiding place?

Great Maeswood snoozed under the summer sun when they arrived, the horses’ hooves throwing up vast clouds of dust. The ladies, together with Marie’s watchful guards, were deposited at the Dower House, for heaven forbid that a bride should sleep under her future husband’s roof the night before the wedding, and the gentlemen then continued to the Grove. Viola and Henrietta emerged with the butler and footman to greet them. Was it Malcolm’s imagination, or was there an unusual calm about the house? Viola was not her usual twittery self.

"Oh, I am very well, brother," she said complacently in answer to his enquiry. "Very well indeed, and all is prepared for your nuptials. Dear Cousin Cornelia has been most helpful in assisting with the preparations. She has rearranged all the curtains."

There was no sensible answer to this, so Malcolm attempted none.

Laurence frowned, however, and said, "Whatever for?"

"Oh, she found the original curtains in the attic — the ones dear Catherine intended to match the decor in each room, you know. Well, you see, when we take them down for cleaning, the old ones are put up temporarily, but after poor dear Catherine died, no one knew just how hers should be hung and so the old ones stayed up. But dear Cornelia has worked it out and she is putting back all the proper curtains. You will be amazed at the difference."

"Since I never noticed they had changed, I beg leave to doubt it," Laurence said, laughing. "I am glad that you are getting along with Charu, though."

"Oh yes! Such a charming girl, and her mother was a princess of some sort in India, you know, *very* high ranking. She told us all about it. Goodness, the servants she had out there! And here she is hanging curtains for us. So very condescending of her. So gracious."

The daughter of a princess — that would account for the sudden change of heart. Laurence and Malcolm exchanged amused glances.

There was no avoiding the revelation that someone had attempted to kill Marie, for Dr Beasley was needed to tend to the wound. He came directly to the Grove afterwards to talk to Laurence and Malcolm.

"This is very concerning, I make no bones about it," he said.

"Is she not healing?" Malcolm said, in sudden fear.

"What? Oh, no, no, nothing to worry about there. The Lichfield sawbones was very competent, and it is a very tiny cut. No, I have no concerns about Lady Mary's immediate health, but a murderer on the loose is what I cannot like. The fellow got away, and since he undoubtedly knows where Lady Mary resides, he will certainly try again."

"Captain Edgerton is organising a full-time guard for her," Laurence said. "There will be plenty of volunteers from around the village, and Edward has given us a good description of him."

"Even so, it is most unsettling. A kidnapping and now outright violence against her ladyship's person. And have you any idea why anyone should wish her harm?"

"Not exactly," Malcolm said cautiously. "There is some family history... an arranged marriage that was disagreeable to Marie. She chose to be a lady's maid to put herself out of reach of importuning."

"An eccentric choice, but these great families are often so. Hmpf. Edgerton protecting her is all very well but we cannot have men scampering about the countryside with knives, and he will come here and all the ladies will be terrified to leave their houses."

"Edgerton will get to the bottom of it, I am sure," Laurence said soothingly. "He and his colleagues are very thorough. And now, if you will forgive us, we have a wedding to arrange."

Truman was expecting them, with wine and pastries laid out ready, but to Malcolm's surprise, Laurence refused the refreshments and had handed over the marriage licences and agreed a time for the ceremony almost before they were well inside Truman's plush drawing room. After no more than five minutes of pleasantries, he jumped to his feet.

"You will forgive us, I am sure, Truman, but we have a great deal to do today."

"Of course, of course. I shall be ready for you tomorrow, never fear, gentlemen." And without the least appearance of pique, he showed them out personally.

"What was that about?" Malcolm said, amused, as they turned out of the parsonage drive onto the road. "What is so urgent that we must needs cut short our visit with such unseemly haste?"

"We are going to pay a call upon the ladies at the Dower House," Laurence said smugly. "That is more to my taste today than Truman's pious prosing. He is by far too oily for my liking. I had a great deal sooner be with Louisa, I can tell you, and I am sure you had sooner be with Marie. And tomorrow we shall be with them as much as we wish. Lord, I cannot wait! I had almost forgotten the delights of—" He paused, and threw Malcolm a sideways glance. "Mal, do you... well, want any advice? I am sure you do not, but if you do—"

"About the wedding night?" Malcolm said, trying not to laugh. "Having had access to Grandfather's private library since I was... oh, about twelve years old, there is little I do not know, I assure you."

"His private library? The locked bookcases we were forbidden from examining? You looked at them?"

"Of course. Most illuminating, I assure you. The keys are in the left-hand drawer of the smaller desk. He was quite a character, Grandfather."

Laurence chuckled. "You devil, Mal! But why did you never tell me? We shared most things, did we not? Why not the secret bookcase?"

Malcolm sighed uneasily. "It was just at that time, not long after your Confirmation, when you had become deeply religious. All you ever read was books of sermons. I was not sure you would approve."

"You thought I would tell tales to Father, I suppose. As if I would have betrayed you! We are brothers, after all, two against the world. Or so I thought, once."

"And so we are again," Malcolm said fiercely. "I am learning, a trifle belatedly, the virtues of restraint and family loyalty."

Laurence smiled, and patted him genially on the shoulder. "And I, too. Perhaps by the time we are in our dotage, we may even have acquired a little wisdom, who knows?"

"Hmm. Sounds boring," Malcolm said. They arrived at the Dower house chuckling together.

Malcolm had expected to find the ladies in a whirlwind of packing, for this was the last night they would spend under that roof. Instead, the brothers were shown into a drawing room of exceptional serenity. Louisa was stretched out on the chaise longue, a book in her hand, and Marie was on the window seat with her needlework. She smiled at him and patted the seat beside her.

"How are you?" he said, as she folded away her work.

"Perfectly well. I forgot to ask, did you get the wedding ring yesterday?"

"Yes, I have it safe. We have seen Truman and we are to be at church at nine o'clock." After a pause, he went on, in what he hoped was a teasing tone, "Still time to change your mind." With a laugh, she shook her head, and he let out the breath he had been holding.

"What about you?" she said, tipping her head on one side.

She looked so adorable that for a moment his throat was tight with love for her, and he lost all power of speech. All he could do was shake his head.

Laurence and Louisa were laughing together on the sofa, quite engrossed, but even so, Marie leaned forward to whisper, "Thank you for the hat. Miss Cokely must have worked night and day to replace it so quickly."

He wanted to tell her how much he loved that hat, how beautiful she looked in it, how much he longed to see her wear it as she became his wife, but he could not yet trust his voice, and she went on to speak of other things and the moment was lost. After a while, when she fell silent again, he dared to raise a matter that had been much in his mind.

"May I... may I beg a favour of you?" he said hesitantly.

"But of course. What is it?"

"May I have a lock of your hair?"

"Ah, such a romantic!" she said chuckling softly, so that he was not sure whether she was laughing at him. She reached into her work bag for a pair of scissors. "There. Snip away, future husband." She turned her head away, to give him access to the back of her head, where several curls fell onto her neck.

He needed no further invitation. With shaking hands, he lifted a single curl, as soft as silk, from her neck. For several seconds, he let it lie in his hand, feeling the gossamer strands, the way it curved about his fingers of its own accord. Beneath it, her skin was smooth and utterly enticing. If they had been alone, he would without doubt have run his fingers over her neck, her shoulders, the cheek that was so close. He would have touched her and kissed her and made an utter fool of himself, and what would she have done then? Would she have pushed him away, or laughed at him, or… something worse?

It was as well that the presence of Laurence and Louisa held him in check, however tenuously. With a sigh of regret, he snipped the luscious curl and handed back the scissors.

"Here," she said, passing him a square of silk. "Wrap it in that to keep it safe."

He folded the silk carefully about the precious hair, and tucked it away in his waistcoat pocket, and not long afterwards Louisa ordered them to be gone so that the ladies might have ample time to look their best before dinner.

Laurence said gallantly, "You always look your best, my love," and she coloured up like a girl.

Malcolm could not think of anything similar to say, and left the house in fretful silence, wishing he could say all that was in his heart. With Catherine, it had all poured out without restraint, but Marie somehow tied his tongue in knots. If only he knew how she felt!

Dinner promised to be a pleasant affair, for Viola had invited a number of their friends to help celebrate, and Captain Edgerton and his colleagues were there too. Mr Willerton-Forbes took Malcolm aside as everyone gathered in the drawing room before dinner, and after offering his congratulations, said, "I trust you will not think me impertinent, Mr Gage, if I mention one or two matters that perhaps may have escaped your attention in all the excitement of recent events. Have you considered the question of marriage settlements, and your will?"

"Ah, there speaks the lawyer," Malcolm said easily. "Your mind naturally considers settlements and wills. Yet to me, such considerations are pointless. I have nothing to settle on my wife, nor to dispose of in a will, so it is hardly material."

"This is where a lawyer's mind is advantageous," Willerton-Forbes said, with a little smile. "How easy it is for a man to say that he owns nothing, therefore what is the need for legal documents? Whereas a lawyer would say that a properly prepared will or marriage settlement will take account not merely of the present, but of the future also, and indeed of all possible futures. For it may be that in August, should young Master Gage succeed in his great endeavour, you will be the possessor of a sizable fortune, well worth the consideration of a will, would you not say? And then there is the Lady Mary's inheritance."

"That is hers," Malcolm said quickly. "It is nothing to do with me."

"On the contrary, it is everything to do with you, for in a very few hours she will be your wife and everything she possesses will, in law, be yours."

Malcolm opened his mouth to refute this, and then closed it again swiftly.

"Yes, indeed," Willerton-Forbes said gently. "And do you have any idea of what precisely she possesses?"

"A competence," Malcolm said. "Enough to live on without extravagance."

"But held in trust, presumably? And under what terms? What, for example, would be the position if Lady Mary marries without the prior consent of her trustees? Who are the trustees? Is her father one of them? Is this her sole dowry, or is there more to be expected? You see, Mr Gage, under normal circumstances, the marriage of an earl's daughter would be a matter of discussion over several weeks or possibly months. Her father and his lawyers would sit down with you and *your* lawyers, and draw up a settlement which would ensure the comfort of Lady Mary and her children, while also protecting their future. *Your* status in society and wealth would be a material consideration. Yet by this hour tomorrow, Lady Mary will be your wife and none of this will be settled. You have not the least idea of the amount of her fortune. In fact, you do not even know for certain if there is any fortune to be had. Do you begin to understand my concern? For it may be that you and Lady Mary will find yourselves in a very few weeks with no income whatsoever, and if you were my client, which you are not, of course, I should most strongly advise you to consider delaying the marriage until these important questions can be resolved."

23: For Better For Worse

Marie found Malcolm unusually preoccupied that evening. He smiled and said all that was proper in the drawing room, but when they moved to the dining room, he fell into abstracted silence.

"Is anything the matter?" she said quietly, under cover of laughter around the table at one of Captain Edgerton's lively tales. "You are not quite yourself tonight."

He sighed. "Willerton-Forbes has thrown up all sorts of concerns that had never occurred to me before. Settlements and wills and so forth, and the terms of your trust fund. Do you know if there are any conditions attached to your inheritance? If you marry to disoblige your family, for instance?"

"There are no conditions," she said at once, with greater confidence than she felt.

"Are you sure? Because Willerton-Forbes said we should delay the wedding until—"

"Then he should mind his own business," she said, so hotly that one or two heads turned in their direction.

"But what if neither of us is able to obtain the expected inheritance? We should be penniless, *ma chérie,* and how would we manage?"

"We would find a way," she said, in a lowered tone. "Between us, we will find a way. Are you looking for an excuse to cry off, Malcolm?"

"Of course not!"

"Then do not concern yourself with imponderables."

"With imponderables, no, but in twelve hours' time, it will be my responsibility to provide for you, and I do not see how I can do that without two farthings to my name."

"You can still teach."

"Schoolmasters at my level cannot marry, and even if it were possible, I could not keep you on fifty guineas a year. I can barely keep myself on such an amount, and with a wife and family, we should be quite destitute."

She could see that he was not receptive to being jollied out of his gloom, so she smiled and laid her hand on his. "We will contrive something, you may be sure. So long as we are *together*, all will be well. You will find some other employment, as a secretary or steward or some such. Or you could take Holy orders and—"

"Not that," he said. "Never that. I am unsuited for life as a man of the cloth. But you are right, *ma chérie.* There will be something I can do. We shall not starve. May I pass you the rissoles?"

He was determinedly cheerful for the rest of the meal, but she thought his smile was rather forced. Poor Malcolm! But she was not about to let him escape her now, not when she was so close to achieving all that her heart desired. She would use every feminine trick to keep him sweet, if she had to.

When the ladies returned downstairs to the drawing room, Marie took up her sewing, feeling rather too ruffled to brave the general conversation centred on Miss Gage and Mrs Middlehope. She supposed she would have to get used to mingling with her social equals again, but five years as a lady's maid had given her a liking for the quiet corners of rooms. There was still enough light from the windows for her to sew without candles, so she settled down with her needle, and while she sewed, she reviewed her discussion with Malcolm and wondered why it had rattled her so badly.

Guilt, she supposed. She had not given a thought to her inheritance since the day she had been told of it, not long after her mother's funeral. The lawyers had travelled back to Springwell Place from London with her father, and explained it all to her. No one had mentioned conditions, or amounts, or anything precise, she now realised. It had all been generalities — a competence, enough to live on without extravagance, and it would be hers at the age of twenty-five or when she married, that was all. No conditions... but what if there were? What if she had misled Malcolm, and she was not an heiress after all? *'Destitute'*, he had said. *'We should be quite destitute.'* Her stomach twisted inside at the thought.

"May I sit with you? Such a lovely light muslin to work on, and your stitches so small and neat," Charu said, bending over the fichu Marie was sewing. "Do you make all your own clothes? And Mrs Middlehope's, too, I hear, and she is such an elegant person, always so stylish, and that must be all your doing. How clever you are! Did you make that figured silk gown she wears tonight? Lovely! Quite lovely! And the gros grain she wore on Sunday - such a wonderful fabric."

It was impossible to dislike Charu, and even though she had wanted to be alone to think her own thoughts, Charu's unflagging good humour was infectious and they were soon talking like old friends. Charu wanted to know all about her work as a lady's maid, and where Mrs Middlehope obtained the fabrics for her gowns, and which journals she read to learn about the fashions, and the time passed amicably until the gentlemen joined them. Then the sight of Mr Willerton-Forbes brought on a renewal of all her indignation. How dared he interfere!

When the tea things were brought in and everyone rearranged themselves, she took the opportunity to position herself beside Mr Willerton-Forbes. "I should like a word with you, if you please," she said.

"Ah." Did he look guilty? "And I with you, my lady. The room next door will be empty if you wish to talk privately. Since it is a legal matter, there is no need for a chaperon."

She agreed to it and followed him from the room. It was the family dining room, unused that evening for the company was large enough to use the formal dining room upstairs. He held a chair for her, and then punctiliously sat on the opposite side of the table.

"You think me officious, perhaps, in speaking to Mr Gage regarding your fortune," the lawyer said, before she could speak. "You would be entirely right, of course, and I can only apologise and assure you that my impertinence arises only from a sincere concern for your wellbeing."

A little mollified, she said, "I do not mind that, for it is natural for him to take legal advice, but you told him to delay the wedding, and that is interference that I cannot accept with equanimity."

"As you should not, of course, but I should perhaps point out that a lawyer never tells a client what to do. I merely advised Mr Gage to consider delaying your wedding until the circumstances of your inheritance should be clear. However, over the port just now, Mr Gage pointed out to me, with some force, I might say, that your very life may depend upon your marriage, and I ceded the point at once. Naturally he wishes you to be safe, above all else, but he also wishes to be able to support you, and not be dependent on his brother's generosity. I was able to assure him that, should he ever find himself in need of employment, I should be very happy to use what influence I have to obtain a position for him in the government, or with a member of the peerage. I am not without connections, Lady Mary." He paused, watching her with perceptive eyes. "I trust this alleviates your concerns a little, and will perhaps mitigate my presumption?"

Marie could not hold out against such contrition. "You are very good, sir."

"Have you notified your trustees of your impending marriage?"

"I have told no one, nor shall I until after the event, Mr Willerton-Forbes. You will think me over-cautious, I daresay, but I do not want anyone to hear of the matter until I am securely wed. Tomorrow I shall write to my father and to Mr Dugard."

"Ah, of Lindley and Dugard? I know Sir Richard Lindley well. Are they your father's solicitors?"

"No, the Winfell family lawyers. My mother was a Winfell, of the Duke of Dunmorton's family."

"That is good, very good," Mr Willerton-Forbes said, in satisfied tones. "They are not connected to your father. Yes, that is very good. So tomorrow you will write, and in a few days... yes, then we shall know."

~~~~~

Malcolm held the pendant tightly in his hand. "I am grateful for a clear day with no rain. I am grateful for my brother's tolerance. I am grateful for Marie..." With a sigh, he rested his forehead against the cool glass of the window pane. "Above all else, I am grateful for Marie, for today is our wedding day."

Then he drew the pendant chain over his head and gently laid it on the window sill. For the first time in years, he fumbled with the tiny latch to open it, and gazed at the curl of Catherine's hair. Such a delicate yellow, yet when he lifted it from its resting place, it was brittle with age, as if he could crush it to dust in his fingers. Tipping the opened pendant into his hand, so that every last strand fell into his palm, he curled his fist around the golden hair. Today was the end of a long, painful era, and a new beginning.

A tap on the door was followed instantly by Laurence's face. "Good Lord, Mal, you are not even dressed yet. Bestir yourself, man, for we have somewhere to be in not much above an hour. You have your lovely bride to meet."

"My lovely bride with the colourful bruise on her face."

Laurence chuckled. "True, but at least everyone knows the blame for that cannot be laid at your door, for the culprits reside in Shrewsbury gaol as we speak. What are you doing? Ah... your pendant."
~~~~~

Malcolm opened his hand to show the golden strands, then, with three quick steps, crossed the room and let them fall gently into the waste paper basket.

"I should have let go of her a long, long time ago," he said quietly.

"As should I," Laurence said, patting him lightly on the shoulder. "Catherine seemed so... *perfect*, the outer shell was so angelic, that one felt honoured to be in her presence, but there was something deeply amiss within that beautiful exterior. Those diaries of hers... so superficially trivial and yet so fundamentally dishonest. I think she wrote them like a novel, the fictitious story of her life, with herself as the heroine. I cannot believe I never realised how little she cared about me. She was no more mine than she was yours, in the end. She held us both captive for far too long, brother, but we are free of her at last."

Malcolm fished under his pillow for the little scrap of silk Marie had given him. Carefully he opened it and gazed at the dark curl that lay within.

Laurence laughed. "Off with the old and on with the new, eh? You could have it made into a ring, you know."

"No, I like my pendant," Malcolm said, delicately tucking the dark strands into the pendant and closing the cover with a click. "There! It is done. Now all I need is John to turn me into a respectable fellow, although not as fine as you are today. Is that a new waistcoat?"

"Yes, do you like it? I had thought to wear the red, but Louisa has a pelisse almost the same colour, and if she wears that today, we should be sadly mismatched. But is it too much, do you think? The blue would be more sober, but I cannot feel that this is a day to be sober, do you? What will you wear?"

"Whatever John tells me to wear. I have very little choice in the matter, for almost everything I own is one of your cast-offs. Ah, there you are, John. What am I to wear today?"

"The dark blue Weston, sir, the black waistcoat with white trim, and the grey pantaloons."

"Do I possess grey pantaloons?"

"You do now, sir."

Malcolm laughed. "Very well. Do your worst, my good fellow, and make me presentable for my bride."

"Oh, we shall aim for a little better than *'presentable'*, sir," John said smugly.

Having not thought much beyond himself and Marie, Malcolm was surprised to find the church packed. Despite the hasty arrangements, everyone knew, of course, and seemingly everyone from the three villages in the parish had taken the day off and crowded into the pews. Everyone smiled, and looked excited. That was for Laurence, of course. Apart from Lady Saxby and her family, Laurence was the highest ranking resident and so his well-wishers had all turned out to see him wed.

Almost before he knew it, Truman was there in his vestments, the two ladies were walking sedately up the aisle side by side with Henrietta behind them, an alert Captain Edgerton bringing up the rear, and the service began. *'Dearly beloved, we are gathered together here in the sight of God, and in the face of this congregation…'*

Marie wore Malcolm's bonnet and the matching pelisse, and oh, her smile! Such a mischievous smile, as if this were a great game, as if life itself were a game.

'...not by any to be enterprised, nor taken in hand, unadvisedly, lightly, or wantonly...'

True! This was not a game, but deadly earnest. Marie's very existence may depend on her marriage now. On Malcolm.

'It was ordained for the procreation of children...'

Well, Laurence and Louisa were already obediently complying with that stricture. As for Marie... that was a matter to be considered carefully. It was bad enough to take a wife when he had not a penny to his name, but children too?

'...wilt thou have this woman to thy wedded wife...'

Oh yes. A thousand times yes! His throat was tight, but he managed to say the words without stuttering.

'...wilt thou obey him, and serve him, love, honour, and keep him...'

Marie's voice was strong, not at all hesitant as she responded. Then it was his turn.

'I Malcolm take thee Mary to my wedded wife, to have and to hold from this day forward, for better for worse...'

For better for worse. Which would it be? The path now opening before them was shrouded in darkness. Would it lead them to sunlit uplands, filled with birdsong and clouds of sweetly-scented blossoms, or to a deep, rocky valley full of pain and despair? It was a leap of faith, for both of them. They had known each other for less than a month, yet here they were, committing to a lifetime together. It could be decades, or it could be mere months... Malcolm shivered.

"...and thereto I plight thee my troth," he said, gazing into those dark eyes, her hand in his.

'I pronounce that they be man and wife together.'

And it was done.

Malcolm was light-headed with relief. It was all slightly unreal, and not at all how he had envisaged his marriage. Of course, his previous imaginings had all featured Catherine's fair head and delicate beauty, and that vision had seared itself into his brain. This marriage had been so sudden that there had been no opportunity to picture how it might be. Yet as he left the church with his wife on his arm — *his wife!* — he had no cause to regret Catherine. Marie's dark curls, those chocolate eyes and the fetching bonnet bobbing along at his shoulder filled him with pride. *His wife.* Her hand rested trustingly on his arm, and she smiled as everyone poured out of the church to congratulate them and shower them with rose petals and rice. Even Agnes Saxby smiled, showing no resentment at being overlooked.

His wife. He felt twelve feet tall.

Then it was back to the Grove for the wedding breakfast, a modest affair since there had been no time to arrange anything grander. Viola spent the entire meal apologising for the paltry scale of it. "If only we had had a little more time," she murmured over and over. "And dear Ursula and Selena not even here, nor anyone from dear Louisa's family, or dear Lady Mary's. It is not at all how we usually do things."

"We shall have some proper celebrations later, when the kitchen has had time to prepare for it," Laurence said placidly.

Malcolm could barely eat while his jangled nerves were so unsettled. Laurence and Louisa laughed and teased each other, Charu entertained the children, and everyone else apart from Viola was relaxed and easy, but Malcolm was silent, toying with his food. Marie watched him with laughing eyes.

"Will you not eat something, husband? A little ham, perhaps?"

And how could he resist the blandishments of his wife? He could not, of course, so he agreed to it and then pushed the ham around his plate along with everything else.

After breakfast, Viola whisked them away to show them to the rooms assigned to them, a pair of rooms on the nursery floor, with Captain Edgerton following watchfully behind, in case an assassin should spring out from behind a curtain.

"It is not quite what I should wish for you," Viola said, twisting her hands together, "not for a newly married couple, but we have so many visitors just now… we could not quite squeeze you in on the floor below… much more space up here…dear Cousin Cornelia thought…"

"It is a charming room," Marie said at once, gazing about her at the pretty wallpaper and hangings, and the light, elegant furniture. Every surface held bowls of roses, filling the room with a heady perfume.

"And your dressing room next door, you see, and Malcolm's through this door. So much more *space* up here, but if you wish to be in one of the principal bedrooms—"

"By no means," Marie said. "This is perfect, and a dressing room, too, and fitted up with a sofa and writing table. How delightful! So much more comfortable than the room I had before."

"Well, that is what we thought… a miniature sitting room, you see. A little retreat from the world. Cousin Cornelia thought of it when she was hanging the curtains. Such a thoughtful person, do you not think? Now, is there anything else you need?"

"Nothing, I thank you. I shall stay here for a while and write some letters, I think."

"Of course, my dear sister." She tittered, hand over mouth. "Naturally you wish... how *romantic.*" She sighed theatrically and, still smiling, left the room. She could be heard murmuring to Captain Edgerton in the passageway outside, before her footsteps disappeared and silence fell.

Marie sat at the writing desk, and searched for paper, pen and ink. "Your sister is so sweet," she said absently. "She fancies us to be some modern version of Romeo and Juliet — one glance was enough to send us spinning headlong into love. Whereas my primary reason for marrying in such haste is to avoid being kidnapped, and yours— What is your reason for marrying, husband?"

Her primary reason? Was there a secondary reason? And he had indeed spun headlong into love, as she well knew. But this was not the time to speak of love. Her tone was light and teasing, and he must answer in the same way.

"I married you because you asked me, wife. And to avoid you being kidnapped, naturally."

She looked up at him, laughing. "Touché! I am repaid in my own coin, I suppose. Are you going to watch me write?"

"I believe I am, yes."

She laughed again, and bent her head to the task, and he settled on the window seat to admire the swift strokes of the pen — she was so decisive, his wife! — and the way a few stray curls of hair lay tantalisingly against the creamy skin of her neck. She was half turned away from him, but he could see the gentle curve of her cheek and the long lashes fringing her eyes, curved down as she wrote then lifting when she dipped the pen in the inkstand, then down again. He could watch her all day.

"There!" she said, sanding the page. "That is the first. What do you think?"

She held it out for him.

"You want me to read your letter?"

"I want you to know exactly what I am saying to my father, so you do not wonder if there is anything secret going on. Read it while I write to my trustee."

He took the page, and read it. It was very brief.

'Lower Maeswood Grove, Great Maeswood, Shropshire. 11th June. Father, I write to inform you that I am alive and in good health. I am also this day married. My husband is Mr Malcolm Gage, whose brother Mr Laurence Gage owns this estate. Mr Gage wishes you to know that you are welcome to visit me here if you should like to do so. Your respectful daughter, Mary.'

The second letter was just as succinct.

'Lower Maeswood Grove, Great Maeswood, Shropshire. 11th June. Mr Dugard, This is to inform you that I am this day married, to Mr Malcolm Gage of this address, the estate of his brother, Mr Laurence Gage. My husband wishes to learn the details of my inheritance from my mother, the Countess of Neston, née Elizabeth Winfell. Your early attention to this matter would be appreciated. Yours, Lady Mary Gage née Fallon.'

"If you fold and seal them, I will take them to the Boar's Head myself," he said.

"Thank you, husband."

Before he left, he wrote a letter of his own, to the *Gazette* newspaper, announcing the marriage of the Lady Mary Fallon. In a few days, the whole world would know the truth. The die was cast and now there was no turning back.

24: A Visitor

Marie could not make out her new husband at all. He had seemed to be a man of passion, who declared on their second meeting that he was going to marry her, had courted her rather charmingly and had declared his love unequivocally when they had kissed. *'Je t'aime, ma chérie... je t'aime, mon doux ange.'* Who could not be delighted by such ardour? But since then, he had shown little sign of it. He had been reluctant to commit to marriage until she had publicly pushed him into it, and that wonderful kiss had not been repeated. Although he had asked for a lock of her hair. That was promising.

But perhaps he merely waited for their marriage before showing the affectionate side of his nature. So she had hoped, and she had even given him the perfect opportunity, yet when she had asked him directly why he had married her, he had answered her flippantly. He was a puzzle, but he showed no sign of regret in this hurried marriage, and there had been a certain look in his eyes as he gazed at her in church that gave her hope.

Whatever the reason for his hesitancy, she was prepared to wait for him. He was a man well worth waiting for, and perhaps he found it as difficult to speak words of love as she did. Once or twice, it had been on the tip of her tongue to tell him the truth, but somehow she always turned aside at the last moment or made a jest instead. But surely there would come a time when neither of them could avoid the question, when they would be alone in her bedchamber and there would be kisses, and surely then the sweet words would come, on her side as much as on his.

So she waited patiently as the endless day wore away, sitting demurely in a room surrounded by the busts of Roman emperors, who gazed imperiously down at her with sightless eyes. It was the day when callers might be received, seemingly, and so she, as a daughter of the house now, must sit with Viola and Louisa and Henrietta to receive the congratulations of those who came. She had her work basket beside her, but she had to lay aside her sewing frequently to join in the conversation. It was so long since she had performed the duties of a lady that she had to summon all her reserves of civility to talk to these strangers, who exclaimed over her and had to have it explained how it was that she had pretended to be a French lady's maid who spoke no English. Some thought it a very good joke, but some were disapproving, she could see, and had she not been an earl's daughter she might well have been subjected to outright hostility.

Fortunately, Malcolm and Laurence returned from some masculine excursion half way through the afternoon, and nobly joined their ladies to take their share of the congratulations. Nothing was quite so dreary when Malcolm was there.

Then there was the ceremony of dressing for dinner, and instead of attending Louisa, Marie had Sarah to help her dress, while Charu helped Louisa. Charu was such a useful person, and by virtue of being both a Gage and a drapery shop worker, managed to float effortlessly between a sort of upper servant status and the family. Marie envied her, and heartily wished she could escape the drawing room sometimes, and the unblinking scrutiny of the world.

Dinner was followed by cards at the Beasleys. Laurence, Louisa and Viola, who loved their cards, were set on going, wedding day or not.

"You two need not come, if you want a quiet evening at home," Louisa said in her matter-of-fact way.

"Oh yes, indeed! A romantic tryst! No one will mind a bit," Viola said eagerly.

But Malcolm said cheerfully, "Cards would be amusing," so there was no more to be said about it. It was almost as if he were trying to avoid being alone with his new wife.

It was indeed amusing at the Beasleys, Marie had to admit, and she was able to have a long chat to Miss Cokely about bonnets and fashions in general, so the evening was by no means a waste. Even so, she was very glad to return to the Grove, where Mr Chandry, her designated guard for the night, accompanied Malcolm and Marie to the bedroom door and then took up his station further down the corridor.

In her dressing room, she could hear Sarah moving about, laying out her night things ready, and no doubt John would be in Malcolm's dressing room. Marie had never thought she would suffer from shyness, but now she was silent, her stomach fluttering with nerves.

"Have you everything you need?" Malcolm said calmly, his tone as placid as if this were a casual meeting and not their wedding night. "Sarah will fetch you whatever you want. Sleep well, *mon coeur."*

"You will come back — will you not?" she said, in sudden distress.

He rubbed his nose. "Not tonight, *ma chérie.* Everything is — too sudden, too unsettled. We need time to grow accustomed to each other."

"But it is your right!"

He smiled then, creating a warmth inside her like a little sun glowing. "True, but I have survived without for thirty-eight years, so a little longer will not kill me. *Bonne nuit, mon ange."*

And then he was gone, the warmth inside her snuffed out like a candle. There was only the brief murmur of voices from his dressing room, and then silence.

~~~~~

For a week, Marie never left the house except to go to church, and even then Captain Edgerton and Mr Chandry marched two feet behind her, and sat either side of her in the Gage family pew. On her wedding day, she had been so caught up in the excitement of the occasion that she had barely noticed their presence, but on the following Sunday she found their close attendance horribly confining. For five years she had tiptoed through life almost unnoticed, and certainly unfettered, but now she chafed at the restriction, even as she acknowledged the necessity.

Within the house, her guards' presence was less intrusive, for one or other of them would lurk outside the door, and occasionally she would glance through the window to spy one of the Rycroft brothers or a groom from the inn patrolling the gardens. She longed for some response from her father, so that this imprisonment might end, but there was no word from him.
~~~~~

At least she was able to spend as much time as she wished with Malcolm, so each morning she sat with her sewing in the day nursery while he and Edward worked tirelessly on advancing the boy's Russian. Even though she understood none of it, she could tell that Edward rarely stumbled and Malcolm seldom corrected him. Instead, they read passages from books in Russian and then discussed what they had read. Nor were they all deeply serious, for one had Edward in gales of laughter, which Malcolm refused absolutely to explain to her.

"Some masculine jest, I presume," she said, but they just laughed all the more.

Edward's other tutors came and went for their lessons — Laurence for Greek, Miss Winslade for Italian and Mr Truman for Latin. Marie had hoped that she and Malcolm might steal away for an hour alone, but Malcolm chose to stay and participate, for he was fluent in all the languages.

"Have you nothing better to do?" Laurence said to him, with a pointed glance at Marie, but Malcolm chose not to understand.

That hurt, for the only construction she could place upon his actions was that he was purposely avoiding her, and why would he do that unless he bore some deep-seated resentment against her? If he truly loved her, as he had said, he would manufacture opportunities to be alone with her, instead of eluding them. But she kept her pain well-hidden. She had achieved her principal goal of marriage, and could wait patiently to advance the hopes of her heart.

One day, almost a week since her marriage, Marie was alone in the day nursery. She was happy to use it as her sewing room, for the big table was ideal for laying out lengths of fabric to be cut to shape and then pinned together. She was busy cutting a delicate silk fabric for Louisa when she heard voices outside the door.

It was Captain Edgerton who came in. "Your father is here," he said quietly.

"Here? He has come himself?"

The captain nodded. "He has Lord Hedlund with him."

"Richard?" She laughed in delight. "How wonderful! I shall hardly recognise him, I daresay. Is he well-grown?"

"A fine, handsome young man. How old is he now?"

"Twelve last March. He is very precious to me, for I have no other brother, nor any sisters. What is Papa like? Is he angry with me?"

"He does not seem so," Captain Edgerton said cautiously. "Where did Mr Malcolm go?"

"He is out riding with Edward." Another new habit with Malcolm. Another way of avoiding his wife's company. She stifled the stab of pain, and thought instead of her father. And he had come himself. That was unexpected.

"Mr and Mrs Gage are out, too, but Miss Viola, Miss Henrietta and Miss Charu are attending to Lord Neston and Lord Hedlund. They have brought a quantity of luggage and several servants, so I presume we are to enjoy a long visit from them. Do you wish to wait for your husband before you meet them?"

"Oh no, but... you will be there, I take it?"

"And Mr Willerton-Forbes also. We will not leave you alone with your father, not for one second."

"Thank you."

How strange it was, to be afraid of her own father, dear Papa who had always been so kind and considerate towards her, until the day he had locked her up to compel her to marry Lord Purval. Even now, she could not quite believe that he had done such a thing, or arranged for her to be seized and carried away by force. It seemed so unlike such a gentle and mild-mannered man.

She made her way slowly down the stairs, almost unwilling, now that the moment had come, to see her father at all. Her life had been so calm until recently, and she had enjoyed the tranquillity. She was not sure she could bear it if Papa were to be angry with her, and surely he must be? Her marriage to Lord Purval had been all-important five years ago, so he was bound to be... *something*. Hostile, perhaps.

Outside the Roman Saloon, she paused, all her doubts and fears rising up to drown her. Papa! Was he truly her enemy? No, she would not believe it. Straightening her back and lifting her chin, she stepped forwards. John opened the door for her, and Captain Edgerton and Mr Willerton-Forbes fell into step behind her. She strode into the room, and there he sat, directly opposite her.

Astonishingly, he looked exactly the same. An extra crease or two around the eyes, perhaps, and a few extra flecks of grey in the dark hair, but otherwise he was her dear Papa, his person as neat and dapper as always.

He saw her, his face lit up with joy and he surged to his feet. "Mary! My dearest daughter!"

Arms outstretched, he flew across the room to embrace her, hugging her so tightly she could scarcely breathe. Almost at once he released her, holding her at arm's length to examine her closely and saying anxiously, "Are you well? You look it. A little fuller in the face, perhaps. Have you been here all this time? Goodness, child, I am so happy to see you, I cannot tell you. Oh, and Richard... come here, my son. There, Mary, is he not growing into a fine young man?"

Richard shyly made a bow, and smiled rather uncertainly at her. He had been six years of age when she had last seen him. Now the rather chubby and angelic child with his mother's golden hair had grown into a gangly boy, already almost as tall as his father.

"Is he not a handsome fellow, Mary?" her father cried. "He takes after his mother in that regard, I believe. Richard, what do you think of Mary now that you see her? Is she how you remembered her? He has so little memory of you, of course," he added to Marie. "Such a long time ago! You have been sadly missed, my dear. I cannot tell you how happy it makes me to have found you again at last, and married! Where is your husband? Is he here?"

He looked quizzically at Captain Edgerton and Mr Willerton-Forbes, and to forestall further confusion, Marie said hastily, "No, Malcolm is out riding with his nephew. He will be back directly."

"What a pity. I cannot wait to meet him," her father said. "And have you known him long? What age is he? Heavens, there is so much I want to know!"

Marie laughed, but it was not an easy laugh. Her father appeared outwardly just as he always had, albeit a little more excitable than usual, and there was nothing in his manner of shame or constraint for what he had done. Was he truly as happy to see her as he claimed?

To cover her confusion, she introduced the captain and Mr Willerton-Forbes, describing them vaguely as *'helping me with some legal and other matters',* and then allowed Viola to sweep back into the conversation, as she had been burning to do. An earl in her house! Her excitement was palpable, making Marie smile. Her father responded kindly to Viola's raptures, but then he had always been so affable in company, so gentlemanly and polite.

Skeates had been busy pouring Madeira for everyone, and now the tray was passed around and Marie sat on the sofa her father had vacated. He sat beside her, beaming with such obvious joy that all her resentment melted away. This could not be pretence! He was thrilled to have found her again, that much was clear, however inexplicable his actions in the past had been. She took a sip of her Madeira, then set the glass down on a table. She was not used to strong drink any more and must keep her head clear when her father explained himself. For an explanation there must be, on that she was determined.

While the servants moved around with refreshments, the talk was general — of the Gage family, and the history of the house, and the usual questions about the neighbourhood. Papa in his turn was questioned about his journey from Northamptonshire, and Marie asked after various family members and some of the long-standing servants at Springwell Place.

After a while, however, the servants withdrew, and Charu tactfully drew Henrietta and Lord Hedlund out of the room on some pretext. There was no dislodging Viola, her curiosity too avid to prompt her to a discreet withdrawal. Captain Edgerton and Mr Willerton-Forbes stayed, too, the lawyer placidly eating macaroons while the captain sat on the edge of his chair watching Lord Neston fixedly, as if ready to spring up in an instant if the earl made any sudden movements.

Marie's father set down his plate and glass, and took her hand with a sigh. "Dearest daughter, tell me truly — have you been in Shropshire all this time? Who took care of you? Your husband? Some other man?"

"Until a week ago, no *man* took care of me," she said acidly. "I took care of myself."

"But how? How could you survive, for you had no income — nothing from your trustees, for I asked them, and they knew no more of your whereabouts than I did."

"I worked as a lady's maid for thirty guineas a year for Mrs Middlehope, who is now Mrs Gage. She lived in County Durham until March, when she moved to the Dower House here."

"A lady's maid!" he cried, shocked. "You worked for a living? My daughter earning her bread? How could you bear it?"

"I could bear it very well, when I consider the alternative. What would you have had me do, sir, sit passively in captivity until I die a shrivelled old maid? At least I have been *free!*"

And to her astonishment he smiled, he actually smiled, with not a trace of remorse. "Yes, you always were a clever little thing. I knew you would find a way out eventually, indeed I hoped you would."

There was no conceivable response to such outrageous effrontery. Snatching her hand from his grasp, she jumped to her feet and strode to the window, her breath fairly catching in her throat at his brazenness.

It was the calm tones of Mr Willerton-Forbes who intervened. "If that were indeed so, one might wonder why you undertook to confine Lady Mary at all."

"I had my reasons," Lord Neston said equably. "Good, sound reasons."

"What possible reason could you have?" Marie cried, whirling round to face him.

"That is immaterial now," her father replied, with unruffled composure. "You are married, and so the question is no longer relevant, and I am glad of it, for your sake."

"How can you say that?" Marie gasped.

"Because it is true, my dear. I never wished you the least harm, I assure you."

"But *someone* does! If not you, then who tried to kidnap me? Who tried to *kill* me?"

His eyes widened. "Kidnap you? Kill you? Good heavens, what is this? You cannot imagine— Surely you do not believe—Mary, my dear daughter, I give you my word, as God is my witness, I have not done any of those things."

"Lord Purval?"

"No! He would no more harm you than I would."

"Then who on earth was it?" Marie said despairingly.

25: A Ride In The Woods

It was Captain Edgerton who recounted to Lord Neston all that had happened in the last two weeks. His tone was clipped, almost curt, and although he was civil, it was clear that he was as angry as Marie at her father's insouciance. Even if he had had nothing to do with the kidnappers or the ruffian who had tried to kill her, he had still kept her a prisoner for a full year in order to force her to marry Lord Purval, and he should at the least demonstrate some contrition, and not pretend to be happy that she had escaped. It was unconscionable.

Lord Neston expressed his horror at the recent events and repeated that none of it was his doing.

"Did you know that Lady Mary had been found?" Captain Edgerton said. "Two of my colleagues took a drawing of her to Northamptonshire and several people identified her, some of them servants in your household, my lord. The matter reached your ears, I daresay?"

"Oh, certainly, and I was relieved to hear it."

"Relieved?" the captain said coldly.

"Indeed. It was the first word of my daughter for five years, so you may imagine how anxious I was for news. Five years without knowing whether she were alive or dead — it almost overset me to lose her."

"Yet she would not have been lost to you had you not kept her a prisoner," the captain said, and now the anger was so visible that Mr Willerton-Forbes raised a placating hand, and murmured, "Michael, Michael," in an undertone.

Lord Neston raised his brows. "I kept her *safe*," he said, in surprised tones. "Did you imagine I confined her for my own amusement? Heavens, Mary, you surely cannot have believed that of me. It was necessary, for the good of the family. If you would not marry Lord Purval, then it was essential to remove you from society altogether to avoid unpleasant confrontation. I told Purval you had gone to Scotland, and he accepted that."

"Unpleasant confrontation?" Captain Edgerton said.

"I could not force Mary to marry, but I could not permit her to marry elsewhere, either. It was better to keep her in seclusion and away from temptation, for her own good. She was well cared for, you know. She lacked for nothing."

Marie was too astonished to say anything, but the captain hissed, "Except her freedom! You imprisoned your own daughter, my lord, but she had the better of you and escaped her captivity. Did you take the trouble to look for her?"

"I did not, for so long as she was hidden from the world she was safe, and any search would jeopardise that. I came at once when she wished it. And now you are of age, daughter, and have taken matters into your own hands. It is a pity, but there we are. It is done now, and all is over. Tell me of your husband. He is a man of means, I take it?"

"He is a schoolmaster," Marie said, rather gleefully.

She could almost have laughed at the shock on her father's face.

"Or at least, he was," Marie went on remorselessly. "He has left his position temporarily to tutor his nephew. Come, Papa, you are not going to despise him for that, I trust. As a younger son, he must needs earn his bread, or marry an heiress, as he is now doing. We shall be comfortable enough once we have my inheritance."

"You refused Lord Purval, yet you would marry a *schoolmaster?"* he said coldly.

"Papa, I am very sorry if Lord Purval still harboured hopes of marrying me," she said more gently. "I know he is your good friend and you wished for the match, but you must see that it is better for me to make my own choice in the matter. The days of arranged matches are long gone. Lord Purval will understand."

"Understand... yes." He closed his eyes momentarily, one hand hiding his face. "Might I be shown my room now? I am very tired, and should like to rest."

Viola whisked him away to the bedchamber assigned to him, and Mr Willerton-Forbes followed them, leaving Marie alone with Captain Edgerton.

"What is your opinion of Papa?" she said. "I cannot make him out at all. I do not like the way he airily dismisses my imprisonment as if it was nothing."

"There is much that his lordship has not told us, I fancy, but one thing is clear — Lord Purval has some sort of hold over him. There is the question of the matter of honour that he spoke of when he tried to persuade you to marry, and that is at the root of the matter, I feel. A debt, perhaps?"

"I cannot imagine it," Marie said. "Papa has always had a good income, which he manages carefully. He is neither imprudent nor extravagant, and he does not gamble except for very modest amounts when obliged to."

"But there is something between them, and there was a change between your sixteenth birthday, when your father laughed off Lord Purval's proposal, and your seventeenth, when it was imperative that you accept," the captain said. "Still, he is to stay for a few days. We will try what Mr Neate can find out from his servants. Have no fear, whatever his secret, we shall winkle it out of him." And he grinned, his teeth gleaming.

Then, with a frown, he went on, "Where is your husband? Should he not be back by now?"

Marie's blood ran cold. A quick glance at the clock showed her that Malcolm had been gone for over two hours. "Yes, he should. These rides with Edward are never more than an hour or so, and even allowing for changes of clothes—"

"I daresay they were distracted by something interesting," the captain said soothingly. "I shall just run down to the stables to see if they are back yet. If not, I will go and find them, to tell Mr Gage that his father-in-law has arrived. I am sure he will be thrilled."

~~~~~

Malcolm told himself over and over that he enjoyed his rides with Edward. His sluggish mount was an irritant, but at least he was out in the fresh air, surrounded by the Shropshire countryside in its summer high bloom, the meadows alive with flowers and the woods a cool, green world of shimmering light and dark pools. Edward was never less than good company, in any language. But for all his lively mind, the boy was no substitute for Marie.
~~~~~

Malcolm ached to be with his bride, but he dared not be alone with her or his resolve would be all too easily overcome. Then she would be in his arms, her lips on his and he knew precisely how that would end — just where he did not want to be. It was bad enough to have married her at all when their future was so uncertain, even though he could hardly refuse under the circumstances, but there must be no child — not yet! Not until they had a home, and an income, and the confidence that the latter would support the former.

Sometimes, in his darker moments, Malcolm pondered what would happen if the worst came to pass. Well, not quite the worst, for that appalling prospect had been averted at Lichfield by Captain Edgerton's quick thinking, thank God, and Marie was well protected now. But the next worst thing would be to find themselves with no means of support. If Marie's trustees cut up rough and refused to hand over her inheritance, and if Edward failed to secure that neat little house in Oxford for Malcolm — what then would they do?

He knew the answer — he would have to return to Harrow in humiliation, and Marie would have to stay under Laurence's care at the Grove, no doubt as Louisa's lady's maid. For all Willerton-Forbes talked of finding him a position in government, or as secretary to some helpless lord, Malcolm had no confidence that he would be able to do it, or that such a post would enable him to maintain a wife, let alone a family. It was the grimmest prospect imaginable, and he could not bear to think of it. To be married to his sweet Marie, and yet separated from her — it was unendurable! Yet it was out of his power to prevent it. Every part of his future prospects depended on others.

And then, when such thoughts overwhelmed him, he remembered how much he had already endured in sixteen years of grief for the loss of Catherine. He had devised his gratitudes to overcome his own wretchedness and would do so again. There was so much to be grateful for, even when he seemed to be drowning in misery.

So he ambled along beside Edward's pony, pointing out a willow-warbler here and a patch of crane's-bill there, listening to the buzz of grasshoppers, trying very hard to enjoy it all, and failing rather badly.

Somewhere behind him a bird skittered up with a cry of alarm. That was the only warning. The next instant, there was a sharp crack and a searing pain in his shoulder. His horse shied, then tossed his head angrily. Before Malcolm had any chance to understand these confusing events, he found himself slipping sideways. He had just time to take his feet out of the stirrups before he flopped like a winged bird to the ground. There was another explosion of pain and then darkness.

~~~~~

Marie escaped to the solitude of the day nursery and her sewing to puzzle over her father, but she was not alone with her thoughts for long. Charu and Henrietta had obviously been taking Richard on a tour of the house, and had reached the upper levels. In they came, Richard smiling shyly at her, but Henrietta was on her best lady of the house behaviour and drew him away to look at the books, the boxes of tin soldiers and the paintings on the walls.

"These are for Edward to practice his language skills," she said. "He can point to the beach in this one, and Malcolm would say the word in many different languages."

"Litore?" he said.
~~~~~

"Or *litus. La plage. La spiaggia. Der strand."*

"Ooh, do the sea!" he cried.

"Das meer, I think. Uncle Malcolm would know. *Il mare..."*

Marie smiled as she listened to them. Henrietta had absorbed a great deal of knowledge from sitting listening to Malcolm and Edward. As for Richard, he was the same good-humoured boy he had always been, quite happy to play along with the game.

Charu came to sit beside Marie, chattering away about the gown Marie was working on, and in raptures about Louisa's clothes, having acted as lady's maid to her since her return from Lichfield.

John came in once to tell her that Malcolm and Edward had not yet returned and Captain Edgerton and Spencer had ridden out in search of them.

"He said to tell you it's most likely that one of the horses has cast a shoe and they're walking home from Woollercott, milady."

"Is that where they went, to Woollercott?"

"I don't know, milady, but it's very likely they went through the woods to avoid the heat, and that's where they'd end up."

But neither Charu's cheerful conversation nor John's reassurance served to remove the growing knot of fear in Marie's belly. Something had happened, something *must* have happened, or they would not stay out so long. When the clock marked three hours since they had left, Marie laid down her needle, unable any longer to pretend not to worry.

"Where *are* they?" she cried.

"Captain Edgerton will find them," Charu said. "One always fears the worst, but usually there is nothing amiss beyond the normal run of trivial mishaps — getting lost, or a lame horse, or some such. When they return, they will be astonished to learn that you were ever concerned about them."

"I suppose so, but... Edward is not a strong rider, so they do not usually go very far. I cannot imagine—"

Thundering feet on the stairs were followed almost instantly by the door bursting open, to reveal John's distressed face.

"Master Edward's brought back senseless, milady. Mr Neate found him."

"And my husband?" Marie cried, jumping to her feet.

"No sign of him, milady, but his horse returned to the stables riderless."

It was Charu who took charge of the household, for Viola was reduced to hysterics, and even Henrietta was in tears, her usual composure torn away by the sight of her brother's motionless body.

"Just got in a bit of a mill," Mr Neate said calmly, surveying the pale face on the chaise longue. "Drew his assailant's cork, though. Full of pluck, he is. I shall run up for the physician."

"I have sent the boy already," Charu said. "John has gone to find Mr and Mrs Gage, and one of the grooms is to ride after Captain Edgerton. Mrs Blenkinsop, that cushion, if you please, then some hot water and cloths. Did you examine him for broken bones, Mr Neate?"

"Nothing broken that I can see, but Dr Beasley will check him thoroughly."

"But if he fell from his horse—"

"Not a fall," he said tersely. "The fellow was running away, and Master Edward chased him through the woods on horseback. By the time I came up with them, he had caught him and laid him out flat, but the fellow got up and started whacking him back. He was much bigger than Master Edward, so it only took him a couple of good punches to do for him. Then he took Master Edward's horse and rode off on it, if you please. I tried to grab the bridle but he as good as ran me down."

"Where was this?" Marie said.

"Maeswood, just at the back of Green Lawns."

"But why was he running away? Why was Edward chasing him? Where was my husband?"

"I can't answer any of that for certain, Lady Mary. What I do know is that this man is a stranger, a man with yellow hair who arrived in the village yesterday and stayed at the inn overnight. I was following him, thinking he might be the same man who attacked you at Lichfield, but I lost him in the woods. Never saw him again until I encountered Master Edward in hot pursuit. As to why he was running, all I can tell you is that just a minute or two before that, there was a sound like a gun being fired. And now, forgive me, but I must go and look for your husband. I shall start in the woods to the south of the Grove, since that, as best I can tell, is where the shot was fired."

~~~~~

Marie found herself in a nightmare that seemed to have no end. Every man of the household, even her father and brother, was engaged on the search for Malcolm, and half the village had been mobilised to help, yet hour after hour passed with no news.
~~~~~

Laurence had gone out with the dogs, despite being desperately worried about Edward. Louisa and Henrietta kept vigil at his bedside, and there at least the reports were promising, for little by little he was returning to his senses, although not yet enough to talk. Not enough to suggest where Malcolm might be lying, or how badly injured he might be.

Viola was still prostrate, and Charu was engaged in directing the household, so Marie passed the endless hours sitting in the Roman Saloon. She was not alone, however. Miss Beasley came with her brother, and sat with her. The other ladies of the village came, too, in ones and twos, spoke in hushed voices, stayed for a while and then went away, but Miss Beasley never left her. She made no attempt to talk to Marie, for which she was grateful, but when there was no one else there, she read aloud from the Psalms or from a book of sermons she had brought with her, her voice quiet but clear. It was a comfort, of sorts, and Marie carefully tended the tiny flame of hope that still burned inside her. Several times it burned low and almost flickered out of existence, but each time she told herself sternly that until she *knew* beyond all doubt that he was dead, then there was still a chance.

It was ten o'clock before they found him, and only the long summer evening allowed them to continue the search so long, for the trees grew too close in Maeswood to risk torches. He was lying in a meadow on the far side of the woods, quite still, the grass around his shoulder stained from his blood. But he was alive. There was still hope.

After so many hours of waiting, the sudden rush of activity was almost too much to bear. The house was full of men, carrying the still form into the hall on a hurdle, and then up the stairs in a blanket to his room.

Oh God, his white face! But he was alive, he still breathed...

Dr Beasley was there, murmuring encouraging words. The housekeeper and maid rushed about with candles, filling the sconces. Another maid with candelabra. Charu with cloths. Hot water, the house medicine chest, extra chairs. A tray of decanters and glasses. So much turmoil. Marie caught a glimpse of her father amongst the other men, but he merely nodded to her, his face serious, and went away with the rest. Then it was only the doctor, Laurence and Marie. And Malcolm.

The doctor settled to his work, checking for broken bones, then snipping away clothing, cleaning, probing, more cleaning. Marie could not tear her eyes away, but Laurence gently shepherded her to a chair, and poured brandy for them both.

"Drink. Have you had anything to eat this evening?"

Mutely she shook her head.

He went to the door, and murmured to someone outside. Then he came back and sat beside her. "Drink," he said again. "I have sent for some food, and I want to hear no nonsense about having no appetite. You will be no use to Mal if you are swooning from lack of food." His voice was soft, sympathetic.

"How is Edward?"

"He will do well enough. Nothing is broken, thank God. Malcolm will be pleased with him, though, for his first words were in Russian."

She smiled wanly at this sally.

"Mal is a tough old buzzard," Laurence said quietly. "He has been lying in that field all afternoon, and here he still is, slightly the worse for wear and with a hole in one shoulder, but still with us. He will be as good as new in a few days, you will see."

She smiled again, and although she was no more confident of Malcolm's survival than before, her spirits lifted a little.

John brought food on a tray, and obediently Marie ate a little, although she could not remember afterwards what she had eaten. The brandy, even taken in small sips, was more effective in soothing her jangled nerves.

Eventually, Dr Beasley sat back with a sigh. "There. I have done all I can for him, poor fellow, and now he is in God's hands."

It was not reassuring.

26: Honey And Cold Water

It was John who stayed with Marie through the dark hours of the night. Charu came and went from time to time, and Louisa and Laurence both looked in with favourable reports of Edward's progress, but mostly Marie and John were alone with the silent figure in the bed.

At six o'clock the next morning, Dr Beasley came, declared himself satisfied with the patient, and went away again.

At seven o'clock, Henrietta came, white-faced, and asked if she could do anything, or relieve Marie while she slept.

"Thank you, but I could not sleep."

At eight o'clock, Viola arrived, supported by Mrs Blenkinsop, but determined to rise from her own sickbed to gaze upon the two invalids. Since the sight of Malcolm's immobile form instantly reduced her to loud sobs, her visit could not be said to be helpful.

At nine o'clock, Mrs Blenkinsop came in. "Begging pardon, milady, but I thought you'd want to know that Lord Neston is preparing to depart."

"Leaving? But why?" she cried. Mrs Blenkinsop looked startled. "No, of course you would not know."

She flew down the stairs. The entrance hall was a maelstrom of servants, but there were no boxes and no carriage outside the door. Nor was there any sign of her father. Richard was standing forlornly to one side.

"Where is Papa?" Marie said.

"Upstairs somewhere," Richard said glumly.

"Is it true? That you are leaving?"

He shook his head. "Not me. Only Papa."

"Oh." That was unexpected. "He is leaving you behind?"

"Mr Gage said he would be very happy for me to stay as long as Papa wishes, although he seemed a bit surprised about it. He said he wondered greatly at Papa. How is Mr Malcolm?"

"Oh... the same. Did Papa say why he must go away in such a rush, and not take you with him?"

Richard shrugged. "He said he had urgent business that could not be delayed."

Laurence and Louisa came swiftly down the stairs, their faces serious.

Seeing Laurence, Marie said, "Do you know why Papa is leaving, sir?"

"He has not confided his reasons to me," Laurence said. "But you may ask him yourself, for here he is."

She spun round. Her father was walking towards her, hat and gloves in hand, while behind him footmen laboured with a large box.

"Papa! What is all this? Why are you leaving so abruptly?"

He frowned, seemingly more puzzled than annoyed. "Abruptly? I always planned to leave as soon as I had ascertained your circumstances. Now that I have done so, I must stay no longer." Calmly he pulled on his gloves, one after the other.

"But why are you leaving Richard behind?" she cried, her voice rising with her anger. "Why are you running away?"

For the first time, his expression showed some emotion. "I am not running *away*, quite the opposite. Daughter, you have chosen your own path in life, as is your right, and we must all bear the consequences of that. Richard, you will wait here until I send word."

"Yes, Papa. How long will that be?"

His shoulders slumped. "I cannot say. And now, I hear my carriage being brought round, so I shall bid you farewell." With a few words of polite gratitude to the Gages, he strode out of the door and down the steps to his carriage. Within a very few minutes, he was gone.

Marie could not make head or tail of it, nor did she much care at that moment. Her husband was teetering on the edge of death, and unless her father could make him well again, she could not summon the slightest interest in him. Only Malcolm mattered now. She spun round and made her way back to his bedside. He had not stirred.

Miss Beasley arrived not long after, with a different book of sermons and her workbag. She dispatched John to get some sleep, and ordered a chaise longue to be brought in for Marie.

"I could not sleep," Marie protested.

"Naturally you cannot," Miss Beasley said in her quiet voice, "but it will do you all the good in the world to rest in a horizontal position for a while, for there is nothing so fatiguing as sitting in a chair for hours at a time, is there? And you may be quite comfortable to rest your eyes from time to time, for I shall sit beside Malcolm and watch over him. I am perfectly used to helping Roland with his patients, so I know all the little signs to observe. I am sure now that Roland has eased the wound and removed every fragment of the bullet, Malcolm will be coming to himself again very shortly."

Marie had not the energy to resist such a kindly offer, so she dutifully lay down and closed her eyes, just to rest them.

~~~~~

When she woke, the sun had moved so far round that the room seemed almost gloomy. Miss Beasley had taken her chair to the window and was quietly reading. Malcolm had not moved.

"How long have I slept?"

"Ah, you are awake again — splendid. You will feel much better. It is almost three o'clock, and Malcolm has not stirred. Roland has been in twice to check on him, and there is nothing at all to be concerned about."

Gingerly, for the chaise longue was not very soft and she was rather stiff, Marie sat up. Miss Beasley closed her book and crossed the room with quick steps.

"There are cakes and pastries over here. Have a little something to eat, just to please me, and perhaps half a glass of wine, and you will feel much more the thing, I assure you."

Obediently, Marie ate a little and drank a little, all the time watching Malcolm. "Has he moved at all?"

"No, but that is quite normal. He lost a great deal of blood, so he is recruiting his strength, as it were. There is no sign of
~~~~~

fever at present, but we shall watch him most carefully. I shall stay and keep watch with you for as long as you want."

Marie tried to reconcile this sensible and competent woman with the little mouse of a creature she had seen scuttling about the village in Viola's wake, head down, clutching her reticule to her bosom. "You are very good, Miss Beasley. You have such a reassuring way about you that I believe you would have made an excellent physician yourself, had you been a man. Thank you for staying with me."

She flushed with pleased surprise. "It is nothing, but of course I have helped Roland so much, sitting with his patients just like this, since he has so many other calls on his time, and I have none. Medicine is so fascinating to me. I read his medical books sometimes, so that I may understand when he talks to me of his patients. He finds it helpful, he says. That is the advantage of having no husband of my own, nor any children to occupy me, that I may be useful to my brother."

"Just as Miss Gage is useful to her brother, also," Marie said.

"Very true. I do not know what Laurence would have done without Viola. So thrilling that he has found happiness again, and after so many years as a widower, too. And Malcolm, of course. He waited all these years until he met you, and I cannot tell you how delighted it makes me. God works in mysterious ways, does He not? Shall I read to you for a while? If you are not tired of my voice, that is. If you prefer silence, do say so. I have the second volume of Dr Deerham's sermons, which arrived only yesterday from Shrewsbury, but I can read quietly if you prefer."

"I should like to listen to you read, Miss Beasley. Your voice is very soothing."

"Soothing! How very kind you are to say so, Lady Mary." And so she picked up her book and read Dr Deerham's words, which in his stentorian tones would have been both rousing and admonitory, but in Miss Beasley's mellower voice were no more than gently reproachful. Marie sat, hands folded, and listened without interruption, all the time with her eyes fixed on Malcolm's inert form in the bed.

This quietude lasted no more than an hour before Malcolm began to grow restless, and before long it was clear that fever was setting in. Dr Beasley arrived, his expression grim.

"I shall have to bleed him," he said. "There is no help for it. Will you find a basin, Phyllida?"

"Is this truly necessary, Roland?" Miss Beasley said. "He has lost so much blood already, he surely cannot need to lose more."

"The body cannot lie," Dr Beasley said firmly. "He is hot, you see? Feel his forehead, and his pulse is tumultuous. He is out of balance and must be bled, and there is an end to it. We will need to build up the fire, too, and flush the fever out of him." He began to roll up his sleeves.

All Marie's instincts rebelled against bleeding. "Dr Beasley, my husband lay in that field for nine or ten hours, as his life's blood reddened the soil around him. He does *not* need to lose any more of it, I am certain of that."

"You would set yourself and your certainty against my years of medical experience?" he said gently. "You would weigh your woman's intuition, based on nothing at all, against my knowledge of the human body?"

Before she could answer, Miss Beasley said in her quiet way, "What about a cooling regimen, Roland? That might answer, do you not think? We could cool him by sponging with water when the fever is hot. And perhaps apply honey to his wound, too. Aunt Marjory used to swear by honey and vinegar, and she said she never had a wound turn putrid in forty years."

"Cold water… hmm, increase the phlegm rather than reduce the choler… that might be sufficient, perhaps, if the fever is not too great. And the honey and vinegar will do no harm. Very well, I shall have Edser send a cooling concoction and some laudanum, but we must watch him very carefully indeed. I shall review the situation in the morning, Lady Mary, but you may call me at any hour if you have concerns. I remember when Malcolm was born, and have watched him grow to manhood — I should be very sorry to lose him now."

"I have known him for precisely five weeks, but I should be very sorry to lose him, too, Dr Beasley," Marie said with dignity.

"Of course, my dear," he said, raising one arm as if to pat her shoulder, then thinking better of it. "We must hope it does not come to that."

That was not reassuring, and for some hours it seemed that the physician's fears might be well founded. Malcolm grew hotter and more restless, occasionally mumbling something unintelligible. Marie and Miss Beasley sponged him regularly, but it seemed to do little good. Nor could Mr Edser's cooling concoction help, for they found it impossible to get Malcolm to take any of it.

Miss Beasley went home as darkness fell and John took her place, and that was better, for he had the strength to lift Malcolm up and hold him so that Marie could help him to drink. He took some of the herbal concoction, and a small dose of laudanum, and after that he seemed more settled.

Marie dowsed most of the candles and lamps, leaving just one candle burning near the bed. John fell asleep in a chair, his gentle snoring the only sound in the room. Marie ate a little from her supper tray with half a glass of wine and then pulled her chair nearer to Malcolm. He had somehow rolled onto one side, so he was lying facing her, the blankets pushed away from him so that his chest was exposed, his injured shoulder uppermost. His nightshirt had slipped open so that she could see a stretch of bare skin below his throat. He looked so vulnerable lying there, his face pale with the sheen of fever upon him, his hands twitching and his lips still restlessly trying to say something.

Her heart ached to see her sturdy husband laid so low. How could she bear it if he died! No, she must not think that way. He would get well, he would smile at her again and gaze at her with those intense blue eyes, and murmur *'Je t'aime'* in her ear, he *must*. If only there were some way she could heal him. If love could do it, if her love could reach out to his injured shoulder and mend it and drive away the fever, he would be well again in a moment, for her heart was so full it overflowed with love for this strange, solitary man. He had seen through her self-imposed mask to the terrified woman huddled inside, and held out his hand to her. She, who had thought her heart made of ice, had melted for him. If only she could wrap her love around him, and keep him safe for ever! If only she could touch him...

She reached out one finger and gently stroked his face. His agitation stilled at once. "Hush, my love," she whispered. "Sssh. Everything will be all right, I promise." Gently she placed her hand against his cheek, rough with stubble. "Hush, now, husband. All will be well."

Again he mumbled something, but she could not make out the words. No point in trying, with Malcolm, for it was just as likely to be Ancient Greek as English.

All of a sudden, she was overwhelmed with despair. How useless she was! There was nothing — *nothing* — she could do to help him, except sit beside him and worry endlessly and pray. And cry, she realised. Tears flooded down her face in protest at her own helplessness. But Malcolm lay still as death under her hand, all his restlessness gone for the moment. His lips moved slightly, but the rest of him was quiescent.

She could touch him. That was something she could do. She could not hold him, not properly, because of his wounded shoulder, but she could touch him and talk to him.

Gingerly she pushed the bed covers back a little way and, with infinite care, slipped into bed beside him. Beside her husband, for where else should she be? That was her rightful place, at his side. He stirred a little, and a sound almost like a sigh escaped his lips.

"Hush, my sweet husband, hush now." Cradling his face, she smiled through her tears. "Sssh. Everything is all right, for we are together now. We will always be together, husband, whatever happens. We will never, ever be parted because I love you, you great big fool of an irritating man. I love you so much, my darling. *Je t'aime, mon cheri. Je t'aime. Je t'aime."*

He murmured something, seeming to lean into her hand. "Hush," she said. He was so close, close enough that she could feel his breath warm on her cheeks. So close...

She kissed him. Then, with a little sob, she kissed him again and yet again, but there was no response.

After that, she could only cry.

~~~~~

Marie woke to John moving around the room, opening curtains and adjusting the windows. The morning light streamed in.

"He's got a better colour on him this morning," John said, from the foot of the bed. "Sleeping soundly, too. Shall I fetch you some coffee? Or chocolate?"

Malcolm had rolled away from her again, and now lay on his back, his head leaning towards her. She pushed the covers back and sat up. She had slept well, she realised, for she felt... not happy, exactly, but more optimistic. The quiet desperation of the dark hours had fled. "Chocolate, I think," she said. "And some buns or pastries, perhaps. What o'clock is it?"

"Between five and six," he said. "I'm sorry I slept for so long, milady. I never meant to drop off like that, or at least not for more than an hour or so."

"We both needed the sleep," Marie said. "If he had grown restless again, we would have woken instantly. No harm done." And she could only hope that was true.

Dr Beasley and Miss Beasley arrived not long after six. The physician declared himself satisfied with Malcolm's progress, and graciously agreed to allow Marie to continue the cold water sponging regimen.

Laurence came to see his brother, and the anguish on his face was clear to see.

"He will be all right, will he not?" he said, looking at Marie anxiously. "He is recovering, yes?"
~~~~~

"Dr Beasley believes so," she said cautiously. "Is there any word on who is responsible?"

"Not yet. Edgerton has people scouring the woods and searching the barns, but for myself, I think the blackguard is long gone. He had Edward's horse, which is no fast mount, but steady enough to get him to Shrewsbury if he wished. He could sell it there and pay for his ticket on a stage coach. Even the indomitable Captain Edgerton will not find this fellow."

"And Edward? Is he any better?"

"Bright as a button this morning. Complaining of extreme hunger, and grumbling at being confined to his bed, so I suspect there will be no lasting ill-effects," Laurence said, a smile lighting his face abruptly.

Marie laughed. "That is excellent news. Has he told you what happened?"

"Only that he heard a shot fired, saw Malcolm fall and when he turned and saw the man running into the woods, he gave chase. But there was one piece of interesting information. He thinks this is the same man he saw in Lichfield who tried to kill you, Marie. A tall young man with yellow hair, quite distinctive. Neate suspected it, but Edward has now confirmed it. But that is so strange, for why would he be so set on killing you, only to then attempt to kill Malcolm? It makes little sense to me."

She considered that. "I think the only person who can shed light on this is my father, who has fled the scene."

And that was exactly what it felt like, a criminal rushing away in guilt. Was he responsible for shooting Malcolm? Had he perhaps authorised someone to act on his behalf, then, faced with the consequences of his actions, had fled? What was it he had said... *'you have chosen your own path in life and we must all bear the consequences of that'.* The consequences of her marriage? But why would that cause him to run away? No, not run away, quite the opposite, or so he had said.

Laurence pulled a face. "True, and we cannot even write to him, since we have no direction for him. This is such a dreadful business, Marie. First you, then Malcolm. He will get better, will he not? He is strong and—" For a moment, he covered his face with one hand. "He *must* get better!"

"He is more settled this morning," Marie said. "The fever seems to have abated somewhat."

"I beg your pardon," he said with a deep sigh. "It is for me to offer reassurance to you, not the other way round, and I have not been here to support you as I should."

"You have had Edward to think about. He is your principal concern, as Malcolm is mine," she said.

"True, but I should have— Well, it is foolish to continually repeat my apology. Since Edward is so much better today, Louisa and I will take it in turns to sit with Malcolm to relieve you."

With Miss Beasley, John, Charu, Laurence and Louisa, Marie had not a moment alone with Malcolm that day until Miss Beasley went home and the others went down for dinner. John would have stayed with her, but Malcolm was sleeping quietly and Marie wanted an hour to herself, so she sent him away, too.

After eating a little from her dinner tray, she brought out a piece of sewing and settled down near Malcolm, with a glass of wine on the bedside table beside her. It was peaceful sitting beside her husband, listening to his soft breathing, as the light from the window slowly dimmed. She rose once to light a lamp, carefully shading it to shield Malcolm from the glare, and returned to her sewing.

"Marie?"

His eyes were open. His position had not changed, but those blue eyes were fixed on her. "Oh, you are awake at last! How do you feel? Are you in pain?"

"Not much. What happened? Did I fall off my horse?"

That made her smile. "In a way. You were shot while you were out riding with Edward."

He frowned, as if trying to remember. "Was I? Why? When?"

"Two days ago, and no one knows why yet. Captain Edgerton will find out."

"Captain Edgerton…" Again, there was a frown. "Two days…" But then he suddenly smiled at her so warmly that it was as if he had lit a fire within her. "I dreamt of you."

"Did you? You had a touch of fever, so it is not surprising if you were tormented by strange visions."

"Not a torment," he said, still smiling. "It was lovely."

"Was it?"

"Mmm. You kissed me and said that you loved me. Who could describe such a thing as torment? But…" Another frown. "You were crying. Did I make you cry, *mon ange?* Or was that just my imagination too? Was any of it real?"

"All of it," she whispered. "All of it was real, *mon amour."*

"Ah." He smiled and gave a little sigh, and Marie thought it the most glorious sound she had ever heard. He would live. Her splendid husband would live, after all, and life was wonderful.

27: Two More Visitors

Marie had imagined her joy at Malcolm's recovery could not be dented. Within a very few hours she found out how wrong she was. The next morning, having taken a little breakfast, Malcolm had drifted back to sleep when Captain Edgerton appeared, his expression rueful. With a finger to her lips, she shepherded him out of the room, closing the door softly behind her.

The captain gave a wry smile. "Believe it or not, Lord Purval has arrived. Mr Gage asks what you would like done with him."

"Lord Purval! Good heavens! But why?"

"To congratulate you on your marriage, possibly?"

Marie laughed, despite herself. "If only it were so! Perhaps he has forgiven me for not wishing to marry him, and in fact disliking the idea so much that I ran away and hid for five years. Does he wish to stay here?"

"He says the Saxbys will accommodate him at the Hall as an old friend of Lord Saxby's, but Mr Gage feels that, under normal circumstances, since he is here explicitly to see you, it would be polite to make the invitation. These are hardly normal circumstances, however, so it is for you to say."

"What is your advice?" she said.

"That it is better to have him here where we can keep an eye on him. I am very curious as to his motives, but you know him better than anyone else. Will you watch out for anything untoward in his person or his manner? Or anything different about him. Mr Gage has some acquaintance with him, too, so I have made the same request of him."

"Of course I will. Do you then suspect him of involvement in these various attacks? I cannot see why he would attempt to kill me."

"I suspect everyone, always," he said, with a wolfish grin. "Since it was his desire to marry you which precipitated all the disturbing events of your life, we must regard him with caution, do you not agree? After all, he could have sent his congratulations in a letter. He must have some reason to travel all this way."

"Very well, I will let you know if I notice anything."

Leaving Miss Beasley with Malcolm, and Mr Chandry patrolling the corridor outside his room, she accompanied Captain Edgerton down the stairs and into the Roman Saloon.

Lord Purval had changed more than her father. His hair that had once been merely speckled with grey now showed no sign of colour at all, and the comfortable, loose-fitting coats she remembered had been abandoned for attire that would not have looked out of place on Bond Street. The smile was unchanged, however, and as she entered the room, it was fixed on Richard. The two sat side by side on a sofa, and Lord Purval had one arm around the boy's shoulders, bejewelled fingers idly playing with his hair.

He turned at her entrance and the smile widened even more. “Ah, Lady Mary,” he cried, leaping to his feet to bow low. “Wonderful, wonderful! Felicitations! Wish you joy, dear girl.”

Marie made some bland response, and they sat and exchanged meaningless courtesies for ten minutes, while she wondered what under the sun was his real motive for visiting. Viola, of course, was all a-twitter, delighted beyond measure to have another lord in the house, albeit only a baron. Marie amused herself by imagining Viola rushing out at the earliest moment, bonnet askew in excitement, to spread the word of the latest arrival at the Grove.

The rest of the family looked bemused, as well they might, although they made sterling efforts to maintain the conversation at the prescribed banal level. They had just moved beyond the state of the roads and begun discreet enquiries about Lord Purval’s estate, enquiries which he would be more than happy to answer for he was never more enthusiastic than when talking about his beloved Strachan Park, when the door knocker sounded again.

“Goodness!” Viola said. “How popular we are today. I shall just go and see— Yes, Skeates, I am just coming.”

The butler bore a silver salver with a calling card. “Beg pardon, madam, but this is for the Lady Mary Gage.”

“For me?” Bewildered, Marie took the card. “It is Mr Dugard, my trustee. At last! I expected word from him long since, but this accounts for the delay — he has come himself. Mr Gage, is there a room free where I might talk privately to Mr Dugard?”

“The library,” he said at once. “Do you wish for anyone to accompany you?”

"I will come with you," Lord Purval said smoothly. "Best have some support. Always good to have a friend by your side, and I have some experience in dealing with men of law."

Now, why should Lord Purval offer to support her? She could not think of a reason, but nor could she find a reason to refuse. "Thank you. That would be helpful."

Mr Willerton-Forbes said smoothly, "You will need your marriage lines, Lady Mary."

"So I will. Thank you, sir."

In the hall, she greeted Mr Dugard, introduced him to Lord Purval and left Skeates to show the gentlemen to the library and furnish them with refreshments while she went upstairs to her room, the silent Captain Edgerton following her. When she returned to the hall with her marriage lines, she found Mr Willerton-Forbes awaiting her.

"Forgive my impertinence, my lady, but have you ever talked to Lord Purval about your trustees?"

"No, never. It can hardly concern him, can it? Why do you ask?"

"I only wondered how he knew Mr Dugard to be a lawyer. Trustees sometimes are, but it is not a universal rule." She was silent, pondering the implications of that, so he continued, "Would you care to instruct another lawyer to be party to your discussions with Mr Dugard? Such as myself, for example?"

His expression was so hopeful that she could not help laughing. "I have not always cared for your lawyerly advice in the past, Mr Willerton-Forbes, but that proves you to be impartial. I should be most grateful for your wisdom on this occasion."

In the library, she found Lord Purval at his ease in one of four chairs arranged in a semi-circle around the cold hearth. Mr Dugard was hovering uncertainly with a small bag in his hand, as Skeates arranged food and drink.

"Mr Dugard, this is Mr Willerton-Forbes, who is—" Marie began, then broke off at the gasp Dugard emitted. "Whatever is it?"

"Willerton-Forbes?" Mr Dugard said faintly, his face ashen.

"You may have heard of my uncle, Sir Rathbone Willerton-Forbes."

"Of course, but... but..." He spluttered for a while, then, licking his lips, said cautiously, "And you, sir. Your reputation precedes you. My lord, this gentleman is the lawyer who acted for the Benefactor after the sinking of... of..."

"The *Brig Minerva*," Mr Willerton-Forbes said smoothly. "A famous case. I was privileged to be of service."

"I recall it," Lord Purval said. "Most tragic. Lady Mary, pray take a seat. Mr Willerton-Forbes? Begin, Dugard."

Mr Dugard pulled a sheaf of papers from his bag, dropped them, bent to retrieve them, dropped a few more. The others waited patiently while he got himself and his papers to the last remaining chair.

"Do you wish for a table upon which to rest your documents?" Marie said.

"No, indeed. How very kind but..." Several more sheets fluttered to the floor.

Marie laid down her marriage lines on the side table beside her chair, rose and crossed the room. Picking up a delicate octagonal side table, she carried it across to the circle of chairs and placed it in front of Mr Dugard. Mr Willerton-Forbes jumped up to assist. While Mr Dugard laid the untidy heap of papers on the table and brought them into some sort of order, Marie sipped the glass of wine at her elbow and covertly watched Lord Purval.

What was he doing there? It was the oddest thing in the world to drive all this way, a two day journey, if all he wanted was to offer his congratulations on her marriage. And then Mr Dugard had arrived hard on his heels, and here was Lord Purval, worming his way into the interview. It was a strange coincidence, if coincidence it was. She was glad she had Mr Willerton-Forbes at her side to protect her from mischief, although what mischief might be afoot she could not imagine.

Mr Dugard pulled a pair of spectacles from some inner fastness of his coat and perched them precariously on his nose. He was a spare man, and his nose was as sharp and thin as a ship's prow. "Now then, Lady Mary," Mr Dugard began. "You are recently married to a... to a Mr... um..." He shuffled papers about in a helpless fashion.

"Mr Malcolm Gage," Marie said. "I have my marriage lines here."

"Ah, thank you, thank you. That is most helpful." He perused the paper for some time, before saying, "By licence? Was there a reason for that, my lady?"

"Yes. Someone tried to kidnap me," she said coldly. "It seemed to me that I would be safer married than not."

"Kidnap?" For a moment he goggled at her, but Lord Purval gestured to him to continue, so he licked his lips and rushed on, "Licence... licence... um... Then your betrothal is of long-standing? It was merely... brought forward?"

"I cannot see— But there is no reason to conceal the truth. I had known my husband for four weeks when we married. Not quite four weeks," she added punctiliously.

"I see." He smiled, and somehow that was more unsettling than the intrusive questions. "So — Mr Malcolm Gage. Tell me about your husband, Lady Mary. This is his brother's house, as I understand it?"

"Yes. My husband is the younger brother."

"Then he has an estate of his own? A profession?"

"No and no."

"His income?"

"Is this relevant?" she said. "He is my legally wed husband, and therefore fully entitled to take control of my inheritance."

"Ah, now in theory, that is so, Lady Mary. Yes, in theory, you are perfectly correct, and it may be so in practice also. Let us hope it is so. But as your trustees, you will appreciate that I and my fellows must take certain precautions... we have to be very careful that all is in order. There is a duty imposed upon us, in law, that requires us to—"

"Mr Dugard," Marie said, tiring of this circumlocution, "my mother left some money to me, is that correct?"

"An inheritance, yes."

"And that *inheritance* is to be made over to me when I marry or when I reach the age of twenty-five, is that so?"

"In principle, yes, but—"

"Very well, let us hear the *'but'*, Mr Dugard."

He pulled at his neckcloth, as if it were too tight. The smile had vanished. When he spoke, his voice was no more than a whisper. "Very well, my lady. There are certain... constraints laid upon us as trustees... upon all trustees... to act in the best interests of the person in whose stead we act. In such a case as yours, the duty laid upon us is very clearly that we must protect you from... from those who would take advantage of you. In short, from fortune hunters, my lady. To that end, we have agreed certain tests which must be met by any man who wishes to become your husband."

With a great sense of foreboding, Marie said, "And these tests — what are they?"

Mr Dugard tugged at his neckcloth again. "Firstly, that he be a gentleman of independent means. Secondly, that there should be nothing underhanded or... or *hasty* in the marriage. And thirdly, that your father agrees to the match."

There was a long, long silence. Somewhere in the distance, a horseman clip-clopped past. In the hall, the long-case clock chimed the half hour, counting out the seconds as disbelief settled in Marie's stomach.

"You are going to refuse, are you not, Mr Dugard? You are going to claim that my husband is disqualified in some way, and therefore I cannot have the inheritance that my mother left to me. You are going to leave me in poverty, all the while claiming that you are acting in my best interests and protecting me from fortune hunters. That bird has flown, sir, for I am already married, in case you had not noticed. You protect me from nothing. I am of age and entitled to choose my own husband, and entitled to the money that is mine by right. Is it not so, Mr Willerton-Forbes?"

"That depends on the precise wording of the terms of the trust fund," he said slowly. "Mr Dugard will not object, I am sure, if I examine the documents?"

"No, no!" he said, eyes widening. "There is no need— I do not have them here— They are private—" He pushed his papers into a neater pile on the table. One slid to the floor and he reached to retrieve it in such haste that he dislodged several more. He got down on his knees to gather them, then scrambled all the papers back into his bag.

"As you wish," Mr Willerton-Forbes said, equably, but his eyes gleamed with interest.

"Mr Willerton-Forbes is my legal adviser," Marie began. "He is surely—"

With a delicate wave of one hand, his signet ring glinting, Mr Willerton-Forbes said, "It is not important, Lady Mary. Mr Dugard has given us all the information we need." He smiled, and reached for his glass of Madeira, adding casually, "Are you staying here tonight, Mr Dugard?"

"Um... I thought the inn?"

"Oh, I am sure Mr and Mrs Gage would be delighted to accommodate you here. So much more commodious than an inn, would you not agree? One is never quite certain if the airing of the sheets has been undertaken to the necessary degree."

Not knowing what he was up to, but game, Marie said, "The food is appallingly bad at the inn. Mrs Brownsmith is said to be the world's worst cook. You had much better stay here. Mrs Gage has a first rate man-cook."

"Oh... then... that would be most agreeable," Mr Dugard said helplessly.

~~~~~

Malcolm gingerly sat up in bed. His shoulder ached appallingly and he felt as weak as a new-born babe, but he was alive and more or less intact. John had washed and shaved him, and helped him into a clean nightshirt, and then Marie had sat with him, composedly sewing and answering his many questions, while John and Captain Edgerton fended off other visitors.

He was glad of it. He could not have borne Viola weeping over him, or Henrietta's anxious face, but Marie exuded calm. She was not someone who fussed over a person, but he recalled her weeping beside him at night and whispering impassioned words of love into his ear, and knew that she cared about him. Was it love that she felt, or was she merely upset that her protector against an enforced marriage might die? He could not say, but she was not indifferent to him, and she was there, by his side, where he could look at her all day, and that was immeasurably cheering. Wherever Marie was, there also was tranquillity and a blissful state of happiness that nothing could puncture.

But now she was gone. They had had breakfast together and then he had fallen asleep, and when he woke, John was there, sorting through handkerchiefs.

"Where is my wife?" That was such a thrill — *my wife.*

"Downstairs with a visitor. A Lord Purval."

"Lord Purval?" What on earth could he want? Then, curiously, "I have not seen him for years. What is he like now?"

"A fine fellow indeed, if you like overdressed dandies," John said. "Now that Mr Willerton-Forbes, he's fashionable too but he
~~~~~

looks as if he thought about what he was wearing and didn't just pull pieces from the press at random."

"You dislike Lord Purval, I think," Malcolm said, amused.

"Can't like a man who wears so much jewellery. Never saw so many rings on one person."

It was an hour before Marie came back, and her face was stormy. "Mr Dugard is here and he is disinclined to make my inheritance over to you, since he believes you to be a fortune hunter. A fortune hunter! The insolence of the man! He tells me in one breath that his duty is to protect my interests and in the next that he will see me starve rather than give me what is mine."

"Well, that is a blow, certainly, but perhaps it may be challenged. Have you talked to Willerton-Forbes about it?"

"Oh yes." She giggled. "He is such a funny little man, but very clever, do you not think? He asked to see the documents relating to the trust fund, and Mr Dugard made some excuse or other. Mr Willerton-Forbes told me not to worry about it, and he has a plan."

"A plan, eh? I wonder what he is up to?"

The rest of the day passed off peacefully. Marie was persuaded to go down to dinner.

"You absolutely must," Louisa said firmly, "for otherwise the gentlemen will quite outnumber us, and the conversation will be all about agricultural methods or the rain barrels at the smithy or some other dreary subject."

"And I know Lord Purval," Marie said, with a wry smile.

"Well, yes, and perhaps you can steer him off the subject of his house. I am sure Strachan Park is very beautiful, but one likes some variation in discourse. Do come! Malcolm will not mind."

Malcolm did not mind, at least not so much as to object. Much as he enjoyed Marie's company, he was not so selfish as to keep her from the livelier society to be found downstairs. Besides, he very much wanted her to take her rightful place in the family.

He had the compensation of dinner with the irrepressible Edward and his new friend, Lord Hedlund. He was a quiet boy, who ate his meal with fastidious neatness, and watched Edward with open admiration as he hopped from one language to another.

"Do you truly not remember being shot?" Edward asked in Russian, as soon as he had established the words for *'shot', 'blood', 'wound'* and *'villain'*.

"Not a thing," Malcolm said cheerfully. "You must describe it to me in full, omitting no detail, and you may embellish it as much as you wish, for I shall know no different."

"Captain Edgerton would be very cross if I... um, embellished anything. He says that a... what is the word for crime? Thank you. When there is a crime, it is very important to tell the exact truth, and only what a person has seen with his own eyes... or heard, perhaps. No inventing or... supposition? What is the word for that? Thank you. But without embellishment, there is nothing at all to tell, except that a shot was fired, you fell off your horse and I chased after the villain and got knocked out, and that is not very exciting, is it? Oh, but my horse has been found wandering the fields near Shrewsbury, and the saddle had the maker's mark on it, and he recognised it for mine and so Little

Star was brought back safely. The villain probably caught a coach from Shrewsbury. He might be anywhere by now." He took a huge mouthful of meat. "This is very good baby pig. Mr Chambers is such a good cook. It is fun eating up here with you. You never get stuffy about manners, like Aunt Viola does."

"No talking with your mouth full," Malcolm said, waggling an admonitory finger.

Edward just laughed, and translated the joke to Lord Hedlund.

They had been dispatched back to the nursery, and Malcolm was playing a surprisingly intense game of piquet with Chandry when there was a knock on the door. It was Mr Willerton-Forbes.

"Pardon the intrusion, Mr Gage, but I thought you should be aware that I have seen the papers establishing Lady Mary's trust fund."

"Oh, so Dugard allowed you sight of them after all?"

"Not exactly," he said, eyes twinkling. "Nevertheless, I have seen them, and I can tell you that the bulk of Lady Mary's inheritance lies in a single estate, to whit, Strachan Park in Warwickshire."

"She owns Lord Purval's estate? Then... he has been renting it from the trustees all this time."

"Precisely so. Furthermore, there is not a single word anywhere in those papers relating to fortune hunters or any conditions of the sort. Interesting, is it not?"

28: An Understanding

"How did Mr Willerton-Forbes get hold of those papers?" Marie said, as they sat side by side on the chaise longue. Mr Chandry had left, John had readied Malcolm for bed and at last they were alone for the night. "I understand now why he wanted Mr Dugard to stay the night, but somehow I cannot see him snooping around the bedrooms in his stockinged feet, can you? He is far too grandly dressed for a thief. Besides, he never left the dining room, at least until the ladies withdrew. No one did."

"I suspect it was the discreet Mr Neate who did the snooping," Malcolm said, laughing. "But I do not see how it helps, for it seems to me that Dugard still has full control of your inheritance, and there is not much we can do about it. Even if we go to court over the matter, it could take years to see a resolution and it might consume the full amount. Lawyers' fees are the very devil."

"But at least I now know precisely why Lord Purval was so keen to marry me," she said. "He wanted to *own* the estate he lived in. His father had it before him, and he was born there. I never guessed that it was only rented to him. He loves the place beyond all reason. It must have been a powerful temptation."

"As if any man would need an additional inducement to marry you," Malcolm murmured, wrapping his good arm around her waist and pulling her so tightly to him that she squeaked in surprise. "Let us not talk about Lord Purval or your inheritance. In fact, let us not talk at all, for here we are quite alone and we should not waste such an opportunity."

"Oh, good. Are you going to—?"

She had the answer to her question instantly, for his lips pressed against hers with an urgency that quickened her pulse and weakened her knees. The world faded away, and there was nothing but his strong arm holding her against him, his robe soft under her hands, the ruffle of his nightshirt tickling her chin and a great conflagration of joy inside her that burned so hot she feared she might fall into a swoon, had he not been holding her so firmly.

"Did you mean it?" he murmured, as his lips sought her cheeks, her eyelids, her forehead, her ears. "What you said in my dream — was it true? You said you loved me... in my dream."

His face was so anxious that she reached up to stroke his cheek. "Why would I say it if I did not mean it? I *adore* you, Malcolm Augustus Gage. *Je t'aime, je t'adore."*

"Oh." His eyes were wide.

"Did you imagine I married you to protect me from Lord Purval?"

"Well, I did actually, yes. You knew I was willing and I was here and it was an emergency so... why are you laughing?"

Willing... she had hoped he was rather more than just willing, but she answered him lightly. "My emergency husband! I spent five years running away from marriage, you crazy man. I could have run away again, but I did not want to. When you first talked of marriage, I dared not think of it — it was too dangerous, for I would have had to tell you everything. But I *did* think of it, all the time, and gradually I came to realise that all my hopes of happiness rested with you. So when the *emergency* occurred, I seized the chance. I hustled you into it rather, *mon chéri*. Are you regretting it?"

He laughed, but in a rather dazed way. "Of course not! In all the chaos of these past days, you are the one shining star of hope in a very dark sky."

"Oh… what a romantic thing to say, husband."

"I probably read it somewhere. I am not much of a romantic at heart. I would like to be, if only I knew what would please you."

"It pleases me when you take me walking through the bluebells. It pleases me when you buy me hats. And it would please me very much if you would come to my bed at night, or let me come to yours."

He jerked away from her. "I *cannot* until our future is settled," he cried.

"But it *is* settled! We are married… we are together, for ever. What could be more settled than that?"

He kissed her forehead again, but it seemed more an act of sorrow than affection. "Marie, I have no money, no income and no employment. Neither of us knows if our hopes for an inheritance will materialise. Mine depends on Edward and yours on your trustees, and we could easily lose both. Our affairs could hardly be *less* settled. I have married you now because it was necessary, but I will not risk bringing another life into this world, not yet. It is my responsibility to provide for you, and I take that very seriously."

"You take everything seriously," she said softly. "But you consider only the practical side. Have you considered that there is more to marriage than a roof over our heads and whether we can afford a carriage or not? There is also the comfort that husband and wife should bring each other, and when there is someone at large trying to murder one or both of us, I am in great need of a little comfort. Do you not wish us to be together as man and wife?"

"Oh, Marie," he whispered, with a little groan, and his arm tightened around her waist. "Of course I wish it! But we must be sensible, and wait until the future is clear."

She sighed. "You have an implacable nature, husband," she said, but the words had no heat in them.

"I am the man who maintained a grudge for sixteen years, remember? Once I have settled on a thing, I pursue it obsessively, right or wrong. Fortunately, my obsessive pursuit of you ended a trifle more swiftly, and so will this obsession, too, I promise, *mon trésor.*"

"Very well, husband, have it your way," she said, kissing him on the nose. "But you will not banish me altogether? I may sleep on the chaise longue again, may I not?"

"I should like that. I sleep better when we are together."

"As do I. Then I shall go and let Sarah wrestle me out of these stays. I shall be back soon."

~~~~~
~~~~~

By Monday morning, Malcolm was feeling almost his usual self again. Mr Dugard had scuttled back to London, but Lord Purval seemed inclined to make a long stay.

"What is being said of him below stairs?" Malcolm asked John as he helped him dress properly for the first time. "What is his man like?"

"Very close-mouthed," John said, smoothing an imaginary wrinkle from the waistcoat. "There's usually some banter between valets but not with this one. His coachman is more forthcoming. Says his lordship used to hold his purse-strings very tight, with nothing wasted, but the last few years he's been splashing out. New carriage, a fancy curricle with prime cattle, lots of new clothes. Whole lot of work done on the house and grounds."

"The last few years? How many years?"

"Not sure... five, six, maybe? I expect he came into some money."

"I expect he did," Malcolm said, wondering how he might have acquired it. Then he laughed at himself. He was getting as bad as Captain Edgerton, viewing everyone through mistrustful eyes. Might a man not inherit a little money, or sell an unwanted piece of land, or make a fortunate investment without falling under suspicion?

Malcolm did not quite feel up to stairs and the inevitable conversation with Viola, so he chose to take breakfast in his room with Marie. Then he ambled along the corridor to the day nursery, with his designated guard for the day, Captain Edgerton, trailing behind him. He was grateful for the captain's care of Marie and himself, but it was still unnerving to be silently followed by a man with one hand on the hilt of a sword and the other holding a pistol. It would be loaded, too, he knew that.

He found Edward and Lord Hedlund seated at the big table, heads together, books spread out around them.

"Oh, famous! You're better!" Edward cried, leaping up. "Can we practise?" he said in Russian. "I have found a poem I cannot quite understand."

In English, Malcolm said, "What about Lord Hedlund? What is he to do while you and I are chattering away in Russian?"

"Oh, he understands how it is," Edward says airily. "We talked about it with Papa, and he explained how important it is that I not get distracted before my examination. He has set lessons for Hedlund to do while we are working on my Russian."

"Has he now. What school do you attend, Hedlund?"

"None, sir. I have two tutors to teach me."

"Are they horrid, your tutors?" Edward said.

"No, not at all. Mr Ambler is great fun, and a terrific cricket player. Mr Yorke likes to collect butterflies and moths... all kinds of insects, really. He has been all over Europe and tells some amazing stories of his travels." He was a quietly spoken youth, with none of Edward's effervescent liveliness, but perhaps he would show more animation when he was used to the Grove's residents. It must be a shock to the boy to be deposited there and abandoned by his father.

"I wish I had a tutor like that," Edward said wistfully. "Mr Hawksbee used to shout all the time, and throw books at me when I got an answer wrong. I cannot see a man with bushy eyebrows now without shuddering and ducking."

"That is very bad. Papa would not allow any tutor to shout at me."

"Oh, Papa got rid of him very quickly but if ever I have a bad dream, it is always him, with those huge eyebrows looming over me. I wish Uncle Malcolm could stay, but he will be going to Oxford to live when I pass my examination."

Lord Hedlund nodded sagely, so clearly he knew the full details of the situation. It was a pity he would be leaving so soon, for Edward was very much in need of a friend, and perhaps Lord Hedlund was, too. A boy of twelve needed a friend if he had no brother. Malcolm had always had Laurence's steady presence as he grew up, and he could not imagine how dreary life would have been without that sensible foil to his wilder follies. Those long, exploratory rambles through the woods and fields, the nights whispering together in bed, the summer games of cricket on the lawn... what times they had had!

Now he could not imagine how he had survived those interminable years when he had willingly chosen to forgo his brother's friendship. They might have squabbled from time to time, but they would have made it up, if they had only allowed themselves to do so. There was a bond between brothers that should have been unbreakable — that *was* unbreakable. He had felt as if a part of himself had been missing all those years, but now he was whole again, and it was wonderful.

For two hours, he talked Russian to Edward, while Lord Hedlund worked at a passage of Greek and Marie sat quietly with her sewing. Then Laurence came to take the boys away for an hour of Greek, and Malcolm sat beside Marie and read poetry to her. Some of it was in English and some was in French and some was in Italian, but she seemed not to mind when it was incomprehensible. She smiled and listened and more than once he found himself so entranced by that little smile that he forgot to read altogether.

"What is it?" she said, tipping her head to one side like a little bird.

"Tu es mon coeur, mon âme. Je t'adore. Tu es ma chérie pour toujours."

"You are my heart and soul, too, husband. Ohh!" she wailed, fumbling for a handkerchief. "Why ever do you say you are not romantic, husband? Now look what you have done."

"Forgive me," he said, gently wiping away tears with one thumb. And then somehow it seemed that the only remedy for such distress to kiss it away. It was not a passionate kiss, nor urgent, for they had their whole lives for such delights. It was sweet and tender, punctuated with sighs and long, smiling glances and gentle touches, and filled with warmth and unconditional affection.

Little by little, under this steady stream of joyous kisses, something inside Malcolm shifted and changed. It was as if he had been an empty vessel and now, very gradually, kiss by delicious kiss, he was filled with some feeling that he could not even name, in any language. A brother, no matter how close, no matter how much a part of him, could never fill him with this glorious feeling that left him fizzing like champagne. Love... yes, it was that, of course, but it was something more than that. It was climbing to the very top of the tallest oak tree, it was galloping hard and fast across the lower meadow and taking the hedge at the bottom without breaking stride, it was hitting a cricket ball all the way to the boundary, it was passing every examination he had ever taken. It was exhilaration and triumph and joy and utter, blissful contentment in his life.

And yet, he knew with absolute certainty that it could be — *should* be — even more than that. There was yet another plane still higher and more exhilarating even than this, the perfect union of mind and body and soul that still awaited them. He drew back a little to gaze into those dark eyes that stared back at him, trusting and unafraid.

"You are right, *ma chérie,*" he said softly. "Sometimes I am wound too tight to see the truth of the matter, but now I understand it only too clearly. In these last weeks, I have learnt not to be afraid of the past, but I should also not be afraid of the future. Whatever the path laid out before us, no matter where it leads, we will walk it side by side, for good or ill. For better for worse. Tonight we will be together as man and wife. You will be mine and I will be yours, and… I suppose God will determine our fate."

"You believe in God now?" she said teasingly.

"I have always believed in God," he said. "I am not totally convinced He always believed in me, however, and religion is— Oh, do not get me started on religion, for I am liable to pace up and down the room, ranting and raving and stabbing the air with an angry finger. I am not rational on the subject of religion."

"By all means, let us not talk about it. In fact, let us not talk at all, husband."

This agreeable plan had barely been put into practice when a knock on the door heralded Laurence's arrival.

He grinned as they sprang apart. "Sorry to interrupt, but there is interesting news. The man who shot you has been caught. He walked into the Boar's Head as bold as you please and asked for his things that he left there almost a week ago. John

Brownsmith recognised him, and he and his boys arrested him. Viola has taken Edward down to the inn to identify him."

"Why would he come back?" Marie said, frowning. "That seems a blockheaded thing to do, if you ask me, to just walk in openly. He must have known he would be recognised."

"Seemingly not," Laurence said. "At least we may now dispense with the looming presence of your armed guard. Lady Mary, I bear a heartfelt plea from Louisa. Mrs Anderson and Mrs Drinkwater have come to call, and with Viola absent and Cousin Charu busy below stairs—"

"Oh yes, reinforcements are urgently required, I see," Marie said, laughing merrily. "Poor Louisa! But I shall be very cross if you continue to call me Lady Mary in that formal way, you know. We are brother and sister now, after all. You must call me Marie — or Mary if you prefer. I answer to either with equal readiness."

"Thank you," he said, with a quick smile. "I shall call you Marie, as Mal does, I think."

She made him a neat little curtsy, then departed on her mission of mercy.

Laurence's eyes fell upon the decanter on top of the low bookcase. "Ah, is that brandy? In the day nursery? How convenient. Would you like some?"

"Are you not going to support your wife through the trial of Mrs Anderson and Mrs Drinkwater?"

"That is ladies' business, although I suggested to Skeates that he might try Purval," Laurence said firmly. "That should appease our visitors. Brandy?"

"Why not."

"I like your wife," Laurence said, handing him a glass. "She will do very well for you. I confess I thought you were mad at first, but you obviously saw something in her that escaped the rest of us."

"That is because you never saw her at all," Malcolm said. "She was a servant and no one ever notices the servants, do they? But I am a kind of servant myself, so I noticed her."

"But you knew she was a lady? You saw beneath the disguise, surely? Or did you truly fall in love with a lady's maid?"

Malcolm laughed. "Truly I did. I knew she was not French, and not some farm labourer's daughter, but beyond that, I had no notion. A parson's daughter, maybe. I never expected her to be of the nobility. But it makes no difference to me."

"There are not many who would speak so, and mean it, but I believe you are truly of their number," Laurence said. "You are remarkable, Mal."

Malcolm raised his eyebrows disbelievingly. "Come now, brother, once one has drunk at the well of love, there is no turning back, whether the object of one's affections is a duchess or a dairymaid. It is character that is of importance, not rank or wealth or any other construct of society."

Laurence grunted, which might or might not be agreement. "On the subject of wealth, it is most disturbing that Lady Mary's inheritance may be withheld. Willerton-Forbes has written to Dugard's head of chambers for his opinion, but it is hard to see what can be done. Trustees have a great deal of power in such cases. And if Edward fails—"

"We will survive," Malcolm said quickly. "Willerton-Forbes talked of a government post. Or I could tutor Edward, perhaps. What did you pay that fellow who terrorised him?"

"Hawksbee? Forty guineas a year and he was not worth half so much. Good God, Malcolm, I will not *employ* you! You may tutor Edward if you wish, and welcome, for he could hardly have a better educator, but you have a place here by right, as my brother, and the allowance you used to have — what was it, three hundred a year? There must be sixteen years' worth due to you."

"With interest?" Malcolm said innocently.

Laurence gave a bark of laughter. "With interest, you old scoundrel! Work out the numbers and write it out fair so that I can understand it, and you shall have it, with pleasure, and a home here, if you need it. I will even build you a house. Louisa wants to renovate the gardens, so she can add a little house into the scheme. That would be such fun, would it not? And if Edward succeeds and you get your house in Oxford, then you and Marie must spend every summer here, so that your children can grow up with mine and Louisa's, as cousins should. Would you like that?"

"I should like that more than I could say," Malcolm said, although it was hard to get the words out through a throat unexpectedly tight.

A knock on the door announced the appearance of Captain Edgerton. "It is a day of surprises," he said, grinning. "You have another visitor. Lord Neston is returned."

"Now what?" Laurence said, with a theatrical sigh. "You may find it hard to believe, gentlemen, but this used to be a sleepy little village where nothing ever happened of greater moment than a box of oranges dropped at Timpson's, or the wind taking off Mrs Drinkwater's bonnet. Now we are awash with the nobility, and beset by murderers and kidnappers. Well, I suppose we had better go and play the welcoming hosts — again."

29: Deductions

Lord Neston's carriage was outside the door when Malcolm and Laurence reached the front door. His lordship was busy directing the footmen on the delicate matter of unloading boxes. On the doorstep, the ladies of the household, together with the interested Mrs Anderson and Mrs Drinkwater, watched in bemusement.

"I had to invite him to stay, of course," Louisa said in an undertone. "I suppose he will take Lord Hedlund away with him, which is a pity, for Edward's sake."

"Perhaps we can persuade Neston to allow the boy to stay for a few weeks," Laurence said, and she brightened. "I shall mention it to him."

Lord Purval stood a little apart, watching warily.

"What do you make of this?" Malcolm murmured to Captain Edgerton, who had followed them downstairs.

"I assume Lord Neston went off to see Lord Purval, and discovered that he had come here. They may even have passed each other on the road. Clearly Lord Neston is very keen to talk to his old friend. Interesting, is it not?"

The boxes were being taken into the house, and the business of introductions had begun on the front step when a small group appeared round the corner of the house, bound for the stables. Edward and Lord Hedlund were there, and Malcolm recognised Neate, Spencer and several men from the inn. There was also a strikingly handsome young man with a head of yellow hair in their midst, his hands tied — the man who had tried to kill him. The fellow looked at the group standing on the steps, his gaze roving incuriously across their faces. Then his eyes widened and he stopped dead.

Lord Neston gave an involuntary gasp. "Nick?" he said, his face ghostly white. "Is it you? Whatever are you doing here?"

"You know this man?" Captain Edgerton said sharply.

He swallowed convulsively. "I do. He... he was a... a footman of mine once... several years ago."

"How many years?"

"Seven. Almost seven years. He worked for Purval before that, but I have no idea what became of him afterwards."

Neate stepped forward from the group surrounding the man. "His name, my lord?"

"Nick... Nicholas Holden." His voice was barely above a whisper and he looked almost ill, as if he might faint away at any moment.

Lord Purval rested one beringed hand on Lord Neston's arm. "Come inside, Neston. Your journey has overset you. A rest and perhaps a little brandy will do you the world of good."

This sent the ladies into a flutter of concern, which swept both Lord Neston and Lord Purval into the house, and the prisoner and his guards went towards the stables. Captain Edgerton deftly detached Marie from the group of ladies.

"Do you remember this footman?" he said in an urgent undertone.

"A little. I should never have recognised him, for he was only with us for a few months, when I was sixteen. I remember being surprised when he left, since he was an excellent footman and Papa never gave a good reason for his going. I do not think he dismissed him, though, so perhaps Holden disliked being so isolated. We were very remote from civilisation."

"Interesting," the captain said thoughtfully. "Mr Gage, I must just have a word with Neate, but will you please stay close to Lord Neston and tell me everything he says."

"You cannot suspect my father, surely," Marie said sharply. "Just because this man was a servant of his years ago does not mean he is responsible for his recent actions."

"Not your father, no. Excuse me, I cannot delay." So saying, he bounded off after Neate and the prisoner.

Malcolm and Marie went back into the house, where the entrance hall was still thronged with servants moving boxes, Mrs Anderson and Mrs Drinkwater agonising over the relative merits of staying as long as possible or leaving with the juicy gossip at once, and Lord Neston looking so ill that Marie rushed to his side. Louisa was already there, and between the two of them and Lord Purval, they manoeuvred him into the Roman Saloon, while Charu emerged from some subterranean fastness in time to efficiently dispatch the two visiting ladies.

"Whatever is the matter with him?" Laurence whispered to Malcolm. "Why should a footman from years ago distress him? And what does that have to do with him shooting at you?"

"I have not the least idea," Malcolm whispered back, "but there is a man who will find it out, if anyone can."

He gestured towards the still open front door, where Captain Edgerton was bounding up the steps with Mr Neate behind him.

"Has he said anything?" Edgerton said.

"Nothing but a few whimpers," Malcolm said. "He has only just this minute gone through."

The Roman Saloon was crowded. Lord Neston sat on a chaise longue, a handkerchief to his face, while Marie held his hand and Louisa proffered a vinaigrette. Charu was pouring brandy, while Henrietta and Skeates looked on anxiously. Lord Purval, Chandry and Willerton-Forbes stood a little to one side.

Captain Edgerton whispered something to Laurence, who nodded, and said loudly, "Lord Neston, I am sure a little quietude will do you the most good. Let me take you through to the library where we will not be disturbed. No, Louisa, I believe we can manage without your good offices for the moment. Come, my lord, let me assist you. Malcolm, bring the brandy, will you. Thank you, Lord Purval, but we can manage. I know I may depend upon you to take care of the ladies. Charu, a glass of something for everyone, if you please. This way, Lord Neston."

It was deftly done, and by the time they had attained the library and firmly shut out the interested servants, somehow Willerton-Forbes was there ahead of them, and Edgerton and Neate had crept in by a different door and stationed themselves so as to guard the exits. Malcolm raised an eyebrow to Captain Edgerton, who smiled and gave the merest shake of the head.

"And now, my lord," Willerton-Forbes said gently, "I think it is time you told us everything, do you not agree?"

Lord Neston moaned, and shook his head.

"Very well, my lord. Let us see if we can work it out. Michael?"

Captain Edgerton moved forward. "My lord, when my colleagues were in Northamptonshire, and discovered that the mysterious French lady's maid Marie Fournier was in fact the Lady Mary Fallon, they made enquiries about her family... about you, in particular. Every report agreed that Lord Neston was a good and honourable man, a faithful husband and loving father, a devout Christian, a kind master and landlord, a generous friend. It was hard to reconcile that image with the man who kept his daughter locked up alone for a whole year, in order to force her into a marriage distasteful to her."

Lord Neston moaned again, but made no comment.

"That raised two questions in my mind. One of them — why Lord Purval was so insistent on the marriage, despite the lady's objections — has now been answered. His estate, his home for many years, was at stake, and he is obsessive beyond all reason about Strachan Park. As a young man, he would have married your wife to secure it, but she chose you. That did not matter, for you were accommodating, and when your wife died and the estate was held in trust for Lady Mary, that arrangement continued. But Lord Purval could not allow Lady Mary to marry an outsider who might take Strachan Park away from him. He determined to marry her himself. And that brings me, my lord, to my second question. Why would *you*, my lord, be so insistent on forcing your daughter into this marriage? It was a matter of family honour, you told Lady Mary, and it was clear that Lord Purval had some hold over you that ensured your compliance. Do you wish to say anything at this point, my lord?"

He shook his head violently, and Malcolm held out the brandy glass to him. He took it, and sipped a little, although his hands trembled.

"Well, let us see what we can deduce," Captain Edgerton went on. "Two weeks ago, an attempt was made to kidnap Lady Mary. That effort failed and the perpetrators were captured, but unfortunately we could not discover who sent them. We may guess, however. Not you, I think, my lord, but Lord Purval — yes, it could have been him. Lady Mary's portrait was shown to many who recognised her, and our people were not as discreet as they might have been, so I believe Lord Purval discovered Lady Mary's whereabouts and sent people to kidnap her. No doubt he intended to force her into marriage."

Edgerton was striding about the room now, in full flow.

"A few days later, another attack on Lady Mary, more vicious, but the villain escaped. A week later, Mr Malcolm Gage was shot by the same man. This raises an interesting conundrum. How are we to explain these seemingly unrelated attacks? Again, they make sense only when seen from Lord Purval's viewpoint. Marriage to Lady Mary is his ideal solution, for that gives him ownership of Strachan Park, but while she remains unwed, he can continue to live there. But if she marries elsewhere, he may lose his home altogether. He cannot permit that and so, in desperation, he considers other, darker possibilities. The death of Lady Mary before her marriage, and the death of Mr Gage after it would have the same effect — to return Strachan Park to your hands, my lord. Had Mr Gage secured a marriage settlement and made a will, matters would have been different, but failing such arrangements, Lord Purval would be safe from the threat of eviction.

"But who is this murderous man who so ruthlessly pursues Lord Purval's interests? He evaded us until today, when by chance he was brought here just as you arrived. You were quite overcome with strong emotion at the sight of him, but were able to identify him as Nicholas Holden, a footman of yours briefly, acquired from Lord Purval. His lordship's coachman confirmed all this, and also told us that Holden returned to Strachan Park immediately after leaving your employ, and has remained there ever since. He is reputed to be highly regarded by his lordship... in fact, they are said to be the closest of friends." Lord Neston started. "You understand me, I am sure, my lord."

He paused, and the only sound in the room was Lord Neston's rapid breathing.

"It would explain the pressure Lord Purval was able to apply to you," Edgerton said.

"Lord Neston," Willerton-Forbes said gently, "blackmail is a great crime, and if Lord Purval—"

"Not blackmail!" he cried, his head lifting suddenly. "Blackmail... such an ugly word. Purval—" He looked at each of them in turn, then said quietly, "The fault was mine, entirely. I have always known that... that I have... oh God! I cannot say it!"

"You prefer men," Captain Edgerton said softly. "Despite your marriage, you find the male form more appealing. You have kept your secret well hidden for your whole life, but then Purval inserted this young man into your household, this very beautiful young man, and you could not resist."

Mutely, Lord Neston nodded, and tears coursed down his cheeks.

"So you sent him away," Edgerton said. "But he went straight back to Lord Purval, who then pressured you to accept his suit for your daughter or word of your actions would leak out."

"It was not like that," Lord Neston protested. "Purval was sympathetic. He understands... he knows... he was... when we were at school... there was an occurrence... that was how I knew the depravity of my nature, and he knew of it, too. But since that time I had been strong, until Nick Holden. Purval was very kind to me. He said he would keep everything quiet, but perhaps in return I could persuade Mary to marry him. That is not truly blackmail, is it? A man helps his friend, and is given some gift in gratitude. And when Mary ran away and Purval lost any chance to marry her, he persuaded me that Strachan Park should have been his by then, so he should have the income from it and not pay rent. That seemed reasonable to me, do you not agree?"

"Blackmail," Willerton-Forbes said firmly. "A capital offence."

"But what I did was far worse and if it were to come out... I should be utterly ruined," Lord Neston said. "It is a capital offence, and I could be hanged for it and the family destroyed! Mary's marriage seemed a small price to pay to escape such a destiny. But now that she has chosen elsewhere... I went to find Purval to determine his mind, prepared to accept my fate. Mary's marriage is not what I had hoped. A nobleman, or at least a man of wealth, could have withstood the buffeting of society following such a catastrophe, but that cannot be helped, and Mary will take care of Hedlund if... if the worst happens. But you can surely understand now why I acted as I did. For all our sakes, it was better by far that Mary should marry Purval, who would have made her a good husband."

"Apart from the small matter of blackmail and kidnap and attempted murder," Edgerton said, with a savage edge to his voice. "You have a strange idea of what constitutes a good husband, my lord."

"Michael, Michael," Willerton-Forbes said, waving one hand appeasingly. "Enough. We have our answer, we have the culprit in custody and although for Lord Neston's sake we cannot possibly accuse Lord Purval of his crimes, he will never trouble any of us again."

"Can you be sure of that?" Malcolm said.

"Oh yes," Willerton-Forbes said softly. "Now that we know all the circumstances, Lord Purval can never reveal his lordship's little secret without also revealing his own part in it. For he sent Nick Holden intentionally to seduce you into sin, my lord, and then blackmailed you afterwards in order to secure Strachan Park. When he discovered Lady Mary's whereabouts, he tried kidnap and then murder, just as the good captain has described. I suspect, although I cannot yet be sure, he also blackmailed Mr Dugard into applying certain conditions to the trust fund to ensure that the estate never passed beyond his control. He is very, very determined to keep hold of Strachan Park, and I am equally determined that he shall not. Strachan Park belongs by rights to you, Mr Gage."

"But what am I to do with it?" Malcolm said. "I cannot simply toss Lord Purval out, for if he loses his precious home, he may well set out to destroy Lord Neston."

"True, and I do not feel that any purpose would be served in removing him. So long as he is paying a reasonable rent for the place let him stay, on the understanding that one word spoken against Lord Neston will see him lose Strachan Park forever."

A flicker of hope crossed Lord Neston's face. "Do you believe that will restrain him from revealing my sins?"

"Has he not proved that he will do anything to keep Strachan Park?"

Malcolm shook his head, bewildered. "That almost seems to reward him for his wickedness."

"I agree," Laurence said thoughtfully. "It is an irony of life that the wicked man who has pursued evil over many years should have the one thing he covets above all, while the good man who fell into sin once and immediately repented of it, is tormented by his conscience for years. We are all sinners, Lord Neston, but God forgives us if we repent and ask it of Him."

"Even this?" Lord Neston said, almost inaudibly.

"Of course. There are many such men, and God understands. Have faith."

He sat a little straighter. "I will try. Thank you, sir."

"And for my part," Captain Edgerton said grimly, "I shall try very, very hard to find some other crime to set at Lord Purval's door, so that justice may be done to him without casting a shadow on the Fallon family. Such evil should be punished, not rewarded."

"Amen to that," Malcolm said.

~~~~~

Marie woke to the not quite dark of the night, those strange hours of midsummer when the sky barely dimmed to twilight before lightening again. The curtain shifted slightly beside the
~~~~~

open window, throwing a puff of cool air against her bare skin. She pulled the covers a little higher. Beside her, Malcolm had rolled away from her in his sleep, his bandaged shoulder and half his back exposed to the air. She leaned over and tugged the blanket across him.

She could not help smiling as she gazed at him. Her husband! And she was his wife, his in every way. It was their third night together — truly together — and her joy in her husband increased with every hour that passed. It was almost too much to be borne, this delirious happiness that was hers, and she saw it in him, too. It was in his eyes as he gazed at her, in his words as he murmured love into her ear, in his touch as they lay together. And when he was not beside her, joy warmed her inside and brought her the utmost contentment. It would always bring her contentment, no matter what happened.

Rolling onto her back, she closed her eyes and imagined their life unrolling at their feet. She could not envisage the house, for there was no knowing yet where they would live, but there would be children, of that she was sure. Boys with Malcolm's long limbs and intense blue eyes, and girls with her own dainty figure and dark curls. Or perhaps, nature being perverse, the other way round. They would play games with them on the lawn, teach them to ride and to fish and to know their letters. The boys would go out shooting with their father, and the girls would—

Was that a noise? Just the house, no doubt, for old houses always creaked and groaned at night, like elderly men stretching themselves, joints popping. But this was not like that. It was a soft sound, almost inaudible.

There it was again, and it was coming from the dressing room.

Silently she slipped out of bed and donned her nightgown. Then she crossed to the fireplace and very, very carefully picked up the poker.

"What is it?" Malcolm said sleepily.

"Ssh!"

Malcolm shot out of bed and shrugged into a robe, hastily picking up a candlestick.

A sudden explosion of sound from next door made them both jump. Shouts... crashing sounds... a thump... a squeal... and then, shockingly, a loud bang that could only be a gunshot.

Then silence. Her heart hammered painfully, as she strained for the least sound from next door.

"Whatever was that?" Malcolm whispered.

Before she could answer, there was a brisk rat-a-tat-tat on the door from the dressing room. "Mr Gage? Lady Mary?" It was Captain Edgerton's voice behind the closed door. "No cause for alarm. Everything is under control, but do not come in here until we have... um, restored order somewhat." There was a sound of laughter from someone else in the room.

"Is anyone hurt?" Marie called back.

"Only Lord Purval's valet, but since he was about to kill you both, you need not concern yourselves over him. I will come and see you when I have... er, tidied myself a little." More laughter.

"Why is that funny?" Marie whispered, as sounds of furniture being moved emanated from the dressing room.

"I have no idea, but I wish people would not laugh without sharing the joke," he said crossly. "It is very rude."

And that made Marie smile at him. "You are just out of sorts because you were woken abruptly."

It was about half an hour before Captain Edgerton appeared, by which time there was a veritable army in the dressing room to judge by the voices. Nor did the captain use that door, entering the bedroom by way of the corridor. He looked slightly dishevelled, reduced to wearing only his shirt and breeches.

"What on earth is going on?" Malcolm said, edgily. "I thought we were safe from further attack. How much more of this can we expect?"

Captain Edgerton grinned. "That is the last of it, you may be sure. I was suspicious when Holden more or less deliberately gave himself up to be captured, and with a blatantly concocted story. He claims he was only trying to get a rabbit and the shot went awry, then he panicked and ran away. He is arrested, off he goes to Shrewsbury gaol to await the magistrates' pleasure, while we assume you are safe and can stand down the armed guard. Meanwhile the valet creeps in at night, murders you two in your bed and Holden is safely under lock and key with the constables as alibi."

"But you suspected something of the sort," Marie said. "How clever you are, Captain."

"Nothing clever about it, my lady. A valet has particular duties to observe and places to do them, and when he has twice been caught sneaking about where he should not be, anyone would be suspicious. Casing the joint, most likely. We have been waiting for him to make his move, and tonight was the night. Unfortunately, I was obliged to shoot him dead. I am afraid your dressing room is... rather blood-stained, Lady Mary."

"And you, too, I gather," Malcolm said wryly. "You have our most sincere thanks, Captain, you and your colleagues. What was so funny about all this? We heard someone laughing."

"I regret to say that Mr Chandry found the vast quantity of blood... somewhat amusing. It is a way some men deal with the horrors of battle, so I have not reprimanded him. I apologise if you found his response inappropriate."

"No, indeed, it must have been dreadful for all of you," Marie said. "I trust we may now sleep easily without fear of creeping assassins?"

"You may. Sadly, I do not believe we can find a way to connect Lord Purval directly to this, but his other servants are honest and he himself is too fastidious to sully his hands with murder. Later today it will be impressed upon him that any further attempts of this kind will inevitably see his name dragged into the business. I think we may safely say that he will not try it. However, the ultimate solution to this problem lies with resolving the matter of Strachan Park once and for all."

"Do you think I should continue to rent to him?" Malcolm said.

"No, I think all he deserves is a bullet through his black heart," the captain said sombrely. "Unfortunately, we live in a world where we do not always get what we deserve, so if you do let him stay there, at least make sure he pays a very high price for it."

"And you will continue to search for some other charge that may be set at his door?"

"You may depend upon it. No matter how long it takes me, I will see him punished for what he has done."

30: Epilogue: Examination

AUGUST

The carriage splashed over the bridge and into Oxford. It was raining, just as it had been for Great-uncle Zachariah's funeral in March. At least the rain was a little warmer this time.

"There, Edward," Malcolm said, pointing through the rain-spattered carriage window. "That is Magdalen College, where you will be examined tomorrow."

"What a beautiful building!" Louisa said. "Medieval, of course."

"Fifteenth century," Malcolm said absently. "The hall is not visible from the road."

They rattled over the cobbles through the busy streets and on into the more peaceful, tree-lined residential streets, where Great-uncle Zachariah's villa was situated. The carriage turned in past the high hedge and rolled to a stop outside the front door. Marie alighted first, then Louisa, Laurence, Edward and Malcolm.

John climbed gingerly down from the box. He was soaked to the skin, but he had insisted on coming with them. "You'll want a valet, sir, when you have your house, and you did promise me, you know."

Malcolm had not had the heart to deny him.

"Good day, Bird," Malcolm said to the elderly manservant holding the carriage door for them. "How are you? This wet weather plaguing you, no doubt."

"Not too bad, sir, not too bad. May I say how pleased we all are to have you back at Maitland House, and to welcome your guests. Everything is ready for you."

"Thank you, Bird. This is my wife, the Lady Mary Gage. Marie, Bird has been here ever since this house was built — what is it, fifty years ago, Bird?"

"Fifty three, sir, fifty three. Only the two owners, from new, and we are all very much looking forward to yourself as the third, sir."

"One final hurdle to jump first," Malcolm said, smiling.

"The house is charming, Malcolm," Louisa said from the shelter of an umbrella. "I had not expected anything so elegant."

"Wait until you see the inside," he said, laughing. "The place has not changed for fifty years, I swear. Fifty three, I suppose."

It was true that the furnishings were old-fashioned, but there was a sturdiness to them that Malcolm rather liked. They were solid and indestructible, rather like Great-uncle Zachariah himself. His visits here had been happy ones, Malcolm realised, but then it had been a bachelor household in those days, just the old man, and most of the servants as old as he was. He could not quite envisage it with children running from room to room, or playing shuttlecock on the back lawn.

"What do you think of it?" he whispered to Marie, as they followed the others in wandering from room to room.

"It is smaller than I am used to, but perfectly adequate," she said.

That was a non-committal answer. "You will be able to refurbish it, if you want... well, if—"

"I know," she said quickly.

If Edward succeeds. It did not need to be said. So much would be different if Edward were to succeed. Malcolm would be a gentleman of means at last, a worthy husband for the daughter of an earl, and the house, while not as grand as the Grove or Springwell Place, was not at all shabby. A gentleman's residence.

"The dining room is a good size," Louisa said. "Room for twenty, I would say."

"Twenty-four, madam," Bird said. "Twenty-four with all the leaves fitted."

"Oh, now this is a lovely room," she cried, as they entered the drawing room. "Which way does it face? South? South-west?"

"Due west, madam. Due west."

Edward, rather pale, gazed around at the high ceiling with its elaborately decorated plaster mouldings, and the walls covered in dark wallpaper and painted panels. A few paintings were dotted here and there, and the chairs were arranged around the walls in the old-fashioned way.

Louisa walked around, examining the paintings. "Very pretty, and next door you have a music room, I see. How many bedrooms are there?"

"Five and a box room on the floor above, madam. Another four above that."

"A very good size," Louisa said, "and plenty of room for a nursery."

Malcolm said nothing, for there was, after all, nothing to say, and Marie likewise followed her sister-in-law in silence. Tomorrow, if things went well, would be the time to talk about the house and whether it was too big or too small or too shabby. Or whether they would even live there at all, or should sell it altogether. Tomorrow they would know.

Not an hour later, Captain Edgerton arrived, his horse lathered with sweat. Malcolm had to talk to him on the doorstep, for he was too travel-stained even to enter the house.

"I thought you would want to know at once," he said. "Lord Purval is gone — fled in the night, having bribed the guards to get Nick Holden out of gaol before the Assizes. We had such a good case, too, managing to tie Holden to the Lichfield knifing as well as the Great Maeswood shooting. He would have been transported at the very least, possibly hanged. Willerton-Forbes is apoplectic with rage at being deprived of his day in court, but it seems rather a neat solution to me. It appears we discovered the one thing Purval cares about more than Strachan Park." He laughed. "A fine punishment, I call it."

"So they get off scot free, do they?" Malcolm said indignantly. "That is not much of a punishment."

"For Holden, no, but then he was only a foot soldier in the enterprise. Purval was the commanding officer behind it and he is being royally punished. Oh, for a year or two he and Holden will be contented enough. They will settle in Italy or some such place, I daresay. But in time, Holden will tire of him and find himself a new sponsor — he is very beautiful, after all. And then Purval will find that he has given up Strachan Park for nothing. What is more, he can never return to England, for fear of arrest. A rather fitting punishment, would you not say? Once Willerton-Forbes calms down, he will see that this is the best outcome we could have hoped for, and the timing is perfect, is it not? Now Master Edward need not feel quite so burdened in his examination. Wish him luck, although I am sure he does not need it."

Some little while later, Colville, the attorney, came to talk to them and assure them that he would be attending the examination to ensure that all was carried out in accordance with his client's will. Then Monk arrived.

"On behalf of the Society of Gentleman Linguists, may I welcome you to Oxford," he said gravely to Edward. "Everything is prepared for you tomorrow. I had thought we would have a quiet meeting, since we are in the middle of the long vacation, but your age has attracted some attention, so a great many members are to bring guests to enjoy the spectacle. You are a wonder, Master Gage, a veritable wonder, and whatever the outcome tomorrow, you may be sure that the attempt will be famous in Oxford's history. Oh, and a person from the *Journal* wishes to attend. You will not mind a report appearing in the newspaper, I daresay."

"I do not mind it," Edward said. "Will there be a great many people there?"

"Perhaps sixty... or a little above. There is great interest from the Fellows of several colleges, so it may be more."

"Not to worry, Edward," Malcolm said. "We have rehearsed before an audience, and I shall be there to support you."

"Ah… now as to that, there is a difficulty," Monk said. "Budanov insists you not attend, to ensure a true test, he says."

"But I am a member of the Society, and Edward's sponsor, as well as his tutor," Malcolm said. "It is usual for the sponsor to be present."

"But not the tutor, and Budanov regards your great-uncle as the sponsor. He takes a strict view of the rules, and since he is to be one of the examiners, his opinion must carry some weight."

"I do not regard it," Edward said stoutly. "Besides, you might distract me, Uncle Malcolm."

Malcolm agreed to it, but it was a concern, and Budanov was not a good choice. He was a clever man, a good tutor to his scholars and very sociable, but he was stickler for correctness. As a native Russian speaker his accent was very strong, and difficult to understand even in relaxed circumstances. However, there was nothing to be done about it now.

They passed the evening quietly, playing a round card game and speaking only in English. "To rest your brain," Malcolm told Edward firmly.

The others saw them off the next morning.

"Just do your best, Edward," Laurence said. "That is all any of us can do, and no one will think any the worse of you if you should fail."

"No, sir. Thank you, sir," he murmured. He had never a high colour, but now he was ashen, looking small and lost and very young in the formal knee breeches that were required dress for Society meetings. Once again Malcolm cursed his great-uncle for laying such a heavy burden on a boy of twelve.

There was no sign of rain today, so Malcolm decided to walk. At least there would be no waiting for the carriage or risk of delay at the last moment by a brewer's dray blocking the road. As they walked, Malcolm went over again the steps by which the examination would proceed. Edward knew it all already, but it did no harm to review it, and perhaps the steady drone of his voice would settle the boy's nerves.

The porter showed them to an ante-room to await the summons. To Malcolm, the familiar smells of polish and dust and smoke and a faint aroma of yesterday's dinner brought back nothing but pleasant memories, and he felt at home under the arched roof, surrounded by bare, polished wood.

They were early, so the room was empty. Malcolm had run out of words, and the silence settled around them like fog.

Edward cleared his throat. "I know you will never... never reproach me if I fail, but I want you to know that I am going to try very hard to succeed."

"I know you are, Edward, but you must understand that the house is no longer significant. I have Strachan Park now, to live in or to sell, as Marie wishes, so if this one is lost... it does not matter. Your father and I will ensure you have every penny bequeathed to you. Do this for your own sake, and not for mine."

"But it does matter," he said earnestly. "Strachan Park was Marie's but this house is yours. I want you to have it. I want to win it for you."

"Houses are not really important," Malcolm said gently. "Money, wealth, all those things... I managed just fine without them for years. I had fifty guineas a year, my board and lodging and all the books I could read, and I was perfectly happy except for one thing, and do you know what that was?" Mutely, Edward shook his head. "My family. I quarrelled with your father and we were both of us too stubborn to make it up. Or too foolish, perhaps. But when your Great-great-uncle Zachariah wrote that will, it was not about the house at all. What he bequeathed me was something far more precious. He forced me to reconcile with my brother, and now I have my family again, and I have a wife, and I need nothing more in my life."

"And I have an uncle," Edward said, smiling for the first time in days.

"Exactly! So you see, forget the house, it matters not a jot. What you have achieved in these last three months is remarkable, and whether you pass or fail the examination, you can be very proud of that."

Edward nodded, and seemed a little happier, so when Colville, the attorney, and Monk came in a few moments later, he was able to greet them with composure.

"The hall is filling up," Monk said cheerfully. "You will have a good audience, young man. Everyone wants to see the remarkable boy who speaks five languages. Now, I am to be the examiner for Latin, so you will have one friendly face, eh?" He laughed jovially. "Ah, here are the others. Challis here will be for French. Lord Banting is for Italian, and Flint for Greek. And here is Budanov, who is Russian. Gentleman, this is Master Edward Gage, your candidate today."

Malcolm heard Edward's sharply indrawn breath as Budanov was introduced. Did he know him? Surely not. But he recovered himself, and as the five examiners asked him about himself and his home and his father's estate, he answered very readily with a clear voice.

And then it was time for him to be led away to meet his fate. He threw one last agonised look at Malcolm.

"Remember to watch the spoons!" Malcolm called out, making Edward laugh. "Good luck."

He was gone, and there was nothing for Malcolm to do but pace anxiously about the room, then sit only to spring up again at once, and examine his pocket watch at one minute intervals. How was it possible for the time to crawl so slowly?

The hour came and went, and Malcolm was still alone. Was that a good sign, or a bad one? Or were they just running late? Had something dreadful happened? If only it were all over!

The door opened, and one very dejected boy came in, his shoulders slumped, his head hanging low.

"I am so sorry," he whispered, and ran straight into Malcolm's waiting arms.

"It is not of the least consequence," he said, hugging the boy tight. "You tried your best, but it is very difficult to think straight when five people are hurling questions at you, all in different languages."

"It was not that," Edward said.

"Oh. Then what?"

"The eyebrows. Mr Budanov has caterpillar eyebrows, and a horrid gruff voice, just like Mr Hawksbee."

"The tutor who used to throw things at you?"

"Yes. Every time he asked a question, he wiggled his eyebrows and it threw me completely off my stride. I mostly kept up until the last part and then I just somehow froze and ignored him, and he still had a spoon up at the end."

"He *does* wiggle his eyebrows, it is true. I can see how distracting that would be. But there, at least it is all over now, and you can have another attempt when you are a bit older."

Monk peered round the door with a smile. "Will you come back inside, Master Gage, and you too, Gage. We are just about to have the vote."

"You have not taken the vote yet?" Malcolm said, suddenly hopeful.

"Not yet. We had a matter or two to discuss privately, but we are ready now."

"What is there to vote on?" Edward said. "I failed. There was still a spoon raised when the bell rang."

"When the bell rang, yes, but the hourglass watcher was so engrossed in your performance that he failed to notice that the sands had run out and so there was some dispute as to the precise situation when the time had expired. There is also the Rule of Last Resort, which Budanov proposed applying in this instance."

"Whatever is that?" Malcolm said. "There is no such rule in the Society's constitution."

"It is an *unwritten* rule that is seldom invoked, but it may be used when there is a question of correct process. The requirement, you see, is that the candidate must exhibit fluency in five separate languages. If fluency in one of the languages cannot be properly determined, then one may use the candidate's *other* language."

"Other language?" Edward said, bewildered. "I do not have any other languages."

"In which languages are you fluent?" Monk said, now grinning openly.

"Latin, Greek, French and Italian. *Not* Russian."

"Possibly. That is what cannot be determined under the rules, for we cannot say whether a spoon was raised at the moment when the bell should have been rung. And what other language?"

"I know no other."

"What language are you speaking at this moment?"

"English, but... that does not count... does it?"

Monk laughed. "The rules say nothing of which languages count. Let us see what the Society thinks, shall we?"

He led the way back into the great hall. The room was primarily used as a dining hall, but today it was arranged exactly as Malcolm had arranged the saloon at the Grove, with the rows of seats for the audience, the long table at the front for the examiners and the single chair for the candidate. This was not Malcolm's college, but the halls were much the same in all Oxford's many colleges, with their high, wood-beamed roofs and arched latticed windows, unchanged since the days of the Plantagenets. There must have been a hundred people seated and many more standing, with a burst of cheering from a group of younger men at the back as Edward was led in.

He looked as if he were attending his own execution, but Malcolm was now tolerably confident of the outcome.

Monk stood before the audience with Edward beside him. "My lords, gentlemen of the Society and guests, Edward Henry Gage asks this day to be admitted to the honoured ranks of the Society of Gentlemen Linguists. Shall he be so admitted?"

The roar of *'Aye!'* was deafening, so that Edward blinked and took a step back in surprise. Arms waved, hats were tossed into the air, and somewhere at the far end of the hall, well-shod feet drummed their approval.

"The said Edward Henry Gage is duly admitted to the Society. Mr Challis, bring forward the gown and cap."

Edward was wrapped in a robe trimmed with violet silk and embroidered with the Society's emblem, and a scholastic cap was placed on his head. The robe was so long that material pooled around his feet. A great surge of onlookers rushed to congratulate him, while streams of servants appeared and began handing round glasses of port, the Society's traditional drink, and trays of tiny biscuits and cakes and pastries.

Malcolm felt rather superfluous, so he edged himself away from the throng. Mr Colville appeared at his side.

"I congratulate you, sir! I confess, my expectations were not high — a boy of twelve, after all! But you have achieved a miracle, sir, a positive miracle."

"Not at all," Malcolm said politely. "Edward's success is entirely by his own efforts, I assure you. He is thirsty for knowledge, and all I did was to allow him to slake his thirst."

"It is a great achievement, which will be talked of for many a day," Colville said. "And you have your house, sir. I shall begin the process of transferring the title to you this very afternoon. Now that everything is settled, I may as well tell you the final charge that your great-uncle laid upon me, by means of a letter to be kept with the will. You will remember that if Master Gage should fail in his attempt to be admitted to the Society, it was laid upon the trustees to dispose of the house in a charitable bequest, at our discretion. The charity was to be you, sir. Mr Zachariah wished you to have the house and his fortune, no matter the outcome today. He wished only for you to reconcile with your brother, and I believe he has accomplished his objective, has he not?"

Malcolm laughed. "The scheming, devious old buzzard. Manipulating us all from beyond the grave."

"But all for the best, eh?"

"Oh yes," Malcolm said softly. "It was all very much for the best."

~~~~~

Great were the celebrations at Maitland House that evening. Mrs Staines had excelled herself in the kitchen, and Laurence had taken the precaution of bringing several bottles of wine to enliven proceedings.

"You should have seen your son, Laurence," Malcolm said, mellow with food, wine and relief. "There he was in his gown and cap, a glass of port in his hand, chatting away to these crusty academics in a multitude of languages as if he had been doing so all his life. It was a sight to behold, I can tell you."

"I wish I had seen it," Laurence said, smiling affectionately at his son. "I am very proud of you, Edward. I would have been proud, no matter what had happened today, for you accepted the challenge and fought like a man to fulfil the terms of this eccentric will, but you have achieved something extraordinary today, and made both your uncle and yourself a great deal richer."

"And I am a member of the Society now," Edward said. "I may attend the monthly meetings. Papa, you will not mind if I
~~~~~

stay here with Uncle Malcolm when there is a meeting on? And perhaps I may bring Hedlund here when he next visits?"

"It is not yet decided whether we will keep this house," Malcolm said.

"Not keep it?" Louisa said. "Why ever not?"

"They might not wish to live in Oxford," Laurence said easily. "There will always be a home for them in Great Maeswood, if they want it."

"Yes, but—" Louisa began, but was quelled by a look from her husband.

"But what was the point of all this, if you are not going to live here?" Edward said, his voice wobbling. "It is a lovely house and Great-great-uncle Zachariah wanted you to have it."

"It is for Marie to decide," Malcolm said firmly. "Ladies make the decisions about houses."

"Do you not care where your home is?" Edward said, frowning.

"My home is wherever my wife is," Malcolm said. "If she is happy to live here, then so am I. If she prefers to live elsewhere, then so do I."

"I like this house," Marie said softly.

"Do you?" Malcolm said. "I thought you were not very taken with it."

"I did not want to say what I truly felt in case it imposed greater pressure on Edward," she said. "But I love it. At Springwell Place, we were so far from the nearest town that I felt cut off from civilisation. Here, we can have all the convenience of the town while still having a lovely big garden and the countryside very near. And the house is lovely — a perfect family house." She blushed prettily, and rested her hand on Malcolm's. "Which will be very convenient next spring."

"Ah," he said, with a smug smile. "I suspected as much, wife. Then that is settled. We will live in Oxford, and raise a great many half-wild children, and host innumerable argumentative dinners for Oxford academics and their wives, and be excessively happy for the rest of our lives. Does that sound like a good plan?"

"It sounds like an excellent plan," she said, gazing up at him with eyes shimmering with tears. "It sounds perfect, husband."

THE END

The next book in the series is *Stranger at the Villa*, wherein a new physician arrives in the village. Susannah Winslade has met him before, but he seems oddly reluctant to talk about the past. You can read a sneak preview after the acknowledgements, or find out more at my website http://marykingswood.co.uk/.

Thanks for reading!

If you have enjoyed reading this book, please consider writing a short review on Amazon. You can find out the latest news and sign up for the mailing list at my website http://marykingswood.co.uk/.

Family trees and maps: Hi-res versions are available on my website http://marykingswood.co.uk/.

A note on historical accuracy: I have endeavoured to stay true to the spirit of Regency times, and have avoided taking too many liberties or imposing modern sensibilities on my characters. The book is not one of historical record, but I've tried to make it reasonably accurate. However, I'm not perfect! If you spot a historical error, I'd very much appreciate knowing about it so that I can correct it and learn from it. Thank you!

The great houses: Most of the houses I describe in the books are creations of my imagination, or 'generic' styles of a particular era, but sometimes I base them on real houses. In this series, Maeswood Hall, home of the Saxby family, is based on Stourhead House in Wiltshire, designed by Colen Campbell. Lower Maeswood Grove, where the Gage family lives, is loosely based on the Queen's House, Greenwich, designed by Inigo Jones. The

Squire's home, Cloverstone Manor, is based on Hatfield House, another Inigo Jones project.

Isn't that what's-his-name? Regular readers will know that characters from previous books occasionally pop up. Lawyer Mr Willerton-Forbes, his flamboyant sidekick Captain Edgerton and the discreet Mr Neate have been helping my characters solve murders and other puzzles ever since *Lord Augustus*. Michael Chandry, first seen helping after the shipwreck in *The Clerk* and more recently in *The Duke,* is now a crime-solving partner to Captain Edgerton and his pals. Dr Butler, the headmaster of Harrow School, is a real person.

About the Strangers series*:* There's a famous saying attributed to John Gardner that authors like to quote: that there are only two plots - a stranger arrives in town, or a person goes on a journey. Most of my books have been based on the latter, in its loosest sense (sometimes a journey of discovery, rather than a literal journey, but a major change, of death or misfortune or even good fortune which propels the main character in a new direction). So I wondered what the other side of the coin would look like - a stranger arriving in town. And there was my series title - Strangers.

Book 0: Stranger at the Parsonage: a new parson arrives at the village of Great Maeswood, and tragedy strikes the baron's family *(a novella, free to mailing list subscribers)*.

Book 1: Stranger at the Dower House: a widow moves into the long disused Dower House and makes a horrible discovery in the wine cellar.

Book 2: Stranger at the Grove: an estranged brother is forced to return to his home and face up to his past.

Book 3: Stranger at the Villa: a new physician arrives in the village, but is he all he seems?

Stranger at the Grove: Strangers Book 2

Book 4: Stranger at the Manor: a destitute man comes looking for help from his cousin, and uncovers some mysterious goings-on.

Book 5: Stranger at the Cottage: an out-of-work governess tries to start a school in the village.

Book 6: Stranger at the Hall: the newly discovered heir to the barony arrives to claim his inheritance.

Any questions about the series? Email me at

mary@marykingswood.co.uk - I'd love to hear from you!

About the author

I write traditional Regency romances under the pen name Mary Kingswood, and epic fantasy as Pauline M Ross. I live in the beautiful Highlands of Scotland with my husband. I like chocolate, whisky, my Kindle, massed pipe bands, long leisurely lunches, chocolate, going places in my campervan, eating pizza in Italy, summer nights that never get dark, wood fires in winter, chocolate, the view from the study window looking out over the Moray Firth and the Black Isle to the mountains beyond. And chocolate. I dislike driving on motorways, cooking, shopping, hospitals.

Acknowledgements

Thanks go to:

John Gardner, whose alleged saying about strangers and plots inspired these books.

Allison Lane, whose course on English Architecture inspired me.

Shayne Rutherford of Darkmoon Graphics for the cover design.

Andrew K Lawston, world famous translator of the Chantecoq books, for French language advice.

My beta readers: Charles Crouter, Barbara Daniels Dena, Amy DeWitt, Rosemary Paton, Quilting Danielle, Melanie Savage and the team from Rachel Daven Skinner's Romance Refined.

Last, but definitely not least, my first reader: Amy Ross.

Sneak preview: Stranger At The Villa: Chapter 1:

JUNE

Miss Susannah Winslade was at her desk on the first floor of Cloverstone Manor. Being a practical soul, she had positioned it to face a wall not a window, so that the summer sunshine and sweet breezes from the river should not distract her from her work. Her mornings followed the same pattern every day. Immediately after rising, she would go to the nursery to check on the children and listen to the long recital of woes from Nurse. Then it was a visit to the kitchens in the basement to discuss the day's menus with Mrs Whiteway, who sampled her own cooking too enthusiastically these days to climb the stairs. Then Susannah went to her office to begin work on her letters, lists and accounts. Mrs Cobbett, the housekeeper, knew to find her there, so any domestic matters could be attended to.

At ten o'clock precisely it was time for breakfast in Mama's room, which was conveniently next door to Susannah's office, so that she could be summoned immediately if needed. Mama's nurse was very competent, and her companion, Miss Matheson, very willing, but sometimes Mama needed her own family about her.

Mama smiled as she always did when Susannah entered her room. She was still in bed, for she rarely left it these days, but she was propped up against a bank of pillows in a lacy robe and silk shawl, her hair neatly brushed and bound up with a ribbon. Against the pillows she looked tiny, as delicate and fragile as a little doll. The room was overpoweringly hot, for a good blaze burned in the hearth despite the season.

"How are you today, Mama?" Susannah said, bending over to kiss her.

"We are a little better this morning," Nurse Pett said briskly, from her position before the open doors of a large cabinet, as she sorted through bottles of medicine and boxes of lozenges.

The lady herself immediately broke into a cough, and Nurse Pett and Miss Madison rushed forward, one each side of the bed, reaching for a glass of water and a vinaigrette, respectively.

"Not a good sign," Nurse Pett said to Miss Madison. "We should ask Dr Beasley to call."

"I agree. Perhaps she is too cold? Build up the fire a little more, will you?"

Nurse Pett was a large woman with a brusque but efficient manner, and Miss Madison was a wisp of a thing, a fluttering ball of anxiety, but they were united in their care for their charge.

Lilian was Susannah's step-mother, her father's third wife, and the birth of eight children in eleven years had exhausted her utterly. Dr Beasley was of the opinion that careful nursing and regular bleeding would restore her health, but in the three years since little Edward's birth, no improvement had been seen, rather the reverse. Every physician in the county had been consulted, and every likely remedy tried, to no avail.

The butler and footman came in with the breakfast trays, followed almost at once by Squire Winslade. Susannah's father was more than fifty years of age, but it was not merely a daughter's fondness that thought him a well-looking man, one who was still sufficiently active to display a very manly figure, and cared enough for his appearance to dress in fine London style.

"Well now, how are you, my dear?" he said, bending over to plant a gentle kiss on his wife's forehead. "You look charming, as always."

She smiled and giggled girlishly. She was half her husband's age, and although they had not a great deal in common, there was a fondness between them that warmed Susannah's heart. Money was in short supply at Cloverstone Manor these days, but no expense had ever been spared by the squire for his wife's comfort.

Susannah and her father ate at a small table beside the bed with Miss Madison, while Susannah's step-mother had a tray resting on her lap, where she crumbled a bun and sipped a little coffee. The squire cheerfully imparted all the news and scandals of the day. Susannah suspected that her father chose to be a magistrate purely to have the earliest intimation of every scurrilous event in Shropshire.

She had more practical matters on her mind. "Papa, James and John both need new breeches, and all the girls need new gowns, and Alice's half-boots are quite worn through. Have the Midsummer rents come through yet? Or can you let me have a few pounds now?"

"I will talk to Jackson, but this is a difficult time of year for our tenants to meet their rent. They have wives and children to feed, and one does not like to be too heavy-handed."

"No, indeed. You are the most generous of landlords, I know, but I must have a little more money soon. We shall need to order coal for the winter before too long and—"

"Caswell will wait. He knows I am plumper in the pocket in the autumn. He will not dun us, you may be sure. We have been good customers for too long."

Susannah frowned. "But he has not yet been paid for last year's supply, and only partially for the year before, and he has a wife and children to feed, just as much as the tenants. They cannot eat coal."

The squire laughed uneasily. "Eat coal? What strange things you do say, my pet, but we must not talk about money, you know, not when your mama is here and looking so fetching. I am sure I have the world's prettiest wife." She blushed and dimpled up at him. "And now I must run off, for Kingly has a little heat in one chambrel and one can never be too careful with a horse of his temperament. Take care and do not overtire yourself, my dear."

And with a quick kiss of his wife's cheek, he was off. She sighed, and her eyes followed his departing back until the door closed with a snap.

"How are we doing with that bun?" Miss Madison said, in her wispy voice. "We must eat a little, Mrs Winslade. A little more coffee?"

"Is Dr Beasley coming today?" she said, in her tiny voice, barely audible. "Will he bleed me? I do so hate it."

"But it does so much good," Miss Madison said firmly. "Is it not so, Miss Winslade? The doctor knows best, and no one understands your mama's constitution better than Dr Beasley."

"I so dislike being bled," said the faint voice in the bed. "Leeches are worse."

"Perhaps you would like to see the new doctor, Mama," Susannah said. "He will be here any day now, and he might have new ideas about curing you."

"No… I am used to Dr Beasley. If only he would not insist on bleeding me when—" A coughing fit interrupted her, and Susannah had to move aside as Miss Madison and Nurse Pett swooped in to attend to their patient. The clock struck the hour, and breakfast was over.

Susannah took her coffee back to her office, and began work on her lists. The butcher, the poulterer, the grocer. The chandler, the ironmonger, the vintner — so much wine consumed! It was astonishing in a house with only two gentlemen and very little entertaining how much wine was needed. Instructions for the man who did carpentry work for them. Instructions to the head gardener. The new items to be added to the list for the children — goodness, how fast they did grow!

Silas crept in with his oily smile. He was the first footman, although he liked to call himself the under-butler, and it was true that he did much of Binns' work now, for poor Binns was very elderly and had trouble with the stairs. He insisted on carrying out the principal butler's duties of supervising dinner and announcing callers, but he left much of the lesser business to the younger man.

Silas asked her to order more candles, and that was another item which should not need to be replenished so often at this time of year. But there, Papa liked to play cards of an evening, and grumbled if the light was insufficient. She could cut back on working candles, she supposed, for there was enough light to sew by until quite late on these summer evenings, if she sat on the window seat.

Dr Beasley came to attend to her mama, and looked into Susannah's little office afterwards. He had a brisk manner that Susannah rather liked.

"She is well enough, and I did not bleed her," he said, with a shrug. "It would do her good, but she hates it so much, and it is not yet an urgent matter. I detected no fever or signs of excess in her appearance today, merely the usual lassitude."

"That is good news. Thank you for coming," Susannah said.

"I shall come again tomorrow, but only to introduce my associate, who arrives later today."

"Mama does not want anyone but you," Susannah said. "She does not quite understand that you have been ill, and must give up your practice."

"Not all of it, I hope," he said, smiling. "I shall still keep on some of my long-established patients, but they will understand that I shall not be riding out to call upon them in the middle of the night any more. I shall leave that to my energetic young colleague. At least, I trust he will be energetic. And my work as coroner — I shall not surrender *that*, you may be sure." He rubbed his hands together with a gleeful smile. Sometimes Susannah suspected he preferred his dead patients to his live ones.

Not long after the physician had left, Binns came in. "Mr Rycroft is here, madam."

"Which Mr Rycroft, Binns?" she said, without looking up from her accounts book, her pen flying across the page.

"Er... the elder... the younger... er..."

She laughed, and raised her head to look at the elderly butler. He had seemed old to her even when she had been a child, and he had not got any younger since then, his accuracy with names receding as fast as his hair, but he was too much a part of the family to be put out to grass. "It is of no consequence, Binns. He will want my father or my brother. Send him to Mearing in the stables. He will know which way they went."

"He asked most particularly for you, madam. A private interview."

"Oh." The elder Mr Rycroft then. "Show him into the Willow Room, and offer him some Madeira. Tell him I shall be there directly."

Carefully, she wiped her pen and laid it down, then sanded the page and closed the book, putting it neatly back on the shelf beside its fellows, adjusting it so that all the spines stood in an exact line. She had no mirror in the room to check her appearance, but she had done nothing which might disturb its symmetry since she had dressed that morning. The Willow Room was seldom used and faced north, so it would be chilled even at this time of year, but it was austere enough to match her mood, and at least it would be private. She picked up a shawl and went to meet her fate.

Jeffrey was gazing out of the window, but when she entered the room he turned and came towards her, hands outstretched, with a warm smile on his face. He was a pleasantly-featured man, not precisely handsome, but personable and good-humoured, when he got his own way. His father had been an improvident man, leaving his family destitute, but his mother had made a fortunate second marriage to Lord Saxby, and so Jeffrey and his brother had been raised as gentlemen, although without the wherewithal to support such a lifestyle. It made him a restless, not to say capricious, man, but in one direction alone had he been steadfast, and that was his devotion to Susannah.

"Susannah! How well you look today."

"Good morning, Jeffrey." She allowed him to take her hands, and for a dreadful moment as he rushed upon her she was afraid he was going to kiss her. He drew back at the last minute, contenting himself with lifting her hands, one after the other, to his lips. Withdrawing her hands carefully, she added, "Has Binns offered you some refreshment?"

"Oh... yes, but I want nothing. Only to talk to you." She sat down on a faded damask-covered sofa and waved him to a chair, but he continued to stand. "I have good news, Susannah. The best in the world, for I have just come from the Grove. The Gages are to build a new house in their grounds, and rework all the pleasure gardens — the whole park, in fact, and they have engaged *me* to oversee the work, contract with builders and suppliers, and so forth. What do you think of *that?*"

His face was so animated, alive with excitement, that she could not but smile at him. "That is wonderful news, Jeffrey. I knew you had hopes of reworking the Dower House gardens, but this is better, far better. It will give you something to occupy you, now that Lord Saxby is no longer with us."

A flicker of annoyance crossed his face. "What has my stepfather to do with anything? I was very sorry about his death, but it hardly affects me, since he would never help me into a career."

"But you used to shoot and ride with him a great deal, and help the gamekeepers and grooms, and all of that will end when the new Lord Saxby is found. It is as well to have some useful pursuit to fill your time."

"Good Lord, Sue, you make me sound like some sort of dilettante, wasting away my days, when you know better than anyone how much I have longed for a profession. Well, now I have the chance to build a career for myself. There is money to be made from it, in time, enough that I shall be able to reclaim Melverley at last, but for now Gage will pay me a salary. It is only a modest amount, but it is a start. Now do you see?" He perched on the edge of the sofa beside her, taking one of her hands in his. "Everything we want is finally within our grasp. Sue, dearest Sue, you know how I feel about you, how I have *always* felt about you, but it was never possible before. I had just about given up hope, I can tell you. But at last we can move forward, and is it not perfect, the way everything has worked out? We can see about the banns any day you like, and be married within the month, but if you want to wait… for your mother's sake… Well, who can say when—?" He broke off sheepishly, and Susannah tried not to be annoyed. Perhaps her mother's days were numbered, but she would never give up hope of an improvement. After the briefest of pauses, he went on, "For myself, I should like us to marry soon, but it shall be as you wish. What do you say?"

To put off the moment when she must answer that question, she said, "You offered for Cass Saxby."

"Oh… well, yes, that is true." He looked uncomfortable, like a boy caught stealing the jam tarts, then abruptly moved closer to her, so close that she had to lean away from him. "I had to make a push for Mother's sake. I mean, Cass has seventy thousand pounds! It would have set us up so splendidly, and I could have cleared the mortgage on Melverley at once and lived like a gentleman, as I should, instead of having to earn my bread like a common tradesman. I had to try, but I knew she would never have me, so I was quite safe. I have never loved anyone but you, Sue. Sweet Susannah!" He ran one finger down her face, smiling at her in a way that ought to have reduced her to water, but somehow did not. "I love you so much, and it would make me so happy to have you as my wife. Please say you will… please?"

His eagerness moved her, but her heart remained untouched. How many times had they enacted this same scene, and yet her part in it never varied? "I am very sorry, Jeffrey, but I cannot marry you. I like you very much, but I do not feel for you that esteem which a wife should feel for her husband. I do not love you, so although I wish you every success with this new venture, I cannot marry you."

"That is no reason!" he cried. "Love… it is not necessary that *you* should love *me*, for that would grow, in time. We get on so well, and the only obstacle has been that neither of us has any money, so—"

"That is *not* the only obstacle," she said crisply. "Really, Jeffrey, I have told you a score of times that I do not love you and can never marry you. Why do you not believe me? I am delighted that you now have a worthwhile occupation, but it does not change my mind in the slightest."

"A worthwhile occupation!" he cried, anger suffusing his face. "You think I have been a wastrel all these years, then. So that is the way of it."

"You are eight and twenty," she said, evenly. "Your stepfather would not *buy* you a career, but there was nothing to stop you making your own way in the world long since. You spent four years at Shrewsbury and three at Oxford, so you are not without friends who could have helped you to a position as a secretary or in government, say. You might even have taken holy orders and found a living by now. Or you could have worked with Barnes to learn to manage the estate properly, got to know the tenants, learnt about farming methods, instead of just dabbling when you had a day with nothing better to do. There are many things you might have done to advance yourself, but you chose not to, Jeffrey."

"I never *needed* to before!" he snapped, but then, with an effort, reined in his temper. "It always seemed easier to drift along, I suppose, in the hope that one day something would happen and money would rain down from the skies." He laughed ruefully. "Foolish, is it not? And one day something *did* happen — my stepfather overturned his curricle and killed himself and his only heir, leaving us nothing, and now we are all to be pushed out of the nest, and must learn to fly whether we will it or no. I am forced to make my way in the world, and I shall! I shall be a success, Susannah. One day I shall be rich and much sought after by those who want a new house or garden, and you will see what sort of man I am. And perhaps, if I do well, you will look more favourably on me?"

His expression was so hopeful that she could have wept, but she had to be honest. "No, Jeffrey. I shall never marry you."

"But why? What is it about me that repulses you?"

"Nothing. In your person, nothing. In your character, I see some weakness, but it would not weigh with me if I had not—"

"Had not what? Are you in love with someone else, Sue? If so, tell me the worst at once, I pray you! Do not spare me."

"No, no! I am not in love with anyone, but I have seen the possibility of love, that is all, and it was nothing like this. It happened when I was but fourteen, and had gone to London with Mama — not this mama, it was Philippa, Papa's second wife. She was in great distress about her inability to conceive, so she consulted a very eminent *accoucheur* in town. That was why she went to town so often, to see that physician, and she was always invited to dine. On the last occasion, the very last visit shortly before she died, I was invited to dine there too. The eminent physician had two or three young men staying, young physicians training under his supervision. That night, when the card tables were set up, one of them offered to teach me to play backgammon, for I had not played it before. He spent the whole evening teaching me, talking to me, treating me just as if I were a lady worthy of his time, instead of a girl of fourteen, the daughter of an impoverished squire from a distant county. His whole attention was on me, and I felt... I cannot tell you how I felt. More alive than I had ever been, somehow. My whole life until then had been spent half asleep, but for that one night, for those few hours, I was awake and alert, all my senses tingling. It felt like high summer in the middle of winter, if that does not sound too fanciful. And I want to feel like that again, Jeffrey. Can you understand that?"

"He was just being polite to you, as a guest."

"Oh yes, of course! It meant nothing to him, I know that. And I was not in love with him... how could I be, when I knew nothing of him? But it felt possible… on that night, with him, anything was possible."

"So you are waiting for this man—"

"*No!* I shall never see him again, I know that, but there will be someone, somewhere… a man who makes me feel alive, truly alive in that magical way, and with whom there is the possibility of love… and I cannot settle for less. I *cannot.*"

END OF SAMPLE CHAPTER OF *Stranger at the Villa*

For more information or to buy, go to my website http://marykingswood.co.uk/.

Made in the USA
Columbia, SC
30 April 2021

37169345R00245